Praise for the novels of USA TODAY bestselling author

ALL I EVER WANTED
"Kristan Higgins has a gift for creating likeable heroines.... I wholeheartedly recommend... Get it. Read it.
—*All About Romance*

"Higgins has a special talent for creating characters readers love... Fun, charming and heartfelt."
—*RT Book Reviews*, 4½ stars

THE NEXT BEST THING
"A heartwarming, multi-generational tale of lost love, broken hearts and second chances."
—*BookPage*

TOO GOOD TO BE TRUE
Winner—2010 Romance Writers of America RITA® Award
"Cheeky, cute, and satisfying, Higgins's romance is perfect entertainment for a girl's night in."
—*Booklist*

"Kristan Higgins proves that she is emerging as one of the most creative and honest voices in contemporary romance. "
—*Romance Junkies*

JUST ONE OF THE GUYS
"Higgins provides an amiable romp that ends with a satisfying lump in the throat."
—*Publishers Weekly*

CATCH OF THE DAY
Winner—2008 Romance Writers of America RITA® Award
"A touching story brimming with smart dialogue, sympathetic characters, an engaging narrative and the amusing, often self-deprecating observations of the heroine. It's a novel with depth and a great deal of heart."
—*RT Book Reviews*, top pick, 4½ stars

Also available from KRISTAN HIGGINS and HQN Books

All I Ever Wanted
The Next Best Thing
Too Good to Be True
Just One of the Guys
Catch of the Day
Fools Rush In

KRISTAN HIGGINS

My One *and* Only

HQN™

Recycling programs for this product may not exist in your area.

ISBN-13: 978-0-373-77557-6

MY ONE AND ONLY

Dear Reader,

Thanks for choosing *My One and Only!* For me, there's nothing like a book that makes me laugh *and* cry. I hope you'll find scenes in these pages that make you do both.

This is a story of finding your way back, of learning to let go of the past and have faith in the future, even when you can't predict it. Nick and Harper had great reasons for falling in love, and they had equally good reasons for breaking up. Finding their way back isn't going to be easy...but nothing worthwhile in life is.

In some ways, this book is a little different—there's a road trip, for example, and my heroine doesn't have terribly romantic expectations for love, as some of my other heroines have. Some things are the same, though...a colorful family, gorgeous settings, and of course, a really cute dog in the form of Coco, a Jack Russell/Chihuahua mix. I had a great time with some of the secondary characters in this story—Dennis was a personal favorite, as well as BeverLee and Carol.

I took some liberties with facts in this book. There is no professional Martha's Vineyard Fire Department... the island is ably served by noble volunteers from the eight towns that comprise Martha's Vineyard. I'm also not sure an attorney could make a living handling only divorces with such a small year-round population. And as far as direct flights from South Dakota to New York City...well, if they're out there, I couldn't find them. But hey. This is fiction.

I'd love to hear from you anytime...visit my website at www.kristanhiggins.com.

All the best,

Kristan

ACKNOWLEDGMENTS

Thanks as always to my agent,
the brilliant Maria Carvainis, as well as
her able and ready staff, who are always in my corner,
always available and always absolutely lovely.

Every writer should be so lucky as to work with
an editor such as Keyren Gerlach, who is insightful,
kind and pushes me to reach higher with every book.
The entire team at HQN and Harlequin Enterprises
has been overwhelming with their enthusiasm
and support for my work. Special thanks to
Margaret Marbury O'Neill and Tara Parsons and the
wicked awesome art department for my beautiful covers.

My heartfelt thanks to Shaunee Cole, Karen Pinco
and Kelly Morse for helping me kick this bad boy off;
to Toni Andrews for her ready and brilliant counsel
on plotting; to Cassy and Jon Pickard for describing
the life of an architect; to Annette Willis for
giving me the scoop on the life of a divorce attorney
(any mistakes...all mine!); to Paula Kristan Spotanski
and Jennifer Iszkiewicz for sharing their
memories and photos of Glacier National Park; to
Bridget Fehon, animal name consultant extraordinaire;
to my dear mom for all her help; Bob and Diane Moore
for the loan of their beautiful home on
Martha's Vineyard. And to my great friends at CTRWA,
thanks for the enthusiasm, support and cheerleading.
The Force is strong within you!

And of course, all my love to my honey
and our two beautiful kids, the three best things
that ever happened to me.

Lastly, thank you, dear reader.
Thank you for spending time with this book, for
writing to me and in many cases, making me your friend.
I just can't tell you how much that means.

My One *and* Only

When I was five years old,
we kindergartners got to bring our art projects
to show the big-kid second graders. As I walked
past my brother's desk, I made my clay turtle kiss him.
He took it like a man, told me it was cute and ignored
the boys who made fun of him for having a dorky little
sister. For that, and for a million other reasons,
this book is dedicated to you, Mike. Love you, pal.

CHAPTER ONE

"STOP SMILING. EVERY time you smile, an angel dies."

"Wow," I answered. "That's a good one."

The man with *the* negative attitude sat at the bar, looking as if he was living a bad country-and-western song—no woman, broken truck, dead dog. Poor slob. "Listen," I said. "I know it's sad, but sometimes, divorce is just the euthanization of a dying relationship." I patted his shoulder, then adjusted his white collar, which was just a bit off center. "Sometimes our hearts just need time to accept what our heads already know."

The priest sighed. "Listen to her with that ridiculous line," he said to Mick, the bartender.

"It's not ridiculous! It's great advice."

"You're evil."

"Oh, my," I said. "You're taking it harder than I thought."

"It's true. After all my hard work, you swoop in and ruin everything."

"Father Bruce!" I said, feigning hurt. "There was no swooping! How cutting!"

The good father and I were at Offshore Ale, Martha's Vineyard's finest bar, a dark and charming little place in Oak Bluffs and a favorite place for locals and tourists alike. Father Bruce, my longtime friend and the immensely popular pastor of the island's Catholic church, could often be found here.

"Now come on, Father," I continued, sliding onto

a stool next to him and tugging my skirt so as not to flash him. "You and I are actually a lot alike." He responded with a groan, which I ignored. "We shepherd people through life's hard times, guiding them through an emotional minefield, the voice of reason when reason is lost."

"Sad thing is, she believes it, Mick."

I rolled my eyes. "Stop being a sore loser and buy me a drink."

"Marriage ain't what it used to be," the priest grumbled. "Mick, a bourbon for the shark here."

"Actually, just a Pellegrino, Mick. And Father, I'm going to strike that last moniker from the record." I smiled generously. Of course I was a shark. All the best divorce attorneys were.

"I take it you lost again, Father?" Mick said, adding a slice of lemon to my sparkling water.

"Let's not discuss it, Mick. She's gloating as it is."

"I'm certainly not gloating," I objected, reaching over to move another patron's beer, which was in danger of being knocked into Father B.'s lap. "I have nothing against marriage, as you will soon see. But in the case of Starling v. Starling, these two were doomed from the day he got on bended knee. As is one in three couples."

Father Bruce closed his eyes.

Though on opposite sides of the divorce issue, Father B. and I were old pals. But today, Joe Starling, a lifelong parishioner in Father Bruce's parish, had come into my office and asked me to begin divorce proceedings. There'd actually been a race to my door, and Joe won. He was… let's see…the ninth parishioner in the past two years to do so, despite Father B.'s best efforts at weaving together the fraying bonds of matrimony.

"Maybe they'll have a change of heart," Father Bruce suggested. He looked so hopeful that I didn't remind him of one hard fact: not one of my clients had ever backed out of proceedings.

"So how's everything else, Father?" I asked. "Heard you gave a killer sermon last weekend. And I saw you power walking the other day. Your new heart valve must be working great."

"Seems to be, Harper, seems to be." He smiled—he was a priest, after all, and had to forgive me. "Did you perform your random act of kindness today?"

I grimaced. "No. It was a senseless act of beauty." Father Bruce, viewing my soul as a personal campaign, had challenged me to, in his words, "offset the evil of your profession" by doing at least one random act of kindness each day. "Yes, yes," I admitted. "I let a family of six go in front of me at the café. Their baby was crying. Does that pass?

"It does," said the priest. "By the way, you look nice today. A date with young Dennis?"

I glanced around. "More than a date, Father." Wincing as John Caruso accidentally-on-purpose bumped into my back, I pretended not to hear his muttered epithet. One grew used to such slurs when one was as successful as I was. (Mrs. Caruso got the condo in the Back Bay *and* the house out here, not to mention a very generous monthly alimony payment.) "Today's the day. I plan to present the facts, make a convincing case and wait for the verdict, which I completely expect to be in my favor."

Father Bruce raised a bushy white eyebrow. "How romantic."

"I think my view on romance is well documented, Father B."

"One would almost pity young Dennis."

"One would, except the boy has it made, and you know it."

"Do I?"

"Please." I clinked my glass against Father Bruce's and took a drink. "To marriage. And speak of the devil, here he is now, all of four minutes early. Will wonders never cease."

My boyfriend of the past two and a half years, Dennis Patrick Costello, was…well. Picture every fantasy you've ever had about a hot firefighter. Uh-huh. That's right. Eye candy didn't even begin to cover it. Thick black hair, blue eyes, the ruddy cheeks of the Irish. Six-two. Shoulders that could carry a family of four. The only fly in the ointment was a rattail…a long, anemic braid to which Dennis was senselessly attached and which I tried very hard to ignore. Be that as it may, his physical beauty and constant affability always gave me a little thrill of pride. There wasn't a person on the island who didn't like Dennis, and there wasn't woman who didn't break off midsentence when he smiled. And he was mine.

Den was with Chuck, his platoon mate on the Martha's Vineyard Fire Department, who gave me a sour look as he headed to the far end of the bar. Chuck had cheated on Constance, his very nice wife. Not just once, either. Nope, he'd pulled a Tiger Woods, eventually admitting to four affairs in six years of marriage. As a result, Chuck now rented a single room in a crooked, 600-square-foot "cottage" out on Chappaquiddick and had to take the ferry to work every day. Such are the wages of sin.

"Hi, Chuck! How are you?" I asked. Chuck ignored me, as was his custom. No matter. I turned to Dennis. "Hey, hon! Look at you, four minutes early."

Dennis bent down and kissed my cheek. "Hey there, gorgeous," Dennis said. "Hi, Father B."

"Dennis. Good luck, son. I'll offer up a Hail Mary."

"Thanks, Padre." Apparently not curious as to why a priest would be praying for him, Dennis smiled at me. "I'm starving. You hungry?"

"You bet. See you around, Father Bruce," I said, sliding off the bar stool. Dennis gave me a smoky once-over—that was, after all, the point of my dress and painfully high heels, which bordered on slutty. I wanted Dennis's full attention, and, as he was male, showing a little breast wasn't going to hurt my case.

Tonight, I was popping the question. Two and a half years with Dennis had shown me that he was very solid husband material. Good heart, steady work, decent guy, close family ties, quite attractive. It was now or never… at almost thirty-four, I wasn't going to hang around and be someone's girlfriend forever. I was a person who made lists and took action, and Dennis, bless his heart, needed direction.

First element of the plan…feed Dennis, who needed to eat more often than an infant. A couple of beers wouldn't hurt, either, because Dennis, though he seemed quite happy with our relationship, hadn't yet brought up the subject of marriage on his own. A little mellowing wouldn't hurt.

And so, half an hour later, a pint of Offshore Nutbrown Ale already in him and a massive blue-cheese-and-bacon hamburger in front of him, Dennis was telling me about an accident call. "So I'm trying to get the car door off, right, and all of a sudden, the thing comes flying off, hits Chuck right in the nuts, and he's like, 'Costello, you asswipe!' and we all just lose it. And the thing is, the old lady's still in the car. Oh, man, it was priceless."

I smiled patiently. Firehouse humor—for lack of a better word—was crude at best. Nevertheless, I chuckled and murmured, "Poor thing," meaning, of course, the old woman stuck in the car while the brawny men of the MVFD clutched themselves and made testicle jokes. For Chuck, I felt only that justice had been served. "Was the driver badly hurt?"

"Nah. Not a scratch on her. We wouldn't have laughed if she was decapitated or something." He grinned cheekily, and I smiled back.

"Glad to hear it. So listen, Den. We need to talk."

At the dreaded words, Dennis's smile dropped. Blinking rapidly, as if I was about to punch him in the face, he groped for his half-pound, overladen burger as if for protection—defensive body language, something I often saw in the spouses of my clients. Best to move in for the kill. I folded my hands neatly in front of me, tilted my head and smiled.

"Dennis, I think it's time for us to take things to the next level, you know? We've been together awhile, we have a very solid relationship, I'll be thirty-four in a few weeks, next year is advanced maternal age, medically speaking, so let's get married."

Dennis jerked back in alarm. Drat. I hadn't sounded terribly romantic, had I? Maybe I should've gone for a more sentimental note, rather than a recitation of the facts. This is what I got for practicing in front of a dog, rather than a human. Then again, there was nothing wrong with being straightforward…closing arguments, if you will.

My boyfriend answered by shoving a good quarter of the giant sandwich into his mouth. "Mmm-hrmph," he said, pointing to his bulging cheeks.

Well, resistance was expected, of course. Dennis was a guy, and most guys, with only a few notable exceptions, didn't pop the question without a nudge. And I had been nudging…I'd admired an engagement ring of one of Dennis's cousins three months ago, commented on Dennis's love of children, telling him he'd be a good dad, mentioned my own desire to procreate…but so far, nada. I assumed Dennis needed something a little more, er, blatant. A kick, for example. Didn't most men need a good swift kick?

"Now don't panic, hon," I said as he chewed desperately.

"We get along great. We spend most nights together, we've been together for more than two years, you're thirty now, you know you want kids… It's time. Don't you think so? I know I do." I smiled to show him we were both on the same team.

Dennis swallowed, his chiseled, gorgeous face now pale. "Uh, listen, dude," he began. I grimaced—*dude?* Really? He noticed. "Sorry, dude," he said. "I mean, Harper. Sorry." Dennis closed his mouth, opened it, hesitated, then took another massive bite of burger.

Fine. I would speak. It was better that way. "Let me go on, okay, Den? Then you can say something. If you still want to." I smiled and maintained eye contact, which was a little hard, given that Dennis's eyes were darting frantically. Also, the Red Sox game was on, which didn't help, as Dennis was a rabid fan. "Den, as you know, I spend my entire day dealing with crappy relationships. I see the mistakes people make, and I know what to avoid. We don't have a crappy relationship. Our relationship is great. It really is. And we can't be in limbo forever. You're at my place most nights anyway—"

"Your bed is wicked comfortable," he said sincerely, stuffing some fries into his mouth. He offered a few to me, but I shook my head, my own salad more of a prop tonight.

"No thanks. Back to the subject…" I leaned forward a little more, giving Dennis a better glimpse of my cleavage. His eyes dropped the way Pavlov's dog drooled, and I smiled. "Our sex life is certainly good," I continued, reminding him of our finer moments. A woman at the next table, who was trying to convince her toddler to eat a fried clam, gave me a sharp look. Tourists. "We obviously find each other attractive, don't we?"

"Most def." He gave me the wide, even smile that rendered so many women speechless. Perfect. He was now thinking with the little head, which would help my case.

"Exactly, hon. And I make a great living, you have... well, a solid salary. We'll have a very comfortable life-style, we'll make beautiful babies, et cetera. Let's make it permanent, shall we?" I reached down for my bag and withdrew the black velvet box. "I even picked out the ring, so we know I love it."

At the sight of the two-carat rock, Dennis flinched.

I closed my eyes briefly. "I paid for it, too, so don't worry. See? This isn't so hard after all, is it?" I gave him my firm court smile, the one that said, *Your Honor, please. Can we stop screwing around and get this done?*

Father Bruce and Bob Wickham, head of the church council, made their way over to the table next to our booth. The priest shot me a knowing look, which I ignored.

At that moment, Jodi Pickering, Dennis's high school girlfriend and a waitress here, shoved the prow of her bosom into Den's jaw. "Are you all set here, Denny?" she asked, ignoring me and giving my soon-to-be fiancé a docile, cowlike gaze.

"Hey, Jodi, what's up?" Dennis said, grinning past her 36-Ds to her face. "How's the little guy?"

"Oh, he's great, Denny. It was so nice that you stopped by the game the other night. He just loves you! And you know, without a father in the picture, I think T.J. really needs—"

"Okay, we get it, Jodi-with-an-i," I said, smiling pleas-antly up at her. "You have an adorable son and are still quite available. Dennis, however, is with me. If you would just take your boobs out of my boyfriend's face, I would deeply appreciate it."

She narrowed her eyes at me and sashayed away. Dennis watched her departure as one would watch the lifeboats paddling away from the *Titanic*. Then he swallowed and looked at me. "Listen, Harp," he began. "You're…you know…great and all, but, uh…well, if it ain't broke, don't fix it, right? I mean, why change a good thing? Can't we just keep hanging out together?"

Again, totally expected. I straightened up and tilted my head a few degrees. "Dennis," I said firmly, well aware that this kind of circular conversation could go on forever. "This isn't high school. We're not kids. We've been together for the past two and a half years. I'm thirty-four next month. I don't want to hang out indefinitely. If we're not going to get married, we need to break up. So…shit or get off the pot, honey."

"That was beautiful," murmured Father Bruce as he opened a menu.

I favored him with a withering glance, then turned back to Firefighter Costello. "Dennis? Let's do this."

Dennis was granted a brief reprieve by a roar from the bar. We both looked over. On the television, various and sundry members of the Sox were spitting and scratching their groins. Did they have no PR department, for heaven's sake? And a game was just what Dennis didn't need… more distraction.

Clearly, choosing a public place for this discussion was a tactical error. I'd originally thought it would work in my favor…even had a little vision of Dennis shouting, "Hey, everyone, we're getting married!" and people (even the people who kind of hated me) cheering and clapping.

Didn't seem like that was about to happen. "Dennis?" I said, my chest tightening just a little. "Can I have an answer?"

Dennis picked up his napkin and started ripping off little pieces.

A small, sharp blade of uncertainty sliced into my consciousness. Dennis was usually so…*agreeable* when I made plans. Yes, I was the one who took control of our relationship, but wasn't that typical? Men didn't plan things on their own. They didn't suggest picnics or trips to the city or what have you. And even if his words tonight indicated reluctance, Den's actions bespoke permanence. Two and a half years—years!—in an exclusive and mutually satisfying relationship without one significant fight. Of course we were headed for marriage. He had all the necessary qualities of a husband…he just needed a little shove into full adulthood.

Actually, I had right here next to my plate a honey-do list to help Den on that front. Get a second job, as he had too much free time as a firefighter and really shouldn't be playing Xbox as much as I knew he did (or downloading porn, which I suspected he did). Get rid of the 1988 El Camino he now drove—one door green, all other parts rust—and drive something that didn't make him look like an impoverished pimp. Cut off the rattail, because please! It was a rattail! And lastly… Move in with me. Despite our four or five nights a week together, Dennis still lived in a garage apartment he rented from his brother. I had a two-bedroom house on the water.

My plan had been to wait till he accepted my offer, then pass over the list and discuss.

But he wasn't accepting.

I confess that I was a little confused. I asked Dennis for very little and accepted him the way he was—a good guy. Sure, he was still something of a kid, but that was fine. Though I wasn't one to get all sticky with proclamations, I loved Dennis. Who didn't? A native Islander like myself, Dennis was mobbed by friends wherever we went, from the guys who worked on the ferry to the road crew to the summer people who occasionally dropped in at the firehouse.

Granted, maybe he wasn't the, uh, most intellectual man on earth, but Dennis was kindhearted and quite brave. In fact, he'd saved three children from a house fire his second week on the job a few years ago and was something of a local legend. And speaking of kids, Dennis was very good with them, natural and at ease in a way I'd never been, despite my hope to have kids of my own one day. Dennis, though—he'd get on the floor and roll around with his seven nieces and nephews, and they adored him.

And—one couldn't rule this out—Dennis *liked* me. Honestly, I couldn't tell you how many men got that retracting-testicles look when they learned what I did for a living. Women too, as if I was a pox on our gender just because I facilitated the end of crappy marriages. There was a fair number of people who'd cheerfully slash my tires after I'd signed on to represent their spouses. I'd been called a bitch (and worse), had coffee thrown in my face, been spit on, cursed, threatened and condemned.

I took it as a compliment. Yes, I was a very good divorce attorney. If that meant a larger-than-normal percentage of the population owned voodoo dolls with red hair and a tight gray suit, so be it. In fact, I'd met Dennis when my car was rammed by an angry wife and the MVFD had to cut me out (no injuries, and a nice damages award from Judge Burgess, who had a soft spot for me). "Wanna grab a beer? I get off in half an hour," Dennis had said, and more shaken than I'd let on, I agreed.

He didn't seem scared by my reputation as a ballbuster. Wasn't intimidated by my healthy paycheck, funded by the dissolution of happily-ever-after dreams. So yes. Dennis liked me. Though I didn't sigh with rapture when I looked in the mirror, I knew I was attractive (very, some might say), well dressed, hardworking, successful, smart, loyal. Fun, too. Well…sometimes I was fun. Okay, sure, there were those who'd disagree with that, but I was fun enough.

All in all, I thought we could be very content. And *content* was vastly underrated.

As I well knew, marriages were fragile birds of hope, and one in three ended up as a pile of dirty feathers. In my experience, the vast majority of those were the *oh-my-darling-you-make-my-very-heart-beat* variety…the type that so often ended in a pyre of hate and bitterness. Comfort, companionship and realistic expectations…they didn't sound nearly as glam as *undying passion*, but they were worth a lot more than most people believed.

There was one more reason I wanted to get a commitment from Dennis. Soon, I'd turn thirty-four, and when that happened, I'd be the same age as my mother the last time I saw her. For whatever reason, the thought of being (*alone, adrift*) single…at that age…it felt like a failure of monumental proportion. In the past few months, that thought had been pulsing in a dark rhythm. *Same age as she was. Same age as she was.*

Dennis was silent, his napkin now confetti. "Dude, listen," he finally said. "Harp. Er. Harper, I mean. Uh, hon…well, the thing is…"

At that moment, Audrey Hepburn's whispery voice floated from my purse—"Moon River," the song indicating a call from my sister. Like Audrey, my sister was lovely, sweet and ever in need of protection. She'd moved to New York recently, and I hadn't heard from her much these past few weeks.

"You wanna take that?" Dennis asked hastily.

"Um…do you mind?" I said. "It's my sister."

"Go right ahead," he answered, practically melting in relief. "Take your time." He drained the remaining half of his beer and turned again to the Boston Red Sox.

Oh, dream maker, you heartbreaker… "Hi, Willa!"

"Harper? It's me, Willa!" Though my stepsister was

twenty-seven, her voice retained a childlike chime, and the sound never failed to bring a smile to my face.

"Hi, sweetie! How's the Big Apple? Do you love it?"

"It's so great, but Harper, I have news! Big news!"

"Really? Did you find a job?"

"Yes, I'm, um, an office assistant. But that's not my news. Are you ready? Are you sitting down?"

A chilly sense of dread laced through my knees. I glanced at Dennis, who was focused on the ball game. "Okay…what is it?"

"I'm getting married!"

My hand flew to my mouth. "Willa!"

"I know, I know, you're gonna have kittens, and yes, we just met a couple weeks ago. But it's like kismet, is that the right word? Totally real. I mean, Harper, I've never felt like this before! Ever."

Crotch. I took a breath, held it for a few seconds, then released it slowly. "I hate to be a buzzkill, Willa, but that's what you said the first time you were married, honey. Second time, too."

"Oh, stop!" she said, laughing. "You're a *total* buzzkill. I knew you'd freak, but don't. I'm twenty-seven, I know what I'm doing! I just called you because…oh, Harper, I'm so happy! I really am! I love him so much! And he thinks I walk on, like, water!"

I closed my eyes. Willa had married her first husband when she was twenty-two, three weeks after Raoul had been released from prison; the divorce followed a month later when strike three came after he robbed a bead store. (I know. A bead store?) Husband #2, acquired when my sister was twenty-five, had come out of the closet seven weeks after the wedding. Only Willa had been surprised.

"That's great, honey. He sounds, um, wonderful. It's just… Marriage? Already?"

"I know, I know. But Harper, listen. I'm totally in love!"

So much for live and learn. "Going slow never hurt anyone, Wills. That's all I'm saying."

"Can't you say you're happy for me, Harper? Come on! Mama's totally psyched!"

This was not a surprise. My stepmother, BeverLee of the Big Blond Hair, lived for weddings, whether in the family, the tabloids or on one of the three soap operas she watched religiously.

"It's just fast, that's all, Willa."

Willa sighed. "I know. But this isn't like those other times. This is the real deal."

"You just moved two months ago, honey. Don't you want to enjoy the city, figure out what you really want to do for a living?"

"I can still do that. I'm getting married, not dying."

There was an edge in my sister's voice now, and I figured I'd dangle a carrot. "True enough. Well, this is exciting. Congratulations, honey! Hey! I'd love to throw you guys a big wedding out here on the Vineyard. All the good places are booked for this fall, no doubt, but next summer—"

"No need, but thank you, Harper! You're so nice, but we already found a spot, and you'll never guess where."

"Where?" I asked.

"Glacier National Park, that's where! In Montana!"

"Wow." I glanced at Dennis, but his attention was still fixed to the screen above the bar. "So, um…when were you thinking?" *Please let it be a long time from now.*

"No time like the present," she chirped. "September eleventh! You'll be my maid of honor, right? It has to be you!"

"September eleventh, Wills?"

"Oh, come on! That day could use a little happiness, don't you think?"

"That's two weeks away."

"So? When it's right, it's right. Will you be my maid of honor or not?"

I opened my mouth, closed it and bit my tongue. Two weeks. Holy testicle Tuesday. Two weeks to talk Willa out of another disastrous marriage, or at least to slow down and really get to know her potential groom. I could do it. Just had to play along. "Well, sure. Of course I'll be your maid of honor."

"Hooray! Thank you, Harper! It'll be so beautiful out there. But listen, I haven't told you the best part yet," Willa said.

My heart stuttered. "Are you pregnant?" I asked calmly. That would be fine. I would support the baby, of course. Pay for college. Make sure the kid stayed in school.

"No, I'm not *pregnant*. Listen to you! It's just that you know the groom."

"I do?"

"Yup! It's a totally small world. Want to guess?"

"No. Just tell me who it is."

"His first name starts with a C."

Men whose names began with C in Manhattan? "I—I don't know. I give up."

"Christopher." Willa's voice was smug with affection.

"Christopher who?"

"Christopher Lowery!"

I jerked back in my chair, my pinot noir sloshing dangerously. "Lowery?" I choked out.

"I know! Isn't that amazing? I'm marrying your ex-husband's brother!"

CHAPTER TWO

WHEN I CLOSED MY PHONE a moment later, I saw that my hands were shaking. "Dennis?" I said. My voice sounded odd, and Father Bruce glanced over, frowning. I gave him a little smile—well, I tried. "Den?"

My boyfriend jerked to attention. "You okay, hon? You look…weird."

"Dennis, something came up. Willa…um…can we just…table our conversation for a little while? A few weeks?"

A tidal wave of relief flooded his face. "Uh…sure! You bet! Is your sister okay?"

"Well, she's…yeah. She's getting married."

"Cool." He frowned. "Or not?"

"It's…it's uncool. I have to run, Dennis. I'm sorry."

"No, no, that's fine," he said. "Want me to drive you home? Or stay over?"

"Not tonight, Dennis. Thanks, though."

I must've sounded off, because Dennis's eyebrows drew together. "You sure you're okay, hon?" He reached across the table and took my hand, and I squeezed back gratefully. Once you cut through Dennis's thick outer layers, there really was a sweet man inside.

"I'm fine. Thanks. Just…well, the wedding's in a couple weeks. A bit of a shock."

"Definitely." He smiled and kissed my hand. "I'll call you later."

I drove home, not really seeing the streets or cars,

though presumably I avoided hitting any pedestrians and trees en route. Since the tourism season was still in full swing, I took the back roads, driving west toward the almost violent sunset, great swashes of purple and red, taking comfort from the endless rock walls of the Vineyard, the pine trees and oaks, the gray-shingled houses. The time I'd spent away from here—college, a brief stint in New York and then law school in Boston—had secured my belief that the island was the most beautiful place on earth.

Martha's Vineyard consists of eight towns. I worked in Edgartown, land of white sea captains' homes and impeccable gardens and, of course, the beautiful brick courthouse. Dennis lived in charming Oak Bluffs, famed for the Victorian gingerbread houses that made up the old Methodist enclave called the Campground. But I lived in a tiny area of Chilmark called Menemsha.

I waited patiently for a slew of tourists, who came down here to admire the scenic working class, to cross in front of me, then pulled into the crushed-shell driveway of my home. It was a small, unremarkable house, not much to look at from the outside but rather perfect inside. And the view...the view was priceless. If Martha's Vineyard had a blue-collar neighborhood, it was here, at Menemsha's Dutcher's Dock, where lobstermen still brought in their catches, where swordfishing boats still ran. My father's father had been such a fisherman, and it was in his old house, set on a hill overlooking the aging fleet, where I now lived.

Through the living room window, I could see Coco's brown-and-white head appearing then disappearing as she jumped up and down to ascertain that yes, I really had come home. In her mouth was her favorite cuddle friend, a stuffed bunny rabbit that was slightly bigger than she was. A Jack Russell-Chihuahua mix, Coco was somewhat schizophrenic, alternating as it served her purposes between the two sides of her parentage—exuberant, affectionate Jack or timid, vulnerable Chihuahua. At the moment, she was in her happy place, though when it came time for bed, she'd revert to a wee, trembling beastie who clearly needed to sleep with her head on my pillow.

I unlocked the door and went in. "Hi, Coco," I said. With a single bound, she leaped into my arms, all eight pounds of her, and licked my chin. "Hello, baby! How's my girl? Hmm? Did you have a good day? Finish that novel you're writing? You did! Oh, you're so clever." Then I kissed her little brown-and-white triangle head and held her close for a minute or two.

When Pops had been alive, this house had been a standard, somewhat crowded and typical ranch. Three small bedrooms, one and a half baths, living room, kitchen. He died when I was in law school and left the house to me, his only grandchild (biological, that was…he'd liked Willa, but I was his special girl). No matter how much I made as a divorce attorney, I would never have been able to afford this view on my own. But thanks to Pops, it was mine. I could've sold it for several million dollars to a real estate developer, who would've torn it down and slapped up a vacation house faster than you could say McMansion. But I didn't. Instead, I paid my father, who was a general contractor, to renovate the place.

So we knocked down a few walls, relocated the kitchen, turned three bedrooms into two, installed sliding glass doors wherever possible, and the end result was a tiny, airy jewel of a home, founded on the hard work of my salty, seafaring grandfather, renovated by my father's hands and funded by my lawyer's salary. Someday, I imagined, I'd put on a second story to house my well-behaved and attractive future children, but for now, it was just Coco and me, with Dennis as our frequent guest. Sand-colored walls, white trim, spare white furniture, the occasional splash of color—a green oar from a barn sale in Tisbury leaning tastefully in one corner, a soft blue chair in front of the bay window. Over the sliders that led to the deck hung an orange lifesaving ring, the chipped letters naming Pops's boat and port of origin—*Pegasus*, Chilmark.

With a sigh, I turned my attention back to my sister's bombshell.

I'm marrying your ex-husband's brother!

Holy testicle Tuesday.

Time for some vinotherapy. Setting Coco back down, I went to the fridge, uncorked a bottle and poured a healthy portion, oh yes. Chugged half of it, grabbed a bag of Cape Cod sea salt and vinegar potato chips and the bottle of wine and headed for my deck, Coco trotting next to me on her tiny and adorable feet.

So my sister was marrying Christopher Lowery, a man I'd last seen on my own wedding day thirteen years ago. How old was he then? Sixteen? Eighteen?

I took a sip of wine, not a gulp, and forced myself to take a deep breath of the salty, moist air, savoring the tang of baitfish (hey, I was a local). I listened to the sound of the endless island wind, which buffeted my house from two directions this night, bringing me strands of music and laughter from other places, other homes. *Calm down, Harper,* I told myself sternly. *Nothing to panic about. Not yet, anyway.*

"I'm getting a glass," a voice said. Kim, my neighbor and closest friend. "Then I want to hear everything."

"Sure," I answered. "Who's with the kids?"

"Their idiot father," she answered.

As if summoned, Lou's voice shattered the relative quiet as he yelled across the small side yard that separated our homes. "Honey? Where's the box of Pull-Ups?"

"Find them your damn self! They're your kids, too!" Kim bellowed back.

This was followed by a shriek and a howl from one of Kim's four sons. I suppressed a shudder. Our houses were only a few yards apart, though happily, mine jutted out past hers, preventing me from having to witness their particular brand of domestic bliss.

"This house is a pigsty!" Lou yelled.

"So clean it!" his bride returned.

"How do you keep the magic?" I asked, taking another sip. Kim smiled and flopped down in the chair next to me.

"You'd never know we were screwing like monkeys last night," she said, helping herself to the wine.

"And how do monkeys screw?" I asked, raising an eyebrow.

"Fast and furious," she laughed, clinking her glass against mine.

Kim and Lou were happily (if sloppily) married. Not exactly my role models, but reassuring nonetheless. They'd moved in a couple of years ago; Kim appeared on my doorstep with a box of Freihofer's doughnuts and a bottle of wine and offered friendship. My kind of woman.

"Mommy!" came the voice of one of the twins.

"I'm busy!" she called. "Ask your father! Honest to God, Harper, it's a wonder I haven't sold them into slavery." Kim often claimed to envy my single, working woman's life, but the truth was, I envied hers. Well, in some ways. She and Lou were solid and affectionate, completely secure in the happy way they bickered and bossed each other around. (See? I had nothing against marriage when it was done right.) Their kids ranged in age from seven to two. Griffin was the oldest and had the soul of a sixty-year-old man. Once in a while, he'd come over to play Scrabble and admire Coco. I liked him;

definitely preferred him over the four-year-old twins, Gus and Harry, who left a path of chaos, blood and rubble wherever they went. The two-year-old, Desmond, had bitten me last week, but seconds later put his sticky little face against my knee, an oddly lovely sensation, so the jury was still a bit torn over him.

"So are you engaged?" Kim asked, settling in the chair next to me. "Tell me now so I can start my diet. No way am I going to be a bridesmaid weighing this much."

"I am not engaged," I answered calmly.

"Holy shitake!" Kim, who tried not to curse in front of her kids, had invented her own brand of swearing, which I'd latched on to myself. "He turned you down?"

"Well, not exactly. My sister called during negotiations, and guess what? She's getting married."

"Again?"

"Exactly. But it gets better. She just met him a month ago, and guess what else? He's..." I paused, took another slug of liquid courage. "He's my ex-husband's brother. Half brother, actually."

She sputtered on her wine. "You have an ex-husband, Harper? How did I not know this?"

I glanced at her. "I guess it never came up. Long ago, youthful mistake, yadda yadda ad infinitum." I wondered if she bought it. Both of us ignored the screeches that came from her house, though Coco jumped on my lap, channeling Chihuahua, and trembled, cured from her terror only by a potato chip.

"Well, well, well," Kim said when I offered no further information.

"Yes."

"So Willa just...ran into your ex-brother-in-law?" Kim asked. "Sure, it's a small world, but come on. In New York City?"

I hadn't asked about that, a bit too slammed by the

mention of...*him*...to properly process the information. After all these years of not thinking about him, his name now pulsed and burned in my brain. I shrugged and took another sip of wine, then leaned my head against the back of the chair. The sky was lavender now, only a thin stripe of fading red at the horizon marking the sun's descent. The tourists who'd come to watch the sunset clambered back into their cars to head for Oak Bluffs or Edgartown for dinner and alcohol—Chilmark, like five of Martha's Vineyard's other towns, was dry. Ah, New England.

"So will you be seeing him again? The ex? What's his name?"

"I guess so, if they actually go through with it. The wedding's supposed to be in two weeks. In Montana." Another sip. "His name is Nick." The word felt big and awkward as it left my mouth. "Nick Lowery."

"Yoo-hoo! Harper, darlin'! Where you at? Did you talk to your sister? Isn't it just so exciting! And romantic? My stars, I almost peed my pants when she told me!"

My stepmother charged into the house—she never knocked. "We're out here, BeverLee," I called, getting up to greet her—bouffanted, butter-yellow hair sprayed five inches off her scalp ("The bigger the hair, the closer to God," she often said), more makeup than a Provincetown drag queen, shirt cut down to reveal her massive cleavage. My dad's trophy wife of the past twenty years...fifteen years younger than he was, blond and Texan. Behind her, my tall and skinny father was almost invisible.

"Hi, Dad." My father, not one to talk unless a gun was aimed at his heart, nodded, then knelt to pet Coco, who wagged so hard it was a wonder her spine didn't crack. "Hi, Bev. Yes, I talked to her." I paused. "Very surprising."

"Well, hello, there, Kimmy! How you doin'? Did Harper here tell you the happy news?"

KRISTAN HIGGINS 31

"She shore did," Kim said, immediately sliding into a Texas accent, something she swore was unconscious. "So excitin'!" She caught my eye and winked.

"I know it!" BeverLee chortled. "And oh, my, Montana! That's just so romantic! I guess Chris worked out there one summer or some such…whatever, I can't wait! Hoo-whee! What color's your dress gonna be, honey? Jimmy, what do you think?"

I glanced at my father. He rose, put his hands in his pockets and nodded. This, I knew from experience, would be his contribution to the conversation…Dad was silent to the point of comatose. But BeverLee didn't need other people to have a conversation, and sure enough, she continued.

"I'm thinking lavender, what do y'all think? For you, Harper, not me. I'm fixin' on getting this little orange number I saw online. Cantaloupe-mango, they called the color, you know? And y'all know how I love orange."

"I'd better go," Kim said. "I hear glass breaking over at my house. Talk to you soon, Harper. Bye, Mr. James, Mrs. James."

"Honey, y'all don't need to call me Miz James! I told you that a million times!"

"Bye, BeverLee," Kim said amiably. She tossed back the rest of her wine and gave me a wave.

"See you," I said to her, then turned to my father and stepmother. "So. Before we pick out the dress, maybe we should talk about the, uh, wisdom of this event?"

"Wisdom? Listen to you, darlin'!" BeverLee exclaimed. "Jimmy, get your butt in that-there chair. Your daughter wants to talk!" She came over to me and pulled my hair out of its ponytail and started fluffing, ignoring my squirm. "Honestly, Harper, the man just doesn't know what to make of this! His little girl getting married to his other little girl's ex-husband! It's just crazy." With that, she took the travel-size can of Jhirmack Extra Hold that was attached to her keychain and sprayed my head.

"Okay, BeverLee, that's great," I said, trying not to inhale. "That's enough. Thanks." She put down her weapon, and I cleared my throat. "Now, first of all, Willa's not marrying my ex-husband," I said in my courtroom voice. "Just to clarify. She's marrying Christopher. Christopher is Nick's half brother. I was married to Nick."

"Honey, I know that." BeverLee fumbled in her purse and withdrew a pack of Virginia Slims. "I was there at your wedding, wasn't I? I misspoke, okay? So try not to take my head off, won't you, sugar? Just because your panties are in a twist since you'll be seeing Nick again doesn't mean you should—"

"My panties are not twisted," I muttered.

"—bite the hand that feeds you. This is a happy day, all right?" The queen of mixed metaphors took a deep drag and exhaled through one corner of her mouth.

"You don't feed me."

"Well, I would if you let me. You're right skinny. Anyway, Willard just loves purple, so lavender would be the way to go, sugar. You wanna make Willard happy, don't you?"

I opened my mouth, then shut it. If I had a soft spot, its name was Willa. Specifically, Willard Krystal Lupinski James.

The summer after my mother had left us, my father went to Vegas for a two-week conference on green building materials…or so he said. I spent the fortnight with my friend Heather, calling her mother "Mom" and pretending it was a joke and not a wish. Dad returned with BeverLee Roberta Dupres McKnight Lupinski and her daughter, Willard.

I was stunned, horrified and absolutely furious at what my father had done. When he'd told me he was going out

West, a little fantasy had played out in my brain—Dad
would find Mom and beg her to forgive him (for whatever I imagined he'd done) and she'd return and we'd
all be happy again. The rational part of my brain knew
that wouldn't really happen...but this? *This* I had never
foreseen. Dad got *married?* To this...this Trailer Park
Barbie? Were those boobs real? Did we have to see so
much of them? And I was supposed to share my *room*
with her *kid?* Was he out of his *mind?* But in typical Dad
fashion, my father's answer was brief. "It's done, Harper.
Don't make it harder than it has to be."

"Willard, go and give your new big sister a kiss, sugar
pop. Go on now!" Willard only tightened her grip on
her mother's hand and refused to raise her eyes. She was
pale and skinny, tangled hair and scabby knees. Please.
I was still bleeding over my mother's desertion, and now
these two were *living* with me? I had a stepmother? A
stepsister? My father was an *idiot*, and there was no way
in hell I was about to make his life easier. I would hate
them both. Especially the kid. The (dare I say it?) *stupid*
kid.

My resolve lasted about eight hours. I went to my
room to choke on the hot and bitter tears that even then I
couldn't seem to shed. I cursed my silent father and railed
against the unfairness of life, my life in particular. Of
course I skipped dinner. I would starve in my room before
going downstairs and eating with *them*. Made plans to
run away/find my mother/become famous/be killed in
a horrible accident/all of the above, which would make
everyone see just how awful they'd been to me, and man,
they'd feel like absolute dog crap, but it would be too late,
so there. My father was an ass. My mother...my mother
had abandoned me, my father barely spoke, I had no siblings. This BeverLee caricature was ridiculous. Her kid...
Jesus. She was so *not* my new sister just because some

blowsy stranger had married my father, who, come on, could have maybe *called* and given me a little warning?

At some point, I fell asleep, curled into fetal position, facing the wall, my jaw aching from being clenched so hard, my heart stony.

I woke up around eleven that night, hoping my new situation was a dream. Nope. From down the hall, I could hear…*sounds*…from my father's bedroom. Fantastic. Not only did he have to marry the disgusting white trash Barbie-on-steroids, he was having *sex*. Beyond revolting. I rolled over to grab my ancient Raggedy Anne doll so I could clamp it over my ears.

Willard—stupid name—was stuffing something under the other twin bed in my room.

"What are you *doing?*" I asked, the adolescent contempt flowing forth without effort.

She didn't answer. She didn't have to.

"Did you wet the bed?"

She just kept stuffing. Perfect. This was just great. Now my room would smell like pee, just in case everything else wasn't enough.

"Don't hide them," I muttered, kicking off my own sheets. "We have to put them in the wash or they'll stink to high heaven. Change your pajamas."

She obeyed silently. I went downstairs with the dirty laundry, ignoring the *nasty* sounds from the master bedroom. Willard trailed after me like a pale, skinny ghost. I put the sheets in the washing machine and poured in detergent and some bleach—I'd become bitterly adept at housework in the past year. Then I turned around and opened my mouth to say something mean and authoritative, to make sure she'd know her place, recognize her status as an interloper and stay out of my way.

She was crying.

"Want some ice cream?" I asked and, without waiting

for an answer, I picked her up—she was tiny and scrawny, like a malnourished baby chick, her short, straight blond hair sticking up all over the place. Carried her into the kitchen, set her down at the table and pulled two pints of Ben & Jerry's from the freezer. "I think I'll call you Willa," I said, handing her a spoon and the Triple Caramel Chunk. "Since you're so pretty, you should have a girl's name, don't you think?"

She didn't answer. Wasn't eating any ice cream.

"Willa? Is that okay?"

"I'm sorry," she whispered, her eyes on the table, and a hot wave of shame and regret washed over me, and longing and sadness and hell, everything else, too.

I swallowed hard, shoved those knife-sharp feelings aside and took a bite of ice cream. "Sounds good, don't you think? Willa and Harper. Willa Cather and Harper Lee are both great American writers, did you know that?"

Of course she didn't know that. I myself had just learned that this past summer, practically living at the tiny library, trying to fill the panicky void my mother had left, avoiding the terrible kindness of the staff. All summer, I'd hid in the stacks and prayed for invisibility, losing myself as best I could in books. And even though I'd exchanged fewer than four sentences with BeverLee, I guessed (correctly, it turned out) that the most intellectually stimulating literature she read was *Us Weekly*.

"I think it sounds good. Willa and Harper, Harper and Willa." I paused. "I guess we're sisters now."

She met my eyes for the first time, and there was a tiny flicker of hope. And just like that, I loved her. And I had been taking care of her ever since.

I shook off the memory. BeverLee was talking about when they'd fly out to Montana, what kind of trousseau she could put together for her babykins on such short notice, and Dad was staring out at the boats.

I cleared my throat. "Is anyone else concerned that Willa's getting married for the third time?"

"Well now, your daddy's my third husband, isn't that right, sweet knees? So I guess I don't see nothin' wrong with it, sugar. Third time's the charm!"

"She just met this guy," I reminded them.

"Well, they met at your wedding, darlin'."

"For six hours," I pointed out.

"And Christopher must be good people if he's Nick's brother." I suppressed the flash of hurt that comment inspired—the immature part of me wanted her to say *If he's related to that stupid ex-husband of yours, Harper, he must be a real ass.*

But no, BeverLee was off and running. "Christopher seemed *real* nice when we spoke on the telephone! Such good manners, and I think that says something about a man, don't you, Jimmy, honeypot?"

My father didn't answer.

"Dad? You got anything here?" I asked.

My father glanced at me. "Willa's an adult, Harper. She's almost thirty."

"She married an ex-con and a gay man. Perhaps one might suggest that she's not the best judge of character when it comes to men?" I said, trying to stay pleasant.

"Oh, listen to you, Harper, sugar! Don't you believe in true love?"

"Actually, no, not in the sense you mean, BeverLee."

"Bless your heart, Harper, you don't fool me. I bet your big ol' Dennis has something to say on the matter of true love! You're just fussing. I think you're a secret romantic, that's what I think. You just fake bein' all cynical 'cause of that job of yours. So lavender's fine, then? I'll do your hair, of course. You know how I love to do hair."

There was really no point in talking to BeverLee. Or Dad, whose failure to have an opinion was a well-documented trait. "Lavender's fine." I sighed. Hopefully, Willa would see sense before then.

"Should we all fly out together? Willard and her young man are getting out there a week from Wednesday, and your daddy and I, we want to get out there ay-sap! He's just dyin' to see his little Willard, aren't you, Jimmy?"

"Sure am." That was probably true. Dad had always gotten on better with Willa than with me.

"So we'll make a reservation for you and Dennis, how's that? We can all sit together, God willin'!"

While technically I did love both my father and BeverLee, the idea of being trapped on a plane with them for five or six hours was as appealing as, oh, gosh…being locked in a sweatbox by al Qaeda. Plus, if things went well, I wouldn't have to fly anywhere. "The wedding's on a Saturday?" I asked. BeverLee nodded. "I think Dennis and I will probably fly out Thursday or Friday, then."

"Come on, Harper, honeybunch, it's your baby sister!"

"And I've been to two of her weddings already!" I said, smiling to soften the words. "I'll come as soon as I can, how's that? Now, I hate to be rude, but I have work to do," I said, standing up.

"Sure now, you are a grade-A workaholic! We get the hint! We don't have to be told twice!" BeverLee hugged me against her breasts, which were the size and consistency of bowling balls, kissed me twice on the cheek, leaving a smear of frosty pink, fluffed my hair and managed to sneak in one last blast of Jhirmack. "Let's grab us some lunch this week, okay? We can talk about all the details. Should we get a stripper for her bachelorette party? Do they have Chippendales out there in…where is it again?"

"Glacier National Park, she said."

"I wonder if they have male strippers out there." Bev pursed her lips thoughtfully.

"I'm guessing not in the park itself," I said. "Teddy Roosevelt would've frowned on that."

"Then I better get on it," she said, and left, my father in tow, a miasmatic cloud of Cinnabar in her wake.

Three seconds later, she was back. "Honey, now may not be the time to discuss, but sweetie, I need a favor." She glanced furtively behind her.

"Um… Okay."

"I need to unburden myself, shall we say, on some-one."

"Sure." I took a deep breath, assumed good listening posture and braced for the worst.

The worst came. BeverLee wrung her hands, her acrylic, orange-painted nails flashing in the dimming light. "Your daddy and me…we haven't had sex for quite some time. For seven weeks, in fact."

"Oh, God," I said, flinching.

"I'm just wonderin', do y'all have any idea why?"

I choked. "BeverLee, you know…well, Dad and I don't really talk about…that. Or anything, really. And maybe you should tell—"

"What should I do? I mean, usually, he can't get enough—"

"Okay! Well. I think you should talk to one of your girlfriends. Or Dad. Or, um, your minister. Maybe Father Bruce?" *Sorry, Father.* "Not me. You two are my…you know. My family."

Bev mulled that over, then sighed. "Well, sure, you're right, honeybun. Okay. But if he does say anything—"

"I'm positive he won't."

"—you just give me a heads-up, all right? Bye now!"

The quiet took a few minutes to creep back to my little

slice of paradise, as if fearful that BeverLee would return. A thrush trilled from a bush, and the eastern breeze carried the sound of a faraway radio. A wisp of laughter came from down the hill, and for some reason, it made me feel…lonely. Coco came over and flopped at my feet, then rested her little head on my bare foot. "Thanks, sweetie," I said.

I stared out at the harbor for a long minute. Late summer is a particularly beautiful and bittersweet time on the Vineyard. Autumn was tiptoeing closer, the island would quiet, the kids would return to school. Nights spent on decks or sailboats were numbered now. Darkness fell earlier, and the leaves had already lost their summer richness. But tonight I didn't really see the view that so often soothed me after a long day's work.

Snap out of it, Harper, I told myself. I did indeed have work to do. Going inside, I saw the light blinking on the answering machine.

Message one, today at 6:04 p.m. "Harper? It's Tommy." There was a gusty sigh. "Listen, I'm having second thoughts. See, the thing is, I love her, you know, and maybe FedEx was just a mistake and we can get some counseling? More counseling, I mean? I don't know. Sorry to call you at home. See you tomorrow."

"You poor thing," I murmured automatically. My paralegal's wife had been unfaithful with the FedEx man, and Tommy was considering divorce. While I wouldn't represent him—it was never wise to represent a friend in a divorce, I'd learned—Tommy had decided mine was the shoulder on which he should cry, though I hadn't been much comfort, despite my best intentions.

Message two, today at 6:27 p.m. "Harper? It's me, Willa! I'll try you on your cell. Wait, did I just dial your cell? Or is this your house? Hang on…okay, it's your house. Well, talk to you later! Love you!" Despite my trepidation over her news, I couldn't help a smile. Sweet, sweet kid. Misguided, sure, but such a happy person.

Message three, today at 7:01 p.m. Right when I'd been proposing to Dennis, which seemed as though it happened last year, frankly.

Message three was just…silence. No one spoke…but the person hadn't hung up right away, either. For a second, my heart shivered, and I stood there, frozen.

Would Nick call me, with our siblings getting married?

No. He didn't have my number—it was unlisted. Even if he had it, he would never call me. Then the machine beeped, releasing me from my paralysis. *You have no more messages.*

I checked caller ID on my handset. Private number. Telemarketer, most likely.

Almost without thinking, I padded barefoot into my bedroom. I dragged the chair from my dressing table to the closet and stood on it, groping along the highest shelf, and took down an old hat box. I sat on the bed and slowly…very slowly…opened the box. There was the silk scarf Willa gave me three birthdays ago, in shades of green that made me look like an ad for the Irish Tourism Board with my curly red hair and green eyes. The black wool cap my grandmother had knit when I went off to Amherst, shortly before she died. My tattered copy of *To Kill a Mockingbird.* I'd always assumed I'd been named after Harper Lee…how many Harpers are out there?… and in the year after my mother had left, I'd read the book nine times, searching for some clue as to how my mother could've loved the story of literature's most steadfast hero but still abandon her only child.

There, underneath everything else, was what I wanted now.

A photo. I picked it up. My hands seemed to be shaking a little, and my breath stopped as I looked at the picture.

God, we'd been young.

The photo had been taken the morning of my wedding day; Dad had been testing his camera settings for the ceremony that afternoon. Nick and I hadn't done that *can't see you till the altar* thing, not buying into those superstitious rites (though in hindsight…). That morning had been cool and cloudy, and Nick and I had gone outside to sit on the steps of Dad's house, cups of coffee in our hands, me in a flannel bathrobe, Nick, a New Yorker, in a faded blue Yankees shirt and shorts, his dark hair rumpled. He was smiling just a little as he looked at me, his dark eyes, which could be so tragic and vulnerable and hopeful all at once, happy in this moment.

You could see it on our faces…Nick, confident, happy, almost smug. Me, a secret wreck.

Because sure, I had doubts. I'd been twenty-one, for God's sake. Just graduated college. Marriage? Were we *crazy?* But Nick had been sure enough for both of us, and on that day—June 21, the first day of summer—for that one day, I believed him. We loved each other, and we'd live happily ever after.

Live and learn.

"You're not a dumb kid anymore," I said aloud, still staring at the image of my younger self. Now I was somebody in my own right. Now I had a job, a home, a dog, a man…not necessarily in that order, but you get my meaning.

I put the picture down and took a deep breath. Straightened my spine and pulled my BeverLee-enhanced hair back into its customary, sleek ponytail. So I'd be seeing Nick again. The tremors that thought had induced earlier were gone now. I had nothing to worry about regarding Nick. He was a youthful mistake. We'd been caught up in each other…and yes, we'd been in love. But you needed more than love. Certainly, eight years as a divorce attorney had reinforced the truth of that idea.

But once, Nick could reduce me to pudding with one look. Once, a smile from Nick could fill me with such joy that I'd nearly float. Once, a day without Nick made me feel as if my skin didn't fit and only when he came home would I feel right again.

No wonder we hadn't worked. That kind of feeling… it couldn't last.

I'd spent years getting over Nick, and over him I was. When I saw him—*if* I saw him, that was—I'd be cool. Dennis and I were solid…maybe not engaged, alas, but solid enough. Whatever Nick had once meant to me, well, that was ashes now.

It almost felt true.

CHAPTER THREE

ELEVEN DAYS LATER, I was about to put the ashes theory to the test. Needless to say, my mood was not in the chipper range.

"Tommy, look. Sometimes our hearts need time to accept what our heads already know." I suppressed a sigh; Tommy was in my office (the eleventh time this week), once more debating whether his wife's transgressions were really that bad.

"It's understandable, isn't it? She's young…we're both young…and I work a lot, right? Maybe she was just lonely." Tommy looked at me across my desk, his birdlike face hopeful. My paralegal was six-foot-four and skinny as Ichabod Crane. In fact, he looked like a crane…long legs, rather hooked nose, small mouth. Despite that, he was awfully cute somehow, all those misfit features working together. He'd been married for seven months to Meggie; I'd been at their wedding, and alas, had known even then their days were numbered. Call it my sixth sense.

"Tom," I said. "Buddy. Let's take a look at the facts. Not what you hope, but just the facts." His expression was blank with a side of confused. "Tommy, she screwed FedEx." Personally, I thought Kevin from UPS was much cuter, but that probably wasn't relevant.

"I know," Tom said. "But maybe there was a reason. Maybe I should just forgive her?"

"You could," I said, sneaking in a glance at my watch. "Sure. Anything is possible." Could a person really forgive

44   MY ONE AND ONLY

and forget a spouse shtupping someone else? Really? Come on. Hell, I hadn't shtupped anyone, and Nick still thought—

I cut the thought off at the knees. Didn't want to think about my ex-husband any more than I had to. I'd be seeing him in…crotch…about twenty-four hours.

This evening, Dennis and I would be taking the ferry to Boston so we could catch a flight first thing tomorrow morning. We'd land in Denver, switch to a smaller plane and head for Kalispell, Montana, which sounded suspiciously tiny. Then we were renting a car to go to Lake McDonald Lodge in the park itself. Christopher, my once and apparently future brother-in-law, had worked out in Glacier once upon a time—I even had a vague recollection of Nick talking about wanting to visit him out there.

"So what do you think I should do, Harper? I mean, I can't help still loving her, and I wonder if I drove her to this…"

"Tom. Stop. You can't blame yourself. She slept with the FedEx man. This doesn't bode well for a long and happy marriage. I'm really sorry you're hurting, I truly am. And you're welcome to stay with Meggie, just as you are welcome to slam your testicles in the car door for days on end." He closed his eyes. "In both cases," I said in a gentler tone, "you're just going to get more hurt. I wish I could say something more hopeful, but I'm your friend, I'm a divorce attorney, so I'm not gonna blow smoke."

He sighed, deflating before me. "Right. Thanks, Harper." With that, he slumped out of my office, listlessly muttering hello to Theo Bainbrook, the senior partner at Bainbrook, Bainbrook and Howe.

"There she is. My star." Theo, dressed in pink pants printed with blue whales and a pink-and-white-striped polo shirt, leaned in my office doorway. "Harper, if only I had ten lawyers like you."

"And for what would you like to praise me this time, Theo?" I smiled.

"You were right about Betsy Errol's account in the Caymans." Theo did a little shuffling dance, humming "We're in the Money." I smiled...not because we were in fact now going to be paid more (which of course we were), but because Kevin Errol was one of those *I just want it to be over, I don't care about the money* types. As his attorney, it was my job to make sure he got a fair shake. He deserved his half, especially having been married to a shrew like Betsy. Betsy had hidden funds...I'd found them. Well, I had found them with the help of Dirk Kilpatrick, our firm's private investigator, bless his heart.

"That's great, Theo. Unfortunately, though, I have to get going. Sister's wedding, ferry to Beantown, remember?"

"Ah. The wedding. If you're going to Boston, you're welcome to stop in the office there and do a little work before you..."

"Not gonna happen, Theo." Bainbrook did have offices in Boston, and sadly, Theo was absolutely serious. He himself hadn't actually practiced law for some time, having found that his minions could do the real work and thus enabling Theo to put in more time on the golf course.

"Would you like to hear who I'm playing golf with, Harper?" he asked, eyes twinkling.

"Tiger Woods?"

"No. Sadly, no."

"Um...gosh. A politician?"

"Yes. Think big, Harper. Backroom deals, war, clogged arteries."

"Is this person a former vice president with a propensity for friend-shooting?" I asked.

Theo beamed and twinkled. "Bingo."

"Ooooh," I said. "Very impressive."

I liked Theo, despite the fact that he was lazy, had four ex-wives and dropped names more often than a seagull poops. He was an amiable boss, especially to me, since I put in oodles more hours than the other three lawyers here in the Martha's Vineyard office. My divorce was one of the last cases Theo had handled himself. As I'd sat in his office, shaking like a leaf, gnawing on my cuticles, Theo's gentle voice had given me a lifeline—*Sometimes our hearts just need time to accept what our heads already know.* He was the one who showed me that divorce attorneys were shepherds, helping the dazed and heartbroken across the jagged landscape of their shattered hope. He hired me the instant I graduated law school—I'd never worked anywhere but here.

"Well, enjoy yourself in Montana, Harper," Theo sighed. "Great fly-fishing up there. Would you like to borrow my gear?"

"That's okay. I'll be back Monday. In and out."

"Watch out for grizzly bears." Theo winked and went off to schmooze Carol, the firm's ill-tempered and all-powerful secretary.

I answered a few emails, checked my calendar for next week, tidied my desk. Then I stared out at the garden my office windows overlooked. Edgartown was the poshest town on the island. Graced with large and tasteful homes, brick sidewalks and our stout white lighthouse, the area was imposing but charming, much like Theo in some ways. In the winter, it was deserted, as most of the homeowners had their primary residences elsewhere. In the summer, it was so crowded that it could take half an hour to drive a mile. Most days above sixty degrees, I rode my bike to and from work; it took me about forty-five minutes of mostly flat pedaling and was a lovely way to get some exercise.

I sighed, unable to distract myself any longer. So. Soon I'd be thirty-four, an age that boiled with significance for me. I had no kids, no husband, no fiancé. Tomorrow I'd be seeing my ex-husband and, no doubt, ripping a few scabs off memories I'd buried long ago and watching my sister marry a man she barely knew. Super fun.

But speaking of scabs and memories...

Very slowly, I opened the top drawer of my desk, took out a little key from where it was taped to the back and unlocked the bottom drawer of the file cabinet to my left.

Last year, on my thirty-third birthday, I'd hired our firm's private investigator for personal reasons. Half a day later, Dirk had given me this envelope.

Just looking at it made me feel a little sick. But I wasn't a weenie, either, so I opened it, just a little, and glanced inside. Town, state, place of employment, place of residence. As if I needed to see the words. As if they weren't already branded on my temporal lobe.

I hesitated, then dropped the envelope back in the drawer. "I have other stuff going on," I told it. "You're not a priority. Sorry." I closed the drawer, locked it, replaced the key.

Then I gathered up my stuff, went into the waiting room, waved to Tommy and told him to keep his chin up—he'd get through this, they all did—and reminded Carol that cell service might well suck out there in Big Sky country and not to panic if she didn't hear from me.

"Have I ever panicked, not hearing from you? Have I, in fact, ever gone twenty minutes without hearing from you?" she said, scowling at me. "Take a damn vacation, Harper. Give us all a break."

"Aw. Does that mean you want some moose antlers as your souvenir?"

"That would be nice."

I tapped the bobblehead figure of Dustin Pedroia on her desk. "Hope the Sox win tonight," I said.

"Did you see Pedey last night? Unbelievable," she said, sighing orgasmically.

"I know," I said, having watched the rerun somewhere around 2:00 a.m. as I battled insomnia. "He's so good now…just wait till he hits puberty."

Carol's dreamy expression turned murderous. "Get out."

"Bye, then," I smiled.

But just before I left, I went back and got that envelope from the bottom drawer, stuck it in my bag and tried not to think of it.

Out on the street, I took a deep breath. School was back in session, and most of the tourists were gone, though they'd be flooding in like the red tide on Friday. Glancing down the street at the Catholic church, I decided to pop in on Father Bruce before herding Dennis into readiness.

The church was quiet. Ah. A sign. *The Sacrament of Reconciliation is held Thursday afternoons from 5:00 till 7:00 p.m.* The little door of the confessional booth was open. I went in. Sure enough, Father Bruce was seated on the other side, apparently dozing.

"Bless me, Father, for I have sinned," I said. Always envied my Catholic friends for this little rite.

Father Bruce jerked awake. "How long has it been since—oh, Harper, it's you. Very funny."

"How are you?"

"I'm fine, dear. But this time is reserved for those seeking the sacrament of reconciliation."

"They're not exactly lining up around the block, Father."

He sighed. "You have a point. Can I do something for you, dear?"

"No, not really. I've just always wondered what you do in here."

"I knit."

"I figured."

We sat there in silence for a minute. One thing about churches—they all smelled nice. All those candles, all that forgiveness.

"Is there something on your mind, my dear?" Father Bruce asked. I didn't answer. "As your confessor, I'm bound by the same confidentiality you give your clients," he added.

I looked at my hands. "Well, sure, in that case, yes, something's on my mind. I'm about to see my ex-husband after twelve years."

As Kim had done when she heard this news, Father Bruce sputtered. "You were married?"

"Briefly."

"Go on."

I shrugged. "It just didn't work out. We were too young and immature, same old story, yawn. Now my sister's marrying his brother. My stepsister, his half brother. Whatever." Suddenly uncomfortable, I sat up. "Well, I should go. I have to pick up Dennis."

"Does Dennis know?"

"Know what? That I was married? Sure. I told him last week."

"And this was the first conversation you had on that topic?"

"It's not really a topic. It's more of a fact. Sort of like, 'I had my tonsils out when I was nine, I got married a month after I graduated college, we were divorced before our first anniversary.'"

"And have you seen your husband since?"

"Ex-husband. Nope."

"How telling."

"You priests. Armchair psychologists, the whole lot of you."

"You're the one sitting in a confessional booth, seeking my wisdom under the guise of curiosity."

I smiled. "Okay, you win this round. Sorry I can't stick around so you can gloat, but I do have to go. Ferry leaves in an hour." But I didn't move.

Since my sister had called, there'd been a thrum of electricity running through me. Not a pleasant thrum, either. Sort of a sick feeling, as if I lived too near power lines and was about to be diagnosed with a horrible disease. As if opposing counsel just dropped a little bombshell about a secret bank account and a mistress in Vegas. For twelve years, memories of my marriage had been locked in a safe at the bottom of some murky lake of my soul. Now, through some whim of fate and through no desire or action of my own, I was going to see Nick Lowery once more.

"Here." Father Bruce pulled something from his back pocket and then opened his side of the booth. I stood as well and opened mine, joining him in the church proper. "It's my card. My cell number's on it. Give me a ring, let me know how things are going."

"I'll be back on Monday," I said. "I'll buy you a drink instead."

He winked. "Call me. Have fun. Tell your sister hello for me."

"Will do." I gave his shoulder a gentle punch and left, my heels tapping on the tile floor.

TWENTY-TWO HOURS LATER, I was ready to strangle Dennis with Coco's leash and leave his body for the vultures or bald eagles or hyenas or whatever the hell else lived up here.

Yes, yes, I'd originally wanted him to come with me. One doesn't face an ex-husband alone when one has a brawny firefighter boyfriend who looks like the love child of Gerard Butler and Jake Gyllenhaal. But the "and guest" idea had played out better in my imagination than in reality. Also, the thought kept popping up that this would've felt *much* better if Dennis been my fiancé instead of boyfriend, but *that* subject had not been broached since the night of the fateful phone call. Plus, I was about to murder him.

Let me explain. We'd been bickering since the moment I found him guzzling a beer and watching a rerun of the 2004 World Series instead of standing at the door with bag packed, as I'd requested. Granted, things had been a little off since my marriage proposal—and by off, I mean we hadn't done it since then, which was causing all kinds of issues. But just because I was unsettled about Willa getting married didn't mean I'd forgotten that Dennis had not exactly been thrilled with the thought of marrying me. Which meant, of course, that he wasn't getting any. But we were still together, and when I asked if he'd come with me to Montana, he said yes. Eventually.

Unfortunately, Dennis, who was prone to back trouble, conveniently suffered a back spasm just before we left his grubby little apartment, which required me to wrangle all our luggage from our respective homes to my car to the ferry to the cab to the hotel, and then again to the cab to Logan, and then from Gate 4 to Gate 37 in Denver, and then from Ye Tiny Airport here in Montana to the rental car. Not just the luggage, but Coco (sulking in her crate with her bunny), my laptop, my purse and Dennis himself, who had a tendency to wander. Add to this that he'd charmed two flight attendants (a straight woman and a gay man) into giving him the last seat of first class due to said back spasms, leaving me to sit wedged between an impressively overweight Floridian and a frat boy who drooled on my shoulder as he slept, oblivious to the sharp elbow I kept jamming into his side. And oh, yes, my sister was marrying a stranger, my father was apparently having marital problems and my ex-husband was at the end of this hellish journey.

I was a little tense.

Which brought us to now, standing in a parking lot outside the Kalispell City Airport, squabbling like third-graders.

"Dude, I'll drive," Dennis said. "Give me the keys." He stretched and twisted so that his lower back cracked, making me wince.

"I'll drive, Dennis." Honestly, concentrating on driving would distract me from what (and who) lay ahead.

"Dude, come on!"

"Stop calling me that!" I snapped. "Please, Dennis! Don't call me dude, okay? I'll drive. You get lost between your house and mine, Dennis, on the island where you grew up—"

"Maybe I'm not really lost," he interjected, uncharacteristically prickly.

"—and we have forty miles to go through grizzly-strewn wilderness," I continued, my voice rising in volume, "so please. Please, Dennis. Can we please get going here?"

Unlike Dennis, Coco obeyed, leaping lightly into the driver's seat. I'd been forced to bring her, as she'd feigned a hurt paw when she heard the word *kennel* and limped around until she saw her travel crate. The dog was an evil genius. She sat happily, sniffing the Montana air, which was strangely clear and pure, unlike the salty winds of Martha's Vineyard, always redolent with the smell of garlic and fish or, in the morning, doughnuts.

Realizing that a spat was not going to advance my case, I took a cleansing breath and tried to unlock my jaw. "Honey? We don't want to be late for dinner."

"My back is killing me," Dennis grumped. "Harp, can't you give me a massage or something?"

Wondering briefly if Father Bruce had a patron saint of patience, I said, "Dennis, we're standing in a parking lot. I'm sorry your back hurts, honey, and I will rub it later, but I can't help you now. Maybe at the hotel, okay? Please, Dennis? Can you please get in the damn car?"

With another sulky (and yes, kind of hot) scowl, he got into the car, grumbling. I followed, and Coco jumped onto my lap. She loved to steer.

I glanced at Dennis, sighed and started the car. "I'm sorry. I'm a little...stressed, Den," I said, adjusting the rearview mirror.

"I guess I would be if I had to see my ex, too," he said with an understanding grin. Then he tipped his seat backward and closed his eyes.

It was, admittedly, stunning out here. Mountains rose around us, patchy with snow—or glaciers, I supposed, great expanses of gray rock and swathes of dense green pine. Already, the trees glowed with autumn color. Clouds stretched through the blue sky, which seemed much higher here, much more vast, for some reason. Big Sky country indeed. I'd never been west before...never really taken a proper vacation, to be honest, just a few days here and there, usually tacked onto conferences in big cities. This... this was different.

A sense of solemnity settled over me, and Coco, as well. Wildflowers bloomed on the side of the road as we quickly left the town of Kalispell behind. Dennis, too, seemed to be struck by the drama and size of the natural beauty, so different from our little island—or no, he was sleeping. Just as well.

Unexpectedly, my throat tightened as I saw the sign for Glacier National Park. I'd watched parts of the Ken Burns special on PBS, but I wasn't quite prepared for the beauty around me...the craggy, sharp mountains, the fields of multicolored flowers, and that air, the sweet, pure air. God bless Teddy Roosevelt. I stopped at the entrance gate, and a park ranger opened her window. "Welcome to Glacier National Park, ma'am," she said, adding "Hey there, cutie" when she saw Coco. I paid and thanked her, nodded dutifully at her warnings to watch out for wash-outs, as the last rainstorm had been fierce, and drove into the park.

The road wove through the forest, then came out into a more open space. My breath caught. To the left, the earth dropped steeply away into a field of long, golden grass twined with blue, red and pink wildflowers. It was breathtaking. After a while, I turned onto Going to the Sun Road...what a beautiful name! A vast, oblong glacier capped the bare and jagged ridge across the way.

Suddenly, my tires caught the edge of the road, and I jerked the wheel a little, adrenaline spurting. The rented Honda veered back onto the road. Coco's tiny feet scrabbled on my lap. "Sorry, baby," I muttered once we were straightened out. "Got a little caught up in the scenery." Den slept on, undisturbed. I glanced at the dashboard clock...heck. Four o'clock already. I'd thought we'd be there by now. Stepping on the gas, I almost immediately caught up to a car in front of me.

A slow car, despite the fact that it was a classic red Mustang, built for speed and midlife crises. Or octogenarian females, I guessed, from the dedicated way the car stayed precisely on its own side of the road, never straying above thirty miles an hour. No more, no less. Great. Why buy a 'Stang if you were going to do the speed limit? Didn't that defeat the purpose of the pointless effort to recapture one's youth and laugh at the specter of death? I couldn't see the driver, as the sun glared off the back window, but judging by the way we were inching along, Eeyore here was one hundred and three years old, blind in both eyes and had already cheated death. Many times.

Glancing at the clock again, I sighed. Everyone else should already be at the hotel…the lodge, I corrected silently. Lake McDonald Lodge, it was called, where Christopher used to work in his youth. Despite the last-minute nature of the nuptials, the happy couple was expecting a fair number of friends. According to BeverLee, Chris was still close to some of the staff at the lodge, strings had been pulled, rates were low as the tourist season was officially over. Willa, who collected people the way a black wool sweater collects lint, expected around thirty guests.

After three phone calls, it had dawned on my sister that perhaps I had some feelings about seeing my ex-husband again. "You're okay with the Nick situation, right?" she said. "I mean, I know you guys werc…intcnsc."

"Oh, I'm fine," I said blithely. "That was eons ago. No, Wills, it's just…honey, I just wonder why you're rushing. You know, I see so many unhappy—"

But my sister was prepared. Sure, I knew her well… but she knew me, too. "Harper, I know you think you're looking out for me. But maybe this time I'm right, did that ever occur to you? Have some faith in me. I'm not an idiot."

And that was the argument that had me grinding my teeth in frustration. Willa *wasn't* an idiot. Except…in a way…she was a dope. A sweet dope, but a dope. If I tried to remind her of the facts of her past marriages or drop statistics, she'd counter that she'd grown up since then. What could I say to that? *No, you haven't, you're still as naive as a baby bunny?*

"So you're okay with Nick being there? Because he's Chris's best man, of course."

Of course. "I'm fine." *So you've seen him? What does he look like? Did he ask about me? Is he still mad? How did he seem? Is he married? Any kids? Does he still live in the city? Still an architect? Is he fat? Bald? Please?*

And by the way…how the hell did Willa meet Christopher, anyway? Was Nick involved? Willa said she'd "run into" Christopher in a city of eight million people and recognized him after twelve years.

Please. I wasn't born yesterday.

Dennis grunted in his sleep, which Coco interpreted as an invitation. She jumped onto his lap, then licked his hand, and he smiled without opening his eyes and petted her. I smiled, too, almost reluctantly. *Exhibit A, Your Honor. Not only is Dennis physically appealing, he's kind to animals.* I turned my attention back to the road.

Crap!

I slammed on the brakes to avoid rear-ending the red car in front of me. "Jesus!" I blurted, leaning on the horn. The Mustang driver had stopped, right in the middle of the road.

"Everything okay?" Dennis asked blearily.

"Yes. Sorry, hon. Some idiot who shouldn't be driving." The woman had just *stopped*. Yes, the ranger had warned about wildlife on the road, but there was no elk, no moose, nothing to explain the delay.

Dennis sat up, rubbing his eyes. Coco licked him on the chin, then poked her little nose out the window, snuffling. She whined and wagged. "You like it here, honey?" I asked my pet.

"It's pretty," Dennis said.

The red Mustang had not moved an inch. We were on a sharp curve, too, so passing would definitely be inadvisable, not that I'd seen many other cars. Should I try it? I tapped the horn again. Nothing. No grizzly bear, no elk, no goat, no response. "Come on," I groaned. The sooner this weekend started, the sooner I could get back to normal. The driver didn't move. Stroke? Heart attack? Flashback to the Civil War? I leaned on the horn again— alas, it was a rather friendly-sounding horn, as the rental was a Honda. Give me a good old-fashioned Detroit-made blare any day.

"Come on, Florence!" I yelled out the window. "Can you please move it?"

The driver of the car extended an arm out the window. And a finger.

It was a male arm...and finger.

And then the car door opened, and the driver got out, and was neither female nor a Civil War veteran. My hands slid off the steering wheel.

It was Nick.

He took off his sunglasses and looked at me and though I was fairly sure my expression hadn't changed—I was rather paralyzed at the moment—my heart lurched, my mouth went dry, my legs turned to water.

Nick. He folded his arms and tilted his head, his eyes narrowed, and my heart flinched as if it had been punched. A roaring sound filled my ears.

Coco yipped.

"Problem?" Dennis asked.

"Um...no." Without further explanation, I put the car in Park and got out.

"Harper?" Dennis asked. "Dude, don't make a scene."

Funny, to be so outwardly calm as I approached my ex-husband. *You're not a dumb kid anymore,* I reminded myself distantly, but the words didn't mean much, not when my entire being burned with electricity.

"Oh, Nick, it's you," I said mildly, pleased to find my voice sounded mostly normal. "I assumed you were an old woman riddled with cataracts."

"And I assumed you were a Massachusetts driver with anger-management issues." His tone was as pleasant as mine. "I see one of us was right."

He was older. Abruptly, there was a lump in my throat. *Of course he's older,* I told myself. *So are you. It's been a long time.* His dark hair was shot with silver, and crow's feet radiated from his eyes, those tragic dark brown gypsy eyes a little cool, a little suspicious. He was thinner now, his face bordering on careworn. His clothes immediately identified him as a cool New Yorker...dark jeans, white button-down with a quality and cut that made him look sophisticated and polished...all the things he'd wanted to be way back when.

Twelve years. What a horribly long time, and yet not even close to being long enough.

Then he smiled the way I remembered—that instant smile that flashed like lightning and had about the same results. Heat, electricity, light and possible injury and/or death, and I was glad I still had my sunglasses on. The last thing I wanted was for Nick to know he could still... affect me. One crack in the armor, and Nick would be in there with a hammer and a chisel, and he wouldn't stop till there was nothing left but a pile of rust. That's how it had been back then, and judging by my staggering heart, that's how it was still.

"You look good," he said, sounding almost surprised.

"You, too." Then, hoping to get him to look away from me, I nodded at the Mustang. "I see you're having a midlife crisis," I said.

"Same to you," he returned, jerking his chin. Ah. Dennis was approaching. Thank God. My boyfriend's overall manly appearance was somewhat diminished by the fact that he was holding my rather tiny dog and stroking her head, and she wore her pink patent-leather collar, but still.

"Is that a rattail?" Nick murmured.

"He's a firefighter," I said, apropos of nothing.

"Of course he is. It was that or pool boy." Nick smiled as Dennis drew near.

I looped my arm through my boyfriend's. "Dennis, meet Nick Lowery. Nick, Dennis Costello."

"Nice to meet you, Dennis."

"Same here." They shook hands. "Are you going to the wedding, too?" Dennis asked.

"Yes, I am." Nick raised an eyebrow at me.

"Cool," Dennis said. "So how do you guys know each other?"

"Biblically," Nick answered.

"Nick's my ex-husband, Dennis," I said a bit sharply. "I'm sure I mentioned it once. Possibly twice."

"Oh, right!" He glanced at me, then back at Nick. "So why'd you stop?"

"Taking in the sights." Nick pointed. About three hundred yards off the road, down the steep meadow, a black bear shuffled slowly along the bank of a clear, broad river. It stopped to sniff the wind, stood up on its hind legs, then dropped back down and continued. Coco whined, certain she could take the beast.

"Dude, is that a dog?" Dennis asked. I closed my eyes. If only Dennis were the strong and silent type…

"Black bear," Nick said.

"Awesome." To Den's credit, the bear did sort of resemble a big, black Newfie. After another minute or two, it disappeared into the long grass.

The two men looked at each other once more. "So you're the ex," Dennis said.

"Yet I lived to tell the tale," Nick confirmed.

Dennis gave a snort of laughter, aborted by my murderous look. He petted Coco, looking a bit like Dr. Evil stroking the hairless cat. Nick just stared at me, his eyes mocking, and my face grew hot. Dragging my eyes off him, I looked at Dennis. "Honey?" I asked brightly. "Want to drive?" I asked.

"I thought you didn't want me to," Dennis answered. Nick's eyebrow rose knowingly.

"Would you like to drive now?" I asked, keeping a smile on my face.

"Uh…sure. Come on, Coco-Buns." The pet name failed to reinforce Dennis's heterosexuality, and I stifled a sigh as my boyfriend obediently walked back to the car and got into the driver's side, letting Coco stand on his lap, her paws on the wheel.

I didn't move. "I hear you approve," I said to Nick.

"I hear you don't." He looked at me a beat or two, steadily. "Take off those damn sunglasses, Harper."

With an exaggerated sigh, I obeyed. "Better?"

He didn't answer, just stared at me with those gypsy eyes, and I looked right back. Twelve years' distance, a career spent in court, staring down idiot lying spouses… *Don't mess with me, Nick.* He seemed to sense it, because he looked away abruptly, back in the direction of the shambling bear. "Drinks later? For the sake of the kids?"

Do not be alone with him.

It was a line I often said to my clients. Seeing him alone would muddy the waters, stir up emotions best left untouched, possibly make you agree to things you shouldn't.

I replaced my sunglasses. "Sure. Are you staying at the lodge?"

"Yes." He had a way of saying *yes,* Nick did. Fast and sure and disproportionately hot, like he knew exactly what you were going to say and couldn't wait to give you an affirmative. I'd forgotten about that.

Crotch.

"Okay, then," I said, and my voice sounded nice and normal. "I'm sure we can find a bar or something."

It wasn't until about a mile or two later, when I was sitting in the car next to Dennis, clutching his hand, that I was able to take a normal breath. That electric hum was downright painful now.

This was a horrible idea. Every aspect of this whole situation was wrong, wrong, wrong.

CHAPTER FOUR

LOOKING BACK AT MY LIFE thus far, I can't say I exactly regret marrying Nicholas Sebastian Lowery. That being said, I knew he was trouble the very first day I met him. The very first second, even.

I didn't regret it because I learned a lot. Well, my time with Nick confirmed a lot that I'd already believed. But when a man comes up to you in a bar and tells you you're the woman he'll marry, it's a little…overwhelming. Plus, it's not the usual come-on line often employed by college students. Even grad students.

I was a junior at Amherst, it was my twentieth birthday, my roomies had gotten me a fake ID, and we were breaking it in. The pub was crowded, hot and noisy. Music thumped, people shouted to be heard…and then I turned and saw a guy staring at me.

Just staring. Steady, unabashed, completely focused. Time seemed to stop for a second, and all those other people, they just faded away, as the dark-haired man… boy…just looked at me.

"You okay?" asked Tina, my closest college chum.

"Sure," I said, and the spell was broken.

But the guy came over and sat at the table next to us and just kept looking at me, and—forgive the nauseating cliché—it felt as if he really *saw* me, because his concentration was so singular.

"What are you looking at, idiot?" I asked, giving him the sneer that had served me so well.

"My future wife. The mother of my children." One corner of his mouth pulled up, and every female part I had squeezed warm and hard.

"Bite me," I said, just about to turn away.

"Anything you want," he answered, and then he grinned, that lightning-flash smile that said, *Sure, I'm a jerk, but we both know I can get away with murder...* and it was hard not to smile back. So I didn't turn away. And I did smile.

"So when should we get married?" he asked, pulling his chair closer.

I checked him out discreetly. Nice hands. Beautiful eyes. Shiny dark hair—I was a sucker for dark-haired men. "I wouldn't marry you if you were the last man on earth, bub."

"Yet you're ogling me," he answered. "What are you drinking, wife?"

I laughed and said, "Crikey, the nerve. Sam Adams Octoberfest."

I didn't love my birthday, given my history with the date, but Tina had dragged me out with two other friends. All of us were in our junior year at Amherst, all of us receiving a stellar education at an extremely feminist-slanted college, all of us absolutely confident that the world held no boundaries, all of us planning to Do Important Things. And yet, those three friends took a respectful and almost envious step back. *Look at Harper! Some guy is hitting on her! And he even used the M-word! Give her some space! Don't blow it!*

And though I now cringe to admit, I was swept off my feet, which came as quite a surprise to me. I guess that's sort of the point of being swept.

Nick Lowery was unlike any of the pale, vague boyfriends I'd had up to this point (and I'd had many and loved none). He was, despite being only twenty-three, a grown-up. In school at UMass, getting his master's in architecture. He already had a job lined up in June—a real job, not an internship, but as a practicing architect in New York City at a place that made huge buildings all over the world. He knew what he wanted, he had a plan to get it, and the plan was working. In a world of vaguely ambitious, overeducated, not-very-employable college students, he was rather thrilling.

We talked for hours that night. He drank without getting drunk and didn't try to get me drunk, either. He listened when I spoke, his eyes intent. And such eyes! Too beautiful and tragic somehow, with a secret pain (cough), a gentle torment only an old soul could feel...well, it was clear *I* had a little too much to drink. Nick had grown up in Brooklyn, couldn't wait to move back to the city, loved the New York Yankees, which resulted in some very fun trash talk (I won, somehow making the Sox sound noble and superior, despite the sorry season they were having). He asked me questions about what I wanted to do, what I loved learning, where I was from. He didn't seem to grow bored, even when I waxed rhapsodic about environmental law, and he didn't stare at my boobs. He just seemed to really...like me.

We were both a little shocked when the busboy asked us to leave, as it was now 2:30 a.m. Nick offered to walk me home, and as we crossed the lovely, still campus, he held my hand. That was a first for me—a boy who took my hand. That was a public statement of romantic intentions, and the boys I'd dated (and they were definitely all *boys*) tended more toward the shoulder bump. Hand-holding, I discovered, was quite the turn-on, though I pretended not to notice.

"Can I take you out sometime?" he asked in front of my dorm.

"Is that code for 'Can I come in and have sex with you?'" I returned.

The answer came almost before I'd finished the question. "No."

Another first.

I blinked. "Seriously? Because I probably *would* sleep with you." Actually, at that moment, I wouldn't have. At least I didn't think so. But those eyes…that rather beautiful hand holding mine so firmly…"Are you asking me out on a *date?*"

"Yes." That fast, certain yes. "Yes, I want to take you on a date. No, I don't want to have sex with you. Not tonight, anyway."

"Why? Are you a Mormon? Suffer from ED? Are you gay?"

He grinned, his gypsy eyes transformed. "No, no and no. Because, Harper Elizabeth James"—crap, I'd told him my entire name (and he remembered, oh sigh!)—"that would be…disrespectful."

I blinked. "Well, now you have indeed rendered me speechless. I can state with absolute certainty that I have never before heard that particular line." Prelaw. What can I say? We all sounded like pompous idiots. Plus, I'd had three whole beers, which made me sound even more idiotic and pompous.

But Nick seemed to think I was cute. "I'll call you tomorrow."

"Now *that* one I've heard before. Full of sound and bullshit, signifying nothing."

He called me nine hours later, having hacked into the college website to find my cell number. "It's Nick."

"Nick who?" I asked, blushing for perhaps the first time in my life.

"The father of your children."

"Right, right." I paused, unable to suppress a smile. "Do I at least get dinner before I have to start breeding?"

He took me to a real restaurant in Northampton... not just a college-kid hangout with four-dollar falafels, but one with tables and waiters and everything, and thus began my first real relationship. He called when he said he would. He sent me little jokes via email, met me for lunch, sometimes showed up outside my classroom to walk across campus with me. We often went to the movies, where we both talked incessantly, much to the annoyance of the other patrons. We dated, as in old-fashioned, 1950s dating, and I couldn't believe how fun it was.

But for an entire month, he didn't kiss me or touch me (aside from holding my hand, for crying out loud), and by then, I was dying of lust. Which, I want you to know, I hid very well. Never mentioned it once. I just waited, more obsessed than I wanted to be, wondering if he was playing some little game. But I found myself waiting for those phone calls, and my heart did this weird leaping thing when I saw his face.

Four weeks and two days after we first met, Nick had me over to his apartment for the first time, a typical grotty little place which was atypically clean. He made me dinner—lasagna and salad and warm bread. Poured me red wine without trying to liquor me up. He'd made a *pie* for dessert, which had me once again wondering out loud if he was indeed gay. He wouldn't let me do the dishes. As we sat on his couch (holding hands but otherwise chaste), he told me why he thought the Brooklyn Bridge was the most beautiful man-made structure on earth and how he would take me there on my virgin trip to New York and we'd walk across it and get an ice cream in Brooklyn and then walk across again, taking plenty of time to worship the world's first steel-wire suspension bridge.

"I've always favored the architecture of Denny's myself," I said.

"I may have to divorce you."

"I call the yacht and the apartment in Paris. It's in the prenup, of course."

Nick laughed. "I don't believe in prenups."

"All the better. I will take you to the cleaners, boy. Paris apartment, you're mine, all mine."

"Why did I marry such a heartless woman?" he grinned.

I smiled back. "You haven't even kissed me yet, Nick. I won't marry you and bear our five healthy sons if you fail to thrill me."

He looked at me, a little smile playing around his mouth, two days of knee-weakening razor stubble, dark hair tousled, and those gypsy eyes. He reached out and touched my lips with one finger. He didn't have to kiss me. I was thrilled anyway. And, quite out of the blue, suddenly terrified. My breath stuttered in my chest, and my heart seemed to contract, and even as he leaned forward, I thought *Don't let him be too good. Don't fall in love.*

But he was, and I did. It was…stunning, really, to be kissed like this, and I felt that I'd never really understood what kissing was before. It was as if our mouths had been made to kiss only each other, and the shock and thrill, the urgent, hot feeling, the little sounds of kissing, the— dang it—the rightness. I never thought I'd be desperate for someone—I'd had seven years and four weeks and two days to teach myself not to love anyone desperately. But when Nick kissed me for the first time, my whole body came alive. It was terrifying how good it was.

We kissed and groped on the couch for eons, until finally, Nick stood up, took me by the hand and led me to his bedroom, kissing me, touching me, his skin hot on mine, his cheeks flushed, eyes nearly black. It was as if we had all the time in the world for this, for this sweet, melting ache that made me shake. I pulled his shirt over his head, and my hands explored his smooth chest, his addictive skin, the lovely space above his collarbone. There was a ragged little scar over his heart, which I traced with my fingers as I kissed his beautiful neck, felt his thudding pulse under my lips, tasted the salt of his sweat. His hands were hot, his mouth was gentle, a small smile playing on his lips whenever he opened his eyes to look at me.

I didn't object when his clever fingers unbuttoned the back of my dress, but when his hand slid up my thigh, I jumped and grabbed his wrist. Time to stop. Time to leave. But I didn't move.

"Far enough?" he asked, his voice husky, his face against my neck.

I swallowed. "Nick?"

He raised his head. *Oh, you're in trouble, Harper,* my brain said. I couldn't manage to speak, as the words were stuck in my throat. Feelings of awkwardness, dorkiness, embarrassment roiled around with the heat and lust and wanting.

"What is it, honey?" he asked, his voice so gentle it hurt my heart.

If he hadn't said *honey,* my guess is that I would've pulled my usual routine and fled, feeling somewhat guilty and completely safe. *Get out, get out, get out,* my brain yammered. I swallowed and looked away.

"I've never done this before," I whispered. God! Being a virgin at twenty and change…in a blue state, nonetheless…at a liberal college…et cetera…!

Nick blinked. Because sure, I was a toughie, very blasé and ubercool. And pretty, let's not forget that, though I didn't spend a lot of time gazing into a mirror. I'd had quite a few guys chase after me, and I'd gone out with many. Guys loved me. My *modus operandi* was to insult and condescend while at the same time flirt, then allow a guy to walk me back to my dorm, where we'd engage in some groping and snogging for a horny hour or so. Then I'd stand up, adjust my clothes, kick the guy out and never speak to him again. This made me extraordinarily popular, for some mysterious reason. Was I a tease? Absolutely. I wasn't sure there was another way to be.

Until now. I couldn't seem to look at Nick, suddenly fascinated with the window shade, the radiator, the crack in the plaster wall. He turned my face back toward him.

"We don't have to do anything," he said. "It's fine." He smiled, and I could see that he meant it, and damn it all to hell, I fell a little deeper.

"I'd like to," I whispered, and my eyes stung a little.

He looked at me seriously. "You sure?" he asked.

I nodded.

"Very sure?" he asked, touching my lower lip.

I nodded again.

He kissed me, sweetly, gently, then smiled against my mouth. "Sure enough to marry me?"

"Nick," I said, unable to suppress a laugh, "can you please shut up and do me?"

And so he did, and it was gentle and slow and sweet, and oh, God…it felt as if we were meant to be together, and suddenly, I could see why all those sonnets had been written, all those Hallmark cards printed, all those movies. Because it was…real. For the first time in a very long time, I trusted someone to take care of me, and he did. Cherished me. Made love to me. All those clichés… true.

When it was over, when we lay twined together, sweaty and breathing hard, my eyes open a little too wide, as the glow faded and my heart rate slowed, a chilly terror crept into bed with me. The fear of being left, or exposed, or judged…or whatever, I was only twenty, not the type who examined emotions, the same way I didn't plunge my hand into a bag full of broken glass. I just knew that I was freaking terrified.

I cleared my throat. "Well, I should…I need to…I have to run," I said, babbling slightly. "That was wicked pissah, as we say here in the Bay State. And, um…I'll see you soon. Thanks, Nick. Bye." I got up, grabbed my dress and panties and pulled them on as I fled. Made it to the living room, opened the door, only to have Nick come up right behind me and push it closed again.

"No, no. No, you don't," he said, sliding around to put himself between the door and me. "Harper, come on."

"I'm absolutely positive you wouldn't keep me here against my will, Nick," I said lightly, not looking at him.

He stared at me a long moment, then stepped aside. "What happened?"

"I'm just going back to my dorm, okay? I have a, um, a history paper due."

"Don't go."

"I just have to. It's not a big deal." I faked a smile and tried to tie the shoulder strap of my dress, but my hands were shaking. Still couldn't look at him. It felt as if something big and dark was pulling in my chest, something that wanted to do me harm, and damn if I wasn't close to tears.

"Harper."

"Nick."

"Look at me."

What could I say? No? I obeyed, glancing at him briefly.

"Harper, I love you." His gypsy eyes were solemn, completely sincere, and that thing in my chest gave a fast, hard, painful twist.

"Nick, for God's sake," I said unevenly. "You barely know me."

"Okay, fine, I take it back. You're a shrew and a pain in the ass, but man, that thing you did with your tongue…"

I gave a surprised laugh, and Nick raised an eyebrow. "Can I see you again? Can I *shag* you again? Please, Harper?" And he grinned, and whatever had been in his eyes a second ago was replaced with an impish light.

I smiled back, and that dark thing subsided, leaving me almost limp with relief. "I'm extremely busy, but you never know."

"Stay a little longer? Even though I can barely tolerate you?"

I hesitated. *We should probably go now,* said my brain. "Sure," said the rest of me.

I know I was supposed to want what normal people wanted. That being loved was supposed to make me feel safe and cherished and happy. And Nick did make me feel those things, sort of. But I never seemed to be able to keep the dark, pulling thing completely at bay. I kept wondering when the other shoe would drop, when this would all end. How much damage would occur when it did.

I was twenty years old, raised by a father who didn't like to talk about messy human emotions, abandoned by a mother who had once adored me. I tried not to think about it, but in the back of my heart, on the tip of my brain, the thought lurked that Nick could ditch me at any time. My own mother had…why not some guy? Best not to fall all the way in love. Best to protect myself as much as I could.

If Nick sensed something was off, he didn't ask, and even if he had, I wouldn't have had the words to tell him the truth. When your own mother deserts you without a backward glance, it's hard to believe you can be truly and unconditionally loved. Love gets used up, you see.

So…Nick and I had fun together. Kept things light, and if he looked at me too…seriously or whatever, I'd tell him to wipe that look off his face, and he would. But the sex, it must be acknowledged, was flipping unbelievable. Not that I had anything to compare it with, but I knew. I pretended it didn't mean anything, and we didn't talk about it, but I knew just the same.

And Nick gave me enough rope to hang myself, never pushed, never again told me he loved me, stopped joking about marriage. When he moved down to the city at the end of the school year, eight months after we'd met, I honestly felt as if I might die. "Drive safely!" I called briskly as he got into his battered car, as the dark thing swelled dangerously. I kept smiling as he started the engine. Took out my phone and pretended to check for messages, which I couldn't actually see, as my eyes were blinking furiously.

Then Nick cut the engine, jumped out of the car and hugged me, and I hugged him back so hard it hurt, and he kissed me fiercely. "I'll miss you," he whispered, and I couldn't speak, it hurt so much to think about even a day without him, let alone forever, because of course I didn't expect things to actually work out.

But they did. He called me every day, and we talked for hours. He emailed me at least once a day, sent me tacky New York City T-shirts and Yankees dolls (I'd stick safety pins through their heads and send them back) and really good coffee from a little place on Bleeker Street. I interned at a law firm in Hartford that summer, and a couple of times a month, Nick would take the train to Connecticut to see me, since I felt a little gun-shy about going down to see him.

His mom died suddenly in October—an aneurysm—and

I drove down to Pelham, New York, for the wake. When I walked in, the look on his face—love, and surprise and gratitude—went straight to my heart. He introduced me to his sparse family, an aunt, a couple of cousins. Nick's parents had divorced long ago, and his mom never remarried. When I went back to school, I sent him quirky cartoons cut from the English department's copies of the *New Yorker*. Baked oatmeal raisin cookies when he came to visit.

He was snarky and smart and thoughtful and irreverent—and a little sad—and the combination was unbreachable. The amount of feeling I had at the sight of him, the rush the sound of his voice could cause, the heat, the everything...it was terrifying. We were, forgive me, soul mates, though I'd have stuck a fork in my jugular before saying that out loud.

So I tried to keep things light, dodged the more serious and intense moments, never said those three little words. Not until one night at Amherst and Nick was up for a rare weekend. I'd been applying to law schools, and applications were scattered all over my room. Not one of the schools I was aiming for was in New York. Even though Columbia and NYU both had great environmental law programs, I wasn't about to apply there. Not when Nick lived in Manhattan, uh-uh. It would be too obvious. Mean too much. Absolutely would not build my life around a man, as my mother had, and look where that got everyone.

Nick looked through the brochures and checklists... Duke, Stanford, Tufts. He gave me a long, silent look. I ignored him and chattered on with some inane story about my roomie and her inability to load the dishwasher. We went to a movie on campus. I pretended not to notice that Nick was bothered.

That night, he jerked awake. "You okay?" I muttered sleepily.

He looked at me, his eyes a little wild in the light from the streetlamp.

I sat up. "Nick?"

"Do you love me, Harper?"

I started a little. Maybe it was the darkness, or the hour, or the slightly lost look in his beautiful eyes, but I couldn't lie. I took his hand and looked at it, traced his fingers, the sweet underside of his wrist. "Yes," I whispered.

He gave a half nod. Didn't say he loved me back. He didn't have to. I knew. We lay back down, and he put his arms around me, and I felt like crying, as if my heart might break if he said anything at all. But he didn't, and the next day, things were normal. We didn't mention law school or love again.

On Valentine's Day of my senior year, I finally went down to New York for the first time, and we did indeed walk across the Brooklyn Bridge. It was frigid and wet and icy, perhaps not quite as fabulous as the experience Nick had envisioned, as I was dying of hypothermia, but he insisted we stand in the middle of the bridge, ostensibly to see if we could spot Mob victims in the East River.

"There's one," Nick said. "Sal 'Six Fingers' Pietro. He never should've boffed Carmella Soprano during the christening."

"Oh, I think I see one, too," I said, pointing and hoping we could go to Nick's soon and have some fabulous sex and then get a quesadilla grande from Benny's. "Right there. Vito 'The Pie' Deluca swims with the fishes, or whatever passes for life in the East River. Can we go now?"

Nick didn't answer. I looked around for him, but he wasn't where he should be. No. He was on one knee, looking up at me with such dopey happiness that my heart nearly stopped. He had on fingerless gloves that day, like some Dickensian orphan, his hair blew in the wind and he held up a diamond ring.

"Marry me, Harper. God knows you're not the girl of my dreams, but you'll have to do."

His eyes, though...they told the truth.

If I had been able to find a way to say no without breaking his heart, I would have. If he didn't love me so damn much, I would've cuffed him and laughed it off. If I said no, that would be the end of it, I knew. And so I shrugged and said, "Okay. But I want a huge dress and eleven bridesmaids."

I knew we were too young. I knew I wasn't ready. I wanted to wait. Years, preferably. But once we were engaged, Nick put on a full-court press to marry quickly, and I lost the battle on that one.

Eleven months after his marriage proposal, and six months after our wedding, we both lost the war.

CHAPTER FIVE

"NICK! OH, MY WORD, you are a sight for sore eyes! Give me a hug this minute!"

Seconds after Dennis and I arrived at the lodge, Nick had pulled in behind me. I was still unfolding myself from the car as my stepmother descended in a blur of blond frizz and spandex. Descended on Nick, that is. Not me.

"BeverLee, you're still as beautiful as ever," Nick said, hugging my stepmother.

"Listen to you, you wide-eyed liar! Let me see you! Oh! Look at you! Handsome as the devil, bless your heart!" She clutched him again, then looked at me. "Harper, did you see Nick?"

"Yes, I did," I answered, turning away as Nick shook my father's hand.

"We met on the road in," Nick said.

"That's wonderful! Oh, you bring back such happy memories, Nick!"

"Or night sweats, depending on your point of view," I muttered. Did my family not remember the pathetic puddle I'd been? Did everyone have to love Nick quite so much? "Dad. Can you give me a hand here? Dennis's back is bothering him." I turned to Nick. "Dennis ruptured a disc while rescuing three children from a house fire. Isn't that right, hon?" *Your Honor, if it please the court, my boyfriend is a genuine hero.*

"All true," Dennis said amiably.

"Way to go," Nick said. He and Dennis bumped fists.

"It was a good day, dude." Dennis grinned as happily as a black Lab.

"How was your trip?" Dad asked, taking a suitcase from the back of the car.

"Hellish. How was—"

"Harper! Harper! Oh, my God, Harper!"

My sister's arms were around me before I even saw her. "Hey, there," I said, smiling my first genuine smile in a week. I kissed her cheek twice, then pulled back. This may have been the longest time I'd gone without seeing my sister, and I had to say, she looked beautiful. "How's the bride?"

"Oh, my God, I'm so happy! Oh, Nick! Hi!" She leaped on him, then on Dennis, hopfrogging around our little circle. "And Harper, you remember Christopher, right?"

I looked up the steps. "Hey, Harper," said the groom.

Wow. Chris Lowery had been cute twelve years ago, but now he was *gorgeous*—Nick, Take Two, sort of. Both men resembled their father...Chris had the same dark eyes, though lacking that *tragic* element that made Nick so unfairly vulnerable. Chris had his mother's reddish-brown hair, and he was a couple of inches taller than his older brother. He may have lacked Nick's electric appeal—well, to me he did—but he was pretty damn attractive.

"My boy, you've become a man," I said, then gave a little *oof* as he hugged me, lifting me off my feet.

"You're still crazy beautiful, I see."

"Everything you say can and will be held against you," I said. "You will, of course, be explaining to me exactly how you plan to take care of my sister, because if you hurt or disappoint her in any way, I will, of course, kill you. Slowly, and with great pleasure."

"Of course." Christopher grinned and set me down.

"I'm completely serious."

"And I'm genuinely terrified." He winked and took my sister's hand.

"Ain't he just gorgeous?" BeverLee asked, fluffing her hair so it was a bit puffier. "Look at all these handsome men! Honest to goodness, no wonder we're all such happy gals! It's enough to make me all swoony! Come on, y'all, it's past five, which means cocktail hour's waitin' on us."

"Dennis and I need a little time to freshen up," I said. "We've been traveling all day."

"Sure enough," BeverLee said. "We'll meet y'all inside." I started up the steps, but BeverLee jerked my arm back. She glanced at the rest of the mob, who was heading in, and then her smile dropped like an anvil. "Harper, darlin', your daddy and me, we still aren't acting as, you know, man and wife. If you know what I'm sayin'?"

"Um," I managed queasily.

"What do you think I should do? I'm gettin' desperate! I just don't know what all has gotten into him. We sure have never—and when I say never, I mean it!—we have never in all our days together gone through a patch like this! The other night, I wore a see-through teddy, and still, nothin'! You think he needs the little blue pill?"

"Bev," I blurted, "I really just don't think I'm the best person to talk about this." Plus, I needed to go wash the image of my stepmother in a teddy out of my squealing brain.

"Why not, honey?"

"Um, because I'm the daughter? And speculating on... you know...it's a little uncomfortable, BeverLee."

Her face fell.

"But you know, BeverLee, people go through...these times, of course. And uh...well, maybe if you look back on past experience, you could…" Okay. Clearly I had nothing to offer. And I wanted to keep it that way.

"No, it's fine, you're right." She slapped on a smile, then checked her teeth in my sunglasses. "See you inside, sugar baby."

The lodge was beautiful. Some kind of post-and-beam construction, but the posts were all rough-hewn trees. A stone fireplace was surrounded by rocking chairs and game tables, and the entire western wall overlooked Lake McDonald and the mountains past it. It was romantic, all right. I practically expected to see John Muir and Teddy Roosevelt smoking their cigars out on the patio.

"Dude, we're on the third floor," Dennis said, handing me a room key.

"Same floor as mine," Nick added. "Dude."

Super.

OUR ROOM CONTAINED two double beds. "It's probably better for your back if you sleep by yourself," I said hesitantly. Better for his back, and better for me. I didn't want the temptation of Dennis right next to me, not when we still weren't engaged. And, for whatever reason, not when Nick was sleeping down the hall. I closed my eyes and took a deep breath. Two days, and this would be over, if Willa really went through with it at all.

"Roger-dodger," Dennis said, flopping on the bed closest to the window. Coco jumped on his chest, then pressed her tiny nose to the window as if admiring the stunning view.

"Dennis, listen," I said as I hefted a bag onto my bed. "I know things are a bit…undetermined with us in the case of our future and all that, but it's a little weird seeing Nick again."

"Sure," he said amiably, setting my dog aside to check his phone.

"Would you mind sticking close?"

"No prob," he said. He was quiet for a minute, then said, "So why'd you guys break up, anyway?"

I took my maid of honor dress out of the suitcase and hung it up. "Oh, you know. Young and impulsive, that kind of thing."

Dennis said nothing. I glanced back at him, and he gave me a quick smile and a nod. "Sure. That makes sense."

"Impulsive marriages...not usually a great idea," I said.

"Right."

"Which is why I'd have a lot of faith in ours, since we've been so slow and steady."

This was met with another long stretch of silence from Dennis Patrick Costello. Silence, of course, spoke volumes.

I sighed. "Okay. Well, do you want to shower before we go down to dinner?"

"Nah. I'm good." He sat up and smiled.

"Okay, I need a little while."

A long hot shower helped ease some of the tension in my neck. I toweled off my hair, then dashed on some makeup, my movements brisk and efficient. Changed into a dress, spritzed on a little perfume and brushed my hair, then secured it into a French twist.

"You look gorgeous," Dennis said when I came out, and with that, we went down to join the others.

"So in case you're unclear on who's who," I said as we walked down the stairs, "Christopher is Nick's half brother, his father's other son. His parents, Nick's that is, got a divorce when—"

"Hi there," came a voice. It was a pretty young mother who was checking in with her two kids and totally scoping out Dennis. The needle on my irritation level, already in the red zone, jumped.

"How you doing?" Dennis said, smiling agreeably. He knew he had an effect on women, and he liked it. "Cute kids," he added, tousling the hair of the male child. The mother's face practically burst into flame.

"I'm Laurie," she said. "Divorced."

"Hello, I'm Harper. He's with me," I said pointedly, grabbing Dennis's arm. "The nerve," I muttered as we continued across the lobby.

"Oh, relax," he said. "I know who I'm with." Then, rather suddenly, he leaned down and kissed me on the mouth, a quick, sweet kiss which I appreciated all the more because there was Nick, standing outside the dining room as if waiting for us. He looked at me steadily as we approached, a mocking light in his eyes. In my heels, I was almost as tall as he was.

"Nick," I said coolly.

"Harper. You look lovely," he said, eyes mocking. "Dennis, my man."

"Dude, how's it hanging?" They shook hands, doing that automatic grip-shifting male handshake that they must teach in the locker room. Must my boyfriend be BFFs with my ex-husband? Huh? I pinched Dennis's arm, but he only gave me a confused look.

We had a private dining room, one big table that seated about twenty, antlers decorating the wall, the windows showcasing the deep blue sky and purple mountains' majesty and all that good stuff. I took a deep breath and tried to relax. Most of the seats were already taken—BeverLee, Dad, Willa and Chris, a few other people I didn't recognize who were, I assumed, friends of the bride and groom.

Tonight was Thursday—the wedding was scheduled for Saturday afternoon, unless common sense decided to put in an appearance. If not, well, crotch. Life was going to be very different with Nick popping in and out again. Really should work on getting Dennis to marry me.

Willa once again jumped up and hugged me. "Guys," she said to the four or five strangers, "this is my big sister, Harper! Harper, this is Emily—" She indicated a dark-haired, pretty woman. "We work together in New York. And that's Colin, he's Christopher's friend from here, same with Noreen there, and this is Gabe, he and Chris went to college together. Guys, this tall drink of water is Dennis, Harper's significant other."

"Hello," I said, smiling.

"Hey, guys," Dennis said.

"And of course, Harper," Willa continued, "you already know Jason."

My head snapped around. Willa was pointing at a rather large man about my own age...tall and beefy with curly, angelic blond hair that made him look like a cherub. A nasty, stupid cherub, that was—Nick's stepbrother, Jason Cruise.

"Great to see you again," he said, giving me a quick once-over.

"Wish I could say the same, Jason," I answered, icicles dripping from my words.

"You married?" he asked.

I ignored him, then risked a glance at Nick, who was taking a seat down near BeverLee and Dad, next to Willa's friend from New York. He didn't look at me. Willa was already chatting with the friends from the lodge, so I took the last seat, which put me between Jason and Dennis and far from Nick.

I hated Jason Cruise for many reasons. Back when I was with Nick, Jason had been obsessed with Tom Cruise, something that had been true for years, according to Nick. Though he was no relation to the famous actor, Jason liked to hint that he was. "Went out to California," he'd say. "Hung out with my Cruise cousins, you know. Saw you-know-who and the kids." Then he'd wait to see if I'd squeal and pump him for star gossip, which he gleaned from the tabloids at the supermarket. When such a reaction failed to ensue, he'd just keep it up. "What's your favorite movie of his? Call me nostalgic, but I still love *Top Gun*." Indeed, I once saw Jason wearing a flight suit. Navy flight suits tended to look great on Navy pilots... on a giant Hobbit of a man, not so much.

But it wasn't just his idiotic fascination with the film star. Oh, no. That was nothing.

Like me, Nick was a child of divorce. His folks had split up when he was eight. Nick's father, Ted, had a honey on the side, apparently, and even before the divorce was final, he'd been living with Lila Cruise and her son, who was the same age as Nick. The same day Ted married Lila, he'd also adopted Jason, which might've been nice if it hadn't meant Ted Lowery then forgot about his other son. Christopher, the child of Ted and Lila, was born a few years later.

I remembered Nick telling me about his childhood one winter's night as we sat on a bench on campus, the stars brilliant, the air still and cold. To sum it up, Ted basically dropped the child of his first marriage. Jason (and later, Chris) replaced Nick in his father's affections. Jason was the son whose picture Ted carried in his wallet, the one whose Little League team he coached, the one who was given a car for his sixteenth birthday.

The divorce between Nick's parents had been ugly; his mother never forgave Ted, and her hatred burned for the rest of her life. Ted retaliated by sticking to the letter of the law on the custody and child support agreements. He was never late with a child support payment, but he never gave a penny extra, either. He never denied Nick a visit, but he never took him any more than what the court ordered—one weekend a month, dinner every other Wednesday. Dinner was always with the entire second family...Nick never saw his father alone.

Early on, Nick had learned to ask his father for nothing, because the answer was always the same. If Nick needed a new baseball glove, if he wanted to go to Boy Scout camp in the Adirondacks, if there was a field trip that cost a hundred bucks, his father would say only, "Your mother got a fair settlement. Ask her." His mother, in fact, got a crap settlement and had to work two jobs to support her boy. If only she'd had a divorce attorney like my bad-ass self.

On the appointed weekend, Nick would take two subways and the train from his home in the working-class neighborhood of Flatbush, Brooklyn, over to the wealthy burg of Croton-on-Hudson. Here, Jason would instantly begin to torture Nick. Jason would gloat over all that he and "Dad" had done. He'd show Nick pictures of their fly-fishing jaunt in Idaho, their vacation to Disney World, their weekend in San Francisco. He'd make sure Nick knew the cost of his soccer cleats, the remote-control airplane, the swimming pool they'd just put in. If Nick was innocent enough to bring some far more humble toy or book of his own, Jason would see to it that the object was broken, or worse, stolen.

Christopher, born when Nick was ten, was in a different class. Nick loved the little guy, and Chris idolized his long-distance half brother. Christopher was, Nick had once said, the only good thing about those awkward, sad weekends spent as the perpetual outsider, watching his father with his new-and-improved family.

"So how is it, seeing Nick again?" Jason asked now, leaning a little closer. He was awash in Polo, a scent I always associated with irritating tourists.

"Lovely," I answered.

"I'm so sure." He raised an anemic eyebrow and leered, sort of a chummy, conspiratorial look. *Poor thing, I understand completely, he's a total shit, isn't he?* "So it's kinda cool we're related again, don'tcha think?"

"We're not related, Jason. We've never been related. You are my ex-husband's stepbrother. No relation, biologically or legally."

"But you're sort of family. Because of Chris and what's-her-name."

"Negative. Willa will be your half sister-in-law, if such a term even exists. As far as I'm concerned, you're nothing." I met his piggy blue eyes with my asshole-lawyer stare, and as ever, it worked.

He sank back into his chair. "Bitch," he muttered.

"And don't you forget it," I returned.

Nick was watching me, and there it was, that quivering hum of electricity. I hoped he had heard me smack down his stepbrother, knew that, in my own way, I'd stuck up for him, but before the thought was even formulated, Nick had turned to the dark-haired Emily, who was laughing at something he said.

"Want some bread, Harp?" Dennis asked.

"Sure. Thanks," I muttered.

"So, Harper, what do you do for work?" asked one of the Glacier friends.

"I'm a divorce attorney," I answered. Everyone quieted.

Nick choked. "Are you kidding?" he asked.

"No," I said coolly. Did Willa tell him nothing? "But I'm available for advice, should the need arise."

"Never," Christopher said, gazing sappily at my sister.

"That's kind of perfect," Nick said. "You found your calling, Harper."

I willed myself not to clench. He really didn't know? He'd never looked me up on Google? Never? In the past twelve years, yes, I'd had a moment of weakness or two (five, actually) in which I'd typed in his name, but before the Internet could torment me with information, I'd had the sense to slap another key and stop my impulse. Apparently, the urge to look me up had never struck Nick.

Whatever. Time to be sociable. "So, Emily, you work with Willa?" I said, favoring the pretty brunette with a smile and taking another bite of bread.

"Mmm-hmm."

"And what do you do?"

"I'm a drafter." At my look of confusion, she added, "I draft the architectural plans at Nick's." She sent a look of bovine adoration his way.

I stopped chewing. "Nick's?"

She glanced at Willa. "Um, yeah. We both work for Camden & Lowery. Nick's firm."

I looked at my sister. "Really. How nice."

I sat there for a minute or two, long enough to say, "I'll have the same thing" when the waitress was done with Dennis, though I had no idea what he'd ordered. Then I excused myself, smiling, kissed Den on the cheek and hightailed it to the ladies' room. Leaned against the sink and pressed my cold hands to my hot cheeks. The door opened a second or two later, and Willa gave me a cute little grimace.

"You're working for Nick?" I blurted.

"Okay, calm down," she said.

"Willa! I—You should've—" I took a quick breath. "Why didn't you tell me? Is that how you ran into Christopher? Why didn't you say something?"

"Harper, chill," she said calmly, scooching up to sit on the counter. "Look. I'd been in the city about a month, not finding any work, okay? Money was running out—"

"Right! Which is why I told you not to leave that stone-masonry program until you had a job! And I also offered to loan you—"

"You already did loan me," she said. "That's the thing. I wanted to make it on my own."

"So you went to him? To *Nick?* To my ex-husband, Wills?" My mouth wobbled, but luckily, the door opened, revealing a middle-aged woman in a sweatshirt that showed a moose dancing over the word *Montana.*

"Occupied!" I barked, and she jerked back. But it gave me a much-needed second to get myself under control. I hadn't cried in years. Wasn't about to now.

"It was literally an accident," Willa said. "I had an interview down in SoHo, which just sucked, by the way, they were so mean and it was for, like, a barista at a coffeehouse, you know, and they were grilling me on the growing conditions necessary for organic arabica and whatever. So I didn't even get that job, I had eight dollars left in the bank, and I'm walking down this little bumpy street, the cobblestones are everywhere in SoHo, you know?"

"Yes, I've been there," I said tightly.

"And I look up and see a sign. Camden & Lowery Architecture. I figured, what are the odds of that being Nick? I remembered him as so nice, you know?"

I gave her a lethal look, which she ignored. "So I went in and there he was, and he was so surprised and happy to see me, and I told him I was looking for work, and guess what?"

"What?"

"His secretary was going on maternity leave. So he hired me."

My stomach was in a knot. "Willa—"

Once again, the door opened, and Dancing Moose

Woman was back. "Still occupied," I said. "My sister's sick, okay?"

"Projectile vomiting," Willa agreed. "Splat. Very disgusting."

"Well, how long do you think you'll be?" the woman asked with a frown.

"Long time," Willa said sweetly. "But there's another bathroom on the other side of the lobby. Oops, here it comes, more barf. You better go."

"Feel better, honey," the lady said, jerking back.

That did the trick. It also reminded me of why Willa got away with what she did. She…well, she was lovable. Good with people, sweet, funny. I could see why Nick would hire her…not just to mess with my head (though one couldn't rule that out), but simply because Willa was awfully nice.

I cleared my throat. "Willa, did it ever occur to you that I'd like to know something like that?"

She sighed. "Sorry. It's just…you and he were so long ago. And I really needed the job."

"So how'd you meet Chris?" I asked.

"He came in on my first day. That's why it was so… you know. Meant to be." She reached out and took my hand. "I'm sorry. I was just a little desperate."

"I would've helped you," I said.

"I didn't want to be helped."

"Well, Nick helped you. Why was it okay to ask Nick and not me?"

"Because he actually needed something I could do," she said gently. "And you never have."

"What utter crap." I caught a glimpse of my face in the mirror and turned away abruptly.

"It's not crap. It's true, Harper. You never need anything from anyone."

We didn't say anything for a minute.

"Willard! You still in there? We're doing a game, honey! Weddin' night Mad Libs! Come on, sluggo! Is your sister in there with you?"

"We're here, BeverLee," I called. "We'll be out in a sec."

"Are we okay?" Willa asked me.

I nodded. "Sure."

"I didn't mean to keep it a secret...I just wasn't sure how to handle it."

"Well, letting me find out at dinner...uncool."

"Sorry." She gave me a repentant little grin.

"Willa," I said, "you know I want you to be happy."

"I know," she said, her smile growing.

"We haven't been able to have a real conversation since you told me the big news. I just want to state for the record that I'm...I'm really worried that rushing into marriage is going to result in another disappointment for you."

"And I appreciate your concern," she said calmly.

"When you marry someone you barely know, it doesn't usually end well. And divorce...sucks."

"I know, Harper. I've been divorced twice as many times as you."

"So why are you in such a hurry?"

"Why waste time? If you love someone, I think you should go for it. And I'm not getting divorced this time. I really love Christopher." Her eyes took on a flinty look.

I tried to make my voice gentle. "You loved Raoul and Calvin, too."

"Christopher doesn't have a prison record, and he's definitely not gay. I'm older and wiser now. Okay? Can't you just be happy for us? I know it's hard for you to have faith in the world, but I do. And you're my maid of honor, so you have to stop being so doom and gloom, okay?"

"Willa..."

"And by the way, do you think you could be nice to Nick?"

I sighed. "I've been very civilized. We're even having a drink later on."

"Oh, that's great! Thank you, Harper!" She clapped her hands and then hopped down from the counter, adjusted her cleavage so it was higher and more pronounced—she was BeverLee's daughter, after all. "You'll see, Sissy. It'll all work out." Then she was gone, her face bright and happy despite our conversation.

What would it be like to be so relentlessly optimistic? I couldn't remember ever having the same lighthearted faith that Willa felt. Not since I was about five, anyway.

I took a hard look at myself in the mirror, almost expecting to see some middle-aged harbinger of doom, Ebenezer Scrooge in drag. Instead, it was just me, the face deemed striking by just about everyone. I stuck my tongue out at my reflection. A few wisps of hair had escaped my clip and were curling, not unattractively, around my face.

My hair was probably my best feature, certainly the one that garnered the most attention. Rich auburn hair shot with coppery highlights from the sun, curling without frizzing, one-in-a-million, pre-Raphaelite hair of an angel which I straightened every day for work. I subdued it once more, secured the clip more tightly and made sure that not one curl escaped.

"Harper, baby doll? You comin'?" BeverLee opened the door. "Oh, sweetie, here. You need a little spray?" She fumbled in her huge vinyl purse for her industrial-sized can of Jhirmack. "Want me to puff you up?"

"I'm good, Bev. Thanks anyway." With my stepmother chattering away, we went back to join the others.

An eternity later, dinner was over. Dad and BeverLee headed upstairs where, please God, they would have sex and thus relieve me of hearing about their marital woes. The rest of the gang drifted toward the bar. Dennis approached me. "Hey, I'm kinda whipped," he said. "I'm gonna go upstairs and ice my back, take a few Motrin. We're going horseback riding tomorrow, I don't want to miss that."

"Horseback riding?"

"That's what they said."

My stony heart sank a bit more. I was actually a little scared of horses. So dang big, you know? "Well. Do you need anything, Den? Want me to come up, get you settled?"

"Nah, I'm fine. Oh, hey, how you doing?"

I turned to look at the party he was addressing. Great. Some pretty woman giving him the eye.

"Harp, this is Bonnie, she's a waitress here."

"Hi, Dennis," she sighed, practically melting on the spot.

I rolled my eyes. "Lovely to meet you." I turned back to Dennis. "Feel better, snooky-bear," I said. "I'll be up in a little while."

Dennis grinned. "'Night, Harp."

"Er. Harp-*er*. You can say it. It's only two syllables."

To my surprise, he gave me a rather lovely kiss. "Good night, Harp*er*," he said. Then he winked at Bonnie and headed up the stairs. I turned around and bumped right into my ex-husband.

CHAPTER SIX

NICK SMILED. "WANT TO get that drink now, snooky-bear?" he asked.

I took a deep breath. "You bet, poopyhead."

"You still like those sickening cosmos?"

"Sue me. I came of age during *Sex and the City*."

"There are tables out there," Nick said, indicating the patio. "Back in a flash."

I went outside. The sun was setting behind the mountains, and the shadows hung long and blue over the lake, turning the water almost black. The wind had died down, and the flagstones held the moderate warmth of the day. I picked a table—the patio was mostly deserted—wrapped my pashmina a little more tightly around me and stared off at the mountains.

It was so beautiful here, so remote. The quiet was like a palpable force, and I felt my soul unfurl a little. Surely Martha's Vineyard was one of the loveliest places on earth, but it wasn't like this—majestic, endless and harsh, a place where you could be killed by nature in a hundred different ways at any given moment. For some reason, the thought was oddly soothing. Out here, you were just part of a bigger plan, one you didn't get to control. Be eaten by a grizzly, have a glacier fall on your head, drown in an icy river—it wasn't up to you.

"Makes you feel a little…irrelevant, doesn't it?" Nick asked, indicating the view as he set down my pink drink. "In a nice way."

"Speak for yourself," I said, a little disturbed that he'd just about read my mind.

"So you found out Willa's working for me." He took a sip of his beer.

"Yes, I did."

"She asked me not to tell you."

"And when would you tell me? During our weekly chats? Don't worry, I'm not mad."

"Sure you are." He flashed his lightning smile.

I looked away. "So Jason's here, huh? I didn't picture that."

"Yeah. Me neither."

"How about your father and Lila? Coming in tomorrow?"

Nick's dark gaze dropped to the table. "No. Dad's got early onset dementia. He's pretty out of it." He began folding the corners of his cocktail napkin.

"Oh, Nick. I'm sorry to hear it." Without thinking, I reached over and put my hand over his.

"Thanks." He didn't look up.

"What about Lila? I can't imagine she'd want to miss her son's wedding."

"Actually, she planned a cruise a while back and didn't want to cancel."

That summed up the memory I had of her pretty well. I didn't know the woman, but I always had the impression there wasn't a lot to discover.

"So does your dad live near you?"

Nick nodded. "I got him into this pretty nice assisted-living place on the East Side. I can check on him that way."

"That's...that's good."

I'd met Ted only three times. He was a consultant to large corporations and Republican politicians, though what exactly he consulted on was never fully explained.

Very successful, very smug, very oily. After rescheduling four times, he took Nick and me out to dinner when we were engaged. "Harper, call me Ted. You are stunning! I can see my son inherited his old man's taste in women." (I know. Nasty.) The next time I saw him was at our wedding, where I was too busy panicking to pay him much attention. The last time was at a Labor Day picnic at his sprawling, soulless McMansion in Westchester County, where Ted invited me to come riding with him sometime. Apparently he was once an alternate on the Olympic equestrian team and said he could tell I had a beautiful seat. (And again…nasty.)

I'd hated the guy, his easy affability with his stepson and younger child, either ignoring Nick altogether or asking him awkward questions that revealed just how little he knew his firstborn. He'd reminisce fondly about Nick's soccer days when Nick had in fact played baseball. He referred to Nick's days at UConn when Nick had gone to UMass. Once he mentioned their fishing trip to Maine, as if he'd ever taken Nick anywhere…Jason had been the son on that trip.

Inexplicably, Nick held no rancor toward him; instead, he'd watched his father with hopeful eyes, waiting for something more than a slap on the back and a "Hey, sport, how you doing?" Whatever Nick had waited for never came. At least, not in the time we were together.

I guessed now it never would.

Nick was staring at me.

Oh. I was holding his hand with both of mine, my thumbs stroking his knuckles. I jerked my hands back, then gave his an awkward pat. Took a sip of my cosmo. *Note to self: don't touch Nick.* The buzz was quite unsettling, and it wasn't caused by alcohol.

"So. A divorce attorney." His hands busied themselves with the napkin. A structure was appearing, Nick's own brand of origami. Sugar packets, toothpicks, asparagus spears—whatever was at hand, Nick would turn into a building, incapable of keeping his hands still.

"That's right," I said coolly. God knows I'd heard every joke in the book.

"Why that field?" he asked.

"Well, as you may remember, Nick, divorcing someone you once loved can be difficult, and it's easy to make a mistake. So I help people get the best result. Hold their hands and shepherd them through a sad time."

Nick raised an eyebrow.

"What?"

"I just find it…fitting."

"I know you're hoping to insult me, but you're not. I help people accept in their hearts what their heads already know." For some reason, my motto sounded hollow tonight.

"Wow. That's some line." The napkin had become a tiny house, complete with roof and folded door. Nick set it aside, then angled it to face the lake, ensuring that it had a water view.

"It's not a line, Nick," I sighed. "If we'd done that, we might've stood a chance or avoided a disaster."

"That's how you think of us? A disaster?" The gypsy eyes flashed.

"Well," I answered thoughtfully, "sitting here with you in this beautiful place, all these years having passed, talking with you again…yes. Disaster covers it pretty well."

"And here I still think of you as the woman I loved more than I've ever loved anyone."

The words had the intended wallop, and my heart shuddered. *Don't be such a weenie,* I told said organ. *He's not trying to soften you up…it's an accusation.* Leaning back in my chair, I gave a half nod. "The past tense is duly noted, Your Honor, as is the soap-opera melodrama. That being said, a simple recounting of the facts would show that you were practically invisible during our brief and unhappy marriage."

"You certainly made me that way, didn't you?" His voice was mild.

This was going nowhere. This was, in fact, where negotiations tended to break down. "Okay, Nick, let's drop it. Ancient history, right?"

"It doesn't feel that ancient, Harper."

I took another sip of cosmo to cover my shiver, but he noticed anyway. "Cold?" he asked, instantly shrugging out of his jacket and offering it to me. "I mean, I know your heart is cold, but how about the rest of you?"

"No, I'm fine," I said. We looked at each other for a minute, twelve years churning between us. I was the first to blink.

"Nick, look. Let's not fight. We're here to talk about our siblings, yes?" He nodded, and I continued. "You and I…we were both obviously hurt by our own bad decisions. We were too young and foolish, we didn't know what to expect, yadda yadda ad infinitum." His eyes were unreadable. "But this is exactly my point. While Willa and Christopher are in fact older than we were, they're still basically kids. Well, certainly Willa is. What does Christopher do for work, by the way?"

"He's…" Nick paused. "He works for me on and off. Well, for my subcontractors, mostly. Finish carpentry, trim, stuff like that."

My lawyerly instinct told me there was more. "And on the off times, what does he do, Nick?"

Nick gave a little wince. *Here it comes,* I thought. "He's…he's an inventor."

I nodded sagely. "An inventor. Anything good? And by good, I'm envisioning Google, just as an example."

Nick sighed. "Well, he does have a patent on a couple things." He hesitated. "The Thumbie."

"And what is the Thumbie?" I asked. My cosmo was gone. Too bad, since it appeared I'd be needing another.

"The Thumbie is a plastic tip you put over your thumb."

"To what end?" I asked.

"To scrape gunk that you can't get up with a sponge."

I paused. "You're not really serious, are you, Nick?"

He sighed. "Chris says you always end up using your thumbnail to—okay, so it's stupid. But maybe no more stupid than the ShamWow."

"The Sham-what?"

"Never mind. At least he's trying."

I took a slow, steadying breath. "And Willa, having quit beauty school, a paralegal course and a stonemasonry apprenticeship, is going to be the breadwinner in this family?"

Nick rubbed his forehead. "I don't know, Harper. It's not for us to decide. Can't you just have some faith in the two of them? Let them make their own mistakes, find their own way, trust that they actually love each other?"

I snorted. "Right. Or maybe—just thinking out loud here—we can actually consider the facts and apply a little loving pressure so our siblings don't end up in the same miserable stew you and I were in."

"There's more to a marriage than the facts."

"Ignoring the facts of a relationship is the reason I have a job, Nick."

"Well, you know what?" he said, an edge in his voice. "I think they'll be really happy together."

"Ah. So I can count on you to pick up the tab for Christopher's divorce attorney?"

He squinted at me, almost smiling. "Wow. I forgot how stunted you are when it comes to matters of the heart."

"Stop, I'm blushing." My voice was calm, though I could feel my heart armoring itself for battle. "I'm not stunted, Nicky dear. I'm a realist."

"A realist, huh. Or we could call it…stunted. Yep, that works." He winked at me and leaned back in his chair.

"Well, I'll tell you this, babe," I said softly, leaning forward with a little smile and lowering my voice. His eyes dropped to my cleavage (gotcha, you dopey man, you), then came instantly back to my face. "At least I haven't had my heart stomped on since you and I broke up."

Nick tipped his head and smiled. "I wasn't aware you *had* a heart, sweetums."

Oh, he was such a pain in the *ass*. My expression may have been—hopefully was—pleasant, but my heart was racing in white-hot fury. That's how it always had been with Nick—zero to sixty in a nanosecond. Before I did something rash like, I don't know, kick him in the nuts, I stood up to leave.

"Well, this has been about as productive as I imagined," I said. "But just for the record, Nick, I do have a heart, you broke it, it mended, the end. Always lovely to see you. Sleep tight."

"Hold on, Harper," he said, standing abruptly. "*I* broke *your* heart? See, this is the same problem as it ever was. You never could acknowledge what you did back then."

"And you never could acknowledge that you played a part, Nick." My voice was fast and quiet…and furious.

He jammed his hands in his pockets. "You just won't admit that you were wrong, and it's really too bad."

"But I *wasn't* wrong," I said. "We were too young, we were not equipped to be playing grown-up, and shockingly, *love*—or whatever you want to call it—just wasn't enough, was it? I was right, and that's what drives you crazy."

With that, I turned and left before he could see that my hands were shaking.

Okay. So that was not productive. I should've known it wouldn't be, should've heeded my own advice to avoid being alone with my ex. Striding through the lobby, I spied a pacifier on the floor. Perfect. My random act of kindness for the day, take that, Father Bruce! Picked it up, spotted a mother/child duo and trotted over. "I think this may be yours," I said sweetly, hoping Nick was watching.

"Oh, thank you!" the mother cried. "Destiny would never have fallen asleep without it."

"My pleasure," I cooed. "And she's just gorgeous." I started to give the child a pat on the head, remembered something about soft spots, withdrew my hand and gave the mother an awkward smile. Then I went outside to the cool and soothing night.

So. Where did one go to walk off some steam out here in the middle of God's country? I strode down the road, away from the warm lights of the lodge and the murmur of people, and tried to breathe deeply, hoping to loosen the vise that seemed to be squeezing my heart.

A few yards off, there was a rock with a relatively flat surface. Perfect. I tiptoed over—not easy to walk in heels out here—and sat down, adjusted my skirt, took three calming breaths and flipped open my phone. Thank God, there was a signal.

He answered on the first ring. "Father Bruce here," he sang.

"Father B., it's Harper."

"Ah! How are things?"

"Pretty rotten, Padre." I swallowed hard.

"Go on, my child."

"You just love saying that, don't you?"

"I really do," he admitted. "But go on. My child."

"Well, I've seen my sister, but she won't listen to me. I just want her to wait a little bit. That's all. To be sure. I don't want her to end up like—" My voice broke off abruptly.

"Like you?"

When I answered, my voice was little more than a whisper. "Yes."

Father Bruce didn't say anything for a minute or two. "You're not so bad, my dear."

"Do I seem stunted to you?"

He laughed. "Well, I've never thought of it exactly like that, no. Ah, shall we say 'guarded'? I like that better."

"See, I just think I'm a realist. I also think there really should be a law requiring some kind of premarriage boot camp. You guys do it, don't you?"

"Pre-Cana counseling," he confirmed.

"Because this is the whole problem. No one thinks anymore. They just assume, hey, I'm in love, everything is sunshine and roses, let's run to Vegas or Montana or wherever and get married and we'll deal with reality later on, and then bam, they're in my office, heartbroken and… stunted." I swallowed again.

"You have a point, dear," he said patiently. "A good point. But what if your sister doesn't get a divorce? What if they make it? Live a long and happy life together?"

"The odds are against them, Father."

"No, dear. The odds are actually in their favor. One in three might divorce, but that means two in three don't."

"Have you run the stats on how many marriages last when the bride and groom have known each other for a month? I bet they're higher than one in three."

"I'm trying to reassure you, Harper. You don't make it easy."

"Oh. Thanks. Sorry."

There was another silence. "Have you seen your ex-husband?" the good father asked.

"Yep."

"How was that?"

"Crappy, Father. Extremely crappy."

"Sorry to hear that."

I glanced at my watch, did the time adjustment. "You have bingo tonight, don't you?"

"I do."

"I'll let you go. Thanks for listening."

"It's what I live for. Call me tomorrow, all right? I want to hear how you're doing."

"Oh, I'll be fine. Have fun. Hope you win big."

I put my phone back in my purse and sighed. Lay back on the rock, using my bag as a pillow.

It would be nice to cry, I mused. Normal people cried and they always seemed to feel better. But, as I was apparently stunted, crying wasn't my thing. And, case in point, if I were crying now, I wouldn't be able to see these stars. Well worth seeing, holy cow. They swirled above my head, the Milky Way in all its vast magnificence spreading out against the deep purple sky. A meteor shot across the sky and was gone, just like that.

Maybe I should move out here. Become a cook on a ranch somewhere...not that I cooked very well. Okay, well, I could...divorce people. All twenty-nine people who lived in Montana. Clearly, if I was going to run away, I'd need some life skills. Maybe I could become a cowboy. Just me and the cattle and my trusty horse, whom I would name Seabiscuit.

Running away...it had its appeal, that was certain. Times like this, I could almost understand doing it. Let the record reflect that Dennis would find another woman in a matter of hours. I had no illusions about that. He loved me, sure, but he was a guy. He might miss me, but he'd find someone else, and fast. Hard to avoid, the way women threw themselves at his head or groin or any other body part they could aim for.

As for BeverLee and Dad, they wouldn't miss me too much. Kim would, but she'd befriend whoever moved into my house, just as she'd befriended me. Willa would call occasionally, maybe swing through on her travels like a bit of milkweed seed, cheerful and light. Father Bruce would find other souls to save. My coworkers would replace me, only mentioning me once in a while when a dusty postcard arrived from Bearcreek or Grass Range.

The sky seemed to settle around me like a giant blanket, comforting and soft and unspeakably beautiful. Somewhere—hopefully very far away—a wolf howled. The wind rustled the long grass, and the nighttime sighed with pleasure.

Dennis would be sound asleep, as once he was horizontal, he generally fell unconscious in a matter of seconds. Willa and Christopher were probably wrapped around each other, gazing with adoration into each other's eyes. BeverLee and Dad, best not to go there.

Nick...I didn't want to think about Nick anymore.

And what was my mother doing tonight? I wondered if she could tell when I thought of her, if there was some primal tingle that touched her heart or brain or uterus.

Probably not. After all, she'd left me the day I turned thirteen. I hadn't heard her voice since. She wasn't dead, that I knew. In fact, though roughly a thousand miles separated us, I was at this moment closer to her than I'd been in decades.

For whatever that was worth. But under this arching, velvety sky, my heart sore from seeing Nick, it was hard not to want my mother.

CHAPTER SEVEN

THE NEXT DAY—FRIDAY—BEGAN with a females-only breakfast. The men were off fly-fishing, which would've made Theo happy. I had to admit, it was nice not to have to deal with Nick. I liked to have at least two cups of coffee before picking relationship scabs, after all.

After the meal, BeverLee, Willa and I went upstairs to the small suite where Willa was staying so the bride could try on her dress, which had obviously been bought in haste. For all my reservations, a lump came to my throat at the sight of her, looking like the proverbial fairy princess in the layers of puffy white. Her eyes met mine in the mirror. "I just know this one will take," she said.

"Of course it'll take! Of course it will! Third time's the charm, just look at your mama, right, sweet knees? Inn't that right? Jimmy and I, well, we couldn't be happier!" BeverLee darted a nervous glance at me, then refocused on her only child. "Oh, my! You're prettier than a spotted pup, bless your heart! I just love weddings!" She rustled in a bag and knelt at Willa's side, tucking up the hem of the dress and pinning it. The gown was a little long, but BeverLee had always been good with a needle.

"Aside from the obvious, Wills," I said carefully, "um, what is it that you love about Christopher?"

"Oh, Harper, he's so dreamy!"

"Okay, maybe something a little more...solid?"

"Nothin' wrong with dreamy, Harper," BeverLee chided. "Your young Dennis, he's pretty easy on the eyes, if you know what I'm sayin'." She paused in her pinning. "Not to mention how handsome that ole Nick is."

I resisted hissing. "Right. But BeverLee, we hardly know Chris. I'm just asking about his qualities."

Willa glanced at me in the mirror. "He's really smart. And so creative! Did you hear about the Thumbie?"

"I *know* I'll use mine *all* the time," BeverLee said staunchly around a mouthful of pins. "I'll buy a whole pack! Willard, hold still, sugar, I need to fix this hem, it's all catty-whompus."

"And what else?" I asked mildly. "Has he ever been married before?"

"Nope. Never married."

"Does he know about your…um…other ventures into matrimony?"

"Sure! Of course! I think we covered that in the first hour," Willa said happily.

"Is he hardworking?"

"Definitely. But you know, most of his work goes on up here." Willa tapped her temple. Super.

"Will he be working at a job where he gets paid?" I asked sweetly. "You know, financial disagreements are a leading cause of—"

"Harper! Darlin'! You just don't know how to let go and let God!" BeverLee cried, shooting me a sharp look. "Now Willard, go and change, honey. I'll get that hem up lickety-split. Brought my Singer for just this reason." Willa slid out of her dress, then gathered her clothes and went into the bathroom. "Harper Elizabeth, don't you rain on your sister's parade!" my stepmother hissed. "Did anyone lecture you on your wedding day? Huh?"

"Well, no, Bev, but looking back, maybe someone should have. Given how things turned out, remember? And today's not the actual wedding day. We still have till tomorrow to talk some sense into her." My voice dropped to a whisper. "BeverLee, I'm not saying that Christopher isn't a good guy. I'm just saying they should take some time."

"How much time? Two and a half years, honey? I don't see no ring on your finger." She shoved her fists into her ample hips and raised a painted eyebrow.

Touché. A pity, because the ring I'd bought myself was bleeping beautiful.

"Willard can make her own choices," my stepmother said more gently. "Besides, I want grandchildren, and I'm not fixin' on waitin' if I don't have to, and since there's no bun in your oven, I figure she's my best bet. Some things are just meant to be, and there's no point in wastin' time." She finished pinning the dress and stood up. "Now turn that frown upside down, missy. We got horses to ride."

AN HOUR LATER, I WAS eyeballing my horse, who was not named Seabiscuit and certainly did not look like he could come from behind to win a race or, in fact, make it out of the corral, as he was too busy dying.

"Is this horse really okay for me to ride?" I asked the person in charge. Alas, the person in charge wasn't a rugged cowboy with gentle laugh lines and dusky blue eyes, as I had imagined…nope. She was maybe eighteen years old, tattooed and pierced, full of eye-rolls and ex-asperated sighs.

"Yeah," she said, stretching it into two syllables of clearly hard-won patience. "The horse is fine." She had a slight lisp from the stud in her tongue. "So like, okay? Can you, like, get on, or do you, like, need help?"

"I'm fine," I said. "It's just…Bob…" And that was another thing. Bob? Bob the horse? "Bob here doesn't look so good."

"He's fine. Does this all the time. Been doing it for eons."

"Yes, that's clear," I muttered, but she was already gone.

Everyone else had already mounted, and only Bever-Lee had required assistance. Dennis, looking wicked good astride a bay horse named Cajun, exuded a Clive-Owen-as-King-Arthur vibe, despite the fact that he was texting someone. Several of Christopher's park friends apparently did this all the time and sat astride horses that didn't seem to have one hoof in the grave. Dad, aboard Moondancer, seemed quite comfortable, reins in one hand, leaning on the saddle horn as if he was about to take a thousand head of sheep up to Brokeback Mountain. BeverLee (steed's name: Cassandra) appeared less comfortable, despite her Texas roots, her pink studded jeans whimpering at the seams, purple leather cowgirl boots at awkward angles in the stirrups, anxiously patting her overpermed cloud of blond hair. Christopher and Willa had claimed Lance-lot and Guinevere and maneuvered their horses together so they could make out, which they were doing quite enthusiastically.

And Nick. Apparently his equestrian-enthusiast father had taught him something about horses, because he looked quite at ease on a black horse, ignoring me and talking with Emily, his employee, whose horse's name was Sweetheart (please). I wondered if she was more than his employee…she was tossing out a lot of doe-eyed looks and dimpled smiles. *Good luck, kid,* I thought. *My condolences.* Oh, and by the way, guess what Nick's horse was named? Satan. I know. You're telling me.

I turned back to Bob, tried to grab the saddle horn and get my foot into the stirrup. Bob may have been at death's door, but he was still standing, and he was very tall. And wide. And somewhat swaybacked. After four or five tries, in which one foot was trapped in the stirrup and the rest of me was hopping madly to bridge the gap,

I finally managed to crawl up Bob's side and sling my leg over the other side. By now, Bob's head was almost touching the ground, as he was fast asleep. I gave the reins a gentle tug, which resulted in absolutely nothing.

"Bob? Time to go, big guy," I said.

"Okay, people, my name is Brianna and I'm your guide today, welcome to Glacier National Park and thank you for choosing Highland Stables," Brianna called in a long-suffering, well-practiced monotone. "For those of you who've never ridden before—" pointed look at me, still trying to wake my steed "—to make the horse go, give a firm kick to the horse's side, you will not hurt the horse, to make him stop, pull back gently and firmly on the reins, to go left, lean the reins to the left, to go right, lean the reins to the right." She heaved a mighty sigh. "Everyone set, okay, let's go, the horses know the way, just sit back and enjoy nature's splendor, please stay in line and in case of grizzly sighting, do not panic."

"That's not very reassuring," I said to Dennis's back. "Don't bears eat horses?"

"They're probably hibernating. Don't worry, hon. I'll protect you." My boyfriend turned around and tossed a confident grin my way.

I gave a reluctant smile back. "Thanks, Den." Such a good guy. And maybe me cutting him off was working, because last night had been full of heavy sighs, tossing and turning from his side of the room. Perhaps a change of heart was coming for young Dennis. One could never rule out the motivation sex provided, after all.

As the other horses left the corral, Bob sleepwalked forward, plodding gloomily and with great effort. Needless to say, I was dead last. The path led into the woods, Lake McDonald glittering in the sunshine on one side, pines and aspen and huge chunks of gray rock sloping upward on the other. Sunlight fell in patches through the forest. The trail was wide and covered in pine needles, the leather of the saddle squeaked, the sounds of the others talking and laughing drifted back to me. The air was so pure here. Even though it was only mid-September, it was cool; someone had said snow was predicted for later in the week, which apparently was par for the course. Clouds scuffed along the mountain on Lake McDonald's far side, and the woods were rich with birdsong.

My reverie was cut off as Bob veered over to a tree and began eating leaves. "Come on, Bob," I said, pulling on the reins and trying not to hurt his mouth. "Let's go, pal. No snacking." Bob, who may have been deaf, ignored me. The other horses continued on. "Bob, come on! Behave." I gave another tug. Nothing.

Just then, Brianna cantered down the line of horses. Thank goodness. Or not…she stopped up ahead at Dennis's side. Perfect.

"Brianna," I called, "Bob here keeps trying to—"

"Have you, like, ever ridden before?" Brianna said to Dennis. "You're totally a natural."

"Thanks," Dennis said, smiling his *I'll save you, little lady* smile. "Nope. This is my maiden voyage. I'm Dennis. I'm a firefighter."

"Shut *up*," she sighed, her face glowing.

"Brianna? Bob keeps eating leaves," I said as my horse once again swiped a mouthful from a tree, practically yanking my arms from their sockets.

"Have you ever, you know, saved someone's life?" Brianna asked.

"Oh, sure. It's just part of the job," Dennis said. "This must be wicked awesome, though, living out here. Man."

"It's cool," she answered. Or I thought she did…their voices were fading as the distance between us lengthened.

Yellow foam dripped from Bob's muzzle as he continued to chew placidly.

"Bob. Enough," I said in my lawyer voice. "Giddyup." That didn't sound very commanding. "Bob. Move it!" He responded by lifting his tail and fertilizing the trail. I gave the horse a gentle nudge with my heel. He didn't move. Tried again, more forcefully this time. Nothing. "How'd you like to be castrated, Bob?" I asked. That and another good swift kick got the horse moving, albeit at the speed of an earthworm. But at least we were moving. The sound of Willa's laughter floated back to me, and I couldn't help a smile. She was so sincere, so well-meaning, so kind-hearted. She'd come a long way from that bed-wetting, pale little ghost I'd first met.

As we got further away from the lake, I could hear the constant shush and gurgle of a stream. Bob plodded along, occasionally favoring me with a grunt or a slight snore. I could see the tail of Dennis's horse ahead of me, maybe twenty yards or so. He didn't seem to notice my lag time. I didn't really mind, to be honest—under the best of circumstances, family gatherings tended to give me hives. Literal hives—I was a redhead, after all. Very sensitive skin. Family events were, in a word, tough. My recalcitrant father, the constant cacophony of BeverLee's often inane chatter, my endless worry over Willa's many ill-fated choices. Dennis made things easier…his easygoing nature and ability to see the best in everyone was a good example for a porcupine like myself.

Despite my being far behind the other riders, it still felt as if a line connected Nick and me. That unpleasant buzz of electricity hadn't stopped humming, and even though I couldn't see my ex-husband at the moment, I felt as if I knew exactly where he was.

I was good at staying in control; you had to be, if you worked in my profession. You got used to people spewing bile or sobbing or hating you. The worst thing you could do was react. It was just harder than I expected, canceling out Nick. Even Dennis's good-looking, brawny presence wasn't helping on that front, and the significance of this wasn't lost on me.

The beauty of the forest began to seep into my prickly soul. Sunlight cut in golden shafts through the thickening cedars and hemlocks, and the woods took on an other-worldly, greenish hue. Birds flitted and hopped in the branches. Their songs were so different from the throaty cries of the gulls or the rasping calls and clatter of the crows back home. A woodpecker drilled into a dead branch, and in the distance, I heard a strange, flutelike trilling overlaid with what sounded like the bark of a small dog. Too bad Coco had to stay behind at the lodge. She would've loved to trot off and investigate. And the smell here! The rich, sharp scent of cedar thickened as we plodded along, and I found myself gulping in great breaths.

God's country. I was almost glad I was here.

Then Bob did an odd little twirl, nearly unseating me, and faced backward on the trail. "Whoa, big guy!" I said, clutching the saddle horn. Bob made a funny noise—blowing hard through his nostrils—and began backing up, off the trail and into the woods, jerking his head up and down. "Bob! Stop, buddy!" It was as if he was having a seizure or something, shaking and jerking. "Bob? We're not supposed to—oh, crotch." All the breath left my lungs in a rush.

About thirty yards behind me, where we'd been just a moment before, right in the middle of the trail, was a bear. A big bear. A grizzly on all fours, looking at his next lunch.

My limbs turned to water. "Oh, no, no, no," I breathed raggedly, clutching the saddle horn as Bob continued to back further off the trail. "Go away, bear, please, please, please. We're…um…way too…big…too big to eat…oh, crap."

Bob came to an abrupt stop. My hair snagged on a branch, pulling hard, and I squeaked in pain, grabbing the lock of hair before it was torn right out. I risked a painful glance behind me…seven or eight tightly knit cedars in a little grove, almost a shelter. Or a trap. Forward was the bear…backward was a wall of cedar.

Swallowing convulsively, I tugged at my hair—damn it! It was really caught. If Bob bolted, I'd be out a fair chunk. Not that I'd mind, of course, it certainly beat being eaten alive. Could I climb the tree? Should I try it? Bears could climb, right? Oh, this day just got suckier and suckier!

Bob seemed to agree. He gave a high-pitched wheeze, then shook violently, as in a death spasm or something, what did I know? "Don't die on me, Bob! Now is not the time! Calm down! It's just a…just a grizzly bear." My voice was tight with panic.

The bear stood there on all fours, shaggy and fricking huge. Even from this distance, I could see its long, gleaming claws. Razor sharp, no doubt. "Not good, not good, not good," I whispered. My heart pounded so hard and fast I thought I might faint. Which would not advance the case of my survival. I took a breath, trying to think.

Okay. So. What does one do when a *grizzly* is contemplating your death? Flee? Fleeing sounded good…a horse could probably outrun a grizzly. Right? Or not? Why did I have the oldest horse in America? Why wasn't Seabiscuit my horse instead? But maybe this was good…after all, maybe I only had to outrun Bob. How about yelling? Should I yell? Yes! I should yell.

"Help!" I peeped, my vocal cords somewhat paralyzed. "Brianna!" Right. Too busy trying to seduce my boyfriend to save me. "Dennis!" Much better—firefighter, big, strong, used to saving people. "Den? Help! Dad? Somebody help me!"

Only the bear seemed to hear. It raised its nose and sniffed. Note to self—shut *up*. Already, images rolled through my head—my lifeless, torn body dragged off to a den where adorable cubs would gnaw on my carcass. My skull being found by a troop of Boy Scouts, who would deem the discovery wicked cool.

Bob, as if sensing my train of thought, gave a little buck, yanking my hair so hard tears came to my eyes. I clutched the saddle horn. "Stop it!" I hissed. "Don't you dare dump me!"

Should I get off the horse? No. Or yes? I had no idea! Plus, my hair was still tangled in the branch. I really couldn't get off Bob. What had Brianna said? *In case of grizzly sighting, don't panic.* Great. Thank you so much for the detailed information, Brianna!

And then, blessedly, I heard hoofbeats. Slow hoofbeats, granted…no one was exactly charging to my rescue. The bear turned slightly, sniffing once more, and all the saliva in my mouth dried up. It. Was. Enormous.

"Stop! Grizzly ahead!" I called weakly. "Be careful!"

"Harper, where the hell—holy crap, that thing is fucking huge."

It was Nick, coming down the path on Satan. And thank *God* he was here, ex-husband or not! He tugged on the horse's reins, and the horse froze obediently, Satan's ears were pricked; he was alert and clearly on edge, but he wasn't moaning in terror, as was Bob.

"Harper? Where are you, baby?" Nick's voice was calm, though why he sounded calm, I had no idea. He was a New Yorker, for God's sake, not exactly a mountain man.

"Nick! We're over here! My horse is stuck! And my hair is caught."

Nick tore his eyes off the bear and looked in my direction. "Try not to panic," he said.

"I'm not panicking. I'm just terrified."

"Yeah. Me, too. Um…what's the plan here?"

"I don't know!" I returned. "I saw my first bear yesterday! You don't have a gun, do you?"

Somehow, this made Nick laugh. "Well, sorry to say I left my Luger at home. Maybe I should I throw a stick at it or something?"

"No! Cripes, don't anger it, Nick! You'd think that stupid guide would do more than flirt with my boyfriend." Bob gave another shudder of fear. One of his front legs buckled, and my hair yanked on the branch. "Oh, great! My horse is about to keel over, Nick." I swallowed. "I'm really scared." Bob managed to right himself.

"Okay, I'm coming. Hang in there." Slowly, without taking his eyes off the bear, Nick leaned the reins against his horse's neck and gave him a gentle nudge. "Come on, Satan," he murmured, and the horse, probably defying every natural instinct, obeyed. My heart squeezed. Nick was coming, and God bless him for it. Even if this meant the four of us—Nick, Bob, Satan and yours truly—were a juicier target, maybe there was strength in numbers.

The bear snuffled at the ground but otherwise didn't move, which was good and bad—on the one hand, it wasn't leaving, but on the other, it wasn't chomping on our femurs, either. Bob gave another high-pitched wheeze, and the bear's head swiveled back at us.

"Oh, crotch. Crotchety crotch crotch," I said, sucking in a shaking breath.

"Try to stay calm," Nick said. He was right next to me now.

"Okay, Nick. It's just a grizzly bear, right? And they

never hurt anyone. Those five-inch claws are for show only—"

"Harper, shut it. And hey. Don't be ungrateful. I didn't have to come back for you, you know."

I looked at him. There was something about being around Nick that reduced me to a seventh-grade smart-ass…even with a grizzly bear staring us down. Nick, on the other hand, looked…ironic. One eyebrow was raised, and a little smile tugged at one corner of his mouth. "True," I said. "Thank you."

"Much better. Here. Let me untangle your hair, at least. If we need to run, we can't have you stuck."

"I don't think Bob's up for running," I said.

"Then you'll take my horse."

"What about you?"

"I'll stay here and whittle a sword and kill the bear or, if that doesn't work, I'll just be eaten alive, happily sacrificing my life for yours." He gave me a look. "Or I'll just stay on the horse and you can sit behind me. Satan can hold two, I'm sure."

"Oh, so you're a cowboy now? I wasn't aware that architects were also masters of horseflesh. You and Satan BFFs now? Practiced your stunt-riding this morning?"

"My dad gave me a few lessons."

"When? When you were six?"

"Well, you know, Harper, maybe we should just stay here and bicker until the bear can't stand it anymore and kills us both. Would that make you happy?"

He moved Satan closer to my shuddering steed, reached over and began working on the task at hand, tugging my hair gently. His body blocked my view of the grizzly, which worried me, as neither of us could see the bear right now, but my options were somewhat limited. I took a shaky breath, inhaling Nick's familiar, spicy smell. Twelve years, and I bet I could've picked him out of a dark room full of men. I'd always loved to burrow under the covers with Nick. Always loved his warmth, his skin, the little scar over his heart where Jason had shot him with an arrow when they were eleven. Nick hadn't shaved this morning. I could see the pulse in his neck beating fast. So he was scared, too. But he was here.

"There. You're free."

His face was very close to mine. Those dark, dark brown eyes…damn. They always held so…*much*. So much humor, so much disappointment, so much hope. It had always been a devastating combination.

Just then the bear stood on its massive hind legs, and terror, true, blinding terror, blanked out every conscious thought. Nick and I both lurched in our saddles, me pushing him away, him trying to pull me onto his horse, ever at odds with each other.

"Nick, get out of here! Go, go!"

"Get on my horse, hurry up. Shit, being eaten by a bear is not how I saw us ending up."

"Stop talking! Just go, get out of here. You can make it, your horse is fast, go!"

"I'm not leaving you, but could you hurry up before we're Smokey's afternoon snack?"

"I can't, you're—"

And then the bear dropped back to all fours, preparing to charge. I clutched Nick's arms. "I'm so sorry," I said, surprising myself with the words. *Your last words,* some quiet part of my brain informed me. *We're going to die.* "Nick, I'm so, so sorry."

He looked at me then. Nick had always been able to stop time somehow. When he'd looked directly into my eyes, when he wasn't goofing around or snarking or fighting with me, the world seemed to stop as some sort of gypsy magic took root. Even now. Even when we were about to be eaten.

"I never stopped loving you, Harper," he said gently.

Oh, God. My heart stopped. The bear wouldn't need to kill me, because those words…they just mowed me down. *It's official. He'd say that only if death were imminent. His face…not a bad last thing to see.* My breath caught. "Okay," I whispered.

A second or two passed. Nick pulled back slightly. "That's it?"

"What?"

"'Okay'? That's all you have to say? We're about to be mauled, I tell you I love you and all you—"

"Oh, good, it's leaving," I said.

Sure enough, the bear…the bear was shambling away, back down the trail. It seemed—dare I say it?—bored.

Nick stared after it. His arms fell away from me. We watched the bear's large backside sway as it walked away—very calmly—down the horse trail, the distance between us stretching farther…twenty yards, twenty-five, thirty. And then it was gone. We waited. Nothing happened. We waited some more. A long line of drilling came from an unseen woodpecker. Bob dropped his head to the forest floor and began to nibble at some moss. Satan sighed.

"Well," Nick said, sounding almost surprised. "No harm done, then."

Delayed fear now put in an appearance, and my arms and legs began to shake. "Should we wait a minute?" I asked.

"I say we should get the hell out of here," Nick answered. He looked at me, swallowed. "You okay?"

I nodded, looking around. No more bears—not that I could see, anyway. "I'm fine." I forced myself to look back at my ex-husband. For a long, heart-rolling moment, we just stared at each other.

He came back for you.

"Thank you, Nick." Then I leaned over and kissed his cheek "Thanks."

His face flushed, and he looked away. "Whatever. Couldn't keep hating you if you were tragically killed."

I smiled. "I thought you never stopped loving me."

"You can only really hate the ones you love."

"That's beautiful. Does Hallmark have a line for that?"

He gave me a look. "Stunted."

He came back for you. He risked his life for you. My ex-husband put himself between a grizzly bear and my person. He could say whatever he wanted. It just wouldn't be cool to use those words for any purpose whatsoever.

"Thanks again," I said.

"We'd better catch up to the others," Nick said, not looking at me, and without further ado, he nudged Satan back onto the path. Bob followed, back to his leaf-snatching ways, his earlier terror (and cowardice) apparently forgotten.

For a while, we just rode, side by side, not talking. Clearly the others weren't concerned...my guess was we were a half hour behind them. For now it was just us, and the squeak of the saddles, the noise of the horses, the constant birdsong and the big sky above us.

"So Emily seems nice," I said.

"She is," he said. "Very nice girl."

"You guys dating?"

"Nope."

I glanced at him, but he was staring ahead. "I think she's got a crush on the boss." No answer. "You dating anyone these days?"

"Not at the moment." He deigned to glance at me. "So. Dennis. An interesting choice for you, Harpy. Not completely unexpected, of course."

"Why is that?" I asked. "Because he's a tall, brawny firefighter? I *am* a woman, you know."

"So they say. No, it's just interesting that you picked someone like…that."

"Like what? Tell me, Nick, since you're an expert on Dennis, having known him for less than a day," I said coolly.

"Happy so long as he's fed and doesn't think too much. Scratch his itchy spot, and he's yours forever." He gave me a mocking look.

I didn't answer. Nick was wrong, of course. I'd scratched Den's itchy spot, but I still wasn't engaged. Not that I'd reveal anything to Nick. The saddle leather squeaked. A rabbit ran across the path, and Nick and I both jumped, then pretended we didn't. "We've been together almost three years," I said mildly, stretching my time with Dennis just a bit. "Same amount of time you and I were together."

"I'm well aware of how long we were together."

"And maybe I love him."

"Sure," he said, clearly unimpressed. "What number is Dennis?"

"What do you mean?"

"Oh, I just imagine a lot of bodies in your rearview mirror, Harpy."

Ooh. "Actually, he's my first serious relationship since you, darling first husband."

"Took you that long to get over me?"

Actually, yes. "Hardly," I said. "I'm just pointing out that you like to make assumptions about me so I'll fit into your world view."

He sliced a razor blade of a look my way. "Why don't you just say what's on your mind, Harper?"

I jerked Bob's head away from a cluster of bright yellow aspen leaves that jutted out into the path. "You script things a certain way, that's all," I said calmly. "When we were married, you were the dedicated young architect who's heartbroken to find that his commitment-phobic wife was, by your definition, at least, unfaithful. Details and facts are irrelevant—your opinion is the only one that matters. Nick, the noble wounded. Harper, the icy bitch."

"Oh, so you were completely blameless?"

"I'd admit to, I don't know…thirty percent of the responsibility for our implosion."

"Yes. Blame me by all means," he said, rolling his eyes. "God knows I was such a bastard, working toward our future, supporting us, adoring you—"

"Adoring? Is that what it was? See, I was thinking *ignoring*. Sounds like adoring, but quite different, in fact."

From up ahead came the sound of voices. The rest of the gang, no doubt.

"Harper," Nick said, pulling Satan to a stop, "I want you to do something for me."

Bob stopped also, his head dropping so precipitously that I almost slid down his neck. "What's that, Nick?"

"Leave Chris and Willa alone, okay? Don't…infect them."

Bull's-eye. I tried not to flinch, but his words clamped down hard on my heart. I didn't say anything. "What I mean is," Nick continued almost gently, "you're cynical, Harper. You don't believe in commitment. Your whole job is splitting up couples—"

"See, that's just ignorant, Nick, not to mention clichéd and unfair," I answered hotly. "I don't split anyone up. They're already apart. I facilitate a legal process, get a fair settlement for my clients and guide them through a difficult time of life. I have absolutely nothing to do with the failure of marriage."

"Except ours."

"Yes. Except ours. Takes two to tango, though, Nicholas, dear."

We stared at each other for a stony minute. This time, Nick was the first to look away. "Whatever," he grunted. "But listen. Christopher's had a rough time in the past few years. Willa's the best thing that's ever happened to him. He's crazy about her, and the feeling seems to be mutual. Can you just leave them alone and let them sink or swim on their own?"

"Rough time how?"

"Let him tell you himself, if he wants to. Or let Willa. But Harper…leave them alone. Okay?"

"It's just that—"

"Harper," he said, his voice fast and hot. "I came back for you today. I was willing to let Gentle Ben eat me instead of you. Can you please do me this one favor?"

Those gypsy eyes were angry. And he had a point.

"Okay," I said grudgingly. "But if Willa asks me for advice, I'm going to tell her what I think."

"Fair enough," he said, and with that, he kicked Satan into a canter and left me to wake my dozing horse and join the others.

CHAPTER EIGHT

THE MAID OF HONOR HAD some very impressive circles under her eyes the next day. I woke up early—well, I'd been waking up all night, Nick's voice echoing in my head. *I never stopped loving you. Don't infect them.* Et cetera. At five-thirty, I tiptoed out of my room to the sound of Dennis's gentle snoring, Coco in my arms. My little dog and I took a long walk along the quiet lake, watching the mist rise silently off the water, the pines dark and wise. A bald eagle swooped silently down and snatched a fish from the water with barely a splash, then disappeared again into the clouds.

I never stopped loving you.

Crotch.

Well, I thought briskly, Nick's feelings were what they were. True or not, they didn't really have anything to do with my life anymore. Soon I'd be back on the Vineyard, and Nick would be safely relegated once more to the land of memory.

As I walked back toward the Swiss chalet-style lodge, I saw a lone figure standing on the shore. It was Nick. Before he could see me, I dodged to the other side of the path and went in the front entrance, avoiding him, and continued to avoid him all through breakfast. Master of evasion, that was me. After the meal, I claimed the need to work—not a lie—and wrote a brief for one of my co-workers and emailed clients as well as Kim and Father Bruce. I sent Tommy a "keep your chin up" note, updated a few files…stalled, in other words, until it was time to get ready for the ceremony.

I made sure Coco had her bunny right next to her on my bed, smooched her tiny head and offered her several bribes in the form of the bacon I'd swiped at breakfast. Then I lugged my dress down to Willa's suite, smiling automatically at the other guests I passed in the hall. Everyone was hurrying downstairs…the wedding was supposed to take place on the patio of the lodge, in front of the achingly blue lake, the clear wind and ragged mountains bearing witness as eagles soared, yadda yadda ad infinitum.

That had been the idea, anyway; Mother Nature had other plans in the form of, as BeverLee put it, a "bluenorther," or, to the rest of us who weren't from the Lone Star State, a huge rainstorm. One could almost say it was a sign. At the moment, the staff of the lodge and a few wedding guests were dragging in the chairs and tables before everything was hopelessly drenched.

"Here you are! Come on, sweet knees, come on, get in that dress. Oh, you got purple, that's just fine, Harper. Good girl." BeverLee swept me into Willa's room and practically kicked me into the bathroom to change.

"Hi, Wills," I called.

"Hi!" she answered. "Can't wait to see your dress!"

"Me, too," I muttered.

Rather hoping that this moment wouldn't come to pass, I'd bought my dress in Boston about two hours before my flight. It looked pretty on the mannequin, and it was the requisite purple…well, lavender. I slid out of my other clothes, pulled the dress off the hanger and tried it on.

Oh, crotch.

The gown fit well enough, but the neckline was…low. Not just low, not just cleavage, but…well…lots of boob, okay? Lots. I looked slutty. Were I a nursing mother, this dress would be quite convenient. Does that paint the right picture? I gave the bodice a tug northward; it didn't move. *Hello, world, I'd like you to meet the girls.* Nothing to be done for it now, unless my father had a little duct tape.

Well. Whatever. No one would be looking at me except for Dennis. And, sure, maybe Nick. Who'd never stopped loving me but also now hated me, due to said love.

And people wondered why I did what I did.

"Oh, my Lord, don't you look *wonderful!*" BeverLee crooned as I came out. "It's about time you showed off your assets!"

"Very pretty!" Willa said, clapping her hands.

"Come over here, darlin', let me give you a little spritz," BeverLee said, holding up her can of hair spray like a weapon.

"I'm good, actually, Bev," I said. "Willa, you look… wow."

Now, granted, I'd seen my sister in wedding regalia before, but even so, it came as a little bit of a shock. Little Willa, getting married.

"Shoot, I forgot to give the caterer the flowers for the top of the cake," BeverLee said. "Harper, can you finish your sister's hair, sweetie? Thanks. Just tease it up a little in the back, 'cause it's lookin' flatter than a griddle cake."

"Will do." BeverLee flew out of the room, her orange church-lady suit flapping.

"Don't tease my hair," Willa said the second the door closed behind her mother.

"I won't," I smiled. BeverLee had always had a heavy hand with the Jhirmack, determined that her bouffant would stand up to the winds of Martha's Vineyard. Back in the day, I'd taken it upon myself to do Willa's hair every day for school, braiding it, brushing it into a ponytail.

Now, I picked up a tiny white flower and pinned it in Willa's smooth blond hair. Just like old times.

Looking at her reflection in the mirror, I could see that her expression was…somber. "So how are you doing, honey?" I asked. This wasn't exactly breaking my promise to Nick, I told myself. No *infecting* going on. Not a crime to ask one's sister how she felt on her wedding day, though I'm sure Nick could find a way to convict me.

She looked up at me, frowning. "Did you want to back out on your wedding day?"

I took another flower and secured it near Willa's temple. "Actually, I did," I said quietly. "I was scared. Everything had happened really fast. I thought we were too young. Looking back, too, it was clear we had…I don't know. Different ideas about what being married meant."

"But you loved him, right?"

I swallowed, looked down, grabbed another bobby pin. "Sure. But loving someone doesn't necessarily mean you can be happily married. And even on our wedding day, I guess I knew that." I paused, then sat down next to my sister and took her hand. "Willa, it would be completely okay if you called this off, honey."

The door to the room banged open, and I jumped. Nick. Of course.

"All set downstairs, Willa," he said cheerfully, then turned to me. "I thought we had an agreement," he muttered, scowling like Zeus with PMS. Zeus with PMS but wearing a tux, which wasn't quite fair. Then again, I had the boobage. So there.

"And we did. Which I've honored." I got back up and resumed my hairstyling duties.

"Hi, Nick," Willa said, smiling up at him.

"So," he said, kneeling next to her. "You nervous?" he asked. As I had a moment earlier, he took her hand.

She gave a pretty grimace. "Well...yeah. A little."

"Excuse me, I need a flower," I said to Nick, nudging him a bit ungently with a knee to the ribs.

"Here." He slapped a blossom into my hand and didn't bother moving. "Willa, I think everyone has a few doubts on their wedding day. Your mind runs through the worst-case scenarios. What if we're making a mistake, what if she doesn't love me enough, what if I love her too much?"

I snorted and slid another bobby pin into my sister's hair. Willa, alas, was rapt.

"Do you regret marrying Harper?" she asked.

"I'm standing right here," I said.

"I know," she said, smiling up at me. "I just always wondered."

Nick still didn't look at me. "No," he said, and my stunted, cynical heart gave a twist. "But I do regret that she didn't have the same faith in me that I had in her."

Heart untwisted quite fast. "Oh, sac up, Nick. That's a lot of crap. Faith, my ass. Willa, I regret not foreseeing how fast Nick would dump me in the middle—"

"Willa, the thing is," Nick interrupted, "you have to listen to what's in your heart. Your heart knows what's right."

Willa smiled and gave a tiny nod.

"Or you could listen to your brain, which tends to be more reliable," I interjected. "Or, here's an idea, you can simply take a few months to get to know each—"

"If you really don't think you should marry my brother, Willa, don't. Call it off. Take some time. But..." here he gave her hand a squeeze, "if you really love him, go ahead. Marry him. Be happy. Take care of each other. Make some beautiful nieces and nephews for me to spoil." He grinned, and that was it. Willa was sold. Her little smile blossomed into full-fledged glory.

"Wills," I said quickly, "I want to spoil beautiful nieces and nephews, too. It's just that I don't want to have you rush into something when there are some very good arguments to be made for waiting. Let your big sister be an example to you. Nick and I also loved each other, and we were done before we'd hit six months. Maybe we could've avoided that if we'd taken, oh, I don't know, a year, two—"

"Your sister and I didn't divorce because we were young, Willa. We divorced because—"

"You know what?" Willa said. "I'm good, you two. I'm all set. I love Chris and we'll get married and sure, have some babies and live happily ever after."

"Great," Nick said.

I glared at him. "Or not great. Willa, listen. If you want to marry Chris, I think that's fine. I'm sure he has some very nice qualities. But there are things you need to know first. Money. Work ethic. A five-year plan. Marriage takes work."

"We can figure it out as we go along," she answered, standing up.

"That's what Nick said to me, interestingly," I answered. "I'm just pointing that out."

"Well, we're not you and Nick." She stood up and gave me a quick hug. "Thanks for doing my hair," she said sweetly. "Now or never, I guess."

"I'll get Chris," Nick said, giving me an evil glance as he left.

"He's really great," Willa said, checking out her reflection once again.

"So great," I replied through gritted teeth.

"Angel baby, y'all ready?" BeverLee was back, along with my father. "Oh, my land! Look at your hair! Harper, you did a bee-yoo-tee-ful job! Just look at you!" My stepmother enveloped her only child in a huge hug. "Oh, this is such a happy day!"

I looked at my father, who was waiting in the doorway, a small smile on his face.

"Dad? Maybe some paternal advice?" I suggested. "Willa's about to marry a man she met four weeks ago."

"Six, actually," Willa corrected.

"Are you having second thoughts, Wildaberry?" he asked, tilting his head.

The slash of jealousy that cut across my heart took me by absolute surprise. Would that Dad had asked me that same question on my wedding day. Would that he had a nickname for me. Then it was gone, and I was just grateful that he'd asked.

"I'm sure, Daddy," Willa said, gliding over to give him a hug.

"You look very pretty," he said. He glanced at me. "You too, Harper."

"Thanks, Dad." I grabbed the two bouquets off the bed and forced a smile onto my face. "Well, if you're gonna do this, let's get going."

It wasn't that I didn't want Willa marrying Christopher Lowery. I just didn't want her to end up divorced *again*, heartbroken *again*, confused and lost and full of self-doubt *again*. My advice was sound. Crikey, this is what I did for a living! And when the shit hit the fan, I'd be cleaning it up, just as I had after every one of Willa's ill-fated moves in the past.

I traipsed down the stairs to the first-floor landing, checked behind me to make sure Willa, BeverLee and Dad were ready, then looked down at the guests.

The main room of the lodge had been transformed into a chapel of sorts…some sort of trellised archway brought in from the yard, buckets of Montana wildflowers here and there. Someone had found some white crepey material and draped it over the arch, and it would've all been very pretty, had it not been such a hugely bad idea. Country music played—something about being in love with your best friend. Right. Willa and Chris were virtual strangers, not best friends.

I could practically feel scales break out on my body as I walked down the stairs and up the makeshift aisle. Nick stared at me, his gypsy eyes narrowed. Jerk. I narrowed my own eyes back, then looked away. Oh, much better—there was Dennis, smiling appreciatively. "You look smokin', dude," he murmured as I walked past.

"Thanks," I muttered.

"And oh, we just get closer," the singer crooned—well, that wasn't hard, given that the bride and groom hadn't been together for two months yet. "You believe in me like nobody ever has…" *Does she, Chris? Does she believe in the Thumbie?* Christopher gave me a shy little nod and a half smile. Sure, he was sweet. All of Willa's husbands had been sweet.

There. I arrived at the makeshift altar and turned to watch my sister approach. Didn't look at Nick.

"I thought I asked you not to infect them," he murmured. "What were you doing? Giving closing arguments?"

"I was trying to infuse some common sense into the proceedings," I ground out through gritted teeth.

"You make me sad," he said.

"And you make me feel like kicking you in the shins," I returned. Christopher gave us an odd look. Nick smiled at him and punched him on the arm.

And here came the bride. Well, she was beautiful, that much was true. Beaming, radiant, yadda yadda. Against all expectations, a lump came to my cynical throat.

"Who gives this woman in marriage?" The justice

of the peace, who appeared to have been dug out of his grave for the occasion, gave a phlegmy cough.

"Her daddy and me," BeverLee said with a hitching sob, her peacock-blue mascara running à la Tammy Faye. As Dad and Bev took their seats, Willa handed me her flowers, then stepped up onto the little dais with Christopher.

Given the small space, Nick and I had to stand very close to each other. He looked calm and wise, but I could feel the irritation crackling off him. He glanced at me, then dropped his gaze to my low-cut dress, where the boobage was generously displayed. "Thanks for the show," he murmured. He pulled back a little and checked out my ass. "I have to wonder, though…where do you hide your leathery tail?"

"Bite me, Nick," I muttered. The justice of the peace gave me a look. His eyebrows would put Andy Rooney's to shame. I returned the look sharply. *What?* He frowned, then cleared his throat.

"Dearly beloved," he said, then broke into another coughing spell.

"One could almost say it's a sign," I murmured to Nick, flashing a smile at my sister.

"Did I mention I like the extra weight on you?" he whispered, staring straight ahead now. "Most women couldn't pull off fifteen extra pounds, but I like you chunky."

"Please, Nick. Sacred vows and all that," I bit out. "We both know how much *those* mean. And it's eight pounds. Not fifteen."

"Will you two shut up?" Chris asked amiably, grinning at his bride.

"Your brother has cramps," I said. "But yes. I'll shut up."

"At last," Nick grunted.

I mouthed an obscenity at my ex, then clenched my teeth and turned to watch the proceedings.

But.

Here's the thing.

As I stood on the altar, next to Nick…well, it obviously brought up some memories. Despite my fears and doubts on my own wedding day, despite the fact that I felt like we'd been making a huge mistake, I had…well.

I had loved Nick with all my heart, damn it.

"I, Willa, take you, Christopher, to be my husband. To have and to hold from this day forth…"

I swallowed. I was so *not* the type to cry at weddings (or divorces, or funerals, or Iams commercials), but those words…I saw that my sister gripped Christopher's hands a little harder.

"…in sickness and in health, for richer and for poorer…"

My snarky cynicism seemed to have deserted me, and I felt a little panicky all of a sudden. Exposed, almost. Willa's voice was husky with emotion, and I recognized the sincerity in her voice…because I'd meant those words, too, when it had been my turn to say them, twelve years ago.

"…to love and to cherish…"

I sneaked a glance over at Nick. He was looking at the floor, and I wondered if he was remembering, too.

"…from this day forward, and for all the days of my life."

God, I'd loved him so much.

He looked up at me, and time seemed to stop. Those dark, sad, beautiful eyes…full of so much…regret? Love? Sorrow? For one long, unguarded moment, we just looked at each other, a sea of emotion and all this time between us.

If only…the saddest words in the English language.

I would never love anyone the way I loved him. My lawyerly brain accepted that fact. My heart…well, my heart couldn't think at the moment. Once, I'd been adored by the man with the gypsy eyes, and those days had been the happiest and most terrifying of my life.

"The rings, please?" asked the JP. Nick looked over at the bride and groom, and the spell was broken, and I was left feeling as defenseless as a newborn raccoon on the Mass Pike during rush hour, because I knew Nick had seen.

The ceremony ended a few minutes later. Willa and Chris were engulfed in a crowd of well-wishers, Bever-Lee's twang slicing through my molars as she squealed her joy. Dennis was already at the bar, obeying his genetic imperative by sipping a Guinness, laughing with Emily. Dad nodded and shook hands. Willa caught my eye and gave that infectious, delighted smile of hers. She waved her hand, and I caught a glimpse of the thin gold band. I shoved down my apprehension, smiled back and said a quick prayer to whatever god, saint or angel might keep her happy, considered sacrificing a goat…whatever it took.

Nick didn't look at me again. There was a stillness about him even as he smiled at the other guests, shook hands and chatted. But he didn't even glance my way.

The storm had ended, and the general consensus was that the party should move back out onto the patio. People picked up chairs and tables, and the party moved outside. The sun broke through the clouds in thick slices of gold, the pines sparkled with raindrops and the lake gleamed an ethereal blue.

I needed a moment.

Running up the stairs, I got a leer from an elderly man in a Korean War veteran baseball cap. Ignoring him, I continued charging up the stairs, all the way to the third floor—hey, I was in good shape, all that bike riding, so this was nothing. No, the knocking and rolling of my heart, that was due to something other than exercise.

My room was blissfully quiet. Coco, curled around her bunny, acknowledged me with two wags but didn't open her eyes, as naptimes were precious to her. I went over to the window and pulled back the curtain, revealing the endless wilderness. My hands were shaking, I noted. What to do about that was another question.

"Harper."

As if summoned, Nick stood in my doorway. "Nick," I breathed.

For a second, I just looked at him—his tousled, nearly black hair, those sad eyes, and it just didn't seem possible that so many years had passed, that I hadn't teased him about his first gray hair, that we hadn't talked every day, that I'd spent so long without him, the last man on earth I ever thought would let me go.

Then he crossed the room, hot, bristling energy gathering in a ball and without word or thought, we were wrapped around each other, mouths seeking and finding, and God, the charge nearly lifted me from my feet, as if I was hovering in the air and melting into him at the same time. He was at once familiar and new, leaner than he'd been and harder, but his mouth, his lovely mouth, was the same, hot and hungry, and it was simply unspeakable, how good it was to feel him again, elemental, fundamental, primally *right* to be with Nick, to kiss him, to…to…to own him again, because let's be honest. We'd only ever belonged to each other.

He held me so hard my ribs creaked, and oh, God, I had *missed* him, missed this, why oh why did we ever let this get away from us? My back was against the wall and Nick shifted, his hand covering my breast, his skin hot on mine, and still we didn't stop kissing, hot, hard, desperate kisses. He felt so *good*, like no one had ever felt, as if we were two pieces of rock that had been split apart by lightning and were now fusing back into one, as we were meant to be. He kissed me as if the end of days was upon us, his tongue sliding against mine so that my knees nearly gave out. Nothing mattered but the two of us, together again. Not one thing. I jerked his shirt from his pants and slid my hands up along his ribs, drinking in the hot glory of his skin, my fingertips seeking out the little scar over his heart, and he groaned against my mouth and shifted so I could feel his full weight against me, and my body hummed with lust and power, because he was shaking a little. I'd done that to him, just as he had to me.

He pulled back, his face flushed, eyes burning, hair standing on end, and then he grinned, and I thought my heart might crack from the sight, so much had I missed Nick's smile.

"Do you want to say something?" he whispered, breathing hard.

"Um…take me?" I said, panting a little, smiling back.

He gave a raspy laugh. "Well, yes, I'd love to." His smile grew. "But maybe you wanted to say something else?" With one hand, he pushed a lock of my now-wild hair behind my ear and just looked at me. His eyes were gentle, and expectant. "Go ahead."

I paused. A trickle of dread cooled the flash fire of just seconds before. Crap. This was where things generally started breaking down where the two of us were concerned. Expectations. "You…you go first."

He cocked his head. "I think you should go first, Harper. After all, you…"

I stood up a little straighter. "After all, what?"

"Well, you're the one who…you know." Clearly he

was hinting that there was some declaration that would be appropriate right about now. I frowned. Nick blinked. "You don't want to say…*anything*, Harper?"

"No, I'm good, Nick." Ardor definitely cooling here.

"Nothing. You have nothing to say to me," he clarified, taking a step back and running a hand through his hair.

I pursed my lips. "Well, obviously, you think I should say something, so why don't you elucidate, Nick?

His jaw grew knotty. "I just figured you'd want to…"

"What?"

"Apologize. I thought you'd want to apologize."

I gritted my teeth. "Oh. This…This is great." I crossed my arms over my too-exposed chest. "For what?"

He blinked. "What do you mean, for what? For ruining our marriage, that's what."

"I—you—Are you kidding me?"

"No," he said, giving me that all-too-familiar look. *Why are you hysterical? I'm only being completely logical here.*

"You want *me* to apologize?" I asked, my voice rising. "That's what you want? Now? Seriously?"

He put up his hands defensively. "Look, I'm completely willing to forgive you and start over—"

"Oh, wow, how generous! Thank you, Nick!"

"—but you have to admit, Harper, that what you did was really bad. I mean, in at least one sense, you cheated on me. Betrayed me. And while I'm definitely open to making a fresh—"

"You know what? Here we go again, Nick. This was the whole problem during our marriage. You were blameless, and everything was my fault. Well, guess what? I'm not playing this time."

"What did I do? I loved you, Harper! I worked a lot. Is that a crime? Was that a stupid plan, for me to work hard so we could have a secure future?"

"You know what's a stupid plan, Nick? This. Us. Look. You're…whatever. And obviously, I'm still…attracted to you. But if you're still looking for me to take the full blame of our fiery crash, no! I won't, Nick! You had a hand in that, too."

"I fail to see what I did that was so wrong," he said tightly.

"And that's the whole problem," I snapped. "I'm sorry you came up here. Too much time has passed. You're still hung up on me being the bad guy. Good night."

"You *are* the one who left," he snapped.

"Actually, you were," I returned through gritted teeth. "Whatever. At any rate, it's clear you're looking for an abject apology and some groveling in addition to some groping and fondling. But guess what, Nick? You'll have to look somewhere else."

And with that, I stomped out of the room, down the hall and back to my sister's wedding.

CHAPTER NINE

"Okay folks, gather round for the latest killer martini—Crillas, in honor of the happy couple!" My voice was bright and chipper—damned if I was going to let Nick know just how much he'd gotten under my skin. "This little number has Kahlúa, to represent our dark and handsome groom…"

"So handsome!" Willa said, kissing her man.

"…and pineapple juice, for the sweet bride." I smiled, getting an "aw" from the crowd. "Now maybe it doesn't sound like those two ingredients go together…" I winked at my sister…"but when you try them, you'll see. Crillas are fantastic! So go ahead, gang!"

This wedding reception was eternal. Faking good cheer was definitely not a specialty of mine, but Nick and I seemed engaged in a war as to who could ignore the other the most effectively. It seemed to be a draw. Here I was, behind the bar—I'd bartended through college, as well as during my brief stint in New York, and was now playing merry maid of honor. Nick, for his part, had claimed the role of available bachelor/uber best man, and had danced with every woman present from Emily to BeverLee to an elderly woman from Wisconsin who wasn't a wedding guest but wasn't complaining, either. Every woman but one, of course. He laughed and flirted and seemed as happy and good-natured as humanly possible, and I'd be damned if I was going to let on that my knees still buzzed from that kiss.

I'd been spared, that was it. In a moment of weakness, of useless, pointless sentimentality, I might've let things go further with Nick, and then I'd be swamped with regret and guilt. It was bad enough…Dennis hadn't even crossed my mind during that kiss, and what the hell did that say, so thank the Lord nothing went any further. There was a reason Nick and I hadn't worked, and it would serve me well to remember that.

As I went to the bar for my third Crilla, Jason Cruise approached, doing that side-to-side swagger so that the friction between his chubby thighs wouldn't cause a fire. "Harper, wanna dance? Old time's sake or whatever?" He adjusted his Wayfarers sunglasses. Wayfarers. Honestly. So 1980s.

"Bite me, Jason," I said.

"Whoa. You don't have to be such a bitch."

"And you don't have to breathe, Jason, yet you continue to do so. Frustrating."

"Why do you hate me?" he asked. "What did I ever do to you?"

For a second, I wasn't going to answer. Jason had, in point of fact, never done anything to me. But letting things go wasn't exactly my forte. "I don't hate you, Jason. You're not important enough to hate. But I dislike you intensely."

"Why?"

"Because I know about you, Jason," I hissed. "How you treated Nick when you were kids, broke his toys, rubbed your life in his face and shot him in the chest with an arrow. Add to this the fact that you're a shallow, irritating twit, and there you have it."

"So? I thought you hated Nick."

I opened my mouth to protest, reconsidered (I did rather hate Nick, at the moment, anyway). "Whatever."

Jason lifted his Wayfarers to better ogle my breasts. "So how about that dance, Harper?"

Men. A friend of mine from law school had just gone the sperm-bank route. She was first in our class, okay? Clearly a brilliant woman.

I was saved from further interaction with Jason in the form of Firefighter Costello, all six foot two of him. "This guy bothering you, Harp?" he asked, looking down at Jason.

"Yes, Dennis. Please beat him to a pulp."

Dennis gave me a startled glance. "Seriously?"

"Dude, I just asked her to dance," Jason babbled, backing up rapidly. "She used to be family or something. That's all. I wasn't trying to, uh…you know. Whatever."

I shot the little toad a lethal glance. "Shoo, Jason. Go back to your swamp." He slumped away, bumping into one of the posts that held up the ceiling, since he'd put the stupid sunglasses back on, and went off to bore more people with his recitation of Tom Cruise's biggest box-office hits.

"Wanna dance, babe?" Dennis asked.

"Definitely," I answered, and so we did, my guilt over kissing Nick causing me to snuggle up against Dennis's broad shoulder. Den smiled and copped a feel, since he was not a man to resist a breast, especially two so obviously offered as were mine.

"What time do you have to leave tomorrow?" I asked.

He grimaced. "My flight's at seven," he said. "Which means I have to catch the five-thirty shuttle."

"You know what? Take the rental car," I offered. "I'll grab the shuttle later on."

Dennis's face lit up. "That'd be great, dude. Thanks."

When I first asked him if he'd wanted to come to this wedding, Dennis hadn't committed right away. The result was that he'd had to book a much less civilized flight than my afternoon departure. Dad and BeverLee were driving to Salt Lake City—I guess BeverLee had some third cousins there she hadn't seen in years—then flying home from there, and so I'd be all alone on my journey back East. That was more than fine with me.

"Gotta hit the head," Dennis said. "Catch you later."

"Roger," I answered.

As soon as he left, BeverLee came over, her Cinnabar so thick that I nearly choked.

"Have you had a chance for a sit-down with your daddy?" BeverLee asked, automatically reaching out to plump up my hair.

"BeverLee, I thought we agreed that I wasn't the best one to interrogate Dad about...you know," I said, resecuring my hair in its twist.

"Well. Sure, now. That's fine and all." She sat there, looking like a large, ungainly chick with that butter-colored hair and blue-mascaraed eyes.

"But I'll...I'll say something to him. Sure." *How's that for a random act of kindness, Father Bruce? That should hold me for a month.*

"Oh, thank you, sweet knees! That's just so...! Oh! Thanks, darlin'! He's right over there. No time like the present!"

"Okay." I sighed, patted Bev's freckled shoulder, then made my way through the dancing crowd. There was my ever-elusive father, handsome and solitary, sitting at a small table with a beer. "So, Dad," I said.

"Harper." He gave me a half nod.

"Having fun?"

"Sure. You?"

"Oh, yeah."

It was turning into one of our longer conversations. After my mother had left, he'd ask such searching questions as "You okay?" to which I'd answer (in a sullen, resentful tone), "No," which would fail to elicit further conversation and served only to make us both feel worse.

I sighed. "So, Dad, how are things with BeverLee these days?"

He slid his eyes over to me. "Why'd you ask?"

"Um...just because?"

He took another sip of his drink. "Actually, I think we may be...heading our separate ways."

"Really?" A prickle of alarm ran up my spine. "Why's that?"

"Just...growing apart."

I sat rigidly. "Does that mean you've found someone else?" It often did, let me assure you.

"Oh, no. No, there's no one else. I'm not the cheating type. We just...you know."

I *didn't* know. BeverLee and Dad had been together for twenty years. Dad was sixty-two. Not that older people didn't divorce. Still, I couldn't help feeling...weird. With a sigh, I asked my dad if there was anything I could do.

"Maybe you could handle the divorce when it rolls around," he suggested quietly.

"Absolutely not, Dad."

"I'll take care of her, don't worry."

"I'll recommend someone for both of you. It doesn't have to get ugly."

"Okay. Thanks."

We sat in silence for a few minutes. My father finished his beer. "Dad," I said eventually, "have you talked to BeverLee about this? I don't get the impression that she knows you're thinking divorce."

He glanced at me and looked away. "I will. Soon."

I started to say something else, then reconsidered. If a person thought he wanted a divorce, well, it wasn't my place to convince him otherwise. Besides conversations about *emotions* and *feelings* and *love* were not something I ever had with my father. Willa and he had always had a much easier time…she'd plop herself down on his lap and tease him and make him laugh. Much more normal than the Mexican standoff I myself had with dear old Dad. After all, I'd always been Mommy's girl. Right up until she left.

I thought again of the envelope, sitting like a tumor in my suitcase.

BeverLee was looking at me anxiously. I gave her a shrug and a smile—*Men, who knows?*—and she nodded back. Sadly. Ah, poor Bev. She loved my father, though I did have to wonder if she really knew him, even after all their time together. According to her, the man practically invented air. Maybe that was the problem. The guy she had in her head bore little resemblance to the person who actually existed. It was a common enough problem.

Suddenly exhausted, I decided to call it a day. My sister and Christopher were locked together on the dance floor, playing tonsil hockey by the looks of it. I went over, tapped Willa on the shoulder and slapped on a smile. "I'm beat, guys," I said. "See you tomorrow at breakfast, right?"

"Actually, we're leaving early," Chris said. "Heading up to Two Medicine for some camping."

I looked at Willa, and my chest tightened. "Well, call me when you can. When do you think you'll be heading back East?"

The happy couple exchanged a glance. "We're kind of playing it by ear, Harper," my sister said.

Great. That always worked out, especially when traipsing around the wilderness with grizzlies and wolves and potential snowstorms. But I held my tongue, and Willa gave me a huge hug. "Thanks for everything, Harper," she said, smooching my cheek.

"Oh, sure," I murmured. Not that I'd done anything other than voice doubt, of course. "Mazel tov, okay?" Lame. "Listen…I hope you'll be very happy." Still lame, but better. I hugged Willa back, always a little awkward where physical affection was concerned. I nodded to my new brother-in-law then headed to my room. Just before I started up the stairs, someone said my name.

"Hey." It was Chris. "Listen, Harper. I know this must've been awkward, seeing Nick and all, me marrying your sister, and I know you don't really approve. I just wanted to say thanks for coming out here. It meant a lot to your sister. And to me, too." He smiled. Not without his brother's charm, this guy.

"Well," I said. "Just be careful, Chris. Marriage is hard. I want you guys to make it, I do."

"I really love her," he said earnestly. "I haven't known her all that long, I realize that, Harper, but I do love her."

"Well, you better. You're married now. All the days of your life." I patted his shoulder. "Good luck. Really."

As I climbed the stairs, I imagined I felt Nick looking at me, but when I turned, I didn't see him.

Though I'd checked on Coco numerous times throughout the day and Dennis had taken her for a couple of walks, she was in full Chihuahua orphan mode, huge eyes, still body, not raising her head from her tragic little paws, looking at me as if I'd just locked her in Michael Vick's basement. Her bunny was on the floor (I was sure this was deliberate), reinforcing the fact I hadn't visited poor little Coco in nearly two hours.

I picked her up and kissed her funny little head. "I'm very sorry," I told her. "Please forgive me. Pretty please."

She acquiesced, morphing back into Jack Russell territory, and gave a wriggle of delight, then licked my chin, letting me know I was forgiven.

"Hey, you're here," Dennis said, emerging from the bathroom, his shaving kit in his hands. On the bed, his suitcase was open, clothes stuffed in haphazardly. I released Coco and began refolding his stuff so it wouldn't wrinkle so much.

"Did you have a good time?" Dennis asked.

I gave him a look. "Not really, Den." Putting his shoes at the bottom of the suitcase so they wouldn't squish anything else, I took a deep breath. "Den, maybe we should talk, what do you think?"

"Um...okay." He sat down on my bed; I sat on his, and we looked at each other—me the principal, Dennis the naughty child. I sighed. It was tiring, always being the one to take charge. But someone had to do it.

"So, Dennis." I took his big hands in mine. "Listen. I asked you to marry me two weeks ago, and you haven't said boo about it since. That probably gives me an answer, don't you think?"

He grimaced but didn't contradict me.

"It's okay. I'm not mad." Oddly enough, I wasn't.

Dennis sighed. "It's just...I guess I'm not really sure this is the way to go, you know?" He looked at me sheepishly. So handsome. His voice had a hopeful note, and this, more than anything, was what hurt me...as though Dennis had been a good-natured prisoner without much hope of reprieve, and I was his longtime jailer, just coming in with news of a gubernatorial pardon. "It's like, if I'm not wicked psyched at the idea, maybe it's not the right thing to do."

Ouch. But he was correct—one should be wicked psyched at the thought of death do us part. Look at my own history. "Right. It's a good point."

"Not that I don't, uh…you know, Harp. Love you. I do."

I had to smile. "Wow. As declarations go, that was pretty lame."

"Sorry."

"It's okay."

"Really?"

"Sure." I squeezed his hands and then let them go. "Just for the record, I think you're really great. You have a very big heart, we had a lot of happy times, and…well, I wish you all the best." *And you thought his declaration was lame.*

He smiled broadly. "Same here, dude."

Well, I wouldn't miss being called dude, that was for sure. But I would miss Dennis. He was like a security blanket, but it was time to put him away, and just because I knew it didn't make it easy. No strapping, blue-eyed children running around, none of the easy, taken-for-granted security in having an amiable companion day in and day out. No uncomplicated contentment. My throat tightened, and I swallowed—and for me, that was the equivalent of a weekend sobbing in bed.

Dennis took my hand and kissed it, an unexpectedly courtly gesture. I reached out and touched his hair. Good old Den.

"Wanna fool around?" he asked, looking up. "A farewell f—uh, fling?"

I choked on a laugh. "Oh, I think…I should pass, Den. Not that it wouldn't be fun. Just probably ill-advised."

"Had to give it a shot," he said amicably. "I'll take Coco out, then. Wanna go for a walk, Coco-Buns?" he asked, and my dog sprang to life as if electrocuted, leaping straight into the air at the *W* word, then grabbing her bunny in her mouth and shaking it exuberantly. "Back in a few," he said, clipping on her pink leash. The door closed behind them.

With a sigh that started in the soles of my feet, I flopped back on the bed and stared at the ceiling. The Plan to Marry Dennis was over. Already, the thought of the big lug's absence echoed around my heart. I had a lot of good things back on the Vineyard, but Dennis had filled a big hole in my life. A big one. Now the thought of my future stretched out ahead of me.

Alone again.

Buck up, I told myself. *You have Coco. You have Ben & Jerry. A job you're great at, friends, a deck and a view. You can still have a kid…adoption, sperm donor, new relationship, whatever.*

But I'd miss Dennis. It wasn't the yawning, bottomless panic I'd felt when Nick and I had imploded, but crap. It hurt anyway.

THE NEXT MORNING I WOKE abruptly and squinted over at the clock. 8:47. The room was empty; apparently I'd slept through Dennis's departure. Indeed, if his flight left at seven, he'd be well on his way home by now. Lucky man. I hauled myself out of bed, the three martinis from yesterday making themselves felt. Coco raised her head from her bunny, affirmed that yes, I looked like utter crap, and rolled onto her back, legs in the air, and feigned roadkill. On the dresser, there was a note from Dennis.

Harp, I took Coco out for a quick walk. See you back home, I'm sure. Thanks for everything. ☺ *Den.*

Well. That was…nice. With a sigh, I checked my phone for messages—blick. Lots. I listened dutifully—six from Tommy, two of them work-related, four of them personal, detailing his roller-coaster feelings about his slutty wife, who, though she had promised to stop seeing FedEx as of Friday, had in fact sneaked off to meet him on Saturday, and Tommy wasn't sure if he should put his foot down. Two messages from Theo, wondering why I hadn't been to work on Friday—the man had a memory like a sieve. A message from earlier this morning from BeverLee; she and Dad were on their way to Salt Lake City and wondered if I'd come to dinner on Friday to relive Willa's wedding. A text from Kim, just checking in. It was nice to have a girlfriend…most of my other female friends were from college or law school, not the day-to-day types. I figured I'd call her back from Denver, where I had a two-hour layover and would have time to chat. And a text from Father Bruce. *Call me when you get back. Hope all is well. Don't forget your RAoKs…your immortal soul can use all the help it can get. As can we all.*

RAoKs. Random acts of kindness. That made me smile. I typed him back a quick answer and hit send. Then, after a moment's hesitation, I texted Willa. *Hope you have a great honeymoon. Here's my credit card number, just in case you need anything. Call me soon.*

An hour later, I was showered, packed and ready to go. I clipped on Coco's leash and went downstairs. My shuttle left at eleven; plenty of time for breakfast. Though the lodge served brunch, no one from the wedding seemed to be afoot. Glacier's season was winding down; another week and snow could easily shut down Going to the Sun Road. Strange that back home, it'd still be summer.

Home sweet home, where I'd be safe and sound. And single, I added with a small dart of self-pity. Soon, no doubt, I'd be seeing Dennis with someone else. Sighing, I assessed my mood. Melancholy…but not ruined, certainly. When Nick and I had gone down in flames… well. No point in revisiting that memory. One didn't really enjoy remembering the time when one had been a quivering, raw, pathetic mess. Surely, simply feeling blue was a sign of maturity. Or something.

I ate on the patio, reading the local paper, occasionally granting Coco bits of toast and an occasional strip of bacon, which she snapped up with sound-barrier speed before she resumed her intent staring. Glancing at my watch, I realized it was time to get moving. The shuttle was due in a few minutes.

I'd miss Montana, I realized with a small shock. Lake McDonald was dark blue and choppy today. On the far side, the craggy mountain loomed, the white of the glacier ruthlessly bright. My heart squeezed. Chances were, I'd never make it back here. For some reason, things felt... unfinished, somehow.

"Oh, well, Coco-Butter," I said to my dog. "Time to go home."

The line for the shuttle was rather long...looked as if everyone was leaving today. I was glad I'd made a reservation last night. The young mother whose baby had dropped the pacifier came up behind me and said good morning, and I nodded back. The shuttle driver took tickets and checked our names off his list. "And twelve," he said, checking my name off the list. "Okay, that's it. Sorry, ma'am," he told the young mother. "Can't take any walk-ons today. These folks all had a reservation. You'll have to wait for the next shuttle at noon."

"Oh, no! Shoot. Do you think I'll make my flight?" she asked him. "It's at twelve-thirty."

"Probably not," the driver said.

Should've thought of that before, I thought, picking up Coco and grabbing the handle of my suitcase. But then I stopped. Glanced at my watch. It took about forty-five minutes to get to the airport; the shuttle left hourly. I had plenty of time.

"You can have my spot," I said magnanimously. "My flight's not till one forty-five."

The young mother's face lit up. "Really? Are you

sure?" But she was already hoisting the diaper bag and grabbing the handle of the baby's car seat.

"Sure. Go ahead." The child stared at me solemnly. Destiny, as I recalled. Quite a name. She certainly was a beautiful child…flawless skin and a rosebud mouth, giant, wise blue eyes.

"Thank you so much! You're a lifesaver!" the mom exclaimed. "Have a great day! Safe home!"

"You too," I said. There. Random act done, and it was a significant act at that. I couldn't wait to tell Father Bruce. Feeling rather holy, I waved to the mother and child, then got another cuppa joe.

Fresh mug of coffee steaming, I went back out on the patio to read a little more.

There was Nick, sitting at the table I'd vacated not ten minutes earlier, staring out at the lake. I jerked to a stop—damn, it was still a shock to see him—then kept going.

"Nick," I said as I passed.

"Harper," he answered, flicking his eyes to me for the briefest instant.

I sat at another table, not too far away. Didn't want to seem like I couldn't stand the very sight of him.

I'd have to accept that should Willa and Christopher stay together, I'd be seeing Nick once in a while. The occasional holiday or birthday or whatnot. And that would be fine. We had a turbulent past, we'd always have some feelings for each other, and so on and so forth, ad infinitum. He was simply a mistake from my youth. Everyone has her heart broken at least once. Didn't mean the heart didn't mend and indeed, grow stronger.

I took out a pen, turned to the crossword puzzle and settled Coco on my lap (she liked to help). Coffee, delicious. Crossword, challenging. Dog, adorable. Ex-husband, invisible, thanks to a senior citizen tour group, which had descended from a motor coach. A veritable sea of white heads prevented me from catching even the slightest glimpse of Nick, and I was grateful.

A short while later, my random act of kindness bit me in the ass.

"What? How can it be shut down?" I asked.

"Ma'am, all I know is what they told me at the airport. The last flight left an hour ago, but since then, the whole fleet's been grounded. Something about a problem with a software upgrade in the navigation system. Nobody can take off, nobody can come in."

"That can't be."

"All they told me is that until this is fixed, no planes are leaving Kalispell City Airport, none are coming in."

"None *is* coming. It's singular." He rolled his eyes and sighed. "Sorry. Um, well, what about the other airports near here?"

"All three of the regional airports have the same problem."

"Are you kidding me?" I yelped.

"No, ma'am." He stared at me, resigned patience clearly running thin.

"When will they be flying again?"

"The controller at the airport said two days, minimum."

"Two *days*?" I screeched. Coco barked, voicing her own indignation. "Seriously, are you kidding me?"

"No, ma'am." I sensed he was about to kick me.

I took a breath. "Okay. Can you take me to the nearest unaffected airport?"

"That would be either Yakima, Washington, or Salt Lake City. And no, ma'am, I can't take you there."

"Crotch." I thought a second. "Well. How about a rental car? Can you take me to Avis? My boyfriend just returned our car this morning. I'll pick it up again and just drive myself to wherever."

"Well, when we got the news, a bunch of folks asked me to take them to the same place, but sure, I'll take you there. You might want to call first and see if they have any cars available."

They didn't. Ten minutes later, I'd tried the other two rental car companies in the area. The surly driver was right. Oh, this was maddening! Apparently, when the fleet had been grounded, the people already at or en route to the airport (and I would've been among them, had I not done my stupid random act of kindness) had been bused to the rental places and snapped up the rather few cars in stock. I was stuck here.

Well. That would be okay. I could stay a day or two. I had my laptop, of course. I could work from my room... let's see, I didn't have court this week, so that was good...I had a meeting with opposing counsel on a case, but I could conference-call that one. And maybe I could even see a little more of the park, and that unfinished feeling would fade.

I wheeled my luggage, Coco in tow, over to the desk clerk. "Hi," I said in my warmest tone, the one I used on Judge McMurtry's clerk when I needed an extension. "Listen, I have a little problem. I don't have a way of getting home, so I'll need to keep my room for another day or so."

"Oh, that's too bad," the girl said. "Sorry to say, we're booked."

"Booked?" I blurted.

She smiled sweetly. "This Elderhostel group has all the rooms. I'm really sorry. Do you want me to try somewhere else in the park?"

"Yes, please," I said, a trickle of panic flowing up my

spine. The girl began typing...and typing...and typing. "Anything?" I asked tightly.

"I'm super sorry," she said after typing seven or eight more pages. "A lot of the park is already closed, and it looks like Elderhostel kind of owns the rest of the rooms we do have this next week."

"Well, what am I supposed to do?" I asked.

"We have tent rentals available," she suggested.

"I'm not sleeping in a tent!" I protested, my voice a tad shrill. "Do I look like the camping type? Plus, I was already almost eaten by a grizzly bear! And I'd freeze to death! It was thirty-four degrees last night!"

"Harper."

Super. Insult to injury. I turned around. "I'm a little busy, Nick."

His face was neutral. "You can come with me."

My mouth dropped open. "You."

"Yes. I'm driving East. I can get you to an airport along the way."

"You're driving?"

"Yep." He folded his arms across his chest.

"How far?"

"All the way to New York."

A prickle started in my stomach, reminding me of something before my brain caught on. Oh. right. There it was. My face flushed.

"Take it or leave it, Harper," Nick said, glancing at his watch. "I'm leaving in fifteen minutes."

CHAPTER TEN

AN HOUR LATER, I WAS sitting in Nick's rented Mustang, Coco and her bunny at my side, a map on my lap. We were heading east on Route 2. The plan was for Nick to take me to Bismarck, North Dakota. All the other airports between here and there had grounded their tiny fleets, thanks to some glitch in an air-traffic-control-software upgrade. Damn computers.

Glacier was behind us, the Rockies towering in the rearview mirror as clouds scudded among their peaks. *Thanks, Teddy,* I thought with a pang as we left the park, and I turned back to say goodbye. Someday, maybe, I'd come back. Sure. My future child and I would vacation here, and I'd show him/her the spot where Mommy was almost mauled by the giant grizzly bear. Or not. That might be upsetting to a child. *Note to self: buy Dr. Spock ASAP.* With a sigh, I turned to face forward and fondled Coco's silky little ears.

Nick's 'Stang was a convertible, of course. A man can't have a suitable midlife crisis without his trophy car being a convertible or his trophy wife being a blonde. The wind ruffled Nick's hair as if directed by the gods of *GQ Magazine.* Add to this the fact that he wore blue-tinted sunglasses, a black T-shirt and jeans and looked irritatingly gorgeous. Coco, who got quite squealy around Dennis, had thus far ignored Nick. Good doggy.

Nick glanced at me, making me realize I was staring at him. "So what happened to Dennis?" he asked.

"He had an earlier flight. We, uh…we couldn't get seats on the same plane."

"Really." His tone suggested he knew something different.

"Mmm-hmm." Abruptly, I shifted my attention to the map. "So, okay, the interstate is about—"

"We're not going to." He didn't look at me.

"But—"

"I know."

"Nick, that means—"

"Yup."

"Seriously, Nick? You do realize that not taking the interstate will add hours and hours to our lovely sojourn together, don't you?"

"Yes, Harper. I'm aware. But this is my trip. You're merely baggage, emotionally and cargowise."

"Ha, ha."

He deigned to look at me. "It'll take about thirteen hours, all told."

I glanced at my watch. "Okay, it's one now, so if we take turns driving and drive all night, we'll—"

"We're stopping for the night."

I gritted my teeth. "Great! Then we can enjoy each other's company that much longer." I smiled sweetly at him, which he ignored. Fine. So we'd stop at some hotel. I'd be in Bismarck…let's see…I could be there tomorrow by ten, assuming we drove till nine tonight and were on the road by seven tomorrow morning. Not bad. Survivable.

But still. Stuck in the car with Nick. The hum of electricity was quite uncomfortable.

"So. A road trip, huh?" I asked.

"Yep."

"Quite the midlife crisis you're having, Nicky."

"I'm thirty-six," he said.

"Almost thirty-seven," I couldn't help saying.

"And it's been a lifelong dream," he said, finally looking at me. "As you well know."

I sure did. Pulling Coco onto my lap, I turned my attention out the window. U.S. Route 2 was no more than a two-way road, though it was a corridor through the entire Northwest. We'd left the mountains surprisingly fast, and around us were only the Great Plains—fields of browning grass as far as the eye could see, and above us, the endless blue sky, streaked with thin white clouds. The air was cool, the sun relentless, and I was glad to have slathered on the fifty-factor sunscreen, as I burned easily. Towns with sweet names and tiny populations were listed on the map—Cut Bank, Beaver Creek, Wolf Point.

Nick had been quiet since offering me the ride. I was rather sure he regretted it now. For someone who'd blurted that he'd never stopped loving me, kissed me into the middle of next week and was now chauffeuring me to the next state, he seemed a bit…constipated. Perhaps therein lay the problem.

"So, Nick, do you want to talk about what happened this weekend?" I offered, turning to look at him. Strands of hair had escaped my ponytail, and the wind whipped them into my eyes.

Nick glanced at me. "No." Then he reached into the backseat, groped around for a second and pulled out a faded Yankees cap. "Here," he said.

I took the extended offering. "Won't I turn into a pillar of salt if I wear this? Being from Red Sox Nation and all?"

He gave me a lightning smile, and my heart answered with a quick trill. "Give it a try and let's see," he said, turning his eyes back to the road.

I put on the hat. Not only did my hair stop whipping around, my face was shaded, too. "Thanks," I said. He nodded. "Okay, well, if you're not going to talk about things, I will," I added.

Nick closed his eyes briefly.

"Here's the thing, Nick. Um, that thing you said when we thought the bear would eat us...pretend I didn't hear. Just a little blast of ubersentimentality, heat of the moment, death imminent and all that."

He sighed. "No, Harper. It was the truth."

Well, crotch. "You still...love me."

"Yes."

My ability to remain speechless lasted roughly three seconds. "And you also said you hated me, too."

"Yes."

"I don't think you meant that. I don't hate you."

"I can't possibly state my relief." He took a swig of water.

"And as far as the kiss...well. We were both feeling very nostalgic. Let's just give each other a free pass on that, okay?"

"Are you going to keep talking about this, Harper? Because I can let you out any place along here." He gave me a look, his expression veiled.

"Okay, fine. Sorry." I looked straight ahead. The road stretched to the horizon, and the fields beside us seemed endless. Not a heck of a lot of scenery, apparently. I glanced at the dashboard. Super. We were doing forty. The speed limit was seventy-five.

Being a native New Yorker, Nick had always relied on public transportation. He got his license only his senior year of college, something I'd often teased him about when we were together. Back then, on the rare occasions when he did get behind the wheel, he was your basic novice...hands at ten and two, eyes fixed on the road, puttering along at the speed of a limping snail. I could see things hadn't changed.

"Want me to drive?" I offered.

"Nope."

"The speed limit's a wee bit higher than you're going."

"I'm aware of that."

"This car is wasted on you."

"Shut up, Harper." He reached forward and turned on the radio. Country music, expected here in the land of cowboys. The singer's woman had left him for another man. Not exactly groundbreaking material.

"I brought my iPod," I informed my driver.

"I brought mine too," he said. "But let's listen to the local station and drink in the scenery, shall we, dearest ex-wife?"

"Oh, of course. So how's life been, Nicky-bear?"

"Very good, thanks."

"You're a successful architect?"

"Yes."

"What type of buildings do you design?" I couldn't seem to stop the interrogation, but crotch. We were stuck in the car together. What else were we supposed to do? Relive our happy times?

"We make corporate buildings, mostly."

"Skyscrapers?"

"Not so much. The biggest building we've done is eight stories. We've done some boutique hotels, two museum wings. But someday, a skyscraper. The firm is still relatively new."

"Do you ever do houses?" I asked.

He shrugged. "Once in a great while. The real prestige comes from the bigger stuff."

And prestige was what Nick had always wanted. Maybe to show his father that he was somebody, maybe because he just wanted to be the best. We hadn't been together long enough for me to find out.

"Good for you," I said.

"And I'm sure you're a big success as well," he said, an edge to his voice. "So many divorces, so little time."

"Speaking of," I said, suppressing a surge of irritation. Flipping open my phone, I was happy to see I had a signal. I hit Tommy's number. He picked up on the first ring.

"Tommy, how are you?" I asked.

"Oh, Harper. Hi. Um…not that good. I'm really sad." He certainly sounded sad. Sadder even than the current singer, whose dog had just been run over by the wayward wife as she stole his John Deere. Was there no Carrie Underwood out here? No Lady Antebellum?

"What's going on?" I asked.

"I just can't stop thinking about Meggie. How happy we were. How do things get so off track, Harper? She loved me once."

Which means absolutely zilch, I thought, glancing at Nick. "Well, I'm not sure."

"I just keep thinking there's something I could do to get our old life back. I don't want a divorce. Christ, it's such a…failure."

"I don't think so, buddy. Sometimes, divorce is just the act that will rectify a mistake." Nick snorted. I ignored him. Sort of. "After all, marriage means different things to different people. *You* didn't go off shtupping the FedEx man, did you? No." I gave Nick a rather smug look. *See? This divorce is a good thing.* "You, Tom, wanted something different. Fidelity. Friendship. Love. You wanted to spend time with your spouse." Another pointed look at my ex. "You put the marriage first, and Meggie clearly didn't. Am I right?"

"I guess," Tommy admitted.

"Right. And as much as I'd like to console you and tell you things will all work out and you'll live happily ever after, I wouldn't be a good friend if I did. If she doesn't want counseling, and she won't take your phone calls, and she's sleeping with another man…I'd say she wants out. I'm really sorry, Tommy. It's going to take some time for your heart to catch on to what your head already knows."

Nick rolled his eyes. Coco sneezed, then rested her head on my knee.

I spent a couple of more minutes murmuring sympathetically to my heartbroken paralegal before losing signal. Sighing, I closed my phone.

"Was that fun for you?" Nick asked. I noted he was gripping the steering wheel rather tightly, though we still hadn't broken the forty-three-mile-an-hour barrier.

"No, Nick. Not at all. Tommy's my friend, and I don't like seeing him miserable." He didn't answer. "Why? What advice would you give to a guy whose brand-new wife was sleeping with someone else?"

As soon as the words left my mouth, my face grew hot, and my stomach lurched. Nick didn't say a word. Didn't turn his head, either. A new song was playing on the radio, something about dead soldiers, in case the mood wasn't bad enough.

Coco whined, then head-butted my hand. "Um, Nick, Coco needs a rest stop."

He took his foot off the gas, clicked on the turn signal (so quaint…we never bothered with that in Massachusetts) and slowly, slowly pulled onto the shoulder, as if we were in heavy traffic on Storrow Drive, rather than out in the wilderness with only a very occasional truck for company. When the car stopped, I clipped the leash to Coco's collar and started to get out, then hesitated.

"I never cheated on you, Nick," I said abruptly, and to my surprise, a lump came to my throat.

He took off his sunglasses and rubbed his forehead, then looked at me. "No, I guess not." For a brief second, something flashed in my chest. He believed me? Then he added, "Not technically, anyway."

My jaw clenched. "Not technically, not in any way."

"That's debatable."

"Okay. Would love to discuss, can't. My dog has to pee." I got out of the car and set Coco down.

It didn't serve to be mad at Nick. He wasn't a forgiving person...well, not where I was concerned. I'd screwed up, sure. But so had he. I'd admitted my wrongdoing. He never would. Hence our divorce. All facts, all in the past. Still, I guessed my blood pressure was in the DefCon Four range at the moment.

Damn it. Accepting Nick's offer of a ride was a huge mistake. I'd be better off fighting grizzlies and shivering in a tent. I walked Coco down the road a bit, as she liked a little privacy, being a girl and all. There was nothing out here, not as far as the eye could see. The Rockies of Glacier had melted into the western horizon. No town was in sight, no buildings, no other vehicles. Just Coco, Nick and me.

I looked back at my ex, and my heart softened unexpectedly. He'd given my sister a job when she needed one, stood beside his dubiously employed brother, probably supported Christopher's efforts at inventing, made sure his neglectful father was near him. And here he was on his much-anticipated road trip, his irritating ex-wife, whom he loved and hated, as a passenger.

At the moment, he was leaning against the car, studying the map as the wind ruffled his hair. I'd always loved his hair. And his hands. Also, his neck. His neck was a thing of great beauty, and I loved it when we lay in bed, postnooky, cuddling, my face against that warm, sweet place—

Okay! Enough of that. I walked back to the car, Coco trotting briskly along beside me. "Where do you think we'll stop for the night?" I asked. It was already midafternoon.

"I'm not sure," Nick said. "I want to see the world's largest penguin statue."

"Very funny."

"I'm not kidding," he said, grinning. "See? Right here."

I leaned in closer. That was a mistake. There was his neck, smooth and tanned and practically edible. Feeling a bit like a vampire resisting the urge, I cleared my throat. "I love maps," I said a bit too loudly.

"Me, too," he said, glancing at me. "All those places you've never been."

"All that mystery," I said. "The GPS is great, but it's not the same."

"My thoughts exactly." His mouth pulled up, my girl parts coiled. I looked away, adjusted the Yankees cap.

"Did you ever do this before?" Nick asked quietly. "Drive across country?"

"No," I said.

"Ironic, don't you think?" He looked up from the map, his eyes steady.

"Very." My heart knocked against my ribs.

He stared back a minute longer, then folded the map. "Okay. Off we go. Penguin statue, here we come."

CHAPTER ELEVEN

NICK AND I WERE GOING to drive across country for our honeymoon. Fly to California, drive back. Neither of us had traveled much. But we were going to do it the summer after our first anniversary, as Nick needed to accrue enough vacation time. And of course, we didn't make it to our first anniversary.

Our wedding was…well, you've been to weddings. They're all the same, more or less. It was very nice.

That's a lie. It was horrible. I was wallowing in doubt, first of all, a chorus of *What the hell are we doing?* ringing under my constant self-assurances. *It's okay. He loves you. He's great. What the hell are we doing? We're too young. It's okay. He loves you. Why am I not in law school? Why am I following a man? It's okay. He loves you. It'll work. What the hell am I doing?*

When I said yes to Nick there on the Brooklyn Bridge, I hadn't envisioned a quick wedding. Figured I'd go to law school at Georgetown, where I'd been accepted, then… eventually…get married. I had no problem with a long-distance relationship; Nick and I had been long-distance my entire senior year, and we were doing fine. But he pushed. Why live apart when we could live together? If I could get into Georgetown, then Columbia or NYU would be a piece of cake. We loved each other. We were great together. We should get married. No reason to wait.

Nick could be very convincing. And relentless. And of course, I did love him.

So, the first day of summer, having been out of college for a month, I was about to get married and sweating blood at the thought. All morning long, as we set up chairs and put flower arrangements on the tables in my father's yard, I waited for Nick to suddenly realize we were idiots to play this high-stakes game of grown-up. I waited for the courage to call things off. For my father to tell me this was a mistake.

I waited, too, for my mother.

See, she'd followed a man, too. My mother, a California girl, had come to Martha's Vineyard at age twenty-one with some friends, met my father—seven years older, tanned and manly. Legend had it that my mother had been doing a modeling gig in Boston. She and her pals had decided to pop out to the island, and Dad was fixing the roof on the cottage one of the friends rented. He was tall, handsome, quiet—the best of the blue-collar clichés. Mom invited him to a beach party. When her friends left the following week, she decided to stay. A month later, she was pregnant and voila…our family.

As of my wedding day, my mother had been gone for more than eight years. In all that time, I'd received four postcards, all of them in the first year and a half of her desertion. They were all similar…*Florida is hot and muggy, lots of orange trees and huge bugs. Hope you're keeping up the good grades!* The second one came from Arizona. *Sure is hot here! You should see the way people water their lawns! Don't they know they live in the desert?* The third from St. Louis (Clydesdales, the arch, a baseball game), the fourth from Colorado (bluegrass festival, Rocky Mountains, thin air). None of the postcards had a return address. She signed them all *Linda*…not *Mom*.

I guess I hated her, except I missed her so much.

I had no real reason to expect her to show up. And yet, our engagement announcement had run in the paper.

Martha's Vineyard had a small year-round community; if she'd stayed in touch with *anyone*, she would've heard that her only child was getting married. So it wasn't impossible that she'd come—it was just extremely, extraordinarily unlikely, and yet every time I heard the ferry's blast, my heart rate tripled.

She didn't come. That made more sense than her appearing, but it was crushing nonetheless. I don't know what I would've done if she had. Still, in the back of my mind, a little scenario played in which my mother, gone these many years, would come home at last, and in all the excitement and happiness (because it was a fantasy, after all), my wedding would be postponed indefinitely.

Then I'd look over at Nick and see his smile, and shame would blast me in a hot wave, because I did love him so. But as much as I wanted that to be a good feeling, it wasn't. It was simply terrifying, as if I'd been walking innocently along one day, and a yawning pit opened in front of me. Ever since he'd knelt down on the Brooklyn Bridge, I'd been scrambling back from a crumbling edge, trying to save myself from whatever lurked in that dark hole, quite sure it was nothing good.

Yet the appointed hour arrived, and there I was, putting on a white sheath dress and painful shoes, my hair worn down for once because I knew Nick loved it that way. BeverLee tried hard to be a good mother of the bride, hitting my hair with Jhirmack every time she walked past, fussing over my flowers, my dress. If my mother had been here—if she'd never left—we'd have gotten matching manicures, as we did when I was little. She'd have worn a pale blue silk dress, not the orange polyester that Bev had chosen. She'd have told me that marrying young was the best choice she'd ever made, and she could tell that Nick and I would be just like her and Dad.

Instead, I had BeverLee, chattering constantly, force-feeding me coffee cake and bemoaning that I'd opted against the dollar dance. While I knew her intentions were good, I'd wanted to tap her with a magic wand and render her silent, stop having her tell me I was "purdier than a new set of snow tires." How could I be getting married without my mother? How I could I be getting married, period? How was it that I'd let things get so out of hand?

No one else seemed concerned. My father told me Nick was "a good kid" and imagined we'd "do all right." Nick's father was beefy and charming and shallow...alas, he was Nick's best man; Jason was already half in the bag, his hair worn long for Tom Cruise's *Interview with a Vampire* look. Christopher, then in high school, flirted with Willa, whom he wouldn't see again for thirteen years.

Even as I walked down the aisle on Dad's arm, that little voice in my brain was whispering furiously. *You don't have to do this. This has disaster written all over it.* Nick's face was solemn, almost as if he guessed what I was thinking. He recited his vows in a somber voice, his dark eyes steady, and even then I thought the words almost ridiculously naive. Did anyone believe that vows meant anything anymore? My parents had said the same things to each other. Nick's parents had also promised till death did them part. Who were Nick and I to believe that our vows would be any more lasting than the breath it took to say them?

Then it was my turn. "I, Harper, take you, Nick..." and suddenly, my eyes were wet, my voice grew husky and I wanted with all my heart for those words to be true. "To have and to hold from this day forth..." We could do this. We could be that little old couple who still reached for each other's hand. "...all the days of my life." And I looked into Nick's gypsy eyes and believed.

After the wedding, we spent a few days in one of those

huge sea captains' houses on North Water Street in Edgartown. It was owned, as are they all, by a fabulously wealthy off-Islander for whom my dad occasionally did some work. He'd generously offered his house for our brief honeymoon, as he wouldn't come to the island till the Fourth of July. And so, for a few days, Nick and I played house as we were playing grown-ups...we drank wine on the vast back porch, planned our trip for next summer—our true honeymoon, we called it. We made love in a room overlooking the lighthouse, cuddled and watched movies, and for those five days, I believed in happily ever after. For five days, it seemed possible that Nick and I would have a house, children, a life, an old age together. Maybe I was wrong to be so...dubious.

I wasn't.

Six days after our wedding, we drove down to Manhattan to the tiny apartment in a desolate part of Tribeca, and everything changed. Nick went back to work. His hours were long. His dedication was impressive. His ambition was boundless. His wife was left alone.

Of course, I realized he had to work, to impress his bosses, to separate himself from the pack of other young and hungry architects. It wasn't the hours—well, the hours didn't help. But Nick had a plan, and that plan went as follows: graduate at the top of his class. (Check). Land job with top firm. (Check). Get married. (Check). And once the box next to my name had been checked off, Nick sort of...dropped me.

Because I'd missed the deadline on applying to New York law schools, I had an unwanted year off. Our plan—Nick's plan, really—was for me to apply to Fordham, Columbia and NYU, make our little apartment a home and fall in love with the city. No need for me to work; he was making enough to pay our bills. Alas, our apartment was a dingy little walk-up in Tribeca, which was something of a ghost town in those days, a place where it was nearly impossible to find a newspaper on the weekend, where no families seemed to live, where the noise of the West Side Highway was endless and the screech of the subway woke me up at night.

I tried to make our apartment homey, but I wasn't really the Martha Stewart type. Painting the bathroom, scrubbing grout with bleach, putting throw pillows on our futon couch…it failed to deliver the promised satisfaction. Though I initially cooked dinner every night, stretching our dollars as best I could, Nick rarely made it home before eight…or nine…or ten.

All the effort he'd put into our courtship, into wooing me, because yes, I was a prickly porcupine of a person, I knew that…all the little ways he'd made me feel cherished and safe…that all ended as soon as we hit the Big Apple. I found myself married to a man I barely saw.

I was alone in a city I didn't know and didn't like, to be honest. It was so loud, so hot and muggy. At night, I'd have to wash my face twice and swab my skin with toner to get it clean. Our apartment smelled like cabbage, thanks to Ivan, the sullen Russian who lived downstairs and rarely left the building, who listened to soap operas at top volume and always seemed to be lurking, shirtless, in his doorway when I came down the stairs. Garbage trucks clattered and banged down the street at four in the morning, and someone had a dog that barked all night. Central Park was a long, tooth-jarring subway ride uptown, and Battery Park, much closer, was dirty then, filled with drug dealers and homeless people sleeping on benches, a sight that never failed to gut me.

I had two friends from Amherst down here…one in law school, one in publishing, and both were caught up in the glamour and excitement of their lives. The fact that I'd gotten married was baffling to them. "What's it like?"

they'd ask, and my answer would be vaguely pleasant. The truth was, marriage thus far sucked.

Nick left for work about twenty minutes after he got up at 6 a.m. If he did make it home before ten he'd spend perhaps fifteen minutes talking to me before disappearing with a smile and an apology behind his computer screen. Many nights, he wouldn't get home till after eleven, and I'd have fallen asleep, realizing he was home only when I rolled over and felt his sleeping form. In the five months we were married, he didn't take off one entire weekend, opting instead to go to the office on Saturdays and most Sundays.

He quickly made himself indispensable at work. His boss, Bruce MacMillan, aka Big Mac, loved Nick's quick wit and work ethic, so Nick was promoted to the wine-and-dine crew, charming clients, schmoozing with the more senior architects, learning from them, kissing up to them, getting in on their projects. He was happier than I'd ever seen him.

I tried to be a good spouse, tried not to be selfish and resentful. I wasn't stupid…I knew this was an investment in the future. But it was Nick's future, the one he'd always envisioned, without room for accommodating another person…or so it seemed. I wasn't a part of his world; he didn't need advice on how to handle people or how to do his job. What I wanted desperately was to feel included but instead, as the weeks passed, I felt more and more as if we weren't really in this new life together. I was just along for Nick's ride. Harper—check. On to the next thing.

I tried, I really did. Wandered the neighborhoods, tried to decipher the massive subway system. I spent all day collecting anecdotes to share with Nick, then began to resent him for not being home to hear them. I hung out at the local library, signed up for some literacy volunteering, but that was just a few hours a week. New York scared me. Everyone was so…sure. So clear on who they were and where they were going. When I voiced my feelings to Nick one morning as he hurriedly shaved, he was baffled.

"I don't know, honey," he said. "Just try to have fun, don't overthink everything. This is the greatest city on the planet. Get out there, enjoy. Oh, shit, is that the time? Sorry, honey, I have to run. We have a meeting with the people from London."

I got out there, if only to please my Brooklyn-born husband. But Nick knew all the neighborhoods, was something of an expert (and pain in the ass) on the city, so my tales of wandering (when I did get the chance to tell them) seemed to bore him.

"Actually, you were in Brooklyn Heights, honey. Cobble Hill's a little more inland. Sure, I've been to Governor's Island. I know exactly where you were. Of course I've been in the Empire State Building. A million times." He'd give me a tolerant smile, his eyes drifting back to his computer.

I think things took an irreversible turn about three months into our marriage. When I forced myself to tell Nick how lonely I was, he suggested we have a baby.

I looked at him for a long, burning minute, then said, "Are you out of your *mind,* Nick?"

His head jerked back. "What?"

"Nick…I barely see you! You want me to have a baby? So we can both be trapped here while you swan off and work your eighteen-hour days? So you can ignore me *and* your child? I don't think so!"

"You're the one who's complaining about being lonely, Harper," he said.

"I wouldn't be lonely if you'd actually spend some time with me, Nick." My throat felt as if a knife was stuck in it, my eyes were hot and dry.

"Harper, baby, I have to do this. I have to work."

"Do you have to work so *much?* Can't you ever make it home for dinner? Can't you ever take one whole weekend off, Nick? Ever?"

It was one of our more impressive fights. I hated it. Hated myself for needing him as much as I did, hated him for not knowing that. He may have been actually a little scared at my reaction; clearly, we weren't on the same page. We weren't even in the same book. He promised to do better. Said he'd take this coming weekend off, both days. We'd go up to the park, have a picnic, maybe go to the Metropolitan Museum of Art or the Cooper Hewitt.

But Friday night, when he came home well after nine, he broke the news. "I have to go in tomorrow. Just for an hour or two. I'm really sorry. I'll be home by eleven at the latest."

I'll admit now that I knew he'd never make it, and thus, wanting to increase my ammunition, went all out preparing a Martha-style picnic for us. Curried chicken with raisins, cucumber salad, a loaf of French bread from a bakery in the Village. Oatmeal raisin cookies baked from scratch. A bottle of wine. At twelve-fifteen, he still wasn't home. At one, not home. At 2:24, he called. "I'm running a little late," he said. "Just have to do one quick thing, then I'm out the door."

He got home at 5:37, a bouquet of browning daisies in his hand. "Babe, don't have a fit," he began inauspiciously. "Big Mac needed me, because apparently Jed totally flaked out with getting the permits from—"

I took a fistful of chicken salad and threw it at him, getting him right in the face. "Here. I made this for you. I hope you get salmonella and spend the next four days puking yourself raw."

Nick took a piece of chicken off his cheek and ate it. "Pretty good," he said, lifting an eyebrow.

That was it. I stomped into the bedroom, slammed the door and clenched my arms over my head.

Of course he came in (we had no locks). With exaggerated patience, he wiped off the chicken salad and put the towel in the hamper, came over, wrapped his arms around me. He didn't apologize. Kissed my neck. Told me he loved me. Asked me to be patient, since this was all, in his words, just temporary. It wouldn't happen again. We'd work things out. Then he turned me so that my face was pressed against his beautiful neck, so that I could smell his good Nick smell and feel his pulse. It worked. I cracked.

"I hate it here, Nick," I whispered into his collar. "I never see you. I feel like…like an appendix."

"An appendix?" he said, pulling back.

I swallowed. "Like I'm here, but you don't really need me. You could cut me out and everything would still work just fine." I had to whisper, it was so hard to admit.

He looked at me long and hard, his eyes inscrutable. I waited for him to understand. Waited for him to remember that I had abandonment issues, that the only other person who was supposed to have loved me forever had left me. I waited for him to realize I needed him to do more than check me off, waited for him to tell me I was no appendix…I was his beating heart, and he couldn't live without me.

"Maybe you should get a job, honey," he said.

That was the beginning of the end.

"A job," I echoed dully.

"You're alone too much, and I hate to say it, but I really can't slack off at work right now. If you get a job, you'll make some friends, have more to do. We can always use the extra money, too, I won't lie. You can quit when you start law school."

He'd wanted me to marry him, I had, and that was the end…to him, anyway.

"I'll ask around the office," he added. "Maybe someone has a lead."

"Don't bother. I'll find something on my own," I said. My heart felt like a rock sitting hard and cold in my chest.

"Great, honey. Good girl."

Then he took me to bed and we had sex, and it was his way of saying, *See? Everything's just fine.* And that, according to Nick, was that. It certainly let him off the hook. Me getting a job was much more convenient than admitting that marriage needed an investment of time, especially a new marriage, especially when the bride was me. This way, Nick didn't have to change his hours or tell his boss sorry, not tonight, he had plans with his wife. No, clearly this was just what the doctor ordered. Harper needed a job. Not a husband who actually showed up.

Almost defiantly, I answered an ad. Bartender, which was old territory for me since I'd worked my way through college bartending. The restaurant was called Claudia's, a trendy new place in SoHo.

The morning of my interview, still angry with Nick for not understanding, I accidentally slammed my hand in the front door. My left hand. No cut, but my fingers had taken the worst of it and almost without thinking, I moved my wedding ring from my left hand to my right. I rarely wore my engagement ring, which was surprisingly large. It was also, to my small-town girl's mind, an irresistible prize for the many roving thieves of New York. Nick only laughed when I told him that and didn't seem to mind.

But my wedding ring…that was a different story. That ring, I loved—two strands of gold woven together, one slightly darker than the other. It was delicate and beautiful and one of a kind, made by a Vineyard goldsmith. It didn't look a lot like the classic wedding ring…especially when worn on the wrong hand. Claudia's manager didn't ask if I was married, and I didn't think to tell him.

You get better tips as a bartender if you're young and pretty…and single. Or if the patrons think you're single. My fingers were swollen for a few days. The ring stayed on my right hand. It meant nothing. Except, of course, that it did.

Work at Claudia's was a lot of fun. Located in SoHo on a cobblestoned street, it drew in the *Sex and the City*-type crowd—beautifully dressed women who wore outfits that cost more than my rent, men who smelled expensive and thought nothing of leaving me a twenty-dollar tip on a ten-dollar drink. And my coworkers…they were just like me. Higher aspirations, temporarily in the service biz, some balancing grad school. None of us planned to be there forever. All of us were in our twenties—Claudia's owner knew that the actor/model staff drew in a better clientele or something, so we were all slim and good-looking.

As the new kid, I watched from the sidelines, but even the sidelines were thrilling. Occasionally, someone would confide in me—Jocasta had dated Ben, then dumped him for Peter; Ryan needed a roommate and Prish was looking, but did they really want to work *and* live together? Especially after that one-night stand? Flattered to be included in their drama, their angst, I'd give a noncommittal answer, didn't take sides and was generally well liked. They fascinated me…they were so free. Big plans, lazy days, a pleasant place to work. The way it was supposed to be at our age.

For the first few weeks, I just watched, did my job, listened. No one asked if I was married, and I didn't offer up the information. Was I punishing Nick? Of course I was. I barely saw the guy. He said he'd drop by one night and see the place, but the weeks passed and he never did.

I was young, stupid, insecure, lonely. Walking home some nights, I'd feel that dark, pulling thing in my chest and I'd wish I could cry, because I hated Nick, I loved him so much. I felt tricked and betrayed, and I kept waiting for him to do *something* that would make me feel the way I'd felt before we were married…that I was cherished, loved, irreplaceable. But he was young and stupid too, and the ocean between us darkened and deepened.

I didn't have the type of bond with my family that would allow me to vomit up my misery over the phone… besides, Willa was only a high school kid and thought Nick and I were the height of romance. BeverLee…no. As for my father, I'd stopped even trying to tell him the truth years ago.

Then one night, a waiter named Dare asked me to hang out with them after closing, and suddenly, I had a group of friends. I don't think I realized how deep my loneliness went until then. My college friends had grown distant, engrossed in their fabulous careers or the challenges of graduate school. But my coworkers…they were right where I was, at this strange phase of life where we worked, but not in our chosen fields, where Real Life still seemed a way off. They were like butterflies, lovely to behold, free to float and flit wherever the breeze carried them, no responsibilities other than making rent.

Of course, none of them was married. In Manhattan, you started thinking about marriage after living together for a decade or so, when you were closer to forty or fifty than twenty. Married at twenty-one? Willingly? I told myself I'd bring it up…eventually. If the gang and I became closer, sure, I'd tell them in some droll, charming way, make a joke out of my *de facto* missing husband. Or maybe when Nick finally showed up at Claudia's, as he continually promised he would. Any pangs of guilt I had on the subject were smothered in the relief of finally belonging.

So I kept my wedding ring on my right hand. Nick didn't notice…but then again, our marriage now consisted of an occasional bout of sex in the wee hours of the morning and a few polite sentences exchanged here and there, mostly via voice mail. I missed him so much that I literally had to turn myself away from it, to stuff it down and ignore it. And hey. I was good at that sort of thing.

My new circle of friends became more and more important. We ate together before work, an early dinner around four-thirty, and we would try to outdo each other with pithy comments and observations of the city and its inhabitants. We might hang out at Claudia's after closing, and I'd make specialty drinks, grapefruit gin fizzes, honey-almond martinis. One day, Jocasta, Prish and I braved the mob at Century 21 and bought cheap designer shoes. We went to a book signing in the Village. When Thanksgiving rolled around, Nick had to go to Lisbon, his first international trip with the firm (or ever). I congratulated him, smiled as he packed, kissed him as the car service came to bring him to the airport.

"You sure you're okay on your own?" he asked, hesitating there on our grimy sidewalk.

"I'll be fine. I'm going to Prish's for dinner. Have fun. Good luck!"

I waved as he left, then called my pals and let them know I was free for the animated film festival at the Angelika theater. We all went and felt very sophisticated indeed. Actually, my friends *were* fairly sophisticated. And shallow and somewhat heartless, but they were better than nothing. I tried to keep up, tried not to feel like such a rube.

The waiter named Dare (short for Darrell, but dear

God, don't ever say that aloud) was a very intense guy... wanted to write the next tormented, twisted, bleak Great American Novel and had plans to get his MFA from somewhere very impressive. Jocasta and Prish both had the hots for him, as did just about every female who walked into Claudia's. He had long blond hair and smoldering gray eyes, and he was tall and thin and made you want to feed him. He took himself very, very seriously, and hey, it worked. He flirted with me...well, not really. Flirting was beneath him. He stared intensely at me (between serving meals, of course). I knew he was interested, but I certainly didn't lead him on.

The need to say something about Nick grew, but for whatever reason, I kept waiting. Maybe for him to remember he adored me, to do something so loving and memorable that all doubt would be forever swept away and we'd live happily ever after. Again...I was young and stupid. And the thing with secrets is, the longer you keep them, the more tightly rooted they become.

By the Night of the Unforgivable Event, I'd been working at Claudia's for almost three months. It was December, and New York is never prettier than at the holidays, Christmas lights in every restaurant and coffeehouse, wreaths on the charming doors of the Village, menorahs winking in windows. Splashy, colorful displays shouted out from the big department stores, and Santa stood on every street corner. Finally, I was falling in love with New York.

As I walked to Claudia's that night, lazy snowflakes swirling in the dusk, I stopped in front of a shop window. There sat a good-sized model of the Brooklyn Bridge, cast in bronze, solid and lovely. Nick would love it. I'd buy it for him for Christmas. For a second, it felt as if I was standing on the bridge again, Nick on one knee, those Charles Dickens gloves, his beautiful, happy eyes...

Something shifted in my chest, as if a rock had rolled off my heart. I loved my husband. We could get through this long, tough time. Maybe I'd even quit Claudia's, find something more compatible with Nick's schedule so we could figure out how to make this work. Tonight, I'd tell my buddies I was married, we'd have a few laughs, whatever.

It was the night of Claudia's staff-only Christmas party, a Monday when the restaurant was closed. There were about twenty of us including the kitchen crew, and the party was in full swing when I arrived. Prish had commandeered the bar and handed me a cloyingly sweet peppermint drink. The restaurant was loud, bright, festive and happy, my coworkers already buzzed and thrilled to see me. Maybe tonight *wasn't* the night for telling everyone about Nick. I'd do it at a more quiet time. That would be better.

Prish's cocktail invention was vile, so I shook up a few special martinis made with cranberries and Grey Goose. The food was smashing, goat-cheese-and-dried-tomato pizzas and crab cakes with remoulade sauce. Ben wore a reindeer hat, Jocasta had on a blinking-light necklace and a glittery red miniskirt.

By 10 p.m., we all sat around the table in the middle of the restaurant, all of us with a few drinks in us (some with more than a few), all quite happy. At some point—I hadn't noticed exactly when—Dare's arm had gone around the back of my chair. Very casual. We were a close bunch by now, and affection was always given freely. We all hugged good-night like a bunch of eighth-grade girls, the guys would do that hand-clasp, lean-in thing and the women would kiss the men's cheeks. Asking Dare to move his arm would only draw attention to it, so I left the subject alone.

This was a mistake.

Something tickled the back of my neck, and I jumped. Dare gave me a half-lidded, steamy glance, but he didn't interrupt himself, just kept talking to Ben about some political battle over a federal court appointee. Taking Dare's hand from my neck, I set it on his lap, and he gave me a sexy little smile. Didn't touch me again.

After dinner, the noise level (and the alcohol level) had risen. Prish was singing into a fork, Ryan was drumming on the table, keeping time, Ben was rummaging for another bottle of wine, and suddenly Dare turned to me and said, "I've been wanting to kiss you for weeks now." Then he took my face in his hands and did just that.

A wet, sloppy, drunken kiss, fairly horrible, tasted like roasted red peppers. The others burst into applause.

"About time!" Jocasta yelled. "He's been giving you the eye for ages!"

I pushed away. "Don't do that again," I said, adrenaline flooding my legs. This was bad. This couldn't...I didn't... he should never have...I had to tell them—

My brain slammed to a halt.

Nick was standing on the street in front of Claudia's, looking in the window. Looking at me. His mouth was slightly open, as if he didn't quite believe what he'd just seen.

The blood drained from my face.

For a second, I thought he'd just walk away, and I jolted to my feet, bumping the table. "Nick!" I called, but he was already opening the door.

"Friend of yours?" Dare asked lazily, pouring me some more wine. I ignored him, but my legs started to shake.

Nick came over to the table. "Hi," he said quietly.

"Hi," I breathed. He didn't seem mad. Or even upset, really. Maybe he could tell that was just a stupid sloppy kiss from an irritating poser. His eyes went from me to Dare, then to the others.

"Um, guys," I said, "this is Nick."

I guess I sounded weird, or scared, because everyone quieted down.

"Nick? Who's Nick?" Ben asked, emerging from the back room.

"You sneaky thing, Harper," Prish said. "I didn't know you were dating someone."

The magnitude of what I'd done finally hit me. Nick looked at me, stunned, as if I'd just shot him in the heart. Which, in a sense, I had. He blinked—twice—I was on hyperdrive with the details here—his gypsy eyes as dark as a black hole. "She's not dating anyone," he said. "I'm her husband."

Somewhere, a fire truck laid on the air horn. Over the sound system, a jazz band was murdering "White Christmas." But otherwise, our party had gone abruptly silent.

"I thought you were only, like, twenty-one, Harper," Ryan slurred. "What, are you in one of those religious sects or something? A sister-wife?"

"You're *married?*" Jocasta asked, incredulous. "Are you kidding?"

And then Nick did walk out.

"Ruh-roh, Scooby-Doo," Ryan said. I shoved away from the table, but Dare caught my hand.

"You don't have to go after him," he said.

"Yes, I do, asshole," I hissed, yanking my hand free. The bells on the door jangled with obscene good cheer as I ran out into the cold night air. No Nick. At the corner, I looked both ways, and there he was, hands jammed in his pockets, walking fast, head down. "Nick! Wait!"

He didn't wait, so I ran after him, tripping on the cobblestones, and caught up to him at the next corner.

"Nick," I said. He didn't look at me. I grabbed his arm. "Nick, wait," I panted. "Please let me explain."

"Go ahead," he said, and his voice was oddly calm.

"Okay, well...I—I obviously didn't..."

"Mention me." The light changed, and he started across.

"Right," I said, trotting after him. I'd left my coat at the restaurant, and it was horribly cold. My teeth wanted to chatter, but I clamped my jaw closed.

"You were kissing that guy." Voice still calm, feet still walking. "What else have you done with him?"

"Nothing! That was nothing, Nick. He's an idiot. He was drunk. That was nothing."

"But nobody knew you were married."

"No...I—see, Nick, I..." Oh, God, what was I going to say? "Let's go home and talk, okay?"

He stopped, finally, and I immediately wished he hadn't. He was *furious*. His eyes were black and hot and burned like a brand. "You never mentioned me."

"No," I admitted in a whisper.

"Not even once."

I shivered, and not just from the cold. Nick didn't offer me his coat. I didn't blame him. "No, Nick. I didn't tell them I was married. I didn't talk about you."

"I see," he said softly. And he started walking again, but he took off his coat and threw it on the ground behind him, and the gesture broke my heart.

"Nick? Please! I'm sorry."

He didn't stop, or pause, or answer. I followed, picking up his coat but feeling unworthy to wear it. I was ridiculous in my shiny silver tank top and high heels, teetering after my furious husband. I was also full of self-hatred. And last but not least...I was utterly terrified.

And if there was one feeling I hated more than any other, it was being scared.

You know, he's got some nerve, a small, evil part of my brain whispered. The seeds of resentment that had been festering for the past few months suddenly found fertile soil, replacing the abject terror and sense of doom. After all, Nick was a fine one to be mad. Really, *Nick* was feeling abandoned? Nick? *I* was the one who'd been dropped into a huge city and basically patted on the head and told to go off and play and not to bother the grown-ups. *I* was the one whose husband had no time for me. Of *course* I'd found friends. Of *course* I'd been hungry for some attention. *He* sure as hell wasn't giving me any. My box had been checked! When was the last time Nick and I had had a real conversation, huh? He didn't *want* real conversations. Not with me. Nope, I was just there to do his laundry, keep the fridge stocked and be available for a quickie in the middle of the night. Some marriage. No *wonder* I hadn't talked about it! Who could blame me?

Oh, Harper, don't do this, the better angel said, but it was easier—so much easier—to be the victim. And so I built the case against Nick—I really was meant to be a lawyer—and found myself innocent. I'd made a mistake, yes, but not a huge one. Definitely forgivable, but what about *his* sins, huh? I let the righteous anger grow while Nick's figure grew smaller and smaller as the distance between us grew. Fine. He didn't want to hear what I had to say? Fine. That was nothing new, was it?

New York was quiet on a Monday night; Tribeca deserted at this late hour. Sirens, almost constant in the city, blared uptown. A single sheet of newspaper tumbled down the cobbled street, the only thing keeping me company. A bitter wind blew off the Hudson, cutting into me, bringing the smell of blood from the meatpacking companies on the West Side Highway.

By the time I reached our apartment building, Nick was already inside. I could see his dark head in the fourth-floor window—our bedroom. I let the door slam behind me and stomped up the stairs, wanting Nick to know I was primed for a fight. Opened the door to our apartment, walked briskly through the tiny kitchen and went into the bedroom.

He was furious, crackling with energy.

And he was packing.

Every thought was immediately sucked from my head. My mouth opened, but no sound came out. I watched as Nick packed with brutal efficiency. Jeans, in. Sweaters, in. T-shirts, socks, boxers…into the suitcases we'd been given for a wedding gift, suitcases that hadn't yet been used.

The last time I'd watched someone pack this way was on my thirteenth birthday. He was *leaving* me, and terror rose up so fast and hard, I thought I might faint…gray speckled my vision and my legs wanted to buckle and my neck wasn't strong enough to hold my head.

And then, just like that, something inside my heart shut off. My vision cleared. My legs and neck worked just fine. Maybe—maybe if I had fainted, or flung myself on him, if I'd begged him to forgive me, if I'd sobbed out how much I loved him—maybe we would've made it through that night.

But I wasn't really the sobbing, flinging type.

"So I guess till death do us part…that was just for fun?" I said. It was the wrong thing to lead with. Obviously.

He didn't deign to look at me. "I'm staying at Peter's tonight."

"For longer than tonight, from the looks of it."

"How long have you worked there, Harper? Two months? Three?" He moved to the minuscule closet and swept out his shirts, hangers and all. "You never, *never* found a second to tell your best buds that you were married? Not once? In three fucking months?"

"Maybe I would have, Nick, if you'd come around. Ever." My voice was cool.

"No wonder that douchebag was kissing you," Nick went on. "Why not? You're free and clear, right?" His eyes dropped to my naked left hand, and his eyes seemed to flinch at the absence there. "Jesus, Harper," he said, and his voice broke, and the case against him took a serious blow.

I bit my lip. "Nick, look. I'm really sorry, I am. It's just…I just felt so freakish—"

"Freakish?"

"Well…yes! It's just…you're never here, Nick! You didn't want to listen to how lonely I was, you didn't care, all you do is work—"

"I'm trying to build a life for us, Harper!" he yelled. "Working so we could have a decent future!"

"I know, but, Nick, I just didn't expect it to be all or noth—"

"I have to do this! I thought you understood!" He threw a pair of shoes into the suitcase. "No wonder you've been so…distant. You've been—"

"Me? Me, distant, Nick? Seriously?"

"—playing around with some 30-year-old loser who's still waiting tables, trying to figure out what he wants to be when he grows up."

"Not that I was playing with anyone, Nick, but could you blame me? You're the one who was on fire to get married, and before the first week is out, you barely remember to come home." I was yelling, too, both of us runaway trains, unable to stop.

He slammed the bureau drawer closed.

"Nick," I said in one last effort to stay calm, to make him see, to make him stay. "Nick. Look. It was stupid and immature—"

"Stupid and immature, okay, so that's a start, Harper. How about deceitful? How about manipulative? How about unfaithful?"

"I didn't cheat on you! That guy, he just…kissed me. I didn't want him to, he just did!"

"Right."

My jaw clenched. "Okay. Believe what you want, Nick. You haven't listened to me for months, why would you now, right?"

Ivan of the Cabbages banged on his ceiling. "Quiet, eediots!" he yelled. Nick continued stuffing his clothes into a suitcase.

"You erased me, Harper," he said. "I don't even exist in your life."

"Right back at you, Nick," I bit out.

"How can you say that?" he barked, slamming closed the lid of the suitcase. "Your picture is all over my office! Everyone knows you at my firm. You're all I ever talk about!"

"And why is that, Nick? Because it makes you look good to have a little wife tucked away at home?"

"This is pointless," he said, moving into the bathroom. He clattered around, grabbing his toothbrush, razor, shaving cream.

He was *leaving* me. After that full-court press to convince me to marry him a month after college graduation, after countering all my fears with assurances that we'd last forever, after all I'd put up with since our wedding day, Nick was leaving me. The first major bump in the road, and the whole "for better or worse" clause was just flushed right down the toilet. My chest felt so tight I couldn't breathe, and my face was burning hot.

I should've known. I should never have believed.

He yanked open the front door and banged down the stairs, suitcase in tow. I followed wordlessly. My brain was a roaring mess. A cab—shit, he must've called a cab, he was really leaving!—turned the corner and slowed in front of our building.

Nick turned to me, jaw clenched, eyes hot with anger. "You never believed we'd work, and guess what, Harper? You seem to be right. Good for you. I'll be at Pete's. Go back to the restaurant. Have fun with your waiter."

At those words, I yanked off the wedding ring from my right hand and threw it at him, and the ring…my beautiful, lovely, special ring…bounced off his chest, went into the gutter and rolled into a storm drain.

"Nicely put," Nick said, and with that, he got into the cab, and not two seconds later, he was gone.

I didn't remember going back inside, but obviously, I did, because some time later, I was sitting on the kitchen floor, shaking so hard my teeth chattered. I didn't fully realize I'd called anyone till I heard the groggy voice on the other end, the voice of the one I knew would help me. "I need you to come get me," I whispered.

"You okay?"

"No."

"I'm on my way." No questions asked. Probably, no questions needed.

I filed for divorce the very next day, sobbing for only the second time in ten years, sitting in Theo's office. But it was for the best. Sometimes the heart needed time to accept what the head already knew.

Nick and I weren't going to make it.

CHAPTER TWELVE

BY THE TIME WE STOPPED for the night after yes, visiting the world's largest penguin statue, I was a little fried—from sitting in the wind and sun all afternoon, and from the memories of our brief, doomed marriage. Nick, too, was quiet, though polite.

The town we stopped in was microscopic, only one intersection (no stoplight), a town hall, a church, a hamburger stand called Charlie's Burger Box and adjacent motel with four units, all unoccupied. Nick paid for both our rooms.

"You don't have to do that," I said.

"No problem," he answered.

"Make sure you check out the dinosaur footprints," the clerk told us, giving me a wink. "Real big. And mind the forecast. Might get some snow later tomorrow."

"Will do," Nick and I said in unison. We glanced at each other, then looked away.

"Where are you folks from?" the clerk asked.

"New York," Nick said as I said, "Massachusetts."

"Oh, yeah? I went to Harvard."

"I went to Tufts Law," I answered, and we had a lovely chat about the wonders of Boston, while Nick stood silently, only contributing an eye-roll as the clerk and I anticipated a Red Sox sweep of the Yankees during an upcoming series. As Charlie's Burger Box was the only restaurant in town, we ate there, the Harvard-educated clerk amiably doubling as the cook as he told us about working as an investment banker amassing and losing millions, then coming back home to Montana. "Never been happier," he said. "You folks enjoy." He passed us our tray of burgers and fries, then went back to the motel.

Nick and I ate at the picnic table at the edge of the small parking lot. Coco sat next to me, statuelike, waiting, waiting for a bite of burger, inhaling it with a snap of her cute little mouth. Occasionally, a pickup truck rattled down the road, but otherwise, we didn't see many people.

"So is this what you pictured for your drive across country?" I asked, wiping my mouth with a paper napkin.

"Pretty much," Nick said, not looking at me.

"Really?"

"Except for bringing you to the airport, yes. Small towns, farmland, the heart's blood of our great nation and all that."

"Said the boy from Brooklyn," I added. "Who, as I recall, couldn't get along with a simple sheep."

It was true...one of the times Nick had visited me the summer I worked in Connecticut, we'd gone to a petting farm in the country. A sheep, assuming that Nick had some of those snack pellets in his pocket, kept ramming her nose into his groin, which made me laugh so hard I actually fell down.

I smiled at the memory and glanced at Nick. He wasn't smiling back. Eyes somber, mouth grim. As if it required physical effort, he dragged his eyes off me and resumed staring at the endlessly flat landscape in front of us. "If we leave by eight, we should be able to make it to the airport by early afternoon," he said.

We'd make it a lot sooner if he'd managed to hit the

speed limit, but I kept those words to myself. "Great. Thanks."

He nodded. Conversation over, apparently. Which was fine.

Since Nick wasn't talking, I took out my phone and texted a few messages…one to Carol with a cc to Theo, saying I'd been delayed and would call them tomorrow. I had both their home numbers, but it didn't feel right, calling on a Sunday evening. They both had families, had a hard-and-fast rule about not working on weekends (unlike myself)…they were normal, in other words. I sent another message to BeverLee and Dad, letting them know the same. Another to Dennis, just in case he worried. I felt a pang at the thought of him back on the Vineyard without me. Our relationship had been…well, comfortable. The thrum, the connection, the depth of emotion I'd had with Nick hadn't been there with Dennis, and I'd always thought that was a good thing. More mature, more lasting, more stable. Guess it showed what I knew. Dennis hadn't wanted to marry me, end of story. I wondered if he was feeling at least a little blue, too. I rather hoped so; what would it say if he wasn't missing me at all?

Though it was home, Martha's Vineyard seemed like a memory. Strange, to be so far away, in a landscape that was nothing like the familiar hills and rock walls of the island, the gray-shingled homes and scrubby pines. Here, the land stretched uninterrupted to the horizon, and the sky was a little merciless in its vastness.

"All right. I'm heading down the street," Nick said.

I glanced down the road. "Stan's Bar. Sounds perfect. Grab a beer, watch some baseball, soak up a little Montana color, is that it?"

"Exactly." He paused. "You can come if you want."

I took a quick breath. "Um…nah. I have to do some

work, actually. I'll just take Coco for a walk and hit the old laptop."

"Okay. Sleep well."

He got up to go.

"Nick?"

"Yeah?" He looked a little careworn, a little creased. He looked his age…not the boy I married. My heart squeezed, and I tried to ignore it. "I really appreciate you doing this."

He shrugged. "I have to. We're related now."

"Oh, God. Is that true?"

His lightning smile flashed. "Well, you're my half brother's stepsister-in-law. So yes. I'll expect presents at Christmastime."

"Got it. One blow-up doll, superdeluxe model."

He laughed, gave my shoulder a squeeze, causing that electrical hum to surge to a thousand volts. "Good night, Harper."

"Night," I said faintly.

I cleared my throat, tossed my trash into the nearby can and took Coco's leash. She had a tennis ball, too, which I retrieved from the car—what Jack Russell didn't love chasing stuff? We walked down the street a little…there was no downtown, no green or park, something I took for granted in New England. But there were fields, endless fields, so we went a few yards in.

"Want to fetch?" I asked, and my dog froze with breathless anticipation, her eyes bright and hopeful. I unclipped her leash, then fired the ball as far as I could, smiling as my little dog streaked across the field. She instantly found the ball and brought it back, tail whipping proudly, and dropped it at my feet so I could throw it again, preferably a thousand or so more times.

It was good therapy, standing in the fresh, cool air, the

sky purpling with the onset of night. Sitting in the car for so long had taken a toll, and I was stiff and a little sore.

What would it be like to live in a place like this? According to the map, there were two hundred and fifteen people who lived in Sleeping Elk. What did people do for work? For fun? How did they meet people? Where did they go on a date, other than Charlie's Burger Box or Stan's Bar?

Maybe this was the type of place my mother had stayed on her long trek throughout the country. Maybe she'd stayed in this very town. Found a job, worked for a while, moved on. I knew very little about what she'd done the past twenty years, but thanks to Dirk Kilpatrick, P.I., I did know she'd been a wanderer. And I knew where she was now.

The wind gusted, and black clouds rumbled in the west. Time to go inside, give Kim a call, make light of my situation with my ex husband, write up a brief and try not to think too much about the people I'd lost.

THE NEXT MORNING, WE learned that "breakfast included" meant a voucher at the gas station next door to the motel, as Charlie's Burger Box didn't open until eleven-thirty. Our amiable Crimson man had left us a note wishing us well. Nice.

"Can't we get some steak and eggs?" I asked as we surveyed the paltry selection of plastic-wrapped Hostess baked goods. "Isn't this Montana, home of beef? Shouldn't I be able to get some steak and eggs somewhere? Isn't this Cheney country? Can't we get some cholesterol somewhere?"

"Can't you limit the number of sentences you say before 10 a.m.?" Nick returned. But he went to the counter and asked the toothless store clerk about restaurants.

The clerk, who looked as if he was never without either

banjo, chewing tobacco or rifle, pondered this difficult question.

"There used to be Sissy's," he said slowly, "but that burned down 'bout six years ago. Maybe seven. Big fire, man, you shoulda seen it. Me and Herb Wilson, you know Herb? Met him yet? No? Well, me and Herb, we was on the fire department back then, and we nearly set ourselves on fire tryin' to hose down the gas tanks, know what I'm sayin'?"

"So no restaurants?" I prodded. Clearly Jethro here didn't get to see real live humans all that often, and I was starving.

"No, ma'am. Used to be Sissy's but that burned down 'bout six, seven years back. You know Herb Wilson, ma'am? Me and Herb—"

"Then we'll just take these," I said, tossing a six-pack of miniature doughnuts on the counter.

"Fill up on pump number one," Nick added. "And I'm sorry for my...companion's rudeness. She's from Massachusetts."

"Where's that at?" Jethro asked.

"It's in New England, and we're not companions," I told the clerk. "I'm his parole officer. Thanks for your time." I slid a five onto the counter, grabbed Nick's arm and led him out of shop.

"Now that's local color," Nick grinned as he filled up the Mustang's gas tank. Indeed, his mood was very jolly this morning, a vast improvement on last night's somber tone. He'd always been...moody. No, that wasn't quite fair. He'd always been *expectant*. He could be sweet and funny and more energetic than a fox on amphetamines. But then, for whatever reason, his mood could shut off like a light. Sometimes, too, when we were dating or engaged, he'd stare at me...not in-love dopey staring (well, there was some of that), but other times, he'd just look at me and…wait. Wait for something I never gave, apparently, because eventually, when I'd had enough and say "Nick, do you *mind?*" he'd look away, clear his expression and act normally.

Communication was never our thing.

But today, he was happy enough. He even petted Coco, who gave him a very disdainful Chihuahua look before turning her head back to me. Nick had never been crazy about animals; one of the (many) arguments we'd had as newlyweds was over whether we could get a dog, which our lease specifically forbade. I was all in favor of breaking the rules; Nick lectured me about how hard it had been to find this place, how expensive housing was here in a "real city"—like so many New Yorkers, he viewed Boston as little more than a poorly laid-out lump populated by obsessive sports fans, which was actually pretty accurate. At any rate, no dog. I'd gotten Coco the day after Theo hired me, and we'd been best friends ever since. As if reading my mind, my little dog licked my hand, then rolled onto her back and allowed me to rub her tummy.

The scenery was much the same as yesterday's. Flat. The sky was beautiful, towering, creamy cumulus clouds drifting over the vast blue. Every twenty or so miles, we'd see a tree. Sometimes we'd spot a few antelope at the side of the road. It was quite exciting. I looked at the map. Looked at the sky. Looked out the window. Occasionally, an eighteen-wheeler would roar past us, rocking the Mustang, as those drivers, at least, were capable of a little speed.

After three hours of driving years beneath the speed limit, I finally snapped. "So, Nick, do you think we could grab life by the horns and go faster than I can run?"

He gave me a tolerant glance with the full power of his gypsy eyes. "My trip, my car. Or, to quote a classic, 'I'm telling you straight. It's my way, or the highway. Anyone wants to walk, do it now.'"

"Hmm, let me guess. Would that be *Hamlet* or *King Lear?*"

"Close. *Road House.*"

"Ah, the classics. But if we're going to make it to an airport before my death of natural causes at age one hundred and four, you're going to have to step on that little pedal down there on the floor. Go ahead, try it. See car go fast. Don't be scared, Nick."

Flashing me a smile, he put on the turn signal, ignoring my groan of frustration. "Time for a photo op," he said, hopping out of the car without opening the door. He reached into the backseat and pulled out his impressive-looking camera.

I clipped on Coco's leash and took her into the field to do her business.

"Surly ex-wife and her dog, somewhere in Montana," he said, clicking a picture of me.

"Your next Facebook entry?" I suggested. Nick came over and stood close to me, showing me the shot he'd just taken. Me, scowling, Coco pooping. Adorable.

"And here we have yesterday's pictures…you with the penguin, don't you look so cute…" I was scowling in that one, too.

Nick smelled good. Edible. This was getting uncomfortable. Apparently Nick felt it, too. "Okay," he said, turning back to the car. "Whenever you and your dog are ready, we can head off to see the world's biggest plastic model dinosaur."

"Maybe we can swing by the Unabomber's cabin," I said brightly.

"Great idea."

"Is this just a plot to spend more time with me, Nick, all these back roads and irritating stops?"

"Oh, definitely. What man alive wouldn't want more time with you, Harpy?" He raised the camera once more and clicked. Well, that photo would showcase my middle finger.

"At least let me drive, Nick." I grumbled, scooping up Coco and plodding back to the Mustang.

To my surprise, he opened the driver's side door and held it for me. "Sure. Be my guest. And here." He bent, picked something from the ground, then presented me with a little blue flower. "For you. A souvenir."

I took it suspiciously. "Nightshade?" I guessed. Nick gave a crooked grin. The flower petals were very soft, and when I touched them, a faint vanilla smell drifted up. Hmm. "Thanks."

"You're welcome."

I tucked the flower in my wallet and got into the car. "Buckle up, Nicky dear," I said to my companion.

Oh, the thrill of sitting behind the wheel of a genuine, made-in-America muscle car! Unlike Nick, I knew what to do. Securing the hat marked with the sign of the devil (NY, that is), I buckled my seat belt and glanced over to make sure Nick was secure, as well. "Hold on to Coco, okay?" I said, and as soon as he had her, I put the 'Stang to the test. Gravel spun, there was a brief screech of tires, and Coco (or Nick) gave a surprised yip.

"Christ, Harper, slow down!" Nick said, clutching the dashboard.

"You're such a weenie, Nick," I said, smiling as the Mustang did what she was built to do.

"Pray, Coco. Dear St. Christopher, patron saint of travelers, please protect Coco and me from this insane Massachusetts driver. Amen." Coco barked and wagged, then picked up her bunny and shook it. She loved speed. Of course she did! She was my dog.

At that moment, my cell phone rang. "Oh, service! How thrilling!" I said, grabbing it. "Hello?"

"You're breaking the law," Nick commented.

"Not in this state, I'm not," I answered, not that I knew either way. The call was from Dennis. Well! How unexpected! "Hi Dennis!" I said brightly.

"Hey, Harp. How you doing?"

"Oh, I'm just great, Den," I said, smiling at Nick. It occurred to me that Nick didn't know Dennis and I were over. Hmm. I decided to keep that little nugget to myself. God knows he would run with that…divorce attorney unable to keep boyfriend. In fact, it might be nice for Nick to be a little jealous. "So, Den, you got home okay?"

"Oh, yeah. But what about you? The airport was closed?"

"Yes. Some computer thing. Software. Whatever. I'm on my way to a bigger city. I should be home sometime tomorrow, maybe even late tonight."

"Cool. Well, I just…I just wanted to check in."

Huh. That was nice. "What are you up to right now?" I asked, hoping to prolong the conversation a little. It was reassuring to talk to Dennis. Uncomplicated. Every sentence wasn't loaded with a quadruple entendre.

"I'm at work," he said. "Might grab a couple beers with the guys."

"Really? That sounds great."

There was a pause. "So you're okay, Harp?"

Did he mean okay about our breakup? "I'm fine, Den. How about you? You okay?"

"This is the most boring conversation I've ever listened to," Nick observed mildly. Coco was standing on his lap, her tiny paws on his chest, obviously having changed her mind about him. One scratch behind the ears, and my dog was a whore.

"Who was that?" Dennis asked.

"Um…that's Nick. He's taking me to the airport."

"Nick? Really?" Another pause. "Your ex?"

Did I have more than one Nick in my past? "Yes. The very same. He offered to drive me, there were no rental cars, it was kind of a mess."

Nick turned to me. "Can I say hi?"

I shifted the phone away from my mouth. "Why? Do you have a man crush?"

"Let me talk to him," he said.

"Den, Nick wants to say hi. I'll see you back home, okay?"

"Okay. Hey, Harp, take care, okay?"

"You too, Den."

Not without suspicion, I passed the phone to Nick. He grinned. "Hey, Dennis, my man. How's tricks? Is that right? No kidding. Nope, actually I didn't know that." He glanced at me and raised an eyebrow.

Well, *crotch*. If Dennis had just told him about our breakup, I'd be pretty pissed indeed. After all, it was personal, and Dennis shouldn't be—

"She has her moments," Nick said with a half grin. He listened for a second. "I know. Really? Huh. No, you don't have to tell me." He laughed, and I shook my head, disgusted. "She's not bad, is she?"

"I hate men," I muttered.

Nick shifted the phone away from his jaw. "Maybe you're a lesbian," he whispered.

"I wish I was."

Nick laughed at something Dennis said. "Well, she's mine for now, anyway." I twitched, and the car swerved a bit. "Oh, yeah. She's sweet, all right. In her own special way. Yep, that, too. Totally. Okay, good talking to you, dude. You too." He closed the phone and put it down. "Nice guy you got there," he said.

"It's so eighth grade, Nick, talking about me when I'm sitting right here."

"How do you know we were talking about you?" he asked.

"Oh, please. You were talking about me. You know you were."

His smile grew. "Coco, is your mommy having a little hissy fit? She is? She has them all the time, doesn't she? You poor thing."

"You know what, Nick? You're an idiot."

"You know what, Harper? You're doing ninety-three miles an hour."

Whoopsy. I took my foot off the gas and slowed down. That was the thing with a car like this. Hard to stay moderate. My face felt hot.

"Coco, tell your mommy that not everything's about her," Nick said to my dog, who was now cuddled in his lap, staring up at him with her big brown eyes.

"Okay, Nick. You weren't talking about me. 'She's not so bad. She has her moments. She's sweet in her own way.' What were you talking about then, huh?"

Nick smiled, his eyes crinkling. Not fair that men got more attractive as they aged. Not fair at all. "Well, you do have impressive recall, Harpy, but the truth is, we were talking about this car."

My mouth opened, then shut. "She's mine for now?" I asked.

"The car." He glanced at me again. "It belongs to a friend of mine."

Crotch! Nick did that on purpose, I just knew. I really did hate men. Especially this one.

After fiddling with the radio and finding no signal, Nick opened the glove box and pulled out his iPod, plugged it into the dashboard. He pressed a few buttons, and the husky voice of Isaac Slade, lead singer of The

Fray, came over the speakers. "You Found Me." One of my favorite songs. One of Nick's too, apparently. The next group was Kings of Leon. I had the same song on my iPod. Not in the exact same order, but damn it, in the same playlist. Then came U2's latest. Had it. Next was "Vida la Vida" by Coldplay, a song I'd probably listened to a hundred times.

"I think I've heard this one a little too much," Nick said. "Mind if I skip it?"

"Nope. Go ahead," I answered. Crikey.

So. We had similar taste in music. Not a surprise, I guess. We were both from the Northeast, both roughly the same age. Whatever. Still, it was a little unnerving.

We stopped twice more, me biting my tongue so hard I nearly drew blood and trying not to fidget as Nick voiced his fascination with the exciting dam and spillway in one town, and several huge grain silos near the train tracks. But eventually, we came to a town—a megalopolis, compared to what we'd seen thus far. Four blocks, a stoplight and everything. And, more important, a restaurant. Two, even.

It was very pretty...brick buildings with some nice detail. Clean. Friendly. If I was looking for a place to hide, I'd pick here. Maybe my mother had, too, at some point.

"You hungry?" Nick asked.

"Starving." The six-pack of doughnuts was a distant memory.

No one else was inside the restaurant, and the bartender welcomed us with an amiable twang, asked us where we were from and didn't mind the fact that Coco was with us. People were nice out here. In no rush, not like us Yankees, always dashing about from here to there.

Nick and I sat in a booth, each of us ordering a reuben, which was surprisingly excellent. Nick read the local paper, idly stealing my fries as if we were an old married couple, occasionally giving one to Coco. He asked the bartender a question about the area. Lou was a local, answered a few questions about the dams we'd just seen, then said he'd been to New York twice, and the two men chatted amiably about restaurants in the city.

Nick had always been good with people. Much better than I was.

When Lou had to answer the phone, Nick took out his book, a manly tome on the great subway systems of the world.

"We probably want to get going, huh, Nick? To the airport? So you can be rid of me and I can get home?"

He didn't look up from his book. "We're only a few hours away, Harper. Try not to stroke out, okay? I want some huckleberry pie. Can't say I've ever even heard of it before." He glanced up. "Life is all about new experiences, don't you think? *Carpe diem* and all that?"

I rolled my eyes. This whole little road trip was getting a little…unsettling. I wanted to be home. All this sky, all this land…it made me feel exposed. Too many memories, too much current buzzing between us. Nick turned back to his book.

A couple came in, greeted the bartender by name and sat at a nearby table. Perfect. I could eavesdrop, one of my favorite pastimes. The man spoke first.

"What does my wittle kitty want?"

Jackpot! A man (and I use the term loosely) speaking baby talk? He reached across the table and tried to take Wittle Kitty's hands. Kitty ignored.

"Is oo a wittle bit mad?"

Oh. Dear. God. I kicked Nick's shin to get his attention.

"No kicking," he said unquietly, not looking up from the book.

"Kitty? Oo wuvs me, wight?"

"Jesus, Alec, can you drop the LOL Kitty talk? I hate those damn things," she hissed (appropriately, I thought).

"I fawt oo wuved da LOL Kitties!" Alec said, making a pouty lip. "Oo wuvs dose kittehs! Wemember, Pwitty Kitty?"

"God. Lou, can I get a beer, please? A Bud?"

"Um, Lainey, sweetie," Alec said, using normal diction. "It's only one o'clock."

"Lou? A Bud?"

"Coming up," the bartender answered, frowning.

The LOL Kittys man recovered. "Well, what looks good, honey? Other than you, that is?"

She sighed pointedly. "I'll have a quesadilla with barbecued chicken."

Alec smiled. "Same for me, Lou."

"You got it," Lou answered, then looked over at Nick and me. "How about you folks? Can I get you anything else?"

"We're fine," I said. "The check would be great, though. We still have a long way to go."

"I'll have a piece of huckleberry pie," Nick said. "And some coffee would be great."

Fine. I'd be patient. It was possible. Taking a slow, deep breath and resisting the urge to kick Nick once more, in a softer part, perhaps, I resumed my eavesdropping. Nothing else to do.

"Should we talk about the wedding, sweetie?" LOL Kitty Man asked.

"Alec, not now!" Lainey snapped. "Okay? Can we just…sit? Please? For crying out loud?"

"Sure, sweetie," he said instantly.

Doomed. There was no way in hell they'd make it.

Alas, Alec apparently reigned supreme in the Land of

the Obtuse. "You know, I think Caroline would be a nice name," he said.

"For what?" Lainey asked.

"For a baby. A daughter."

She stared at him, disgust and incredulity painted on her face with a heavy hand. "What*ever*."

"Hi, there" I said, waving to the happy couple.

"Don't," Nick muttered, still reading.

"My name's Harper, and I couldn't help overhearing." I stood up and approached. "Mind if I sit for a second?"

"Not at all," Alec replied. "I'm Alec, and this is my fiancée, Lainey."

"Hello. Harper James. I'm a divorce attorney."

"Harper," Nick called, glancing up from his book. There was a note of warning in his voice.

"I couldn't help overhearing you two," I said, ignoring my ex. "Alec, you seem like a nice guy. And Lainey, you seem…well, listen. I'm just wondering how you two are doing."

"We're great!" Alec said with tragic sincerity. "Um… why do you care?"

"Call it professional curiosity. See, I hate to be rude, but I feel compelled to point out that if you two are already having trouble, it's not a great sign."

"Mind your own beeswax, lady," Lainey said, baring her teeth at me. She had braces.

"Let me guess, Alec," I said quickly, ignoring her. "At first, Lainey was so nice, right? But then, once you proposed and gave her an Amex with her name on it—"

Nick materialized at my side. "Okay, we'll just get going here," he said, giving me a tug. "Sorry to bother you folks."

"How'd you know I gave her an Amex?" Alec asked me, frowning.

"Car, too, I'm guessing?" I asked.

"Mind your *business*, lady," Lainey snarled.

"Alec, I wonder if you have to work this hard now, when you're supposedly in love—"

"Shut it, Harper." Nick's voice was low.

"—just imagine how—" My words were cut off as Nick clamped his hand over my mouth. He hauled me out of the chair and began steering me to the door, Coco following obediently, her leash trailing.

"Oh, that dog is so cute!" Lainey exclaimed. She looked up at Alec, her steely eyes morphing to calculated softness. "I wish I had a wittle doggy like dis one."

"Want me to buy you one?" Alec asked.

"Wiwwy? You would? Faw me?" she said. She reached out for Coco, who wisely dodged away. Nick let go of me and picked up my dog's leash.

"She's just after your money, Alec," I said quickly. "Make sure you have a prenup!"

"Sorry," Nick said to the happy couple. He grabbed my arm again and practically dragged me out the door, then released me. Coco sat down and stared at me as well, as if in a collusion of disappointment. "Did you have to do that?" Nick asked.

"What? Tell the truth? Try to save that guy some misery?"

"It's not your job to decide, Harper," he said, rubbing his eyes.

"It's like watching a car head for a telephone pole at sixty miles an hour. I couldn't just say nothing."

"Just let them be. They're strangers, for God's sake. You don't know anything about them. Maybe their... thing...works."

I took Coco's leash out of his hand. "Right. And you know what else, Nick? The Brooklyn Bridge is for sale."

"You sell everyone short, Harper. You're such a cynic."

Oh, those words…that condescension! "I'm a realist, Nick," I said. "This is what I do for a living—deal with crappy relationships every single day. He's crazy about her, and she can barely stand him. But he's pretty well off, as we can see from this brand-new Chevy pickup, Exhibit A, Your Honor." I pointed to the shiny black truck in front of us. "She might have a three-carat diamond on her hand, but Mom and Dad couldn't afford dental care, because she's only got braces now, Exhibit B. I bet we both know who's paying. He's a nice guy, bending over backwards to make her smile, and she can hardly look at him. It's not fair. They shouldn't get married. I'd bet you a thousand dollars she'll cheat on him. I bet she's cheating on him right now."

I stopped, a little out of breath. Nick was looking at me oddly. "The window's open," he said softly.

Oh…crotch. I turned my head…yes, crotch. Indeed. Lainey looked nervous, her eyes darting between me and her fiancé as she twisted her ring. Because of course, I was right.

Alec was staring at me, his mouth opened slightly, as if I'd just clubbed him with a shovel. *Sorry, mister.* Slowly, he turned to his fiancée. "Do you love me, Lainey?" he asked.

She hesitated, then fixed a smile on her face and took his hand, her acrylic nails gleaming like claws. "Of caws me wuvs oo! Oo's mah favewit cowboy!"

He bought it. Of course he did. Well, any man who spoke LOL Kitty clearly had no self-respect, and soon, another of my divorce-attorney brethren would have a new client.

"Take a walk," Nick said in a low voice. "I'll meet you at the car in twenty minutes."

I walked. An unfamiliar sensation sloshed in my stomach, and it took me a minute to name it. Shame. I was right, I knew. Everything I said would come true, I'd bet my liver with a side of kidney. Was it wrong to try to save LOL Kitty Man some heartbreak? Granted, maybe the truth shouldn't have come from a stranger, but at least he heard it. Maybe late at night, he'd have a revelation. Dump her, find some kindhearted woman who really appreciated him and end up happy.

But probably not. Probably, he'd marry that manipulative little money-grubber and live miserably ever after.

The disappointment on Nick's face…that hurt. Crap.

Being right wasn't everything.

Coco trotted neatly along, her strong little legs a blur. She stopped to sniff a streetlight, one of four in the downtown area. Townspeople were out and about on their errands, the men clad in jeans and flannel shirts, green John Deere caps or, in the case of a few, cowboy hats. The women were similarly attired, sturdy and capable. In my linen pants and pink silk shirt, silver bracelets and expensive shoes, I definitely stuck out.

I missed Kim, who liked me, and Dennis, who had never once been disappointed in me, or made me feel as if I was wrong, or misguided. I missed Willa, who always loved me, even when I was telling her what not to do. Then again, she saw potential in everyone.

What would it be to think like that? Trusting the universe, believing in the goodness of people the way Willa did, going with the flow…she made it look so easy. Not that it always paid off, of course. And now she was married. Would we stay as close? Since we hadn't spent our whole lives together, since we'd missed out on those early formative years, maybe our bond wasn't as strong as blood sisters.

I pulled my cell phone out of my pocket and hit her number. Much to my surprise, she answered.

"Hey!" I said. "How are you?"

"Hi, Harper," she answered. "I'm okay. How are you? Chris said that you and Nick went to South Dakota or something? Flight problems?"

"Yeah. We're almost there. North Dakota, actually. But don't worry about that. How are you? *Where* are you?"

"Oh…I'm okay. We're somewhere in Glacier. Somewhere cold. It's…fine."

My ears pricked up. "You sure?"

"Well, yeah. This isn't quite…you know. It's a little tough. We're camping. Actually, we're just sort of huddling in a tent. Christopher can't seem to make a fire. Not a warm one, anyway."

"Well, you'll be home soon, right? Back in New York?"

She didn't answer for a minute. "I don't know. Chris wants to stay."

Her tone was not promising. "You okay with that?"

"I don't know. I'm just…adjusting." She hesitated, then spoke again, her voice decidedly more chipper. "So how'd you end up with Nick?

"I was kind of stuck. Flight problems. I might have had to camp, too."

"Well, camping sucks, so I'm glad you didn't have to," she said, a smile in her voice. "I should go. My battery's dying."

"Okay." I paused. "You have my credit card number, right? If you need anything?"

"Yeah. You're great. I'll call you soon, okay?"

Feeling a little melancholy, I went into the small gift shop down the street. "Is it okay if I bring in my dog?" I asked. Coco, sensing she was being judged, wagged her tail and tilted her head adorably, then lifted her front paw.

"Sure thing," the woman behind the counter said. "Oh, aren't you a cute puppy!"

I browsed the shop…dream catchers and fossils, Native American souvenirs and silver earrings. Belt buckles that could slice a person in half, they were so big. An array of T-shirts.

"Can I have one of those?" I asked, pointing to a display.

"Sure can," the clerk answered. I paid, she handed me the bag and off we went, Coco and I, down the street.

Nick was waiting for me, leaning against the car. "I'm sorry I made a scene," I said, handing him the bag. He took out the gift. It was a T-shirt, emblazoned with the words *Montana. There's nothing here.*

A reluctant smile came to his face. "Thanks," he said.

"You're welcome." I looked at the ground.

"They're fine," he said, reading my mind. "I told them you'd just gotten out of a relationship and were a bitter, jealous hag, and I was taking you to an ashram in North Dakota."

"Does North Dakota have ashrams?" I asked.

"You're welcome," he said pointedly.

"Thanks. I guess they can implode on their own."

"That's my girl."

Strange, that those words made me feel as good as they did.

CHAPTER THIRTEEN

NICK CONTINUED TO LET me drive, mercifully, and the fields flew past. The sky turned gun-metal gray, and the temperature seemed to be dropping. Gusts of wind occasionally walloped the car, but the classic Mustang hummed along with a satisfying growl. Sweet, in Nick's words. Wasted on one who rode the subways and hadn't learned to drive until college, but sweet nonetheless.

We passed into North Dakota, which didn't look too different from Montana. It was flatter, maybe. Distant clumps of trees shivered in the wind like a mirage under the gray sky. Once in a while, I'd catch a glimpse of an antelope or deer, but otherwise, we seemed to be alone out here.

Two more hours till Bismarck, according to the map. Almost there. Almost safe.

A few miles in the distance, some impressively black clouds seemed to be gathering on top of each other. "Nick, maybe we should stop somewhere. The weather looks pretty bad."

He was engrossed in the map. "Don't get your panties in a twist," he said after a mere glance at the gathering clouds. "Women."

"Yes, Nick, I am a woman, and no, Nick, my panties are not twisted," I said calmly. "It's just that we're driving right into a storm and I really would like to avoid it, as I'm quite eager to get to Massachusetts in one piece."

"Don't worry. That storm is miles off. Just some gray skies."

The skies were not gray. They were black, the clouds swelling. Lightning flashed inside them and thunder grumbled menacingly in the distance. "Are you just contradicting me for fun, Nick, or do you have a factual basis for your opinions? Which would be a first in our relationship, of course."

"Calm down, Harper. It's maybe a little rain."

"Or a tornado. Have you ever heard of one of those?"

A flock of blackbirds—dozens…no, hundreds of them—suddenly wheeled out in front of us. Fleeing the storm.

"Let the record reflect the Biblical signs of doom," I said.

"Relax. Coco's not nervous, is she?" I glanced at my dog. She sat on Nick's lap, bunny in her mouth, staring at Nick, trying to hypnotize him into worshipping her for the rest of his life. Bad enough that my father, BeverLee and Willa all adored Nick. Now my dog had fallen, too. Suppressing a sigh, I looked ahead at the endless, straight road. It was now three o'clock. Had Nick broken the little-old-lady speed barrier and/or taken the interstate, I'd be on an airplane right now.

This was not good. Being around Nick…it was like taking a lovely stroll in the forest, sun shining all around, birds serenading, flowers perfuming the air, and then a rabid wolverine leaps out of nowhere and rips open your jugular.

"You ever regret divorcing me?" he asked, looking up abruptly.

See, Your Honor? I rest my case. "Nick, let's not do this, okay? We divorced each other many years ago. In two more hours, maybe less, we'll be in Bismarck. Two hours till we part ways. Can't we all just get along?" I glanced over at him. The wind ruffled his hair—we still had the top down, as Nick was living the dream and all that—but his eyes were steady.

"Do you?"

"I regret that we got married so young, Nick. We were naive, if not breathtakingly stupid."

"That's not how I remember it."

"How lucky for you."

"Remember our honeymoon?"

Crotch! "No. The electric shock therapy has done its job. Please, Nick. Let's not talk about it."

"Scared?"

"No! I'm just sensible. There's no point in doing this. We're different people now. Why pick scabs, huh? Huh, Nick? We've moved on."

"Right. You're with Dennis now."

I didn't correct him. He shifted in his seat, facing forward once again. Mercifully, his cell phone chimed, and I forced myself to unclench my fists from around the wheel. Nick glanced at the screen and his smile flashed like the lightning up ahead. "Hi, honey," he said.

Honey? *Honey?* Who was honey?

"I'm fine. What's new with you? Oh, yeah? That's great." I glanced over at him, but he was smiling, petting Coco's head as she now slept on his lap. "Oh, I'm fine. I'm in…let's see…North Dakota. It's flat. Open. A little spooky, maybe." He laughed. "Okay. Love you, too. Bye."

So. He had a honey. And he *loved* his honey. Why hadn't he said anything? I was finding it a little hard to take a normal breath. *Calm down, Harper,* I told myself. Nick had a girlfriend. To be expected, after all. Just… surprising. We'd been together for the past four days, and he hadn't said a word.

"So what's her name?" I asked.

"Isabel."

Isabel. Not a name one could mock, like Farrah or Bitsy. Nope. A real name.

"What does she do for a living?"

"She's a student," he answered.

Well! A little *young,* wouldn't we say? A student. Really. What a cliché. *Successful older man who drives red convertible Mustang also dates younger woman to demonstrate continued virility.* Or maybe she wasn't that much younger. Maybe she was getting her degree part-time. "Where does she go to school?"

"NYU," he answered. "She's a freshman."

"Nick!" I sputtered. "A freshman? That's just…gross. I'm sorry. You're dating an 18-year-old? She's half your age!"

"I'm aware of that, Harper," he said. "But I'm not dating her. She's my stepdaughter."

My mouth fell open, my head whipped around to look at him. "You're *married?*" I screeched.

"Watch it, Harper!" Nick said, and there was a thudding sound, and we bounced up and down. Coco yelped in surprise, and then there was a hiss, some steam, and the engine just died, and we coasted to a very anticlimactic stop.

Then the heavens opened, and hail rained down upon us like God's wrath.

"Shit!" Nick yelled. "Harper, you ran over an antelope!"

"What? Oh, no!" I grabbed Coco to shield her little frame from the hailstones, wincing as they pinged off my head.

Nick turned around and grabbed the Mustang's top, hauling it into place, clamping it to the top of the windshield. The noise of the hail was deafening. Coco barked.

I glanced at Nick. "An antelope?" I had to raise my voice to be heard.

"Roadkill," he said, sweeping hailstones onto the floor.

"It was already dead? You sure?"

"I'm guessing it wasn't just napping there, Harper."

"In the road?"

"No, in the clouds! Yes, in the road! You ran over it! Don't you remember?"

"Okay! I'm sorry! You shocked me, that's all." I paused. "So why did the car stop?"

"How should I know? I barely know how to drive."

"At least you admit it."

He gave me a dark look, and then I was laughing, so hard I was just squeaking, tears spurting out of my eyes, and Nick shook his head and started laughing, too. For a long time, there was just that—the rough drumming of the hail on the car, thunder rolling across the endless sky, my occasional squeak and Nick's lovely, lovely laugh.

When a clap of thunder broke right over our heads, I shrieked a little and Coco reverted from fearless Jack Russell to vulnerable Chihuahua. Faithless mutt that she was, she chose Nick as her shelter, burrowing against his ribs, almost trying to hide behind him.

"Don't worry, pooch," he said, adjusting her a little.

"Give her the bunny," I said, and Nick did, tucking Coco's stuffed animal against his ribs. My dog nestled under Nick's arm and sighed. For a second, I felt a little flash of jealousy. Toward my dog. Yes, I was jealous of Coco, nestled against Nick, his clever, beautiful hand stroking her from head to tail, head to tail. *Okay. That's enough, Harper. Snap out of it. He has a stepdaughter. Which means he also has a wife.*

Scanning the horizon for a twister, I saw none, but my visibility was impaired as the hail ended abruptly and the rain began. It fell in sheets, streaming over the windshield. I cleared my throat. "So. Think we should try to find a ditch or something?"

Nick opened the door for a second, looked out, then closed it again. "I think we should stay put. Tornado Alley's farther south, right? If we get out, we'll just get soaked. And I don't see any ditches or bridges, even if we did need one."

"Okay. Call for help, then?"

"Sounds like a plan."

I flipped open my phone. "No signal."

He checked his phone, as well. "Me, neither. On to plan B, then. Sit here and wait for the Children of the Corn."

This brought on another round of giggles. "I think it would actually be the Children of the Sugar Beets," I said, peering out the rain-streaked window.

"Doesn't have the same ring to it," he said, flashing a smile. His eyes crinkled, gorgeous crow's feet framing those lovely dark pools. (Crikey, listen to me, but there it was, his eternal effect on me.) And Nick was still looking at me, still smiling, and damn. My face felt a little warm. And my face wasn't alone. Girl parts tightened, legs weakened. I sat up a little straighter and ran my hands along the leather-coated steering wheel. The rain was gentler now, which was reassuring.

"So. You have a stepdaughter, Nick. Does that mean you also have a wife?"

He didn't answer for a minute, just turned his attention to Coco, who appeared to be sleeping. Another roll of thunder barreled across the sky, and rain streaked the windshield.

"We're divorced," he said.

Divorced. Twice—once from me, once from Wife #2.

Knowing Nick, that must've hurt. A lot. "I take it she's older if she has a kid in college?" Why, that didn't matter.

"Right. She's...let's see. Forty-three? Yeah."

"How long were you married?"

"Three years. We've been apart for almost four now." He glanced at me, smile now gone. "Her name is Jane, she's very nice. Works in finance. Amicable split." He paused. "Still friends."

I sat, listening to the rain drumming on the roof of the car, and swallowed carefully. First, I was jealous of my dog. Now I was jealous of his second ex-wife.

For a brief second, I tried to imagine having Nick as my friend over these past twelve years. It wouldn't have worked, but still. The image of being able to think of him without a razor slash to the heart...that would've been nice, to have heard his laugh, to have been able to talk to him, meet him for coffee. I pictured the two of us walking down the street, arm in arm, old friends, a warm and easy affection between us.

Yeah, right.

But it surprised me, how much that image squeezed my heart.

"So why'd you break up, since she's so nice?" I asked, and my voice was a little tight.

He didn't answer for a few seconds. "We grew apart," he said finally.

Ah. How many times over the years had a client said that to me? It was code for infidelity, and knowing Nick, I'd bet anything he wasn't the one who strayed. "But you're still friends?"

"Yes. Isabel didn't deserve another disappearing father figure. Jane works on Wall Street, not far from me, so we wanted to be civilized."

How mature. Childish resentment blossomed like a

fungus. Probably they all had dinner together and went to the Metropolitan and Yankees games and all that. "And what's Isabel like?" I asked.

Nick smiled, and my stupid jealousy flared again. "She's great. Smart, outgoing, cute as a bug's ear. She's got a beautiful voice. Her group sang at Carnegie last fall. Here." Like any good father, he pulled out his wallet and flipped it open. "That's high school graduation."

She was *very* pretty...china-blue eyes, straight blond hair, sweet, genuine smile. "Beautiful," I said truthfully. I petted Coco for reassurance, but she didn't take her face out of the crook of Nick's arm. Traitor.

"Thanks. Not that I had anything to do with it." He put his wallet away.

My heart felt a bit...sore. Not, I told myself, because Nick had married someone else (though you'd think he could've mentioned it *one time*, right?). But because somewhere out there was a child (albeit a nearly grown child) who loved him, not to mention her mother, whom Nick once loved and maybe still did but certainly didn't hate.

But I wouldn't say anything. No. I'd just bite my tongue on this one. "So you and your ex-wife...Jane, you said?" Ah, my iron resolve. Nick nodded, and there was a little smile around his mouth, which I felt like a poison dart to the throat. "You and Jane get together, go to Izzy's concerts, have Sunday brunch, stuff like that?"

"Yep," he answered.

There was nothing but the sound of rain. The windows had fogged up, isolating us from the outside world. I traced the path of a melted hailstone on the dashboard with one finger. "So Nick," I said eventually.

"Yes, Harper?" He must've sensed something in my tone, because he shifted to look at me more closely.

I put my hands on the wheel, ten and two, and

looked straight ahead. "I guess I'm wondering about something."

"And what is that?"

"Your father was a rotten parent, but you take care of him, keep him near you, visit him even though he never gave you the time of day." I glanced over at him. His earlier smile was gone. "Your idiot stepbrother did everything in his power to make your life miserable, but you shook his hand and treated him nicely at the wedding."

Another glance revealed that he was frowning now.

"You and Jane grew apart," I continued softly, "by which I'm guessing she fell for someone else and quite possibly had an affair." I paused, returning my gaze to the middle distance. The silence from Nick confirmed my suspicion. "But you're still friends, still see her, still love her daughter."

"What's your point, Harper?" he asked tightly.

I swallowed. When I spoke, my voice was very, very quiet. "I guess I'm wondering why you can forgive everyone except me."

The rain gentled, the pitch of it softening to a whisper. I looked at Nick. His eyes were lowered to Coco, his hand still on her back. The current that thrummed between us intensified and seemed to wrap itself around my heart and pull. *Please, Nick,* I thought. *Tell me.*

He didn't look up. "I don't know, Harper," he said in a low voice, and I knew he was lying. My throat tightened abruptly.

Sometimes the past was too far distant to revisit. And some things were better left untouched. I knew that. I did.

Suddenly desperate for something to do, I turned the key—the battery still worked, even if the engine didn't—and switched on the defrost. The windows cleared. The rain tapered off, and a golden bar of sunlight sliced through the clouds. Coco raised her head and yawned. "Guess I should check the car," Nick said.

"Guess you should," I said, my voice normal once more. "Not that you know anything."

Nick flashed me a grin and got out, and I followed.

The air was pure and sweet after the thunderstorm, and if there'd been any antelope gore stuck to the side of the car, it had mercifully been washed away. I walked over to Nick's side, where he was now lying on the ground, looking under the car. Coco licked his knee.

"See anything?" I asked."

"Metal. Tires. A hose dripping stuff. Oh, and here. A souvenir." He worked something loose and stuck out his arm, and I leaped back and shrieked.

"Nick! That's nasty!" It was the poor dead antelope's horn.

"You don't want it?" he asked, standing up with a grin.

"No! And Coco, you can't have it, either. Yuck." Nick tossed it to the side of the road. "Here," I said, rummaging in my purse. "Purell. Use a lot." He obeyed, looking at me steadily. Making me nervous.

"So," I said, "Car death by goring?"

"Looks like it. Too bad you failed to see the large mammal lying in the road, horns up."

"Nope. I was too busy being shocked over your little bombshell. Your adorable stepchild."

"Jealous?"

I faked a smile. "Not really. Dennis and I plan to have kids. Strapping, brave, black-haired children, six or eight of them."

"Name one after me." He grinned, knowing I was lying on some front. Jerk. Couldn't he act jealous, just a little bit? Huh? I narrowed my eyes and didn't respond. What was the point? Nick and I bugged each other. We bickered, scrapped, fought, resented and blamed. Mad skills, all, especially where the two of us were concerned. Whatever moment had happened back in the car a few minutes ago, whatever I'd hoped to hear, what he might've said…it was best left alone.

That being said, I didn't fail to recognize that we were in East Bumfuck, Nowheresville. No cars, no trucks, no living antelope to ride to civilization. Nick reached into the backseat of the car, rummaged in the cooler and emerged with two Snapples. He handed one to me.

"Should we ration these?" I asked, only half kidding.

"Nah. Someone will come."

"Really, Nick? Because I haven't seen a car in an eon or two."

At that very moment, we heard a motor. Nick gave me a smug look, then stood in the middle of the road, ready to flag down our rescuer.

CHAPTER FOURTEEN

"SURE, WE GOT A MECHANIC, you betcha. Lars Fredricksen. He'll get you set up, don'tcha worry 'bout a thing."

Coco and I were sitting in the truck between Nick and Deacon McCabe, our rescuer. His words were balm to my battered soul. With a sigh of relief, I felt my shoulders relax. Deacon seemed about as nice as a guy could be, full of folksy phrases and the rounded vowels of the region. The truck was old and smelled pleasantly of oil. A crucifix swung gently from the rearview mirror, and Deacon himself smelled like hay and tobacco, a very pleasant combination.

The fact that I was squished against Nick…well, that felt pretty damn good, too. He had his arm around me— well, not technically. Technically, his arm was resting on the back of the seat, but it was…cozy. The air had turned quite chilly. Unfortunately, my sweater was packed in my little red suitcase, which currently resided in the back of the pickup. Nick, however, was nice and warm. And he smelled good. And he seemed irritatingly unaffected by my presence for a man who loved and hated me.

The plan was for us to go into town (Harold, North Dakota, population 627) and get a tow for the poor Mustang, then have the mechanic assess the trouble.

"You folks'll stay with us tonight," Deacon said. "Our town doesn't have a motel, don'tcha know, but you're real welcome with me and the missus. We don't get many folks coming through, no sir. And tonight just happens to be our very own Harvest Festival, so you'll have to do us the honor. Real Americana. Where'd you say you folks were from again?"

"Martha's Vineyard, Massachusetts," I answered. "We're headed to the airport in Bismarck. Is that far?"

"Oh, gosh no, not at all. Couple hours, three tops."

"Great!" I said. If Nick's car wasn't fixed by then, maybe I could pay someone to drive me to the capital. By this time tomorrow, the odds were excellent that I'd be in the air, headed for home, back where I knew what I was doing. I couldn't wait.

"So what's it like in Martha's Vineyard, Massachusetts?" Deacon asked, and I happily told him about Menemsha and the fishing fleet, the wind and the pines, the rain, the ocean, the cheerful pastel Victorians of Oak Bluffs, the tidy streets of Edgartown.

"Sounds like you folks have a real nice life out there," Deacon commented.

Nick said nothing, just looked at me, his eyes unreadable.

"Yes," I finally said after a minute. "Coco likes it, don't you, honey?" She wagged her tail agreeably, then resumed trying to hypnotize Deacon into becoming her love slave.

Thinking about home reminded me that I needed to call Dad. Should check in on Tommy. See what I could do for BeverLee. Make sure Willa had enough money. Court next Tuesday. My bimonthly lunch with Father Bruce. It was different from here, where the endless fields were punctuated with huge spools of hay, the flatness of the landscape nearly unbroken by trees. My home seemed so safe by comparison, the ragged coastline and snug little towns, the solid stone walls and whispering pines. No exposure, no relentless sun. No Nick.

A COUPLE OF HOURS later, I was the queen of the Harvest Ball. Well, maybe not queen. But I was holding court, at least in the judicial sense of the word. Six women had me cornered at a picnic table as we ate a tasty yet unidentifiable casserole called "hot dish" by my hosts. Coco, well fed on the same, snoozed at my feet, her leash tied to one leg of the picnic table.

"So if I move out, he could get the house? Gosh, that doesn't seem right," Darlene said. She was twenty-six, married for seven years, two kids. Husband was a trucker who enjoyed a side of hooker with his rest stop all-you-can-eat buffet, apparently.

"It'd be better if you stayed put, especially with the kids," I answered, taking a sip of my Coke—strike that. A sip of my soda pop. Sounded much nicer that way.

"Okeydokey," she said. "Stay put, you betcha. Think I should change the locks?"

"Well, that would certainly send a message," I concurred.

Darlene nodded, and my next consultation approached. "Hi, there, Harper hon, didja see that rain before? I'm Nancy Michaelson, so nice to meetcha."

"Hi, Nancy," I said, taking another bite of hot dish. One could only imagine the cholesterol count, as the primary ingredient seemed to be mayonnaise, but man, it was good! "What can I help you with?"

She sat. "You're a regular doll, answering all our questions, don'tcha know. So, okay, my mother, bless her heart, she just married some old geezer from the nursing home over in Beulah. At first, we thought he was, y' know, not so bad, but turns out, he's taking money out of her savings account! What can we do? I think she should divorce his scrawny old carcass, but Mom, well, she's saying she's in love! At her age, can you imagine!"

I squashed a smile. "Well, if you've got power of at-torney, you can stop that. But if she's competent—"

"Whatja mean, competent?"

"In her right mind? You know…sane?"

Nancy sighed. "Well, I think she's crazy, having a ro-mance at her age and all, but I guess I don't get a vote. Thanks, hon."

"Okay, okay, let's give our guest a little breathing room, what do you say, girls?" Margie Schultz bustled over, my new best friend/bodyguard. She seemed to be in charge of the event; after Deacon had introduced Nick and me to her, she'd towed us around, introducing us to dozens of people, all of whom had seemed ridiculously happy that misfortune had led us here. Midwestern hospitality at its finest, putting us Yankees to shame.

The Harvest Festival was pretty much what you'd expect—the lot behind the Lutheran church strung with lights, a few booths and mouthwatering smells as hot dogs, hamburgers and bratwurst cooked on a grill. A giant table held dozens of casseroles, Jell-O molds and plates of cake and cookies. Soda pop and milk…no beer. A small band was setting up…just a guitarist, a bass player and a fiddler. This year's real Harvest Queen, a sturdy and beautiful lass decked out in a pink prom gown, work boots and a John Deere cap, collected money for the school's football program. Kids ran around with sparklers in the fading light, and the whole scene could've been taken from a Ron Howard movie.

"So is the Harvest Festival always on a Monday night?" I asked. Hard to believe it was only Monday—I felt as though I'd been in the car with Nick for years, but Monday evening it was.

"Oh, gosh no," Margie said. "It was supposed to be Saturday, but oh, we had quite a storm blow through! And here there was that cloudburst today, I nearly wet myself,

Harper, I did, thinking we were gonna have to reschedule again! But the Lord must've heard my prayers, because it just turned out fine, didn't it?"

"It did. And the weather couldn't be prettier," I agreed.

"Well, it's a little nippy, that's for sure. I'll have to bring my plants in tonight. Might be a frost, can you believe it?"

I smiled. I found myself a little in love with Harold, North Dakota, to be honest. Granted, I'd only had Nick to talk to these past couple of days, but these people had to be the friendliest, nicest people ever. Martha's Vineyard wasn't exactly a simmering hotbed of evil and malice, of course…but it was an extremely wealthy area, and with great gobs of money came a lot of…well, let's be honest. Snootiness. Here, life seemed a bit more even, more clearly defined, which was, I admitted, ridiculously condescending and naive of me. Wishful thinking. Then again, I was only here for the night, and if I wanted to cling to some stereotypes, there was probably no harm in that.

"Can I take your dog for a walk around the church?" a girl asked. She was about twelve, tall and slender, hair in French braids. My mom had braided my hair that way when I was small. "I'm very responsible," she added.

"Well, in that case, sure," I said. The girl thanked me and roused Coco, who leaped up with joy at the sight of another fan.

"Your fella's quite a looker, isn't he?" Margie commented.

Oh. Right. One more thing about Harold, N.D. Everyone here was under the impression that Nick and I were married, despite the fact that neither of us wore a ring. I hadn't corrected that impression, and though Nick and

I hadn't talked much since Deacon picked us up, I was pretty sure he was letting it ride, too.

I glanced over now at Nick. He was a looker, all right, standing there with his hands in his pockets, an easy half smile on his face as he talked to the mechanic and Deacon. Dennis was undeniably gorgeous, but Nick... Nick *did* things to me.

"How long have you two been together?" Margie asked.

"We got married when I was twenty-one," I said. "\ There. Not a lie. Let them think we were married. Introducing the facts...that would diminish the glow of this sweet night.

"Any kids?" another lady asked.

For a second, the image of a dark-haired, brown-eyed boy appeared in front of me. He'd be skinny. Impish, irresistible smile. The kid would get away with murder and I'd let him, because he'd look just like his daddy..."Nope. No kids."

"There's still time," an older lady said.

"You betcha," I answered.

"But you better get on that, don'tcha know," she added. "No time to waste."

As if aware that I was lying about him, Nick turned his head and met my eyes. Boom. There it was, that locked-in feeling, like two magnets that had been quivering around each other before the forces of nature finally smacked them together. For a long moment, we just looked at each other. Then I smiled, reluctantly, maybe, and Nick started over to our corner of the lot.

"Breaking up marriages again, darling?" he asked.

"Your wife has been so patient there, Nick!" Margie exclaimed. "Oh, Harper, you're a good sport, aren'tcha? Now, I have to run over there and get those boys up on stage. If they don't start playing soon, people'll go home. See you later, kids!"

The remaining two ladies wandered off as well, leaving Nick and me and my hot dish alone together.

"Care for some soda pop?" I asked.

"Wife, huh?" He cocked an eyebrow.

I shrugged. May have blushed. Then the microphone squeaked, and a man's voice came over the PA. "Folks, let's get things started off, how'd that be? Here's a classic—Patsy Cline's 'Crazy.'"

"Want to dance, wife?" Nick said.

"Not really," I said.

"Great." He took my hand and towed me to the dance area, which was outlined with hay bales.

"Typical of you, ignoring my opinion and doing what you want anyway," I muttered as he put his hand on my waist.

"Shush, woman, you're ruining the moment," he said, pulling me a little closer.

There were a few other couples out there. The little girl who'd taken Coco was now dancing with my dog, and Coco was apparently all for it, since she had her head on the girl's shoulder, braid in her mouth. The white steeple of the Lutheran church glowed against the cobalt sky. And despite the fact that Nick wore my last nerve down to a nub, my heart was nonetheless fluttering away like it was 1950 and this was the prom.

Nick was smiling that faint, wry smile that turned his eyes from tragic to mischievous, as if we had a secret that only we knew. He wasn't much taller than I was, and I had a disconcerting view of his face, those too-seeing eyes. I moved a little closer so I wouldn't have to look right at him…mistake. Now I could feel his heat, and he held me a little tighter. His neck was right there, next to my cheek, and the urge to bury my face there, kiss the hot, velvety skin—damn. My eyes closed. No one had ever felt this good. No one had ever felt this right.

"Hey there, Harper and Nick. Didja meet my husband, Al? Al, this is that nice couple who broke down out on Route 2."

"Hello," I said.

"How are ya?" Al said.

Nick released my hand to shake Al's. "We're great," he said. "Lovely town you live in."

They smiled in unison. "Oh, we couldn't agree with you more, there, Nick," Margie beamed. "It's so nice to have you kids join us."

"That it is," Al agreed, winking.

They swayed away, and Nick took my hand once more.

"How's the car?" I asked briskly and not at all as if I was melting from the bones out.

"Well," he said softly, and we were now so close that I could feel the vibration in his chest as he spoke, and my knees went weak with longing, "Lars said we—and by we, I mean you, of course—ripped out a hose." His arm tightened a little—my imagination? "But he thinks he can either replace it or patch it enough to get the car running. We should be good to go."

"Good to go. Good. That's good. Great," I breathed. "Excellent."

Crazy for crying, crazy for trying, crazy for loving you.

You said it, Patsy. Nick + Harper = Disaster. Been there, done that, had significant emotional scarring from said event. But it was easy to ignore in this moment, Nick's arm around my waist, his clean, spicy smell, the gentle rasp of his unshaven cheek against mine, the slide of muscle under his warm skin. He held my hand the way he always had. With certainty. With commitment. As if I belonged to him.

I swallowed, then gulped in a quick breath of the cool night air. The band had morphed into another sweetly melancholy song. "I'm Not Supposed to Love You Anymore." If that wasn't the voice of God, I didn't know what was.

I stepped back. "That was nice. Thanks, Nick," I said, my voice a little loud. "I better find Coco." And without giving myself the chance to do something stupid, I slipped off to reclaim my dog and some peace of mind.

DEACON McCABE'S HOUSE was a tiny little one-story house in the middle of a lot of land. There were a few trees clustered around the house, and the earlier storm appeared to have stripped them of their leaves. Margie had been right—it had turned quite cold, and the wind gusted around the house, swaying the squat little bushes that crouched outside the door. I picked up Coco and kissed her head. Wondered what she thought of our strange little trip.

Inside the house, the living room was decorated with knotty pine paneling and mounted elk heads, which made Coco growl most adorably. Orange shag carpeting, a woodstove that, judging from the chilly temperature, had gone out some time ago. A pug came trotting in to greet its master, and Deacon bent down. "Lilly, this here is Coco and her mommy and daddy," he said, scooping up the chubby little package of dog. Lilly made wheezing, snuffling noises at my dog. Coco gave me a quick Chihuahua look...*Seriously? I have to let this thing slobber on me?*...but then decided to allow Lilly a few ecstatic licks, which delighted the pug no end.

"The wife'll be in bed already," Deacon said, scratching his dog's head, causing Lilly to wriggle madly with joy. "She'll be sorry to miss you tonight—her rheumatism was acting up, which is why she skipped out on the festival. A shame. But she'll be eager to meetcha come morning. Now, if you don't mind, I'll get you folks settled and hit the hay myself."

"No, that's fine," I said.

"We're both beat," Nick said, cutting a glance at me. It was nine-thirty.

"I'll take you into town in the morning, Lars should have you all set up," he said, ushering us down a narrow hallway. He stopped, reached into a room and flicked on the light. I jumped back a little. Behind me, Nick made a strangled noise.

The room contained a double bed, a small bureau and…um…well…

"Wife's kinda devout," Deacon said by way of explanation. "This room's her, uh, special place. Sorry if it's a little chilly in here."

"No, it's great," Nick said in a carefully controlled voice. The room was, in fact, frigid.

"You and your wife are so nice to put us up," I added. It was true, of course.

"We really appreciate it," Nick seconded, tearing his eyes off the decor. "Hope it's not too much trouble."

"Not at all, not at all. Well now, there are clean towels in the bathroom," Deacon said. "You need anything, you just let me know, all right?" He took a deep breath, surveying the room as if seeing it for the first time, gave his head a little shake. "Okeydokey then. Good night, you two."

The door closed, and Nick and I just…well, we just took it in.

Pictures—dozens of them—of a blond-haired, blue-eyed Jesus decorated the walls, and apparently, Jesus had a very strong resemblance to Brad Pitt circa *Legends of the Fall*. Amen!

"Is it wrong to find the Lord attractive?" I asked, earning a rush of Nick's warm laughter as reward. I turned in a slow circle…more Jesus. Wow. And not only pictures, but, oh gosh, a small area where unlit candles sat on a long, low table in front of the biggest crosses I'd ever seen outside a church. A big church.

"Think they're planning to crucify us?" Nick whispered, his eyes bright with laughter. He set our suitcases down. "I mean, what do we really know about these people?"

There was only one bed. One small double bed that, had Nick and I actually still been married, would've been quite cozy. I set Coco down, and she jumped right onto a pillow, as was her custom. She curled into a ball and ignored the two of us and our silent machinations.

Then, as if reading my mind, Nick said, "You can take the bed. I'll sleep…on the, uh…altar." A squeak of laughter escaped from me, and Nick gave me a lightning grin.

I sobered up a bit. "I'm gonna brush my teeth. Back in a flash."

In the bathroom, I stared at my reflection. The past few days had taken their toll; I hadn't had a good night's sleep in days, and I wasn't about to get one, either. Shadows lurked under my eyes, and out of its ponytail, my hair looked scraggly. Good. The last thing I wanted right now was to look alluring in any way, shape or form.

Of course, in the movies, this was where the hero and heroine hooked up, trapped in some little motel or whatever. But Nick and I were not going to hook up. "You and Nick—not gonna hook up," I whispered to my reflection, just in case I forgot. Because come on. Nick *stirred* things in me, damn the man. Once I'd become turned on watching him empty the trash. I'm serious.

With a sigh, I scrubbed my face without tenderness or mercy, brushed my teeth and pulled on my pajama bottoms, which were bright yellow and printed with laughing monkey faces. About as unglam as you could get, luckily. A vast Red Sox sweatshirt (my Christmas present from Dennis) completed the *don't touch me* look, about as close to a chastity belt as I could manage at the moment.

Nick was in the hall when I came out, toothbrush in hand, and we did that awkward *step-to-the-left-step-to-the-right* dance for a second until he grabbed my shoulders and just held me still, hands warm and strong, causing my girl parts to croon. He brushed past me with a half smile and went into the loo.

Sober up, Harper, I told myself briskly, dragging my gaze off the bathroom door. Was he shaving in there? If so, I was a goner, because honestly, was there anything sexier than a man shaving? Was he brushing his teeth? *Frooow.* Granted, he could be hunched over the toilet, retching, and I probably would've found him incredibly hot.

"You're pathetic," I muttered, shaking my head at my own stupidity.

Back into the bedroom. Under the Brad-like gaze of Jesus, I climbed into bed, lifting up Coco and earning her *please don't beat me* look. "Warm my feet, doggy," I whispered, setting her down. "It's freezing." Then I pulled the covers to my chin. The bed was comfy, if icy. I'd always hated getting into a cold bed, the shock of the sheets bringing on dramatic bouts of shivering that I was unable to control. I huddled under the blankets, waiting to get warm. Coco, deciding that she really wasn't the foot-warming type, moved to another corner of the bed, faithless diva that she was.

It was very quiet out here on the outskirts of town, on the prairie. The wind blustered outside, and the branch of a tree tapped against the window. In my little cocoon of blankets, the sheets smelled sharply fresh and clean, a testament to line-drying, but the usually lovely scent failed this time to slow my thudding heart.

A minute later, Nick came back into the room, and I closed my eyes, not wanting to see him, chicken that I was, then opened them. He wore plain green pajama bottoms and a faded Yankees T-shirt, thank God.

When we were married, he'd always slept in the buff. And I'd always worn one of his shirts, which he'd always enjoyed removing. Which I'd always quite enjoyed him removing.

This is the kind of rhetoric that leads to certain disaster, I told myself. Swallowed. Tried looking at Brad at Gethsemane to dull the thoughts of Nick and me back in the good old days.

Nick sighed, ran a hand through his unruly hair and went over to the other side of the bed. He took the other pillow off the unoccupied side of the bed and opened the closet. Withdrew a blanket and looked at me for a second. "You all set?" he asked.

"Mmm-hmm," I answered.

"Goodnight, then," he said.

"Night."

He turned off the light, and shafts of cold white moonlight sliced into the room. I listened as Nick lay down on the floor, there in front of the makeshift altar.

The wind gusted again. Coco sighed.

One blanket.

It was awfully cold in here.

"Nick."

"Yeah?" The answer came instantly, and my heart clenched.

"Come to bed," I said, my voice blessedly matter-of-fact. "It's too cold to sleep on the floor."

There was a pause. "You sure?"

"Yep."

Mistake, dumbass, my brain told me in no uncertain terms. But crap. It wasn't as if we were hormone-inflamed teenagers. We weren't about to sleep together—well, of course we actually *were,* but nothing more. *My goodness, you're stupid,* Brain informed me, and it was true. If a client had told me she was about to let her ex climb into bed with her, I would've been screechingly against it. But this was different (as all women tell themselves right before they make a huge mistake). This was just a mission of mercy.

The bed creaked as Nick got in. Coco gave a tiny growl, then jumped off the bed, disgusted that we'd had the nerve to disturb her. I lay on my side, facing away from Nick, a good foot between us, but I could already feel his warmth over there, like the sun, taunting me.

"Thanks," Nick said.

"Oh, sure. It's nothing. Couldn't let you freeze, not with Jesus watching." I grimaced in the dark, glad he couldn't see my burning face.

"You cold?"

"I'm fine," I lied. "Nice and toasty."

"You're freezing," he stated.

"No, I'm good." My feet were blocks of ice.

"Admit it. You're dying over there."

"I'm not. Very much alive."

Then his foot slid over and touched mine. "You call that alive?" he asked, and then the covers rustled and his arm was around me, my back against his chest, his hand smoothing back my hair.

My throat tightened, and the nearness of him, the only

man who ever made me feel cherished…it just sucker-punched my heart.

"Sleep tight," I whispered.

"You, too."

God, I'd missed him.

Nick was quiet, his skin as warm as I was cold. We lay like that for a long while, not talking, not moving. The wind blew, Coco adjusted herself and gave a little doggy snore. Nick's breathing was slow and even, and this…the two of us lying together, was as comforting and wonderful as anything I'd ever felt. And horrible, because it brought such a pain to my heart. We'd had something special and rare, Nick and I. There'd been more to our marriage than loneliness and tunnel vision and wretched communication skills. There'd been times like this, lying together in the dark, together. Those times hadn't been enough…but they'd been so precious nonetheless.

When I was sure he was asleep, I touched his hand. Just a little, just a little brush of my fingertips against the back of his lovely, wonderful hand.

"You asked why I couldn't forgive you," Nick said, very quietly, and I jumped a little. "It was because you were the love of my life, Harper. And you didn't want to be. That's hard to let go."

The words were like a ragged shard of glass in my heart. I swallowed, the sound loud in the dark. "That's not exactly true, Nick," I whispered, turning around to face him. "I did want that. But…"

But what? I'd loved him with all my tattered, puny heart, but the fear I'd felt had trapped it inside, stunting me, ruining us. "It would've been easier to believe if you'd been around a little, Nick. If you'd…helped me believe it."

He nodded, and that surprised me. "You're right. My hours didn't help. But I thought once we were married, you'd feel…safer." He stopped, gave a rueful shake of his head. "I'll tell you something, Harpy," he said, his voice almost a whisper now. "It never even occurred to me that we wouldn't make it. And it never occurred to you that we would. You were just waiting for us to go down in flames. I thought we could get through anything."

"Except you left me, Nick," I whispered, my heart tight. "That night. You packed your things and left."

"I needed to cool off, Harper. I was staying with a friend for a couple days. I never would've asked for a divorce. You know that. You, though…you saw a lawyer the next day, Harper. The next day."

For the first time in a long, long time, I felt as if I might actually cry. Instead, I gave a half nod of acknowledgment. Coco must've sensed her mommy was close to the edge, because she jumped up on the bed and wormed herself against my legs.

"Can I ask you something else?" Nick's voice was very soft and horribly gentle.

"Oh, of course," I whispered. "Why not?"

He gave a little smile at that, and then grew serious once more. "When I asked you to marry me, Harper… why did you say yes?"

Oh, God. This wasn't scab-ripping. This was a bone-marrow harvest. "Nick…" My voice was uneven, and I stopped.

"I know you loved me," he said, his eyes steady. "But you didn't want to get married, that was clear in hindsight. So why did you say yes?"

"I couldn't say no," I blurted, the truth rushing out. "I didn't want to…hurt you."

"It hurt when you divorced me," he said, raising an eyebrow.

"I know! I know it." I lowered my voice so as not to wake the McCabes. "And you're right. I knew it was just a matter of time before things blew up in our faces, but I couldn't figure out how to say no and still keep you, and so...I just...went along."

He looked away for a second. Scrubbed his hand through his hair, making it stand on end, then looked back at me, his eyes sad. Very, very sad. "Okay. Thanks."

"For what?"

"For telling me the truth."

There was nothing left to say.

How unspeakably sad that small, hard fact was, so awful and so true. Love hadn't been enough to save us, and though the thought wasn't new to me, the world suddenly seemed awfully big and empty and hollow nonetheless.

Carefully, slowly, I turned back on my side. Nick put his arm around me once more, and his breath tickled the hair on my neck. Coco sighed.

I lay there, watching the blue numbers of the digital clock change as the moonlight slid across the room. Eventually, Nick's breathing slowed, and his hand twitched, telling me he was asleep at last.

But I stayed awake for a long, long time, not wanting to fall asleep, because tonight was the last night of the two of us.

CHAPTER FIFTEEN

WHEN I WOKE UP THE next morning, I was alone in bed, not even Coco for company. I could hear Nick's voice down the hall, a feminine voice answering—Mrs. McCabe, I presumed. For a second, I just sat there, looking at Nick's pillow, an unfamiliar sense of loss clanging around in my chest.

Time to get myself in gear. In a couple of hours, I'd be on my way home, back to work, back to my island. I checked my messages, zapped off a few texts, then padded into the loo to wash up and dress. I found Nick, freshly showered and shaved, sitting in the kitchen with Mrs. McCabe.

"Mornin', hon," he said with a little smile, and just like that, he let me know we were…well. We were okay, or as okay as the two of us got. He introduced me to Mrs. McCabe, an attractive woman with a blue tinge to her white hair.

"Ruth and I were just talking about baby names," Nick said. "She and I both lean toward the Old Testament."

"I've always loved Zophar," I said. Comforter of Job, six letters. I did crossword puzzles, after all.

"Now, sweetie, you know my heart's set on Jabal," he said. Ah. The former altar boy struck back.

"We can always compromise. Esau," I said, grinning. Jacob's twin, son of Isaac and Rebecca.

"Or Nebuchadnezzar," he returned.

"I do love that one," I said, nodding thoughtfully.

"Well, now, you might want to think of how the other kids will, um, react," Mrs. McCabe advised, frowning. "Nothing wrong with David or Jesse, don'tcha think? Harper, hon, have some coffee cake."

We had a lovely breakfast, and then Deacon drove us into town. Lars the mechanic had no problem replacing the hose on the Mustang. Had the part in stock. Easy fix. It was rather disappointing.

"Sure hope you folks'll make it back here someday," Deacon said as I paid the bill (I insisted, and Nick let me).

"It's a lovely town," I said sincerely. "And you've been wonderful, Deacon."

"Well, we enjoyed the company," he said. "Any time you swing through North Dakota, you look us up, won'tcha?"

"We sure will," Nick said, shaking his hand. "Thanks for the hospitality."

"Take care, kids! Send us a Christmas card!" Deacon called.

And that was that. Goodbye, Harold, goodbye sweet, brief pretense that Nick and I were—or ever had been—happily married, goodbye whispered truths in the moonlight. Coco curled up on my lap—Nick insisted on driving, making numerous roadkill jokes, started the engine and we were off. According to Nick's portable GPS system, the airport in Bismarck was two hours and forty-two minutes away.

"There's one stop I want to make before I take you to the airport," Nick said. "Do you mind?"

"No," I said instantly. "Nope. That's fine."

Time, which had seemed so sluggish the past few days, suddenly sped up. Nick and I chatted carefully—nothing deeper than the weather forecast—and listened to NPR. As we neared the capital city, the trees and buildings grew denser, and Coco perked up as if realizing we were reaching a destination. Bismarck was a new city—well, compared with the East Coast, that is. The trees were turning here, and many of the houses were from the Arts and Craft period, or solid old Victorians. Lots of yards, lots of gardens. It was quite lovely…and quite flat. Shocking, really, how far you could see out here.

The Mustang's top was down, and sky gleamed pure blue. I wore Nick's Yankees hat, but the breeze managed to free some locks of hair anyway. I guessed it didn't matter. We passed restaurants and shops, and the city turned into blocks. Finally, we came to a college— Whalen University. Nick slowed, then turned into the entrance. The manicured campus grounds sprawled in front of us, green and lush, dotted with shade trees and college students lounging on the grass. Nick knew where he was going; he turned right, then left and finally came up in front of a building. The Hettig Library & Media Center, the sign announced.

"Need something to read?" I asked.

He didn't answer, just got out of the car. I followed, Coco trotting at my side, her pink patent leather leash catching the sunlight.

The library was made of brick and glass, very clean and open, with graceful lines and an arched glass roof. How nice it must be to study in there, I thought, the endless Midwestern sky above you as you pored over books or computer screens. There was a slate courtyard with a very modern-looking fountain, all angles and corners, the smooth fall of water splashing down in a wonderful rush of noise. At one end of the building, there was a four- or five-story tower that nicely echoed the more traditional, older architecture of the rest of the campus. I caught up to Nick, who was staring up at the tower, squinting in the sun.

"It's yours, isn't it?" I asked.

"Yes," he said in that immediate way he had. He turned to face me. "I just wanted you to..." He paused. "To see something of mine."

My heart swelled. I never had seen one of Nick's buildings...not that I knew of, anyway. "Well, then. Show me around."

For the next hour, we walked around the building, inside and out, and for the first time, I saw him in full architect mode, talking about light and angles, expansion and symmetry, commonality and conservation. His voice was New York fast, his lovely hands pointing and framing, and he smiled as he spoke, his eyes bright. When a librarian came over to kick Coco out, Nick introduced himself, pulling her name from his memory banks—apparently they'd met five years ago when the building was actually being constructed—and Coco was allowed to stay. Kids looked at him, recognizing that this was a guy who knew something; one even approached him and asked if he was the architect of the library, and the two of them talked for a few minutes about master's programs. In the end, Nick gave him his business card and told him to drop him a line if he wanted a summer internship.

It was something, to stand in a building that Nick—my Nick—had dreamed up and made real.

"Is this one of your favorite buildings?" I asked as we headed back into the sunshine and scudding clouds.

"Well, in some ways, yes," he said. "Mostly because it's a library. What happens here is generally positive, you'd hope, anyway. Better than a parking garage."

"I'm glad you showed me, Nick," I said as we stopped near the fountain. "It's beautiful. I'm...I'm proud of you." My cheeks prickled with heat. Great. I was blushing.

Nick looked at me somberly for a minute. "Thank you."

Then he flashed his smile, and I smiled back, relieved
that he didn't tell me what a dork I was.

But we couldn't stay here forever. I glanced at my
watch, and Nick lurched back into gear. "Guess you want
to get to the airport," he said.

"I probably should."

"Right."

It was a very quick ride to the Bismarck Airport. Nick
pulled up in front of the terminal, popped the trunk and
towed my suitcase inside. We waited at the counter, a
little awkward now, smiling at each other, then looking
away.

"So you're looking to get to Boston?" the ticket agent
asked. Her name tag read Suzie, and she gave Nick an
assessing glance. He was wearing the blue-tinted sunglasses, a close-fitting black T-shirt and faded jeans—the
king of cool, in other words, and Suzie smiled brightly.
"Just you, ma'am?"

"That's right. As soon as possible, okay? I got tangled
up in that mess in Montana."

She dragged her eyes off of Nick. "What mess was
that?"

"The software glitch? Grounded the fleet for a few
days at all the little airports in Montana on Sunday?"

She frowned. "Oh, that. That only lasted a couple
hours, hon. You'd have done better to stay put. They were
flying later that same day."

I blinked. "Oh." Glanced at Nick, who shrugged.

"All righty, then," Suzie said. "Well, it's a little tricky,
since you'll have to change planes a few times. You'll go
from here to Denver, and from Denver you can go directly
to Boston, but you're gonna have to wait five hours. Or
you can go on to Dallas, and from Dallas to Atlanta.
Quick layover in Hot-lanta, and then on to Beantown.

That'll get you to Boston at, let's see, 10 a.m. tomorrow morning."

Twenty hours of hell, in other words. I glanced at Coco, who stared back.

"Are you staying in Bismarck?" Suzie asked Nick. "We have some super-duper restaurants, if you need a recommendation or two. I get off at—"

"And how much will that be?" I asked, just a bit tightly.

"Okeydokey, let me just check there…" She typed for the next minute or so. Clickety clackety clack. Click. Clack! Clickety click. I sighed, she paused, gave me a look of thinly veiled tolerance, flashed a supersunny smile at Nick, who returned it, I noted with irritation. "Suzie? Any time would be great," I said sweetly.

"Well, now, I'm working on it, don'tcha know. I'm sorry if it's not going fast enough for you, ma'am," she said with an equal dose of saccharine. She gave Nick a sympathetic smile. *Gosh golly, isn't it just so awful that we both have to deal with her?* Clickety clickety clack. For God's sake! Was this her novel? Emails to her BFF? *Hey there, Lorna, you should see this bitchy redhead I have to take care of, she's not even letting me flirt with my future husband, which is so unfair, don't you know, when I've gone to all this trouble and named our kids and everything!*

Finally, she gave me a perky and very phony smile. "Well, with the fee for your little doggy and yourself, that comes to $2,835.49."

"Holy testicle Tuesday!" I exclaimed.

"Oh, my," Suzie chided. "Well, it takes all types, I guess. Shall I book that for you, then? We accept all major credit cards, of course."

I gave her my best lawyer stare, then opened my wallet.

"Harper," Nick said. He took my arm and pulled me a few paces away. "Listen. I'm heading…I can take you to Minneapolis. It's a straight shot, maybe seven hours." He paused. "I bet you could get a better flight from there."

The possibilities flashed in red through my mind. Seven more hours with Nick. Seven more hours revisiting the past. Bickering. Fighting attraction. Bone-marrow harvesting.

Laughing. Talking. Maybe we could find another church festival.

Seven more hours of falling back in love with Nick.

It had taken me years to get over him. Years. The case could be made that I wasn't over him yet.

His dark eyes were waiting for an answer.

"I better just get going, Nick," I said.

His gaze dropped to the floor. "Okay. Sure. That's probably a good idea." He folded his arms across his chest and nodded.

"I just need a driver's license, ma'am," Suzie said. She was really starting to wear.

"You don't need to hang around, Nick," I said.

He looked up. "Okay. Well. Safe home, Harpy. See you around."

"You too, Nick." My throat hurt. "Thank you for driving me."

He gave me a very brief hug, and my cheek brushed his neck, and I breathed in his clean, lovely smell, but before I was even able to get my arms around him to hug him back, he'd stepped away, then bent to pet my dog. "Bye, Coco," he said as she licked his hand with her fast little tongue. He straightened up, looked at me and stopped time. "Take care," he said, his voice soft.

"You too, Nick."

I watched him walk away, and it seemed as if a chunk of my heart went with him. Coco whined.

"Didja want that dinner recommendation, then?" Suzie called after him, frowning fiercely. Nick didn't answer, and in another second, he was gone. Suzie huffed. "Okey-dokey, then," she muttered. "Can I have a credit card and your license, ma'am?"

"Sure." I opened my wallet.

The little blue Montana flower Nick had picked for me fell out, flat and creased after two days. Still pretty, though. I picked it up and stroked a petal.

"Your flight to Denver leaves in forty minutes, ma'am," Suzie informed me tightly. "And as you might know, they like you to get there a little early."

I ignored her. Looked back toward the entrance of the airport, and before I knew I'd made a choice, was towing my suitcase behind me, Coco leaping along beside me.

"Oh, that's just great," I heard Suzie say. "A complete waste of my time."

The sun was so bright outside that for a moment, I couldn't see. But then I could, and there he was, leaning against the red Mustang, hands in his pockets, looking at the ground. He looked up, saw me, froze for a second… and then his lightning smile flashed, and I realized I was smiling, too. Coco barked and jumped.

"Land of Ten Thousand Lakes, here we come," I said, and Nick's laugh made my heart swell in a painful, wonderful way.

Maybe I needed closure. Maybe I needed something else. Whatever it was, I wasn't ready to say goodbye just yet.

CHAPTER SIXTEEN

BUT OF COURSE, IT wasn't quite that straightforward.

"Okay, there's one thing I didn't mention," Nick said as we headed away from the airport.

"What's that?" I asked, pulling the Yankees cap back on.

He took a deep breath and held it for a second. "You know the library I just showed you?"

"Yeah?"

"Well, I have a meeting with the dean of the college. They're thinking about a new engineering building, and they wanted to talk."

"Oh."

"It's not a big deal. Just an hour. Maybe two."

"Right. Okay. Sure. Maybe we can find a Laundromat or something? I didn't plan on being away this long."

"Sure, sure." He glanced over at me.

"What time's the meeting?"

"Two. I had to reschedule it from yesterday, after you ran over the antelope."

So. A meeting that just happened to be in Bismarck, North Dakota. I should've remembered. As carefree and meandering as he may have wanted to seem on our little jaunt from Glacier, Nick rarely did anything without a plan.

An hour and a half later, I sat in the BubbleNSqueak, watching my laundry through the porthole of a washing machine. For some reason, I was feeling vaguely...tricked.

Not that Nick had owed me any explanation; he'd done me a huge favor by driving me here. But still.

"Snap out of it, Harper," I said aloud. A woman about my age gave me a look, then glanced down to make sure her daughter was safe. "Talking to myself," I explained.

"Oh, you betcha. I do it all the time," she said kindly. Midwesterners. So bleepin' nice.

Time to return some phone calls. I had the usual slew of messages. Tommy, Theo, Carol, BeverLee (my heart clanged at the thought of poor Bev; I hoped the divorce wouldn't drag out), Willa and ah! Kim. Just what I needed. A girlfriend. I hadn't talked to her since Sunday night, which felt like an eon ago.

"Kim, it's me."

"Who's me?" she asked. "Gus, stop biting your brother! Stop it! Stop! Thank you! Hello?"

"Hi. It's Harper."

"Well, holy ovaries, Batman, it's about time! Where are you?"

"I'm in a Laundromat in North Dakota."

"Fascinating. Is your ex around?"

"He's at a meeting, actually."

"And tell me, what would Dr. Freud say about the fact that you two are still together? I mean, sure, you're in the middle of nowhere, but there's got to be a plane somewhere, right?"

"Actually, I'm in the capital city, and it's quite lovely."

"Yeah, yeah. But you're still with what's-his-name."

"Nick."

"Right. Gus, do I have to put you in a cage or something? Because I will! Don't push it, mister!"

"As an officer of the court, I feel obliged to speak up and tell you that child imprisonment is against the law," I said.

"Right. Well, then, I'll take that as your offer to babysit all four of my precious angels when you get home."

"Then again, cages can be very comfortable," I said and smiled. Kim was all talk. She could barely stand to have the kids lose dessert, let alone shut in the dog's crate (which, it must be noted, the boys used as a fort).

"So, back to you. Have you done it yet? You and the hot ex-husband? Nick?"

"How do you know he's hot?" I asked.

"Isn't he?"

"He's…um…yes," I admitted, rolling my eyes. "But no. Nothing's happened yet." Then, hearing myself, I quickly added, "And nothing will. We're just…see, the flight was really—"

"Right, right, no need to make excuses. So what are you doing with him?"

I sighed. "Not sure."

"But you want something from him, or you wouldn't be washing his shorts."

"I'm only washing my own stuff, just for the record."

"God, you're a master of evasion, Harper! You called me. Spill. Make it quick. The twins are gnawing on each other."

"I'm just…I have no idea what I'm doing. I'll bring the boys something sharp as a souvenir. Gotta run."

"Bye, you coward," she said amiably.

My next call didn't go through—Willa was out of range. I had a momentary pang of anxiety, remembering my brush with the grizzly bear. Why people camped was beyond me. But Willa's last call had been this morning, when Nick and I were out in Harold, so chances were good that she was still alive.

Next on the list of people to call: BeverLee. "Sugar baby, how are you?" she answered.

"Hey, Bev," I said. "Where are you guys? Still in Salt Lake City?"

There was a pause. "No, sweetheart, we…we came home." Another pause. "Listen, Harper, darlin'. I'm real sorry to tell you this over the phone, but your daddy and me…looks like we're partin' ways."

Her voice was steady and gentle. Horribly so. "Bever-Lee, I'm so sorry," I said, my voice surprisingly husky. "You okay?"

"Well, now, of course I am! You know me! Land on my feet, that's what I do." But her usual exuberance was muted.

"Sure. Right." I bit my lip. Where would she go? Would she want to stay on the island, a displaced Texan in the heart of New England? What about money? "If you need anything, just say the word," I offered, immediately disgusted with the lameness of my words.

"You bet, sugarplum. You wanna talk to your daddy?"

"Um, that's okay, Bev…oh. Hi, Dad."

"Harper. Everything okay?"

"Oh, sure. I'm just…taking the circuitous route to the airport, seeing this great country of ours."

"Nice."

"So Dad…everything okay there?"

"Yep."

"BeverLee doing okay?"

"Yep."

"And how are you, Dad?"

"I'm fine."

How could he be fine, divorcing his wife of twenty years? And people thought *I* was emotionally constipated. The apple didn't fall far from the tree. "Okay. Take care, Dad. Hey, have you heard from Willa?"

"Here. I'll put you back on with BeverLee."

There was some whispering on the other end, then BeverLee's voice once more. "What's up, sweet knees?"

"Just wondering how Willa's doing."

"Oh, she's *fine!* She and that handsome hubby of hers, they're just havin' the *time* of their *lives!*" This may or may not have been true, of course—it was BeverLee's nature to assume the best until the facts kicked down her metaphoric front door…and even then, it might be hard to get her to change her mind. Case in point: Clifford "Jimmy" James, my dear old dad. "It's just so beautiful in Montana, don't you think? Seems so small back here by comparison. Not that I'm complainin', of course, I just love being a Yankee—" Her voice broke off abruptly, as if remembering her status in the Northeast was now tenuous.

"Well, I'm in North Dakota," I said to cover the awkward silence.

"Oh, that's nice. What's it like?"

"Flat," I said. "Pretty." I closed my eyes. "Let's have lunch when I get back, okay, BeverLee?"

"That'd be real nice," she said softly.

"Take care."

"You too, sweetheart." She hung up, and a wave of absolute panic seemed to wallop me out of nowhere. There was something horribly final about her voice…Damn it! Why did people have to split up?

Asked the divorce attorney.

Right. Right. There were excellent reasons to divorce. And plenty of reasons not to get married in the first place.

I felt a flash of gratitude for Dennis's reluctance to marry me. Maybe he knew something I didn't. The memory of my list made me cringe in shame. *Once you've fulfilled my requirements, Dennis, I'd be happy to let you marry me.* Nice, Harper. Dennis, with his big heart and good soul, deserved someone much better. Someone who thought of him as the love of her life. Not someone who handed him a list.

At least he got off the hook.

I called two clients next and rescheduled for the following week, then called the office. My cell battery was low, and I hadn't been able to find my charger in my suitcase last night, so I had to make it quick.

"Hi, Carol, it's Harper. Put Tommy on, okay?"

"Well, good flipping morning to you too, Harper!" she said, slapping me on hold before I could apologize for my shortness.

"Harper! Hey! How's it going?"

Tommy sounded much improved, that was for sure. "Tommy, hi. Things are fine…just, um, I'm just taking a little side trip."

"Theo's having kittens," he said.

"Well, kindly tell him I'll be back in another day or two, remind him that I must have at least two months of vacation accrued and let him know I'm working when I can…my schedule's pretty light this week, anyway. How are you?"

"I'm *great!*"

Oh, dear. He sounded sincere. My doom-o-meter fired into the red zone. "Great?"

There was a meaty pause. "Meggie and I are back together!" he said joyfully.

Oh, crotch.

"We talked the other day, and it was just like old times, Harper. I mean, it was great! And she's really sorry and stuff and she wants to move back in!"

I took a breath, held it, then proceeded with caution. "Tommy."

"Isn't that great, Harper?"

"Um…Tom. Couple things. Counseling immediately,

okay? And don't—do *not*—put your money back into the joint account. Promise?"

"Why?" he asked. "I mean, we're really past the bad stuff."

"You already did, didn't you?" Visions of LOL Kitty Man (and every other naive spouse I'd dealt with) danced in my head. "Okay. Get to the bank and put everything in an account with only your name. Okay? Just trust me on this one." My phone beeped, signaling the end was near for my battery (and Tom's marriage).

Tommy didn't answer for a second, and when he did, his tone was decidedly frosty. "Look, I know it's your job to be cynical," he began. "But Meggie and I, we *love* each other."

"Well, that's…interesting," I sighed.

"And *I'm* capable of forgiveness. I ran into Dennis, by the way. He told me you guys broke up. Sorry, boss. So I understand if you're feeling a little…down on love these days."

"Down on love? Tommy, I'm not down on love, I'm the voice of experience. If she moves back in with you, her claim on the house will be stronger. And that house has been in your family for how long? I'm not saying it won't work, buddy—" but it wouldn't "—I'm just saying to take things slowly here." *Because Meggie will clean you out faster than a cat can lick its ass,* I thought, borrowing one of BeverLee's favorite phrases.

"Gotta run, Harper. Is there anything else?"

I took a breath. "Yes, please. Reschedule Joe Starling, tell him I'm sorry, make it for Tuesday, okay?" *Beep.*

"Want me to send you the depo notes for the Mullens? You have Wi-Fi, right?"

I paused. "Sure…actually, no. I'm in the middle of nowhere right now. That can wait till I'm back. Oh, and would you send Carol some flowers for me? Have the card say 'Sorry you work for such a pain in the ass, love Harper.' Okay?"

"Sure, boss," he said, chipper once more. "Have a great trip home. Gotta go, Meggie's on the other line."

I hung up and rubbed my forehead. Well, this sucked. Tommy would be out his life savings any minute now, not to mention a claim for half the value of the house built by his great-great-grandfather. Once again, he'd have his heart stomped on by Meggie and her trashy shoes.

Tom was the poster child for why divorce could be a good thing. My father and Bev...that was another story. BeverLee loved him, even if she viewed him through rose-colored glasses. Granted, her endless chatter could match a Republican filibuster, and her unique blend of Cinnabar, Virginia Slims and Jhirmack could cause black lung, but BeverLee...she was okay.

I sighed and got up to switch my laundry. The mother and daughter were folding their laundry at the wide counter. The mom passed the little girl dishcloths and hand towels, praising her for being such a good helper, and the little girl smiled smugly, as if well aware of her prowess at laundry. They talked amiably about the girl's upcoming birthday party and how important it was to thank everyone for coming.

I guess I was staring, because the mother caught my eye. She gave me the smile of a woman content with her life, aware of her child's wonderfulness, rock solid in her devotion.

I'd always thought my mother felt those things, too.

When Nick arrived later that afternoon, Coco and I were the only ones in the Laundromat, the mother and daughter having left an hour before. He smiled as he pulled up in front of BubbleNSqueak. "Yo, Harper, get in the car, woman," he called, pushing his sunglasses on top of his head.

"The mating call of the Brooklyn male," I grumbled, but my laundry was already folded and stowed in my suitcase, so I hefted my bag into the trunk and got in the passenger seat. Coco curled up in my arms, resting her teensy head on my collarbone. "Where now, chief?" I asked. "Back to the thrill of the open road?"

"Actually, no. Can Minneapolis wait till tomorrow?"

"Another meeting?" I said, a twinge of irritation flashing. Should've bought the damn plane ticket.

"Nope." He gestured to the backseat. "A picnic."

"Oh."

Nick and I had never been on a picnic together. I remembered that one time we'd tried, the ill-fated chicken salad, the fight that marked the beginning of our end.

"Is that okay?" Nick asked, and looking up at him, I saw that he remembered, too.

"That's great," I said, clearing my throat.

Half an hour later, we were down by the Missouri River, looking at some rather odd, cut-out statues of Lewis and Clark and Sacagawea as they pointed to a parking lot…or the river, more likely. Nick pulled a blanket out of the trunk and grabbed the cooler that ostensibly contained our food.

We found a place near the train bridge and sat looking out at the wide, blue Missouri. "What do you think of the bridge?" I asked, and Nick smiled.

"Not bad," he said. "It's not Brooklyn, but it's okay." It had always been Nick's habit to compare bridges to his beloved Brooklyn Bridge and find them wanting. Not even the Golden Gate could measure up. "Orange is orange," he used to say, "no matter what you call it."

We let Coco off the leash to explore, which she did for approximately four minutes before deciding a nap was in order. She lay next to me on her back, her paws in the air, sneezed twice, wagged her tail and fell asleep.

"Hey," Nick said, nudging my arm with something. It was a little package. Gift-wrapped. "Happy birthday."

I sucked in a quick breath. He was right. I guess I'd sort of forgotten the date, being on the road, not constantly on the computer. And of course, it wasn't my favorite day of the year, given my history and all. Funny that neither my father nor BeverLee had mentioned it. Well. Other things on their minds.

"Open it," Nick said.

It was a pendant, a polished stone, gray and lovely, framed with silver twists. It was somber but lovely, one of a kind. "Thank you," I said.

"The stone's from the river here," he said. "A souvenir."

"It's beautiful."

"Want me to put it on?" he asked, then, at my nod, knelt behind me. Nick's hands were quick and gentle, barely brushing my skin. "Happy birthday," Nick repeated, and for a second, it seemed as if he might kiss me. But he didn't.

"Thanks," I whispered, not quite able to look him in the eye.

But my heart was sweetly sore, because September 14 wasn't just my birthday or the day my mother had left me…it was also the day I'd met Nick.

"So what do you want to do tonight?" Nick asked after a few minutes.

"Let's go to the movies," I said, and that's just what we did. First we checked into a chain hotel. Two rooms, of course. I left Coco in mine with Animal Planet on and strict instructions to limit her room service to three desserts and three only, then met Nick in the lobby. We walked down the street to the theater. Two horror flicks, three romances, one cop movie.

"*Nightmare on Elm Street*, or *Saw*?" Nick asked.

"Oh, *Nightmare*, definitely," I said.

"So romantic," Nick murmured. Without asking me if I wanted any, he bought me a vat of popcorn and a root beer. We found seats and did what we'd done in the olden days—proceeded to talk incessantly throughout the film's murders.

"Ten bucks says the virgin dies before the slut," I said, taking a sip of my soda.

"You're on. Oh, hey, don't go in the shower, for God's sake," Nick advised the scantily dressed college student on the screen as she tiptoed into the bathroom. He stuffed a fistful of popcorn into his mouth. "Well, okay, there you go," he added as she was slashed to death by Freddy's fingernails. "Can't say I didn't warn you. Your poor parents."

"Do you mind?" asked a kid in front of us.

"Listen, son," Nick said. "I'll save you some suspense. Everyone dies."

"Ass," the kid muttered, getting up and moving ten or so rows away. We ignored him.

"Nick," I murmured, "should I ever head into the cellar armed only with a ladle after the police have just warned me that a psychotic killer is on the loose, please slap me."

"Shut *up!*" someone else hissed.

"Will do, Harpy, will do. Oh! Yuck! Okay, I didn't see that one coming. Can you actually do that with a corkscrew?"

The hisser moved.

God, it was fun! The popcorn was fresh, the root beer wasn't watered down, and sitting there in the theater, giggling inappropriately as teen after teen was hacked, the thought came to me that if only Nick and I had done things like this when we were married—picnics and movies and harvest dances—we might never have gotten divorced.

If only.

When the movie was over, we returned to the humble hotel. Nick walked down the hall with me, murmuring something about seeing me safely to my door. Uh-huh. I slid the card into the slot and opened the door. Checked to make sure Coco was okay—she was sleeping on her back in the middle of the bed—then turned to my ex.

"Thanks for a great date," I said, my knees suddenly buzzing.

"You're welcome. Happy birthday," he murmured. His eyes dropped to my mouth. I swallowed.

Sleeping with him is definitely ill-advised, said the lawyer part of my brain. Unfortunately, the blood flow had redirected to my girl parts, which gave a hot and sudden throb. Nick looked at me, his eyes as dark as an abyss into which I would cheerfully throw myself. The lawyer part of me gave a distant, outraged squeak.

His lashes...they were so pretty, thick and unexpected, and when he smiled, which he was doing now, the loveliest lines spread from his eyes, and those eyes, so often tragic and gypsy-sad, were happy now.

A week ago, I wouldn't have dreamed of sleeping with Nick. Now though...now...okay, the brain was definitely struggling for survival as the girl parts continued to croon...Nick and me, naked and in bed...that seemed like a *wicked* good idea.

The lawyer part committed hari-kiri.

Nick reached out and touched my cheek. "Good night, Harper. See you in the morning."

"Yes! Okay! Right. You too, Nick. See you, I mean. In the morning."

He glanced back at me as he walked down the hall to his own room, a half smile on his face, and if he'd been two steps closer, I would've grabbed him by the shirt and dragged him into my room, common sense and history be damned.

Okay, why did he leave? Huh? Hmm? Huh? Men. I mean, really! Men! Who knew what went on in their tiny brains? Had he just saved me from myself, or completely insulted me? Hmm? Should I be grateful or furious? I yanked on my pajamas, washed my face, brushed my teeth and got into bed, frustrated…and yes, maybe a little relieved.

Suffice it to say I didn't get a lot of sleep. Tangled thoughts battered me like a debate team on steroids.

Nick and I lived in different states.

So? Try the long-distance thing.

We have completely separate lives.

They don't have to be separate.

We already tried this, and it was an epic failure.

You've changed.

Please. People don't change.

He still wants you.

He just walked away from me.

Don't be coy.

We'll never get over our past.

Hmm. That might be true.

The past certainly haunts me.

Yes. Okay, you win.

With a sigh, I kicked back the covers, got out of bed and clicked on a light, earning some very tragic and confused blinking from my dog. Great. It was 3 a.m., not an hour when sound decisions are often made.

Then I did something I hadn't done in a long time. I sat down in front of the mirror and took a good hard look.

I knew—intellectually, anyway—that I was pretty. Beautiful, even. My hair was envied by most of the population on earth. Eyes were green and clear. Bone structure quite strong yet still feminine.

It's just that it was my mother's face, too.

I didn't simply take after her…I was practically a clone. My father was tall, thin, dark and handsome. I was tall, red-haired and fair. Every day for the past twenty-one years…every *day*…I'd had to look in the mirror and see the face of the woman who walked out on me. I hadn't heard her voice in more than two decades. In all that time, she had only managed to send four postcards with a combined total of twelve sentences.

And as of today, I was the same age she was the last time I'd last seen her.

That was quite a thought. Quite a thought indeed.

The envelope was still in my computer carrier. Slowly, I got up and withdrew it, sat back down and, with another glance at my reflection, opened it up.

CHAPTER SEVENTEEN

NICK WAS ALREADY drinking coffee and staring out the window of the little hotel restaurant when I came in from walking Coco the next morning. My dog jumped up on the seat next to him and stole a slice of bacon, and I ruffled his hair before sitting down.

"Hey," he said, looking a little confused at the gesture of affection.

"Hey yourself," I answered. "Sleep okay?"

"Not really," he said. "I lay awake for hours, horny as a teenage boy."

"Duly noted," I said. "So. Are you bound and determined to get to Minneapolis today, Nick?"

His eyes narrowed. "Why?"

"Feel like a little detour?"

He must've sensed something was up, because he gave me a long, speculative look, as if reading my soul. (Wow. Corny. Sorry.) "Where would you like to go?"

"Aberdeen, South Dakota. Maybe three, four hours from here. If I drive, that is."

"And what's in Aberdeen?"

"You mean in addition to the Sitting Bull monument?" I asked, having spent some time on Google a few hours ago. I took a sip of his coffee, which he noted with a wry look.

"Yes. In addition to that."

"My mother."

Saying those two words out loud...it took something

out of me, because suddenly, I couldn't keep up the cute banter and my hands were shaking, Nick's coffee sloshing over the rim. He took the cup from me and held both my hands in his, held them tight.

When he did speak, it was brief. "Ready when you are."

MY THIRTEENTH BIRTHDAY had fallen on a Saturday, but my parents and I headed to Boston on Friday. On a plane, oh, yes. The ferry only went to Woods Hole, whereupon we'd have to take a bus or drive our aging Toyota, which just didn't fit the glamorous night my mother had planned.

She and I had spent weeks researching the very best restaurants in the city, comparing views, decor, street desirability, menus and wine lists...not that I'd be drinking of course, but just to assess the *class* of the place. Class was a very important noun to my mother. And so we'd come up with Les Étoiles. "Perfect," she pronounced. "Harper, this is definitely our kind of place. Now we just have to clean up your father, and we'll be all set."

She let me stay home from school that day, and I was thrilled. My mother was my absolute favorite person and always had been. She was much younger than most mothers of kids my age; in some cases, almost a generation younger. And she was so beautiful! She'd been a model, of course, and never lost her love of looking fantastic. Still a size four, that glorious hair, those green eyes. My mother looked ten years younger than thirty-four and she knew it. She was a wonderful flirt, and all the fathers loved her, of course, discreetly checking out her ass or her boobs, which she showcased in low-cut tops and tight jeans or miniskirts. She had flair, she had style, and she was *fun*. I was so proud to be hers, it was impossible to voice. The only real difference between us was that I was a really good student, and she hadn't been. Otherwise, we were practically twins.

When my schoolmates voiced their hatred, disgust, despair over their mothers, I listened in disbelief and horror. Seriously? They weren't allowed to see *Pretty Woman*? Why? So what if the main character was a ho? They still had bedtimes? Heck, my mother let me stay up as late as I wanted, and we'd watch TV and eat junk food and do each other's nails. Their mothers didn't let them wear makeup? Huh. Imagine that.

My mother wasn't like that. She was miles cooler than those other, frumpy, aging women with short bobs held back by pink plaid hairbands or, even worse, those "I give up" types who carried fifty extra pounds, had gray roots and wore baggy, sagging jeans and voluminous sweatshirts. Yawn. No, *Linda*—I'd been calling her that since I was nine—Linda was special. She taught me how to dress, was always coming home with classy little outfits… no Madonna-style fishnets for me, uh-uh. Linda and I had *class*. Though we were far from rich, we *looked* rich, and being mistaken for summer people was a special point of pride for my mother. She coached me on how to diss boys and then make them like me, how to flirt, how to be popular and powerful with both genders. And God knew, she taught me how to make the most of my good looks because, "let's face it, Harper. We're knockouts." As other girls my age sulked through adolescence, I stood out. Prettier. More confident. Better dressed. More fun. All because of my mother, who taught me everything she knew.

And so, the night before my thirteenth birthday, I came downstairs in my strapless blue minidress and three-inch pumps, smoky eyes and just a touch of clear gloss to my lips. My hair was Grecian tonight, loose curls piled on my head to better show my long, graceful neck. My father choked on the beer he was sipping.

"Linda!" he barked, turning away from me. "She's thirteen, for God's sake!"

My mother came out of the bedroom. "And she's gorgeous! Look at you, Harper! Oh, my God! We look like sisters!" It was true. She wore a silver dress with pearl jewelry, killer pumps encrusted with faux pearls. Her makeup focused on her red, red lips—so daring, so Hollywood.

"It's a little…sophisticated, don't you think, Lin?" my father tried again. "She looks…twenty."

"Did you hear that? Your father thinks you look twenty! And you do! You should order a martini tonight, just to see what the waiter says," Mom said, adjusting my necklace.

"Linda!"

"Jimmy, I wouldn't let her drink one," my mother sighed, rolling her own beautifully made-up eyes. "Maybe just a tiny sip," she added in a low voice, winking at me. I grinned in happy conspiracy against dopey old Dad. Sweet but…you know. So provincial.

Dad was quiet all the way to the airport and during the short flight to Boston. Linda and I ignored him, cooing and clutching hands as our cab neared the restaurant. "Okay, we're here. Be cool, and Jimmy, try not to act like a bumpkin." Linda and I giggled, united as always against my dad, though I did give him a pat on the cheek.

Looking back on that night, I would see things differently. My father, a general contractor, made a decent living out on the island, but we weren't wealthy by any stretch. Spending all that money—the designer dresses bought at full price ("We deserve it," Linda had said), the shoes, the jewelry, the mani-pedis at the uberluxe day spa, the cab to and from the airport, the flight, and my God, the meal…it probably cost him more than a month's pay. Quite possibly more than two months' pay.

But on that night, it was all about Linda and me. We acted blasé as we got out of the taxi, though secretly both of us were darting looks to take it all in…the sleek decor, the legion of restaurant staff—the captain, the waiters, the busboys, the sommelier—the soft clink of crystal and murmur of voices. And yes, heads turned as our party of three was led through the restaurant to the best table in the place, up on the second level, overlooking the rest of the diners. We were a gorgeous family, it couldn't be denied.

"Too bad we couldn't afford New York," Linda said as we sat down. "Better yet, L.A. Harper, you'd be a star right this minute if we lived in L.A." She shook out her napkin with authority. After all, she'd grown up in California. She knew about these things.

We ordered drinks…tonic and lime for me, which tasted weird but which my mother had told me would look way cooler than a Shirley Temple or ginger ale. Dad had a Sam Adams, causing Linda to sigh patiently before ordering a grapefruit martini, dry, for herself.

Then Dad looked at the menu and tried not to blanch, but holy crap, the prices! Forty-five dollars for a piece of fish? Seriously? Fifteen dollars for a salad?

"Order whatever you want, Harper," Linda said, gazing blandly at the menu. "It's your special night. Mine too, since I did all the work." She gave me a wink and proceeded to order a lobster and avocado appetizer, a caesar salad and filet mignon. She always could eat. Never needed to diet.

Dinner was…well, it was fine. The truth was, my feet hurt in my new shoes, and I was kind of cold in my strapless gown. Food-wise, I'd have secretly preferred Sharky's Super Nachos back on the island. But I pretended it was the best meal of my life as my mother regaled Dad and me with stories of her life in California, making us laugh, charming us with her tinkling laugh, even flirting with my father, laying her hand on his arm and talking in her animated, talk-show host way.

And that part...that part was wonderful.

My parents had a rocky marriage. I knew that. Linda spent too much, didn't do a lot around the house, and Dad was often frustrated. Sometimes, late at night, I heard them arguing, Dad's voice loud, Linda's defiant. But Linda wasn't like other mothers, or other wives, and surely he could see that. She was special, more fun, more lively, more envied. Dad's appreciation for her was far less than mine, but on this night, we were really happy. We were having a ball. Even in this beautiful city, even at this very fine restaurant, we were clearly the people to be.

We ordered dessert (no candle on my cheesecake, it would be so gauche) and were winding down when a man approached us.

"Excuse me, do you mind if I take a minute of your time?" he asked. He had graying blond hair, a wicked expensive-looking suit, and he took my mother's hand the way Lancelot took Guinevere's.

He introduced himself, sat between my parents in the unoccupied chair at our table. His name was Marcus something, and he was from New York. He worked for Elite Modeling Agency.

At the name of the agency, my mother's eyes got the slightest bit wider. Her perfect lips parted, and her eyes darted to my dad, who already looked thunderous.

"Of course we've heard of Elite, Marcus," Linda said, tilting her head a bit. "Who hasn't?"

The man smiled. "Mr. and Mrs. James, your daughter

is a very lovely young woman," he said, turning to me. "How old are you, sweetheart?"

"I'm thirteen. Well, tomorrow, I will be. It's my birthday," I said.

"You'll be thirteen tomorrow?" he said.

"That's right," I answered. I could tell it was a good answer, because he gave an approving nod.

"How tall are you, Harper?"

"Five seven and a half. Still growing, I think." I smiled, and he smiled back.

"I don't think I want my daughter modeling," my father said, his familiar frown lowering.

My mouth opened, and I glanced at my mother for solidarity. Surely, we weren't going to let a chance like this pass us by, were we? Hadn't my own mother taught me her runway walk? Modeling...for *Elite*? This would be a dream come true! My friends at school would die! Linda and I would travel all over the world, and I'd—

"Well, before you make a decision, consider this. Some of our younger models have put themselves through college, just working part-time," Marcus said smoothly. "Of course we'd like some pictures taken. At our cost. We'd fly you all down to the city for a day or two, take you out for dinner, get you some tickets to a show and see what the pictures say."

Despite the fact that I was pretending to be terribly sophisticated, I jumped a little in my seat. Was he kidding me? Come on! This was the best birthday ever!

"I can see you're having a special dinner, and I don't want to take any more of your time," Marcus said. "But this is my job, and I have an eye for these things." He gave me a little wink. "I'm in town with Christy Turlington. Do you know who that is?"

Of *course* I knew who Christy Turlington was! The Calvin Klein model? We must've had at least ten magazines back home that were *littered* with pictures of Christy Turlington!

"I think you could have a very bright future, Harper. Here's my card. Please call my secretary whenever you're ready." He handed me the card, and it was the real deal, embossed, expensive. He shook my parents' hands as well as mine, then left, smiling and pleasant. A minute later, a waiter came over with a round of drinks and broke the stunned silence that had fallen over our table.

"Courtesy of the gentleman who just left," he said.

"Thanks," Dad muttered.

"Can you believe it?" I squeaked.

"I can't," my mother answered, and it was only then that I noticed her face was white underneath her perfectly applied blush.

"Can I?" I asked. "Can I call him, Mom?"

"Harper! Show a little *class*," my mother hissed. She took her drink and drained it. "We'll discuss this later."

We never did discuss it later.

For a long time, I thought it was because I called her "Mom," not Linda. Or maybe it was because the guy had interrupted our dinner, and we'd been having such a nice time.

It took me years to realize that my mother thought he'd come over to talk to her.

The evening was over, the mood gone. Our trip back to Logan was quiet, and oddly enough, it was Dad who tried to fill the silence. When we got home, I got into my pajamas, washed off the makeup that had been applied with such care and went to bed, hoping that my mother would be in a better mood tomorrow, and that I could call Marcus's secretary. But even then, the thought of going to the city was tainted.

The next day, I found a note on my pillow from my dad, saying happy birthday, he was finishing up a house in

Oak Bluffs and he'd see me later. I went into my mother's room to say good morning.

She was packing.

"I'm taking a little trip," she said blithely. "Gotta have a little *me* time, if you know what I mean. Last night was fun, wasn't it?"

Once—only once—my mother had gone away without me. To California to visit her family, leaving Dad and me alone for a week. She came back three days early and said only that her family was made up of idiots and she was right to get the hell out when she did. So a trip…"Where are you going?" I asked.

"Not really sure yet," she answered, not looking at me. "But you know how it is, Harper. I wasn't really meant for small-town life. Time to stretch a little, get away from your father and this *provincial* little island."

"But…when will you come back, M—Linda?"

"M…Linda?" she asked, and her voice was cruel. "Well, I've been here for thirteen years and nine months. I guess I'll come back if and when I want to."

Ten girls had been invited over to our house this afternoon. Mom and I spent half of yesterday getting ready for that party before abandoning our efforts to prepare for our glamorous night in Boston. We were supposed to be going to the beach, then come back and have virgin margaritas. We'd dipped strawberries in chocolate, a whole tray of them.

She yanked open another drawer and began tossing clothes in, her movements sharp and angry.

"Can I come with you?" I asked, and I hardly recognized my voice, it was so small and scared.

Only then did she spare me a glance. "Not this time," she said, looking away. "Not this time."

Half an hour later, she was gone.

NICK LET ME DRIVE. It took three hours and fifteen minutes to get to the exit for downtown Aberdeen, and by then, my hands were stiff, sweaty and clenched around the wheel.

Back when we were dating, I had told Nick a very sketchy version of my mother's desertion, kept a blasé and cool attitude about it, sort of the "Ah, well, shit happens" take on the event. But I'd told him in the dark, in the middle of the night, and when I was done, I made him promise never to bring it up, a promise he honored.

Today, though, on the ride to Aberdeen this day, he got the full version. He let me tell the whole story without interrupting once, and when I was finished, he'd simply taken my hand and held it.

And now we were here.

According to the report Dirk Kilpatrick, P.I., had given me, my mother had worked in Aberdeen for the past three years as a waitress at a place called Flopsy's, home of the best milkshakes in the Midwest. The navigational system directed us to the restaurant, which turned out to be a rather cool-looking retro diner, chrome on the outside, a sign with *Flopsy's!* in big green letters, an ice-cream cone outlined in neon jutting into the air.

Was she in there? My gorge rose at the thought, but my outward movements were smooth and controlled. I continued past Flopsy's and pulled over onto a side street about half a block away, turned off the engine and just sat for a minute. The day was cool and cloudy, but I was sweating like a racehorse nonetheless. Pretty.

"Harper," Nick said, turning to face me. "What exactly do you hope is going to happen here?" It was the first time he'd spoken in some time.

I took a deep breath. "Well," I said, and my voice was strange, "I guess I just want to see her again. Ask her why she left and never...you know. Came back. Or wrote. Well, she did write. Those four postcards."

Nick nodded. "Do you know what you want to say?"

"I guess just...'Hi, Mom.' Do you think I should say that? Or 'Hi, Linda'? Or maybe something else?"

He shook his head. "You say whatever you want to, honey. Spit in her face if you want. Kick her in the shins." He gave a smile that didn't quite make it.

I nodded, but the truth was, my heart was kicking so fast and hard in my chest it felt as if I'd swallowed an enraged mule. When she'd first left, I'd spent night after night twisting in the chilly arms of insomnia, wondering what I'd done to ruin everything. Why hadn't I been different? Or better? Or sweeter? Why hadn't I seen her unhappiness and stopped it? Why was I so stupid? Later, I could see—intellectually, anyway—that it wasn't my fault...I was just a kid, just thirteen years old. I hadn't done anything wrong, but that knowledge seemed to float above my heart, whereas blame sliced effortlessly right to the center.

I had pictured our reunion thousands of times. When I was still young, I'd imagined the joy, the *bliss* on her face as she saw me, whereupon she'd explain everything—she was a Mafia princess, you see, and she'd had to testify against her family. Or she was a CIA agent, and staying with us would've endangered our very lives, but now it was safe, and we could be together again. As the years passed, the fantasy changed—she'd be the one to track me down (it was probably no coincidence that I'd stayed on Martha's Vineyard). She'd be full of remorse and grief that so many years had passed without me, and she'd tell me what a huge mistake she'd made, that she'd thought of me every day, never stopped loving me, I was the one and only thing in her life that mattered.

And then, in recent years, I'd imagine learning that

she was dead, and how I'd react to the phone call that told me the news. How broken I'd be at all that would never happen now. I guess that's what made me ask Dirk to track her down.

Now that the moment was finally upon me, I wasn't sure what to do.

Nick squeezed my hand. "I'm coming with you," he said.

"That'd be great," I whispered. "What about Coco?" I asked, suddenly panicked. "What if they don't let dogs in?"

"Why don't we just leave her in the car?" he suggested. "She'll be fine. We'll leave the windows open a few inches. It won't get too hot."

"Really? Are you sure?"

He nodded. "I'll come back and check on her if you want."

"Okay. Thanks, Nick."

He gave me a little smile. "You ready?"

"Not really," I said, but I opened the door anyway. My legs felt made of water, and Nick took my hand in his as we walked down the street, toward my past, toward my answers, toward *her*.

We came to the crosswalk. Right over there, across the street, my mother might be inside. Would she look different? What if she wasn't scheduled for today? What if she'd quit? I swallowed.

"You sure about this, honey?" Nick asked.

I looked at him. "Yes. Yep. I'm sure."

And then we crossed the street, and Nick opened the first set of doors into the restaurant foyer. I froze. "I don't see her," I said.

"Want to go in anyway?" he asked. I nodded, and he opened the second set of doors. A cash register. Green-and-white décor. A counter with stools. Booths.

There she was.

My mother.

Nick must've seen the resemblance, too, because I heard his quick inhalation. His hand found mine once more.

She wore black pants and a lime-green shirt. Her hair, once the same shade as mine, was redder now, and cut in a wedge style. She wore peach lipstick. White Keds. She was fifty-five years old, but she looked younger. She was still beautiful, and it was so *strange*, looking at her, seeing myself in twenty more years, I felt a flash of gratitude that I'd age well, and then a flood of longing so hard and fast my knees almost buckled and I couldn't breathe.

"Welcome to Flopsy's!" cried a voice, causing me to jump. "Can I help you?"

I turned to see a girl of about sixteen or so, her hair French-braided tightly back from her face.

"Table for two," Nick said.

"Right this way!" she chirped, grabbing two menus.

My heart rolled and flopped in my chest as the girl led us to a table by the windows. She was so close now, but she was turning away, had she seen me, was she leaving?—no!—but it was okay, she wasn't leaving, she was just talking to the cook.

"Two coffees," Nick said.

"Your server will be right over," the teenager said, practically skipping away.

"Harper," Nick said in a low voice. "Harper, are you okay?" He reached across the table and took both my hands in his. "Honey?"

"I'm really glad you're here," I whispered.

And then the kitchen doors swung open, and my mother came over and took out her pad, groped in her apron for a pen. "Hello there," she said, and her voice!

My God, I hadn't heard that voice in so long! It was still the same, and my heart flooded with love and hope.

"Hi," I breathed. I drank in every detail...her still perfect makeup, her eyebrows, waxed thinner than they used to be, that mole on her cheek...I'd forgotten that mole! How could I have forgotten that mole?

"Can I get you folks a drink to start? We have the best milkshakes in the Midwest!"

Then she looked at me, right at me, and I waited for it—the shock, the recognition, the tears, the explanation, the utter and complete joy. The same love I felt right now.

"Or maybe just some coffee?" she said.

She was looking at me, but her expression remained the same. Pleasant. Querying. She glanced at Nick and smiled. "Anything to drink, folks?"

"Coffee will be fine," someone answered. Oh. It was me.

"Coming up!" she said merrily. "We've got a tuna melt special today, and save room for some blueberry pie, because it just came out of the oven. Back in a sec!"

And then she was gone.

"Christ," Nick breathed.

I didn't say anything. My heart slowed and calmed... and seemed to freeze. Maybe it had stopped completely. But no, it was still pumping away. Right. I was fine. It didn't matter. Then, realizing I hadn't blinked in some time, I closed my eyes for a second.

"Oh, honey," Nick said gently.

"Bye, Carrie, you have a great day, okay?" my mother called to someone. She came back to our table with two mugs, set them down and poured our coffee. "You folks decided what you want?" she asked.

Did she really not recognize me? But I was her baby...

her only child. I was her little girl. And damn it to hell, I looked exactly like her.

"I'll have the tuna melt," I said, and my voice was normal.

"Same," Nick said.

"Fries or cole slaw?" she asked. I *hated* cole slaw. I hated it. Didn't she remember that?

"Fries for us both," Nick answered.

"Coming up!" she said, scooping our menus from the table. She strode away, stopped to chat with someone at the counter, then disappeared into the kitchen once more.

"Harper, say something to her," Nick said. He got out of his seat, slid around to my side and put his arm around me. "Tell her who you are! I can't believe she doesn't know."

My mouth opened, then closed, then opened again. "No, it's okay. If she doesn't want…uh…" My brain was having trouble operating. "I think we should go," I whispered.

"Honey, you deserve something from that woman," he said fiercely. "Do you want me to say something? Tell her who you are?"

"No!" I hissed. "No, Nick! Let's just get out of here, okay? Please, Nick? Take me somewhere else, please. Please."

He hesitated, then nodded and reached for his wallet.

"No. Let me." I yanked my purse open, grabbed my wallet and took out a hundred dollar bill, tucked it under the sugar bowl. "Let's go."

It didn't feel like walking…it was more like floating, slowly. Would she stop me? Call my name? Grab my arm and pull me into her arms, kiss me, crying, apologizing?

Nope. Nope to all of the above. Nick opened the door for me, and I went outside.

If my mother even noticed, she didn't say a word.

CHAPTER EIGHTEEN

I DIDN'T SEE THE street as we walked back, but here we were, right by the car. Nick opened the passenger door, and I got in, clipped the seat belt. My mind seemed to be an empty white space, and yet I noted everything. Clouds to the west. A yellow Mini Cooper, just like mine back home. Cool. Nick was doing something on his phone. Coco's little nose against my chin, because apparently I was holding her. I kissed her silky head, felt her sweet little body, strong and fragile both. When we got back to the Vineyard, this dog was getting whatever she wanted. An hour of tennis-ball chasing on the beach. An evening of belly rubbing. Filet mignon for dinner, and lots of it.

"You sure you want to leave?" Nick said, looking at me.

I stared straight ahead. "I'm sure."

"Okay." He started the car, and off we went. A few minutes later, we pulled up in front of a large brick building. The Ward Hotel. Seemed nice. Nick went to the front desk and asked for a room. There was some discussion about Coco. Nick opened his wallet and took out some bills. The discussion ended.

I'd seen my mother today.

This huge swell of...*something*...rose up inside me like a gushing oil well at the bottom of a once-pristine ocean. Oh...crotch. I wasn't going to...I couldn't...I wasn't the wailing type, was I? No. Of course not. I took a breath and tried to squash it, that dark and hungry thing, and I managed, shoving it down with all the strength I had.

Nick was back, our bags in tow. "All set?" I asked, and he gave me an odd look and said we were, then took my hand and walked to the elevator. Ding. Perfect. No waiting.

I tried to blank out any thought and focus on the wallpaper, the buttons, Coco. We got to our floor, walked down the hall. Patterned carpeting. Very pleasant.

Nick opened the door to the room. We went in. Huh. Nice. Nicer than I expected. Coco began sniffing the corners for werewolves, then, satisfied there were none, jumped into the middle of the bed.

Nick turned to me and opened his mouth.

"Stop. Wait," I said, taking a step back. My face scrunched up, that dark thing surged again, and my hands went up defensively. "I need to say something."

It was a little hard to breathe, suddenly. My lungs felt empty and tight. My mouth opened, closed, opened again. "Nick," I said, and my voice was low and harsh. "Everything you said about me…being stunted and heartless… it's true. I'm so sorry. I'm so sorry, Nick, for everything I did back then. I thought I could be…normal, I guess, but I guess…I mean, when you look at what I come from…I'm just like her."

My throat was so tight I could hardly breathe. "She didn't even recognize me, Nick," I whispered. "I'm her only child, and she didn't recognize me. Or even worse, she did. My mom…my…I'm so sorry, Nick. I'm so sorry."

Then Nick's arms went around me and he held me hard against him. "Oh, sweetheart," he said, and that kindness, it just broke me. Something was wrong with me, I was choking and my eyes were hot and wet and my chest was jerking up and down and these strange noises were coming out of my mouth. I mean, there was crying, and then there was...*this*, and even as one part of my brain was pretty damn disgusted, the rest of me couldn't get it under control. Holy testicle Tuesday, I don't know how he could stand it, these caterwauling, elk-like sounds that ratcheted out of me, my clawlike grip on the back of his shirt, my sloppy face buried against his neck.

Then he bent a little and lifted me, carried me to the bed and put me down. I curled onto my side, fetal position, how ironic. This crying was bloody *awful*, sobs splintering out of me, they *hurt*, and there didn't appear to be a thing I could do about it.

Nick took off my shoes, then lay down next to me and gathered me against him, tucking my head against his shoulder, stroking my hair. He reached over to the night table and handed me a box of tissues, then kissed my head and held me close as I cried, and cried, and kept crying. There was just one word in my heart, one horrible, cruel, cheating, primal word.

Mommy.

For so, so long, I thought my mother would come back for me. I was her best friend, her little doll, her daughter. As the years passed, my hope scabbed over, and I learned that people hurt each other all the time, that even if you scrape your heart on the rough brick of their indifference, the skin grows back, so to speak. Shit happens, you get over it.

That's what I thought until today, when I remembered how much I had loved her, how I'd yearned for her, how I'd prayed for her to come back. How even today, I had hoped to win back my mother's love.

It wasn't going to happen.

She didn't know me. Or even worse, she did.

I didn't know there were this many tears in a human body. Nick kept passing me tissues and kissing my hair, and Coco curled up against my back, whining—she'd never heard me bawl like this, God knows—and still I cried.

But apparently, the thing about crying is that you can't keep it up forever. Dehydration sets in, whatever. Eventually, my gulping sobs became squeaks, and the torrent of tears became a patter, then a trickle. My breathing went from gulping to jerky to shaky…and finally, I was quiet.

Then Nick moved so he could see my face and looked at me with his gypsy eyes, the dark, dark brown framed by those thick lashes. "You're nothing like her," he said. "Nothing like that."

Well, shit. So much for no more tears. More tears slipped out. "But I am, Nick," I said, my voice frayed from crying. "I broke your heart, I divorced you, I never came back. I'm exactly the same."

"No. You're not. You're not, honey."

"How am I any different, Nick? Because I think I should probably throw myself under a train if that's the kind of person I am."

Nick smoothed his thumbs under my eyes, pushing away the tears. "You loved me, Harper. You did, I know that. And sure, you're a tangled mess, aren't we all, and yes, you did divorce me, but Harper, you loved me." He kissed my forehead. "Whereas that woman saw you only as an extension of herself, and the very first day you outshone her, she ditched you. After what I just saw, I don't think she's capable of loving anyone."

I swallowed noisily. "I don't know that I am, either," I admitted in a whisper.

"Well, I do know, and you are. So don't argue with me, woman," he said, his eyes smiling. "You love Willa, right?" I nodded. "And your father, and BeverLee. I bet you have friends and coworkers you love, and I bet they love you, too."

I swallowed noisily and closed my eyes. "Nick, if I were in your shoes, I'd just drop me off at the nearest convenience store and lay down some rubber."

"Well, it's a thought."

My eyes opened. Nick was smiling. "I know you," he repeated. "You're nothing like her." Then his voice dropped to a whisper. "And look at you now. You're still here with me. You could be home now, but you're with me."

My eyes filled yet again. "Run, Nick."

"I can't. Harper, you're emotionally autistic, it's true, but I love you."

My jerky breathing returned. "Don't pity me, for God's sake, Nick."

"I don't pity you. I have sympathy for you, having had that selfish bitch for a mother, but I don't pity you. And I do love you."

"Shush, Nick. I can't—"

"Harper, I love you."

"I just think—"

"You're the love of my life. I've loved you since the day we met, I never stopped, I can't help myself, you're like crystal meth or something, though that's probably not the most flattering comparison, but there it is, I love you, Harper. Even if you are a pain in the—"

There was really only one way to shut him up, and so I did. I kissed him, just pressed my mouth against his, then pulled back and looked at him.

His eyes were so gentle, and the smallest smile lifted one corner of his mouth. "I see my evil plan is working," he whispered, and I kissed him again, for real this time, not just to shut him up, and the second my lips touched his, a swell of feeling seemed to lift me off the bed. He was still so familiar after all these years, his mouth perfect on mine, hungry and gentle at the same time, and I'd missed him, missed this, could not believe that somehow we'd let this get away, this desperate, wonderful feeling that being with Nick was—forgive the melodrama—my destiny. The only man I'd ever really and truly loved. My first love, my one and only. I knew it now, and the truth was, I'd known it always.

He held me harder, his hand sliding through my hair, turning my head for more access to my mouth, kissing me fiercely, practically crushing me against him. His tongue brushed mine, and I clutched him tighter. Mine. He was mine, and I was his, and that's all there was to it. "I love you," he said again, and then we were kissing again, and it was just essential, this kissing, this being together, him and me, Nick and Harper, together again, at last. At last.

Nick pulled back with difficulty, kissed me again, then stopped. "I have to…I can't…" He closed his eyes for a second before looking at me once more. "I can't do this to you. Not now, not when you're upset."

"Do what?" I asked, running my finger along his neck. He was so beautiful, his face flushed, his eyes heavy-lidded.

He was breathing hard. "Make love to you."

"You can't?"

"No."

"I think you should." I pressed a kiss to his neck, tasted him, earning a shudder.

"Stop. Damn it. Harper, stop. It would be wrong. I'd be, uh, taking advantage of you."

That made me smile. "I'm thirty-four years old." I pulled his shirt out of his jeans.

"Well, I still shouldn't. It's not fair. You're, uh, vulnerable." God, his skin was beautiful. "Harper, honey—"

I rolled off the bed. "I'm taking my clothes off now, Nick Lowery," I said, pulling my shirt over my head. Oh, goody, pretty bra, light blue with a little lace. Nick swallowed, and his eyes looked very dark. "You can do what you want, but I plan on lying naked here next to you, and I will not keep my hands to myself."

I unbuttoned my skirt and let it float to the floor.

"Okay, you win," he blurted, and with that, he leaped off the bed and practically tackled me, and that was the thing. No matter what, no matter when, we could always make each other laugh. Even when we were mad, or sad, or horny. When he undid the clasp of my bra, when his mouth found that spot on my collarbone, when his fingers laced with mine, the laughter faded, though, and something even sweeter took its place.

Nothing had ever felt as right as this. When I felt his hot skin against mine, the delicious weight of him on top of me, his mouth, his hands, I understood once again what making love really meant.

CHAPTER NINETEEN

LATER THAT DAY, WHEN the shadows lengthened and cast our room into shades of gray, I lay awake, looking at Nick's sleeping face. He lay on his stomach, his arms over his head, lashes dark smudges on his cheeks, which were flushed like a little kid's. Unlike Nick, I hadn't slept after Round Two. I'd been watching him instead, memorizing his face once again, the effects of the passage of twelve years, the glints of silver in his thick hair, the lines around his eyes. And yet he was the same, the boy who had approached me so long ago and told me I'd be his wife.

The debacle with my mother was pushed firmly into the cellar of my consciousness, where it belonged, replaced with the feelings I had—and, let's be honest, had always had—for Nick. I didn't know what would happen between us now, didn't know where this was going, and the very thought caused a cold trickle of fear. Maybe this was a mistake, sleeping with my ex. But it didn't feel that way. It felt like...love.

Nick jerked awake, as he always had, looking briefly confused. Then his eyes found mine. "Hey," he said.

"Hi," I whispered.

"I thought you might've left," he said, reaching out to push a strand of hair behind my ear.

"Um...nope. Still here."

For a long minute, we just looked at each other. "Nick... that night. Back then."

There was no need to explain which one. He knew. My

throat was still a bit raw from all the sobbing earlier, so I kept my voice at a whisper. "I didn't tell anyone I was married because I was punishing you. I was going to say something, I just…well. But I never would've cheated on you, Nick."

He nodded, and I continued. "When I saw you packing…I just…I just couldn't handle it. I couldn't believe we could get back to where we were before. It felt like you were leaving me forever. So I left, too. I left more, you know? That way, I could be the one doing it, not having it done to me."

"Harper," he said after a beat, "it was my fault, too."

This was new. In all our arguments, Nick had never acknowledged any wrongdoing; it had always been me who was supposed to change, accept, understand. He was just working for the future he'd always wanted, and I was the bafflingly miserable wife.

"I took you for granted," he admitted, taking my hand and studying it. "You tried to tell me you weren't happy, I didn't want to hear it, and I should've done better." He paused and looked into my eyes. "It wouldn't happen again."

Then he slid his hand into my hair and pulled me closer, and when he kissed me, my heart hurt from happiness, if such a thing was possible. "I missed you," I whispered against his mouth.

"Don't sound so surprised," he said, smiling.

"I guess I'll have to throw away my Nick voodoo doll."

He pulled back and looked at me, his eyes smiling. "Really? You'd do that for me?"

"Maybe."

"Good start." He kissed my chin. "Can I get an 'I love you, Nick'?"

"I think we've had enough sappy proclamations for the day," I answered.

He rolled onto his back, pulled me on top of him, his fingers trailing down my spine. "Say it, woman."

"It. Woman."

"God, you're a pain," he said, but he was laughing.

"I love you." The words, which had never come easily, slipped out of my mouth.

His laughter stopped abruptly, and his gypsy eyes softened. "Well, then," he whispered.

Then he kissed me again, and we didn't talk again for a good long while, unless you counted "Oh, God, don't stop" as real conversation.

Which I kind of did.

WHEN WE WERE STARVING and could no longer ignore Coco, who was staring at us from the foot of the bed without blinking, we showered and dressed and took her for a walk. Found a little park nearby and just sat under a tree and held hands, taking turns tossing Coco her ratty little tennis ball.

I didn't worry about running into my mother. For some reason, I was sure I wouldn't. Besides, I wanted to just be here, in this moment. The future was unclear, the past was a bog, but now...now was pretty wonderful.

"Harper. About Dennis," Nick said, his expression somber.

"Dennis and I broke up before we left Glacier," I said.

"What? Why didn't...never mind. You broke up, huh? And why was that?"

I glanced at Nick, then threw Coco the ball for the four hundred and seventeenth time. "Well, to be honest, because I wanted to get married, he didn't."

Nick cocked an eyebrow. "Really? You want to marry that guy?"

"Not anymore," I said. Thinking about Dennis still gave me a pang of guilt—that numbered list, my less-than-heartfelt marriage proposal. I was almost surprised I hadn't done a spreadsheet on the pros and cons of our relationship or devised a mathematical formula for our success potential.

"Are you sure you're done?" Nick asked.

I kissed the back of his hand. "Yep."

"Really sure?" he repeated.

"Asked and answered, Your Honor. Can we proceed, or do you need constant reassurance that I've chosen to be with you? For the moment. If you play your cards right."

Nick smiled. "Why do I put up with her, Lord? Come on, I'm starving. Let's eat."

We found a little restaurant that didn't mind a well-behaved dog and ordered dinner. Played footsies as we ate our burgers. We talked a little (and very carefully) about Chris and Willa, drifted into other subjects, places we'd been, places we wanted to see. Knowing Nick loved buildings of all types, I described the courthouse of Martha's Vineyard, its essential New England feel, the beautiful blue ceiling, the rows of benches, curving staircase and portraits of glowering judges. Nick in turn told me about the building he hoped to build for Drachen Industries, a German investment company.

"It would be our biggest project yet," he said. "They want it on the banks of the Volme River, and we'd use hydropower wherever we could, you know? And glass, of course. No point in being on the water if you can't see it from everywhere." I smiled, listening to his fast, New York way of talking, his clever hands flying. "Anyway, we're up against Foster, and they tend to kick butt wherever they go. But it's a little small for them, so you never know."

"Build me something," I said. "Right now, mister."

He cocked an eyebrow at me, then took my plate—the restaurant had provided enough fries to feed me for a month or so—and got to work. He trimmed some of the fries, laced a lettuce leaf with a toothpick, shaved off the remainder of my bun. Occasionally, he'd glance at me for a minute, as if assessing my needs as a client, but I kept quiet, just watched his beautiful hands cut and stack. Even at a silly task like this, he looked so…brilliant, so intent and focused as he carved a door out of a pickle.

"There," he said. "Your home. All green construction, of course."

And there it was, a surprisingly sophisticated little house made of French fries, cantilevered and shingled, complete with windows and a little bridge leading to the front door.

"Such a talent," I said, and he grinned.

"It's a little small," he said. "We'll have to expand when the triplets are born."

A small wriggle of warning danced through my knees. Nick, I knew from experience, never said anything that didn't mean *something*. This was, after all, the guy who'd called me "wife" before he even knew my name. The man with a plan that brooked no deviation. Not that I didn't want some kind of…something…with Nick, but as my feelings had been through the food processor in the past twelve hours, I—

"Oh, my God!" the waitress said, saving me. "Did you make that?"

We ordered coffee and a slab of chocolate lava cake for Nick. The subject of children, or the future, was not broached again. It was different, this night—in some ways, like a first date, in others, dinner with an old friend.

The buzz that always hummed between us was no longer painful, now that I wasn't pushing it away.

Maybe we could work this time.

It was raining softly when we left the restaurant, and we held hands as we walked, Coco pattering beside us, stopping to sniff a tree once in a while. The hiss of tires on the passing cars, the murmur of water in a drainpipe, the distant roll of thunder all seemed like a blessing.

"What do you want to do tomorrow?" Nick asked as we approached the hotel. Coco shook, droplets of rain spattering my already soaked jeans.

I thought for a moment. Work was stable for the moment; I'd emailed the clients who were affected by this week's sojourn, and the sky wasn't falling as far as I could tell. "I just want to be with you," I said, and realized that not only was it true, it felt pretty damn good to say out loud.

Nick seemed to like the answer, because he pressed me against the still-warm and wet brick wall of the hotel, and kissed me till my knees didn't work anymore. And when we went upstairs to our room, it felt like coming home.

WE WOKE UP IN A LOVELY tangle of limbs before dawn the next morning, spent quite a long time untangling, then decided to see the Sitting Bull monument on our field trip du jour. We said a fond farewell to the hotel, bought muffins and coffee from a little bakery, got some dog food, water and potato chips at the grocery store, and headed for the gravesite of the famous hero.

While I followed my New England imperative to apologize for all the wrongs committed by my ancestors and was murmuring "wicked sorry" to the statue, Nick got a phone call. As soon as he answered, I could tell something was wrong; his voice was terse and fast.

"Hello? Yes, this is he. What? When was that? How did he just walk out? Why wasn't…oh. You did, good. No, I'm in South Dakota at the moment." He was quiet for a minute. "No, he's on his honeymoon. Jason should be…oh. No, that's fine, I'm on my way."

My heart sank. "Everything okay, Nick?"

He looked at his phone for a long minute, then turned to me. "I have to go back to New York. My father's missing."

"Oh, no!"

He frowned, still not looking at me. "Apparently, he wandered off early this morning when the staff was dealing with another patient. The police are looking for him, but it's been two hours." He raised his eyes to mine. "I'm sorry, Harper. I have to get back. As soon as possible."

"No, no, of course. You have to go." I paused. "I'll come too," I added.

His eyebrows raised. "Really?"

"Sure. Let's go."

Because of course, what else was I going to do? Let him go alone? I couldn't help feeling a little sad that we had to go back so soon, just when we were together again. But it couldn't be helped.

Knowing my Massachusetts lead foot would get us to the airport faster, I drove while he made some calls—his office, a message for Christopher, one to a friend in the city. Last, he tried his stepbrother. "Jason, this is Nick. Dad's missing; he wandered away from the Roosevelt, and I'm in South Dakota, on my way to the airport. Call me when you get this." He hung up and tried another number, repeated the message. Tried a third, still to no avail. "Shit," he muttered.

"Is your stepmother still around?" I asked, vaguely recalling the unnaturally smooth and expressionless face of Lila Cruise Lowery from the two times I'd met her.

"She can't deal," Nick said shortly. "She said her heart was too broken to see him like this, so she hasn't been around. Moved to North Carolina a couple years ago. And anyway, she's on a cruise of the Greek isles at the moment."

Right. Her reason for missing Chris and Willa's wedding. "Where does Jason live, Nick? Is he any closer?"

"Jason lives in Philly, but he's not picking up right now." Coco, sensing Nick needed some sugar, licked his wrist. He gave a reluctant smile and patted her head, which she took as permission to curl up in his lap.

"They'll find him, Nick," I said, reaching over for his hand.

"I'm really sorry about this," he said again.

"By the time we get to the airport, you'll probably get a call saying he's back, safe and sound," I offered.

That wasn't the case, unfortunately, but the good news was, Nick's travel agent had found us a direct flight to New York. Coco was not pleased to have to go into her crate and looked at me mournfully through the bars before curling around her bunny with a reproachful sigh.

By far, the worst part of an emergency is the inability to act. As the plane finally took flight, Nick grew more and more tense. We held hands, but we didn't talk much as the minutes ticked by. The no-cell-phone rule kept us in limbo as to what was happening in New York, but as soon as wheels touched tarmac, Nick was on the phone again. No sign of his father.

When we emerged into the terminal, the noise of the JFK was deafening. I'd forgotten how loud the city was, the languages, the colors, people streaming in every direction. After a week on the road through beautiful nowhere, it was a shock. Nick, however, had reverted into the fast-walking New Yorker he was. We picked up Coco and our bags, and after walking for what felt like miles, made it outside, where the heat and noise and smell of jet fuel welcomed us to New York like a punch to the head.

A car service was waiting; Nick greeted the driver by name and helped heft our bags into the trunk. Then we headed toward Manhattan, which had briefly been my home. The skyline glittered, sharp and unforgiving and beautiful in the blazing sunshine.

Poor Mr. Lowery. He may have been a callow jerk in life, but now he was a confused old man, alone in the teeth of the city. Coco seemed to agree…she whined and trembled, though it was probably in response to the roar of the jets overhead, the cars surrounding us. The driver nudged the car onto the Queensboro Bridge, ignoring the blare of horns from behind.

"So what's the plan, Nick?" I asked. He was staring out the window, his mouth tight, eyes sharp.

"The officer in charge is waiting for us at the nursing home," he said. "He'll fill us in then. How my father could just wander out—" He shook his head and said no more.

Coco sat quietly on my lap, shivering occasionally as we headed up Park Avenue. It was a very posh area, of course; once I'd spent the afternoon around here, a lonely newlywed trying to fall in love with the city that was such a part of Nick. I pushed the memory aside and stared out the window, hoping against hope to see Nick's dad.

By the time we pulled up in front of the Roosevelt Center on East 65th Street, it was three-thirty in the afternoon, a miracle of efficiency on the part of Nick's travel agent and assistant, and still Nick's father was missing. A detective and the director of the facility, an understandably anxious woman named Alicia, greeted us and brought us into a sitting room.

"Mr. Lowery," she said to Nick, "you have my deepest apologies on this. Apparently, one of the new staffers inadvertently shut off the front door alarm, and—"

"We'll deal with how this happened later on," Nick said tersely. "What are you doing right now, where have you looked, what was my father wearing, how many people are out looking?"

They filled us in on the efforts thus far—an APB, photos, news coverage, neighborhood canvassing, K-9 unit. They handed us the flyer they were passing out, which featured a large, clear photo of Nick's dad. My heart lurched. Mr. Lowery—*Call me Ted*—had aged shockingly. His hair was thin and white, and his face held a slack, sweet expression. He couldn't have been more than sixty-five, but he looked eighty.

"Is there anywhere he might've wanted to go, Nick?" I asked when the briefing was over. I didn't watch *Law & Order* for nothing.

"I was just about to ask that," Detective Garcia said.

Nick ran a hand through his hair. "Did you call his old company?" he asked. "Maybe he went there."

A quick phone call ascertained that Mr. Lowery had not shown up at his old building on Madison Avenue. Though it seemed unlikely that he'd have the ability to find his way back to his old house in Westchester County, the current owners were notified and asked to call immediately if they saw him.

Neither Lila nor Jason had returned Nick's calls.

"Any sentimental places he'd go, Nick?" I asked. "Central Park? Maybe his favorite restaurant? The zoo?" I hesitated. "Places he took you boys as kids?"

Nick glanced at me, then slumped back in his chair. "I don't know," he admitted. Because of course, Ted hadn't taken him many places at all. "Jason might have a better idea." He closed his eyes. "Well, I'm not going to just sit here," he said. "I'll head for the park. What was he wearing this morning?"

The director glanced anxiously at Detective Garcia. "Well, here," she said. "We have the security tape, in which you can clearly see your father leaving and heading west."

The tape was already loaded; the director clicked the remote, and we saw the front entrance of the Roosevelt Center. A second later, the film showed a man simply walking out the door.

The quality of the film was good; it was definitely Mr. Lowery, clad in what appeared to be a sport coat, dark T-shirt and sneakers.

No pants. None at all. I clutched Coco a little more tightly.

"Oh, shit," Nick muttered. "He's wandering the city bare-assed?"

I bit my lip, and Nick glanced at me. "Don't laugh," he warned, but his mouth twitched.

"No. Not funny at all," I agreed. "I'll go with you, Nick."

Coco, Nick and I took a bunch of flyers and headed west, toward the park and Museum Mile, past the limestone and brick townhouses adorned with wrought-iron balconies, down the tree-lined streets of the wealthy. We passed a homeless man, sleeping next to the garbage cans in front of a beautiful brownstone. It wasn't Mr. Lowery, but Nick took a good look anyway, then took a twenty out of his wallet and tucked it into the guy's boot.

"I thought the mayor discouraged that," I said.

"Screw the mayor," Nick answered. I had to trot to keep up. Coco, however, loved the pace and galloped joyfully on her leash. Despite biking to and from work each day, I was panting by the time we reached Fifth Avenue. It was so hot, and the air was heavy and damp.

"Nick, can you slow down a little?"

"My father's out there somewhere," he said tightly, walking across the street against the light. Swallowing, I dashed after him—I'd never mastered the art of jaywalking.

"Nick, wait," I said. I grabbed his hand and dug in my heels, stopping him. "Just…wait."

"Harper—" His voice choked off, and I wrapped my arms around him and kissed his neck.

"This will turn out okay, you'll see," I said. "But it's a big city. Let's try to be smart about this, because we can't just run all over Manhattan. Where do you think he'd go?"

He pulled back and rubbed his eyes. "I don't know, Harper. I just…we never did that much together. If that idiot Jason would call, maybe he'd know, but I just can't think of anything."

"Okay, well, what do we know? He's not at work…anything he's always loved? Like, I don't know…dinosaurs? Maybe he'd head to the Museum of Natural History?"

Nick shrugged. "I don't think so."

"What about horses? He rode, right? Isn't there a stable somewhere in the park?"

Nick's face lit up. "You're a genius, Harper." With that, he hailed a cab.

TWO HOURS LATER, WE'D come up empty. No sign of Mr. Lowery, not at either of the two uptown stables, not at the recreation center in the park itself where the trail rides began. Nick had called the police with the idea that his father might've sought out a place with horses, and they were doing the same thing we were, with unfortunately the same results.

We passed out a bunch of flyers, spoke to everyone we could, but things were looking bad. At this point, we were simply walking through Central Park, which was full of the usual suspects—tourists from all over the earth, runners, students lounging on the grass, kids climbing on the rocks. I'd forgotten how loud New York was, the endless noise of traffic, horns blasting, sirens calling, the chatter of people, the blare of radios and street musicians.

Nick had been checking in with the nursing home and cops every fifteen minutes. Apparently, there'd been a few reports of a man matching Mr. Lowery's description, but none had turned out to be the real deal.

I myself was sticky, dirty and getting more and more anxious as the day wore on. And starving—my last meal, for lack of a better word, had been a pack of pretzels on the airplane. I bought a hot dog from a street vendor for Coco while Nick was on the phone, but only had enough cash for one. I carried Coco now, concerned about the effects of asphalt on her little paws, and my arms were aching. She may have weighed only eight pounds, but she felt like an unconscious Great Dane at this point.

It was hard not to picture the worst-case scenario... poor Mr. Lowery wandering onto the West Side Highway or falling into the East River or being hurt by an evil thug. My heart ached for Nick—such a devoted son, despite his father's shortcomings.

Jason had called; apparently he was at a casino in Vegas and had no suggestions on where to look for his adoptive father. Chris was still out of reach, though Nick left him another message.

"We'll find him," I said, not at all convinced of the truth of that statement. Nick nodded, clearly disheartened.

Then his phone rang. "Nick Lowery," he answered. His expression changed. "Where? Okay. We're on our way." He hung up, grabbed my hand and started running for the street. "You were right about the horses," he said. "Someone spotted a guy with no pants down by the carriages and called it in. Taxi!" A yellow cab veered out of traffic and Nick opened the door. I slid in, Coco in my arms, more grateful than I could say at getting off my feet.

"Fifth and Fifty-Ninth," Nick told the cabbie, then turned to me. "By the time the cop got to the spot where the guy had seen him, Dad was gone, but someone maybe saw him heading down Fifth, so…" His voice was hopeful, his knee jiggling with nervous energy.

It was clear the cops were on the job, because there was a glut of black-and-white cruisers there on Fifth where horse carriages lined the sidewalks across from the Plaza Hotel. Nick's phone rang again. "Yeah? Okay. Okay, sure." He clicked off. "Another possible sighting by St. Pat's." He knocked on the Plexiglas divider. "Keep going down Fifth, okay?" he asked. "Real slow. I'm looking for my dad."

We passed FAO Schwartz and CBS, Bergdorf Goodman and Tiffany's, as well as places that hadn't been there when I'd lived here—Niketown and Abercrombie. There was Rolex, Cartier Jeweler's, St. Thomas, the beautiful Episcopal church with the blue stained-glass windows and white marble altar, a place where I'd sought refuge from the heat one summer day. Midtown was packed, as it was now well into rush hour.

"You'd think someone would stop an old guy without pants," I murmured, looking out my side of the window. Then again, this was New York City.

"Yeah," Nick said, gnawing on his thumbnail. At St. Patrick's Cathedral, his phone rang again, just as we were pulling over. "Shit. Where? Okay." He hung up. "Keep going, okay?" he asked the cabbie.

"Whatever you want, mister," the driver answered, glancing in the rearview mirror.

"They got a call from someone who might've seen

him farther downtown," Nick informed me, looking out the window. "The cops are all over St. Pat's, but nothing yet."

Half a block farther, Nick lurched forward. "Stop! Pull over! There he is," he said, pointing.

And sure enough, Mr. Lowery—though I wouldn't have recognized him—was shambling along in front of the flag-bedecked building that was Saks Fifth Avenue. Still no pants, I noted. Traffic was thick, and Nick didn't bother waiting for the driver to make it to the curb. He threw a few bills at the driver and was out of the car before it stopped. A good number of horns blasted as he dodged through the heavy traffic to the sidewalk. "Be careful!" I shouted.

The cabbie pulled over—on the opposite side of the street from Saks, alas, but traffic was like a solid wall. "Good luck," he said as I got out with Coco.

"Thanks," I called. Dang. I couldn't see Nick or Mr. Lowery—wait, there was Nick, just disappearing into Saks. Surely the security guards would grab Mr. Lowery.

Clutching the ever-heavier Coco to my chest, I ran to the corner to cross the street with the light, dodging people, bumping into more than a few. "Sorry, sorry," I said, waiting impatiently for the light to change yet unwilling to defy death by crossing against it.

Then I saw Mr. Lowery. He wasn't in Saks…he was across the street in all his pantsless wonder, sport coat still on, scratching his, um…okay! Where was a cop when you needed one? And of course, Nick was inside the store.

At least now Mr. Lowery was getting some attention; passersby stared, grabbed their kids and steered well clear of him as he crossed the intersection, looked up at the store on the corner, and went inside.

It was American Girl Place, that bastion of juvenile

femininity. Dolls. Dress-up clothes. Tea parties. And now, a half-naked old man.

"Oh, shit," I muttered.

Then the light changed, and I flew across the street and into the foyer of the store, which was packed with, oh, hell, *dozens* of girls and their parents, red-and-white bags everywhere. Holding Coco tightly as she wriggled in excitement, I stood on tiptoe and peered in each direction. No Mr. Lowery. Come on! Where'd he go? He hardly blended in here.

There he was, just disappearing around a display of cheerful dolls all dressed in purple leotards.

"Mommy!" said a little girl. "I can see that man's—"

"OMG!" I shouted as loudly as I could. "Justin Bieber is right outside! I just saw Justin Bieber!"

The air split with high-pitched squealing, and suddenly, several dozen girls stampeded for the door. I dodged, twisted, got a little trampled, but then again, I just saved about a hundred girls from learning far too much about the aging male anatomy. Dodging shrieking females, I ran to where Mr. Lowery had disappeared. Coco barked as I passed a tired-looking security guard (who obviously wasn't all that good at her job!). "No dogs in the store, ma'am," she said wearily.

"Yeah, and no naked old men, either, but that's what you have, so let's shake it, okay?" I called over my shoulder. There was an escalator in front of me, a hallway to my right. I hesitated, then charged up the escalator, and there he was, right in front of gift wrapping. His thin white hair was disheveled, his shoes filthy. The young woman behind the counter apparently couldn't see that he had nothing on below the waist except Nikes, because she asked very sweetly, "And what can I do for you today, sir?"

"Mr. Lowery?" I said. He didn't turn my way. The security guard arrived, panting a bit. "Can you get him something to wear?" I whispered.

"Like what? Felicity's nightgown?" she muttered. "My shift ended two minutes ago."

"Be helpful," I said. "Random act of kindness, okay?" I cleared my throat. "Mr. Lowery? Ted?"

He turned, and my heart broke a little.

"Hi," I said. "How are you? Haven't seen you for a while." I smiled past the lump in my throat. He didn't much resemble the man I once knew, that smug, confident schmoozer who neglected his firstborn son. No. This man was confused, lost and old before his time.

"Do I know you?" he asked hesitantly.

"I'm your son's wife," I said.

"Jason? Jason's married?" He frowned.

"No. Not yet. I'm Nick's wife. Harper. Remember?"

"Nick?"

"Yes. Your son Nick. Your oldest boy." I smiled again and approached slowly—after all, this guy had been dodging NYPD all day, and I didn't want him cavorting through the store, flashing little girls.

"Oh, yes. I have boys. Sons."

"Good guys, too. Handsome like their dad, right?"

He smiled at that, and I saw a hint of the man he'd once been. "That's a nice dog," he said, reaching out to pet Coco. Bless her noble heart, she licked his hand and wagged, and Mr. Lowery smiled. "Can I hold him?" he asked.

"Sure. But she's a girl."

"I only have sons," he said.

The guard came back with a blanket. "Best we could do," she said, much less grumpily.

"I'm gonna call Nick, okay, Mr. Lowery? He's been on a trip, and he's dying to see you," I said.

The man who was once my father-in-law looked up at me and grinned, the ghost of his old personality flitting across his face. "Call me Ted."

CHAPTER TWENTY

THREE HOURS LATER, I was alone in the very comfortable sitting room of the Roosevelt Center, Coco snoring on my lap. She was happy—she ate a cheeseburger as big as she was, then morphed into a therapy dog, charming the residents with her tricks of paw-raising and leaping straight up and down. Nick had been busy getting his father settled, then had to go off with the director to fill out forms, receive apologies, inspect the alarm system and God knew what else.

I sighed, bone-weary. It was hard to believe today had begun with Nick and me in bed together, somewhere in the heartland. Yesterday (yesterday!), I'd seen my mother. Less than a week ago, my sister had gotten married. My father was getting divorced, and God only knew what would happen to BeverLee.

I thought of my little house in Menemsha, of sitting on the deck with Kim and a glass of wine, the sound of the water splashing against the hulls of the fishing boats, the wind shushing in the long grass. It seemed like a lifetime since I'd been home.

Apparently, those thoughts were just too much to be wrangled with, because I dozed off. Next thing I knew, Nick was kneeling in front of me. "Hey," he said with a smile.

"Hi," I answered, lurching upright. "How's your dad?"

"Sleeping. He's doing okay. He was a little dehydrated,

but otherwise, fine." He looked at me, and the clock seemed to stop. "You were great today, Harper," he said. Then he put his head in my lap and closed his eyes, and a wave of love washed over me so big and strong it took my breath away.

"Well, chasing after pantsless men has always been a hobby of mine," I whispered. "There's a website for us. PantslessMenLovers.com." I stroked Nick's hair, and as always, the glints of silver in the dark brown gave me a pang. Who took care of Nick? I wondered. He looked after everyone else…Christopher, Willa, his father…and, for this past week, me. Well, for tonight, anyway, I'd take care of him.

"You ready to go home, big guy?" I asked.

Nick looked up, his eyes crinkling. "Yeah. As fun as it's been, I'm ready for this day to be over."

We got a cab, and when Nick gave the address, my mouth fell open. "Really?" I asked.

He shrugged. Maybe he blushed, though it was hard to tell in the erratic light as we headed downtown. Coco yawned, then jumped as a horn blasted.

Twenty minutes later, I saw that it was true.

Nick had never moved from the building where we'd lived together.

As I got out of the cab, the screech of the subway split the air, just as it had so many years ago. Coco twitched and shivered in my arms.

Still a little stunned to be back in the neighborhood, I stared at the building as Nick got our bags from the trunk of the cab. Same pillars, same tall, narrow windows. Nick hit the code on the panel and opened the front door, and as I stepped into the foyer, the same cool smell of stone greeted me. And cabbage. "Don't tell me Ivan still lives here," I said.

"I'm afraid so," Nick answered.

We went up the stairs—four flights, same as when we'd lived there. My heart pounded at the memories…a lot of lonely days, a lot of doubt and fear and homesickness.

A lot of missing Nick.

Inside, though, everything was different, and that… well, that was a relief. I put Coco down, and she trotted off to explore and sniff.

Previously, the apartment had occupied a quarter of the fourth floor in a cramped, awkward design, but the co-op builders had made what had been four apartments into one. Gone were the graying plaster walls, the linoleum that peeled up in the corner of the kitchen, the tiny closet where we'd had to stuff our coats.

Instead, the apartment was much more what you'd imagine for a Tribeca co-op—exposed brick walls, distressed hardwood floor. Nick had always suspected that under the cheap carpeting lurked oak, and while he'd planned to find it, he'd never had time. At least, not while I was around. There was a generous galley kitchen with stone counters and stainless-steel light fixtures, a counter with two very modern-looking stools. A small but comfortable office, impressive computer screen and an entire wall of books on architecture. Dark leather couches in the living room punctuated by steel and glass end tables. On one wall hung an old black-and-white subway sign listing the stops of one of the lines.

"Pottery Barn?" I asked.

Nick shot me a look. "Original, thank you very much. So. This is it. What do you think?"

"It's very nice, Nick. Very…you."

"Thanks."

And it was…or I guessed it was. Back when I knew Nick, he'd wanted all this so much—to prove himself to his father, to be successful at the job he loved, to be financially secure, well regarded. But it was freaking me out a little, too, to be in the home where we'd been, forgive the honesty, so miserable.

We looked at each other for a minute. "You hungry?" I asked. "I'm excellent at making peanut butter sandwiches."

"That's okay," Nick said. "I ate at the nursing home." Drat. I'd kind of been looking forward to cooking for him. So 1950s of me. "Do you want anything?" he added.

"No, I'm good."

We stood there another beat or two, and it occurred to me that maybe Nick felt a little uncertain, too. Should we cuddle? Shag? I was fairly grimy. "Well, how about a shower?"

"Absolutely. Right this way." Down the hall—we'd had no hall, it was too small for that—and into a wicked awesome bathroom tiled with speckled brown granite. A glassed-in shower area, a sink that looked more like a piece of modern art than somewhere to spit toothpaste. "Towels are here," he said, and there they were, plush and inviting. "Anything else you need? I'll put your suitcase in the, um, in the bedroom."

So he *was* nervous. For some reason, I found that quite the turn-on. Aw…he was blushing, and his hair was standing almost straight up, so many times had he run a hand through it in frustration and fear this long day. Right now he looked both hopeful and weary.

I turned on the water and stood for a second, watching it gush out of the generous showerhead. "Nick?"

"Yeah?"

I undid the first button of my shirt. "Wanna save water?"

He looked at me for a second, then smiled, that flashing, transforming smile. You see, back when he was a grad student and I was in college, back before so much had gotten in our way, that had been our little joke—save water, wash up and oh, yes, maybe indulge in a little steamy sex, as well.

"We *are* in a drought," he said, then crossed the small distance between us, wrapped his arms around me and moved so that we were both in the shower, fully clothed and now soaking wet. I smiled against his mouth and then unbuttoned his shirt and did my best to take care of him.

CHAPTER TWENTY-ONE

THE NEXT MORNING AFTER breakfast (bagels, of course...
New York did have a few things going for it), Nick called
the nursing home to check on his father. While he was on
the phone, I booted up my laptop and checked my messages. There was my real life, waiting for me to return.
Tommy was still in wedded bliss with his faithless wife
and had attached a picture of the two of them standing
in front of the Gay Head Light. He was smiling. She was
not. I grimaced, wondered if it would be crass to advise
him to get checked for herpes, and typed a brief, noncommittal reply. Theo was curious as to when I'd grace
the office with my presence (code for *get your ass back
here*). I reminded him that I had nine weeks of time off
accrued and would be happy to point out the firm's policy
on vacations in the manual I myself had written a few
years back. I also wrote Carol a note with a cc to Theo,
telling her that if Theo didn't relax, she was free to slip
him a few horse tranquilizers and we'd just see what that
did to his golf game.

There was nothing from Dad—that wasn't a surprise...I
don't think the man had ever sent me an email or called
of his own volition. But nothing from BeverLee, either,
which was unusual. And nothing from Willa, which
struck me as ominous.

With a glance down the hall at Nick, who was speaking
now to a doctor, I logged in to my credit card account.
Just for the heck of it. There, dated yesterday, was a $108

charge to Bitter Creek B&B in Rufus, Montana. Huh. Well, good. The kids had left the great outdoors for a shower and a bed. Couldn't blame them.

In the past when she used my credit card, Willa was always very specific about what exactly she'd be doing... not asking permission, but letting me know she wasn't going wild, either. This was a first.

My computer beeped; an email from Carol. *Horse tranquilizers administered. Miss your grouchy ass. Where the hell are you?*

New York City, I typed back. *Yankees fans everywhere. Will do my best to cull the population. See you Monday.*

Then I dropped a note to Kim, asking her to water the one houseplant I owned (a cactus, go ahead, make the joke) and if she wanted anything from the Big Apple. Another inbox chime. *Is Derek Jeter available?* she wrote. *And why are you in New York? You still with your ex-husband? Are you sleeping together? I'm calling you right now.* On cue, my cell phone rang—Ozzy's "Crazy Train," Kim's favorite song. I opted to skip the call and kept typing.

Can't talk now, long story. Will be back this weekend. Gotta run. Sorry.

"Want to come in to the firm? See where I work?" Nick asked, appearing in the doorway with a cup of coffee in his hand. The man was irresistible, and damn if he just didn't improve hourly. Dressed in a crisp white shirt and tan pants, he hadn't shaved today. Sigh!

"Sure, I'd love to." I snapped down the lid of my laptop, then remained seated. "But Nick, I have to get back to Martha's Vineyard, too." I paused a second. "This whole...um, trip wasn't on the calendar. I need to think about home."

"Oh, sure. But not today, right? I mean, yesterday didn't

really count. You should stay till Sunday. Actually, traffic sucks on Sundays. So stay till Monday." He paused and looked into his coffee cup. "Or longer."

The first warning bell chimed, far off but still audible. "Well, I have court on Tuesday, and I need to prep for that. And you know, my regular stuff back home."

"Right. Unless…well. Never mind. Let's go."

"BOSS! YOU'RE BACK!"

Within seconds of walking into the fifth floor of the Singer Building, Nick was swamped by employees. He greeted everyone by name, shook hands, answered questions about the wedding. I recognized Emily; she offered a tentative smile, and I gave her a little wave back, feeling oddly shy.

"This is Harper," Nick said. "Willa's sister." His hand rested lightly on my back—a message, perhaps, that I was to be treated well. The seven or eight people clustered around the reception desk fell silent. Ah.

"Holy shit," said someone. "I don't believe it."

I found the owner of the voice. "Hi. Peter, right?"

Pete Camden had worked at MacMillan with Nick. They'd been the two anointed rookies, the *wunderkinds*. Though I had met him only once, his name was burned into my memory…the night of our big fight, Nick had gone to stay with Peter Camden.

"Jesus Humphrey Christ. It really is you." He gave me a cold look.

"Pete, you remember Harper," Nick said.

"Oh, I remember, all right," Peter answered. No one else said anything for a second.

"Want the tour?" Nick asked, then took my hand and started to lead me away from the gaggle.

"Nick," Peter called, "stop in my office when you have a sec, okay? I've got something on Drachen." He slapped

Nick on the shoulder. "Great to have you back, buddy."
He ignored me.

"So my legend precedes me?" I asked Nick as we went
down the hall.

He shot me a look and didn't answer. "Here's my
office," he said, opening a door. The room was spacious
and open, decorated with blond wood furniture and a
red leather sofa. An antique drafting table anchored one
end of the room, a large desk and ergonomically graceful
chair on the other. The windows overlooked Prince Street,
and I could see the wrought-iron facade for which the
building was rightly famous. In the center of the room was
a huge smoked-glass conference table laden with neatly
rolled blueprints and a model of a ten- or twelve-story
building.

"So this is the Drachen model?" I asked.

"Yeah," Nick said. "What do you think?"

It was like a really sophisticated dollhouse, charming
and detailed. I bent to get a better look, smiling at the
little details inside, the models of people outside, the trees
and walled gardens that would line the entryway, should
Nick get the job. "It's beautiful, Nick."

"Thanks," he said with a smile. "Here are some of the
other buildings we've done." He pointed me to the photos
hanging on the wall.

They were stunning. I didn't know too much about
architecture other than what I'd absorbed during my time
with Nick, but I could tell his stuff was special, modern
yet not ridiculous, if you know what I mean. Nothing
was shaped like a penis, in other words. Nick's buildings echoed the surrounding architecture of the neighborhoods, but they were unique, too, in some indefinable
way. I looked long and hard at the photos, aware of Nick's
eyes on me. "I like the curves on this one," I said, pointing
to one.

"That's a little hotel in Beijing," he said. "I wanted it to feel soft, you know, since it overlooked the botanical garden. The foyer is done in the shape of a gingko leaf… see?"

I nodded, charmed.

"And where's this one?" I asked, pointing to the next photo.

"That's a private museum in Budapest. That one was really fun. We used this curved facade out here, and again over here. There's a solar-powered waterfall in the café, over here…" He moved on, pointing and commenting, like a kid during show-and-tell, his enthusiasm and love of his job lighting up his face. He belonged here, doing this.

"Nick? Gotta sec?" Peter appeared in the doorway. "Sorry to interrupt." He flicked his gaze toward me, obviously not sorry at all.

"Go ahead," I murmured. "I'm fine."

"Okay. Back in a flash," Nick said, leaving me alone.

Behind the desk were a few other framed photos that caught my interest—a nice one of Nick and Christopher, both in tuxes. Maybe at Nick's other wedding.

Crikey. I'd almost forgotten about that. Somewhere in this city was the other former Mrs. Nick—and her much adored kid. Sure enough, here was another photo— Isabel, if I recalled correctly—standing next to Nick in front of the Guggenheim. And voila, another one. Nick, an attractive woman with a sleek blond bob, and Isabel, perhaps twelve, all smiling on a white-sand beach. A family vacation.

Guess Nick wasn't always a workaholic.

Stifling the flash of jealousy, I stuck my head out the door. No sign of Nick. I wandered down the hall to the foyer. Two of Nick's employees, a man and a woman, were in a huddle over the reception desk, their voices low.

"So apparently," the man was saying, "they used to be married, and she cheated on him, broke his heart."

"Are you serious?" she asked.

"I didn't cheat on him," I said clearly. They jumped, totally busted. "Anything else I can clarify for you?" I tipped my head and smiled my angel-killing smile.

The woman scuttled back to her desk. The man, unfortunately for him, was the actual receptionist. Nowhere to run.

"Worked here long?" I asked cheerfully.

"Five years," he mumbled.

"So you know my sister, then?" I asked.

"I sure do," he said. "Sweet kid." He paused. "I'm Miguel. Sorry about the gossip. It's just…well, we all love Nick." He gave a rueful smile.

"Nice meeting you," I said, opting for the high road (and considering it my random act of kindness for the day). I offered my hand, and Miguel took it.

"You don't seem nearly as evil as Pete says." He cringed. "Jesus, what's wrong with me today? I'm not even drunk."

I laughed. "So, Miguel, how many people work here?"

"About fifteen. We subcontract out a lot, depending on where the job is."

I nodded. "So did Chris Lowery work here, too?"

"Sometimes," Miguel readily answered. "Nick gets him stuff with our finish carpenters once in a while. He worked here full time a while back, but Nick finally fired him and wouldn't take him back until he got sober."

The word slammed into me like a cannonball, but the receptionist didn't notice and kept talking. "He came back, let's see…a year ago? A little less? Yeah, it was just after Christmas, and he looked great, you know?"

"Christopher's an alcoholic?" My voice was flat and hard.

Miguel's eyes widened. "I…did I say that? I…um… you know, maybe you should ask Nick."

I stared at Miguel unblinking, my heart rolling in slow, deliberate thuds. Vaguely, I recalled Nick saying something about Chris having a hard time lately. Ah. Mystery solved. Did Willa know about this?

"Nick!" Miguel chirped nervously. "Speak of the devil! Hi! You guys going to lunch? Want me to make a res somewhere?"

Nick looked between Miguel and me. "Hungry?" he asked me.

I didn't answer.

"Harper? Want to go somewhere?"

"Sure," I said.

Nick cocked his head and frowned at me. "Okay. Let's go, then. See you, Miggy."

"Have a great time! Boss, will you be back later?"

"No," Nick said. "I'll check in, though."

I didn't speak as we left the building.

"Harper?" Nick asked as we walked down the street. "Everything okay?"

"Not really," I said.

"Yes, I get the impression you're ready to murder a kitten," he said, taking my arm to steer me around a broken chunk of sidewalk.

I pulled my arm back. "I'm not going to murder a kitten, Nick. I'm just…"

"Just what?"

"Sucker-punched."

He stopped. "How?"

"I just learned that my sister married an alcoholic who

hasn't even been sober a year." It was difficult to keep my voice calm. "I have concerns."

Nick looked at the sidewalk. "And somehow this is my fault, yes?"

"It would've been nice to know, Nick."

"Come on. Let's not fight on the sidewalk." He steered me into a restaurant. "Table for two, please," he said to the young woman at the counter.

"We're closed," she muttered, turning the page of her magazine. She had a tattoo on her shoulder—Hello Kitty wearing an eye patch. "We open at 11:30."

"It's 11:29," I pointed out a trifle sharply.

"Fine." She snatched up a few leather-bound menus and led us to a table under a large clock, then stomped away.

I took a breath, then another. Nick didn't look at me, just began building a tower out of sugar packets.

"All right," he said, "Christopher checked into a program last winter. He's been sober for about ten months."

"And how long has he had a drinking problem?" I asked, calmly. Felt as if I was in a deposition.

"Since high school."

Crotch. Half his life, in other words. I took a long sip of water, not able to look at Nick.

"Harper, I know it's not what you want to hear, but it's not really your problem, is it?" Nick asked. "Chris has a good heart, and he's trying really hard." More sugar packets were put to use.

I unclenched my jaw. "Nick, Willa's been married twice before to good-hearted men who tried really hard. Husband Number One tried really hard to stay out of jail. That lasted three weeks. Husband Number Two tried really hard not to be gay. That lasted about a month and a half."

"She knows how to pick 'em," Nick said, glancing up with a grin.

I bit my lip hard, started to say something, then broke off. "Nick," I said in a harsh whisper, "I don't want to see my sister go through another divorce. Divorce sucks, as we both know. It's not funny. She has terrible judgment when it comes to men."

He added another layer to his tiny building.

"Will you stop doing that?" I said, reaching over and grabbing the packets.

"You just wrecked Taipei 101," he said. Then he sighed, sitting back in his chair. "Look, Harper, I don't know what to say. I know you want to protect Willa, but she's an adult. So is Chris."

"Really, Nick? The inventor of the Thumbie and the girl who hasn't held any job for more than two consecutive months?"

His mouth tightened. "Not your call, Harper."

"And here's the other thing, Nick." I tried to keep my voice neutral. "We're…together now. Sort of. You slept with me, but you didn't tell me about this, and I just feel… blindsided."

"There hasn't been a lot of time, Harper," he said.

There'd been time. That dinner in Aberdeen when he made me the house out of French fries. Last night, when we'd raided the kitchen around midnight. "Well," I said, opting to let those go, "would you have told me eventually?"

He didn't answer. Which was, of course, an answer. "So you have no problem sleeping with me, but I'm only privy to some things," I said. "And you decide what those things are."

He held up his hands. "Okay. Just…stop. Just for a minute, okay?" He looked up, smiled his thanks at the waitress. "We're not quite ready to order," he said.

"Fine," she said. "You guys were, like, the ones beating down the door to get in here."

"Back off, missy," I snapped.

"Fine," she repeated, rolling eyes and storming away yet again.

"You know she's going to spit in our food," Nick said.

"Nick, back to the subject at hand," I ground out.

He sighed. "Look. Let's not argue about Chris and Willa, because that gets us nowhere."

"Does Willa even know?" I asked.

"You mean, did I sit her down and tell her about Christopher's drinking? No. I didn't. It wasn't my place."

"Are you aware that concealment of addiction can be grounds for annulment, Nick?"

His mouth tightened. "Harper, their marriage and issues and problems are theirs. Not ours. So please, let's not ruin things by talking about another couple."

I tried not to grind my teeth. "Nick, two things. First, given the fact that I constantly bail Willa out of disastrous situations, I think I should've known about this. And I'm feeling a little…hurt that you didn't see fit to tell me. But I'll let that go. Or I'll try. Secondly, their issues *do* affect us! These are our siblings, Nick. Not some strangers. If they get a divorce, that matters to us."

"You're such a cynic." He shook his head.

"Don't start. I'm a realist, okay? Don't forget what I do for a living."

"As if you'd let me."

We stared at each other across the table. The feeling of impasse was very familiar.

"Let's change the subject, okay?" Nick suggested gently. He reached over and took my hand.

"Sure," I said briskly. "What would you like to discuss? The weather? Baseball?"

Nick grinned. "The Yankees beat the Sox last night. Ten to three."

"You're hardly getting on my good side, Nick." But I allowed a small smile.

His smile grew. "Okay, well, let's talk about your law practice. You could pass the New York bar exam in a heartbeat, don't you think? Or would you even have to, since you're already practicing in another state?"

And sucker-punched again. I blinked. "The bar?"

Then Nick's phone chimed gently. "This might be the nursing home," he said, pulling his phone out. He glanced at it. "Nope. It's just Pete."

"Take it," I replied without thinking.

"It can wait."

"No. Go ahead. I could use a minute anyway."

He hesitated, then stood up. "Okay. Be right back." He went outside, and I watched through the window as he talked, then listened. He glanced at me, then spoke some more. Shook his head. Looked my way again, waved, kept talking.

The New York *bar exam*? That one came right out of left field. My knees were still buzzing with surprise. The electrical current that ran between Nick and me…it had always carried the danger of electrocution.

I took a shaky breath. The last time we were together, Nick had rushed ahead with a lot of plans. Get engaged, quick wedding. He'd found our apartment and signed the lease before I even saw the place, saying that to wait would've meant losing it. And of course, when we were married, it had been all about his plan, his schedule, his career.

This time…this time would have to be different. The last thing I wanted was to make the same mistake twice.

Nick came back to the table and sat back down. His knee started bouncing.

"Everything okay?" I asked.

"Sure. Everything's great." He hesitated. "You know the Drachen project?" I nodded. "The company's CEO is in New York. Peter managed to pin him down for a late lunch."

"Great," I said.

"I won't go," Nick said. His knee continued to bounce. "Do you want to order?"

"Um...no." I took another deep breath. "Nick. You should...you should go. To the lunch."

"No," he said quickly. "I'm with you today."

"No, you should go. You really wanted this one. This is your chance."

He didn't answer.

"I'll be fine," I added. "Does the CEO come to the States that often?"

"No," he acknowledged.

"So you should go!"

Nick just looked at me, his dark eyes assessing, and as ever, time seemed to stop. Except it didn't—the clock above us chimed softly.

"I have a million emails to return," I said, "and Nick, you know you want this deal. So go. Okay? I'll see you back at your place." I stood up, kissed his cheek and left.

CHAPTER TWENTY-TWO

BACK AT NICK'S APARTMENT, I took Coco for a walk. She hated the noise, jumping back from the curb when a car passed, quivering at the sound of air brakes or the clatter of a jackhammer. I ended up carrying her most of the way. She could probably adjust, but it seemed rather cruel to ask that of her. She was used to the wind and sand and salt air. Not this.

When we got back, I checked my email, answered a few, then wandered around the apartment, feeling a little stir-crazy. Opened a cabinet here, a drawer there. There were a couple of framed pictures of Isabel. One of Nick, Christopher, Jason and Mr. Lowery. Another of him and Peter in front of a temple. Japan, maybe.

On his desk was a leather-bound day calendar. I flipped it open. Funny, that in this age of phones with every conceivable app from foot massages to ghost whispering, Nick kept a handwritten record of his appointments. There was last week…in his blocky architect's handwriting, Nick had written *C&W's wedding*. Later that week, *Whalen U., School of Engineering*.

This coming week, it appeared he'd be going to Dubai. Later in the month, Seattle. In October, Nick was scheduled to be in Houston, London and Seattle again.

Business was good.

I sat in his chair for a little while. Coco, sensing my melancholy, jumped into my lap and put her head on my shoulder. She seemed blue, too. The subway screeched from down the block, and my dog shivered in fear. "You'd think they'd have fixed those brakes by now, huh, Coco?" I asked, petting her sleek little back. From the floor below, I could hear the strains of bouncy music and some muffled voices—Ivan, watching the soaps.

Some things never changed, and I wasn't just talking about Ivan's taste in daytime television. Nick's business was thriving; God knows, he worked hard enough and deserved every success. I wouldn't want it any other way... and yet...and yet, things were feeling awfully familiar. He wanted me to move to New York, to fit my life in around his. Again. And the way he'd mentioned it, so flip and assured—*You could pass the New York bar in a heartbeat.* We didn't even know what next week would look like, but he was already assuming I'd uproot everything and move back to his city.

And that whole thing with Chris...that didn't bode well, either. Nick deliberately withheld something critically important from me. Not without reason—I could see his point about it being Christopher's to share or not share—but still. It didn't feel good. The way he'd had that meeting scheduled in Bismarck but hadn't mentioned it, had made our trip feel completely spur-of-the-moment, while all the time, he'd had a plan and a schedule.

Ivan's soap cut to commercial, and the merits of Huggies diapers were extolled at an excruciating decibel. It was so odd to be back here, so disconcerting. Different, but still the same. Gone was the small kitchen where Nick and I had shared so few meals, where the steam radiators had ticked and hissed as I'd waited for him to come home. Gone was the tiny alcove in the living room where Nick had ensconced himself in front of the computer on the rare nights he made it home before nine or ten. Gone was our old bedroom where we'd fought so often. And yet, here we were, same building, same structure, same foundation. It was glossier and more sophisticated, but it was still the same.

And so were Nick and I.

God, that thought was *petrifying*. I realized I was gripping the leather arms of Nick's chair in a stranglehold. But sitting here alone in this apartment, it was far too easy to remember the bitter solitude of my early days here. The helplessness I'd felt as I became invisible to the man I'd loved more than air. The utter terror that paralyzed my heart as I watched him pack. I could still hear the clink of my ring hitting the storm drain, could still see the accusing glare of the cab's taillights as Nick left me.

My inbox chimed with a new message. Exhaling abruptly—apparently I'd stopped breathing—I heaved myself out of the chair and took a look. BeverLee. I clicked on it, then squinted to make out the curly pink typeface she always used.

Hey there, Sweetheart how are you doing? I've been just the tiniest bit worried about you, it being you've been gone such a while. Let me know where you're at, okay? Miss you bunches. xoxox BeverLee. By the way give me a call if you can.

My heart squeezed. I'd never thought of BeverLee and me as being particularly close, but in her eyes, we were tighter than Joan and Melissa Rivers. If she deemed you her BFF, that's how she'd act, and it would take a SWAT team and a junkyard dog to keep her away. And now she was having to deal with her recalcitrant-to-the-point-of-mute husband telling her their marriage was over. My family life, if odd, had been pretty stable these past twenty years…and now it would be broken once more.

I needed to go home. At the thought, my eyes filled with completely unexpected tears. I didn't want to leave Nick…but I really had to take a step back. Nick wouldn't be happy about it. He might even be furious, and my heart died a little at the thought of disappointing him again, of being away from him. I loved Nick, had always loved him, that was undeniable. But maybe…maybe we both needed to step back a little and think. If we were going to work out, we had to be smarter than we were last time. Not to mention the fact that I had a family, a career, people who were waiting for me to come home. I had a cactus, damn it.

I wiped my eyes—holy testicle Tuesday, look at me, crying twice in the same decade, would wonders never cease? Coco cocked her cunning little head and looked at me as if affirming my thoughts. "Time to go home, Coco?" I whispered. She licked my elbow. The hammering of my heart told me I was running away…but sometimes flight was the best course of action. I'd never been able to win a fight with Nick, after all. He could sell a swimming pool to a dolphin.

Taking a deep breath, I typed a quick reply to Bev—*I should be home tonight, Bev. Call you later, okay?* Then I clicked open my browser and went to the Expedia website. Booked a flight on the five o'clock shuttle to Boston, then a seat on the puddle jumper that would take me to the island. Emailed the office. Packed up my clothes, noting distantly that my hands were shaking. Looked for Coco's bunny rabbit, which she enjoyed hiding so I could fetch it. She trotted beside me, amused that I couldn't just sniff the air and find the ratty old thing.

There it was, under the sleek couch in the living room. Coco barked twice, congratulating me. "Found it," I confirmed, groping for it. Just then, my cell phone rang, then chirped to indicate the low battery. Right. I still hadn't found my charger; may have left it at one of our stops across country. I handed Coco her beloved and then ran to answer the phone. The screen read *Dennis,* and an unexpected wave of guilt washed over me. "Hi, Den! Everything okay?"

"Hey, Harp! How are you?"

Beep. "Um, I'm doing fine," I answered. "Hey, my battery's low. What's up?"

"Everything's fine. Um, I was just wondering if you knew when you were coming home. You've been gone kind of a long time, that's all."

This was...new. Dennis generally wasn't the type to call and check on anything; he'd always left that to me. "Well, actually, I just booked a flight for later today."

"Oh, great! I'll pick you up!"

Beep. "No, no, that's okay, Dennis. You don't have to. I'll just grab a cab. It's only ten miles."

"No, dude, it's totally okay! You'll need a ride, right? What time?"

"Um...seven-thirty? But Dennis, please don't—" *Beep.*

"Cool! See you then." With that, my battery gave up the ghost. With a growl of frustration, I picked up Nick's phone and called Dennis back. I really didn't want to see Dennis first thing upon landing; life was enough of a snarl. And it wasn't like him to be so...helpful. Maybe he felt some guilt of his own for not accepting my proposal. Whatever. My call went straight to voice mail...typical. "Dennis here, leave a message!"

"Hi, Den," I said. "Listen, that's really nice of you, but I'll take a cab home, okay? Thanks anyway. Talk to you soon." I hung up and sighed, then looked down at my little brown-and-white buddy. "You want to go home, Coco?" She cocked her head and froze with anticipation, as if the word *home* was almost too good to bear. "I know just how you feel."

When Nick got home, it was almost four. I was staring unseeing at a copy of the *New Yorker,* and at the sound of his key, I lurched to my feet, nervous as hell. "Hey! How was your meeting?" I called brightly. "Everything go well?"

He didn't answer, unfooled by my chipper tone. Instead, he dropped his gaze to my suitcase, parked there by the front door, and folded his arm across his chest. "I probably shouldn't be surprised," he said tightly.

"Uh, well, I need to—"

"You're leaving me." His voice was flat.

"Nick, don't jump to conclusions. But yes, I have to get back. I have a lot going on." Nick cocked an eyebrow, and my temper stirred. "It's actually true, Nick. I do have a life separate from you."

As if saying her own form of goodbye, Coco began leaping straight off the floor as if spring-loaded. She launched herself into Nick's arms, and he grabbed her a bit awkwardly, unused to her forms of devotion. My dog licked his chin, unaware that the grown-ups were about to have a serious talk.

"So," Nick said, putting Coco back on the floor. He took a deep breath, and I could tell he was trying to keep calm. "What about you and me?"

I nodded. Sat down on the couch. Crossed my ankles. "Well," I whispered, "I think it's a little soon for us to talk about the New York bar."

"Right." His gaze dropped to the floor.

The silence seemed to stretch, pushing us apart bit by bit. "Maybe you could come out to the Vineyard sometime," I suggested, biting a cuticle. "Um…next weekend. If your schedule's clear."

He just looked at me for a long moment with those tragic eyes. "I'm not leaving you, Nick," I blurted. "I just…I just don't know how this is going to work. I don't want to make the same mistakes again."

In a second, he was on his knees in front of me, gripping my upper arms. "Harper, I love you."

God, those eyes, those damn gypsy eyes. "I know. And I…I love you back, Nick, you know that. But how does that translate? I mean, everyone loves everyone, right? But so many relationships don't work out. We didn't, Nick, loving each other or not."

"And she's off," Nick muttered, letting go of my arms.

"I'm not off," I protested, biting my poor cuticle yet again. "I'm just being realistic. I can't drop everything I've got back home just because we still have feelings for each other."

His eyes narrowed. "I'd think that those feelings would matter, Harper. They do to me."

"They definitely matter," I said in a small voice. "They're just not…they're just not the only things that do."

He ran his hand through his hair, then rose from the floor and sat next to me. We didn't say anything for a minute. "Look," he said in a gentler voice. "I love you. I want us to work. Last time, you had one foot out the door the whole time we were together. I can't take that again, Harper. You have to decide if you want this or not, and judging from the suitcase by the door, you don't."

I swallowed. "Nick," I whispered, "I think we need time to…think."

"I don't need to think, Harper. I know. But you…" His voice rose. "I'm in this, I want us to be together, but you… your bags are already packed. You're leaving. Again."

"I'm not, Nick!" I barked. "I have to deal with things at home, okay? I have a life there, and…I can't just not go back. You're traveling all over the planet, anyway, and I won't throw caution to the wind and make all the same mistakes we made last time and end up miserable again. I won't do that, Nick."

There it was again, that look. I'd let him down, even though everything I said made perfect sense.

From the street below, a car horn honked. "There's my cab," I said.

"That was fast," Nick muttered.

"I didn't think your lunch would last for four hours, either," I snapped. "Okay?"

Déjà vu all over again. When had I ever gotten an inch from Nick, after all? Never, that's when.

Nick walked to the door and picked up my suitcase and laptop carrier, his movements sharp and angry. He stood back to let Coco and me go through the door and down the stairs. The ripe smell of the city greeted us out on the street, the roar and the humidity.

"I'll see you soon," I said briskly, turning to Nick.

He nodded.

Then, without another word, we were in each other's arms, and I was hugging him as hard as I could, my face pressed against his beautiful neck, and he held me so close that for a second, it seemed as if he would never let me go, that he'd say something that would make everything okay.

But he didn't say anything, and he did let me go.

So THAT WAS FUN. My brain decided to play Debate Team again for the entire bleeping plane ride to Boston.

Leaving was the right thing to do.

Are you insane? How could it be the right thing?

Please. Let's not get hysterical here. It's not as though Nick and I are done, we're just—

Oh, God, go back, what are you thinking, that man is the love of your stupid life!

As I was saying before you so rudely interrupted, we're

just figuring things out. I have other responsibilities, don't forget.

Didn't you see the look in his eyes? You did it again. You left him.

Finally, I grabbed my laptop case. There was the yellow envelope that contained my mother's information. Fat lot of good that did me, huh? So much for closure—more like a reopening of the jugular. What would I have done without Nick that day? *(See, idiot? Can we turn this plane around?)* Veering away from the tarry emotions that paved the path of maternal memories, I flipped open my laptop and looked at my calendar. Court on Tuesday, Schultz v. Schultz, Judge Keller. Easy peasy…a couple who'd parted ways without so much as a whimper. So civilized. Lunch with Father Bruce. Kim and I were supposed to have a night out on Thursday. That would be great…I could use a little girlfriend time.

What about Nick? When will you see Nick again?

I have no clue, I answered. *I will call him tomorrow. Or even tonight. So can you please leave me alone?*

We landed in Boston, and I got the resentful Coco from steerage. "I'm sorry. You deserve much better," I told her as I lugged her crate, my suitcase, laptop carrier and purse to the Cape Air gate. She ignored me, and who could blame her? "It wasn't much better where I was," I assured her. "One quick hop, and we're home again. Bear with me."

A short while later, we were flying over the Atlantic. No sooner had we taken off than the plane seemed to begin its descent to Martha's Vineyard. A lump came to my throat at the sight of the island. There were the cliffs of Gay Head in variegated streaks of brown and white, the scrubby green bayberry and beach plum gentling the ragged shore. Waves broke against the beach, and I could see gulls flying and fluttering as they dropped shellfish onto the rocks. Just around the curve of Aquinnah was Menemsha, Dutcher's Dock and home.

Our plane landed without fanfare, and as I got off, I sucked in a deep breath of the salty, pine-scented air. It seemed as if I'd been gone for a year, not just a week. The sun beat down hot on my hair, and the wind blew strands into my eyes. A mockingbird sang from on top of the gray-shingled terminal.

This was where I belonged. Fourth-generation Islander, granddaughter of a fisherman.

I sprang Coco, clipped on her leash and managed to wrestle my luggage out the door. Coco paused, never a fan of automatic doors. "Coco, come on, honey, don't get Chihuahua on me—oh, my God."

Oh, my God indeed. Oh, *crotch*, in fact.

Because there, in front of the terminal, was a Martha's Vineyard fire truck, eight firemen, a small crowd of regular people and quite a few kids.

And Dennis Patrick Costello, on bended knee.

CHAPTER TWENTY-THREE

"DENNIS," I BREATHED. "Holy testicle Tuesday."

The horror of the situation splayed out in front of me. After two and a half noncommittal years together, one dodged marriage proposal and a breakup, Dennis was about to pop the question.

My eyes, which felt stretched way too wide, took in the scene. Jeez Louise. Were those Dennis's—yep. His parents. His nice parents, Sarah and Jack. His two sisters, their spouses, too. Various and sundry children, aka Den's nieces and nephews…all present. There was his brother, who owned the apartment where Den lived. My father, who gave me a somber nod. The guys from Platoon C—including Chuck, who hated me, as well as Fire Chief Rogers—all present.

"Hey," Dennis grinned. He was holding something. Two things, in fact. A piece of wire, was it? And a small black velvet box. Which he now opened, revealing the ring I'd bought for myself four weeks ago.

Crotch. Crotchety crotch crotch. This was bad. Plagues of Egypt bad.

Coco, seeing her buddy, bolted forward, and as I appeared to be in a state of paralysis, the leash slipped from my limp fingers.

"Hi, Coco! How are you, cutie? Did you miss me?" Dennis, still on one knee, allowed himself to be licked by my bouncing little dog, then passed the leash to one of the nieces.

KRISTAN HIGGINS   325

"Dennis, what are you doing?" someone squeaked. Oh. It was me.

He grinned up at me. "Harper," he began.

"Den—" I said. Then words deserted me, leaving only strange little airy noises coming out of my mouth.

"She's speechless," said a familiar voice. Theo. My boss was also here. "Now that's something you don't see every day." There was Carol, grinning. Tommy, too. Crikey.

"Harp," Dennis said, smiling broadly. "This week apart has taught me some big lessons. Big lessons, dude."

"Dennis—"

"Yeah, no, let me finish. Um…" He paused, frowned, then remembered the rest of what was clearly a rehearsed speech. "I guess I didn't realize what a…jewel?" He glanced at his mother, who nodded encouragingly. Chuck made a rather loud choking noise. "What a jewel I had in you," Dennis continued, "but now that we've been, you know, away from each other, I…uh…" He paused, thought, then looked up again. "Well, shit, I wrote this all down but I can't remember now. Whatever. Harp, I think you're awesome, I love you, and I know I haven't been the greatest boyfriend ever, but I found your list—"

Oh, *crotch!* The list! I *hated* myself! Dennis fumbled in his shirt pocket and pulled out a folded-up piece of paper and handed it to me. "Go ahead, he said. "Take a look."

As if observing myself from above, I unfolded the paper. There was my list. Ah, damn it. Dennis had put check marks next to all of the items…Get rid of rust-bucket car, move out of brother's garage, get second job. All the things I'd felt the need to detail.

Shame made it difficult to lift my eyes back to Dennis.

He was grinning from ear to ear and holding up the black wire—oh, no. It wasn't wire. "Here you go, baby," he said.

It was his rattail. Automatically, I accepted the nasty little braid, the sense of the surreal growing by the nanosecond.

"See?" he said. "Dude, you got your way."

Everyone laughed. Well, I, of course, did not laugh.

"So, Harper. Baby. Will you marry me? Make me the happiest guy in the world and all that?"

He did seem happy, his blue eyes gleaming. Everyone looked thrilled—his mom, dad, siblings, all those kids, his coworkers, even Chuck, were smiling. Only my father was solemn.

I looked back at Dennis.

And then, because I couldn't bring myself to humiliate him in front of everyone he loved…I said yes.

"SEE, YOU LEFT THE LIST that night. When you, uh, proposed," Dennis said as he drove me home in his new truck. Unfortunately, the ride was brief, too short to tell Dennis there was no way I could marry him. Coco, unaware that her mistress was up Shit Creek *sans* paddle, snuffled happily at the familiar breezes as we drove from the airport to my place. "And anyway, with you away all this week, well, I guess I finally figured out what a good thing we had going." He reached over and squeezed my knee with his big hand. I forced a smile.

"Um, so, your parents…How long are they staying?" I asked.

"Just for the weekend. Then they'll stay with Becky in Boston for a couple days. Mom wants to talk wedding shit with you, so get ready, okay?" He glanced over and smiled.

I swallowed sickly. Obviously, I wasn't going to marry

Dennis. But what had happened? I couldn't believe he'd done everything on that stupid list. Maybe he'd gotten a little…well, jealous, knowing I was off with Nick in parts unknown.

Whatever the case, he'd gone to some real trouble, arranging this (debacle) proposal. His parents had flown up from North Carolina! And they were such nice people—basically, Ye Wonderful American Parents, the type I didn't have, full of pride for their offspring, adoration for their grandchildren, enjoying retirement with book clubs and golf games. "Well, it took him long enough, but he came around," his mother had said as she hugged me, wiping away happy tears. "I hated that rattail, too. Harper, you're the best thing that's ever happened to him."

If you only knew, lady, I thought, cringing internally as I hugged her back.

"We should talk, Dennis," I said now, biting my lip as we pulled into my driveway.

"Oh, yeah. Absolutely," he said. "But everyone's here, so…maybe later?" He flashed another grin.

Dennis had even arranged a party—an engagement party, *chez moi,* and the driveway was lined with cars. Music played, people were crowded onto the deck. Kids flittered about, someone had found a kite…a beautiful summer scene, minus the black dread seeping out of my heart.

The instant I got out of Dennis's new truck, Kim cantered toward me, her youngest on her hip.

"Harper!" she cried, widening her eyes at me. "Hey! I've been calling you! A lot!"

"Hi!" I said a bit desperately. "Oh, hi, Desmond! How are you, my, um, little man?" The toddler regarded me suspiciously. Didn't blame him.

"Hey, Kim," Dennis said amiably.

"Dennis! So!" She glanced at my left hand, where the

diamond winked like a malevolent eye (not that I was *freaking out* or anything). "Wow! So! Congratulations are in order, then?"

"Totally," Dennis said, slinging an arm around me and pulling me in for a kiss. I ducked.

"Den, could you get my stuff inside? I—I'm kind of whipped," I said. "Thanks, um…hon."

"You bet, dude," he said. "Come on, Coco-Buns!" He hauled my luggage out of the back of the truck and went in the house.

Kim put her tot down and kissed his curly head. "Go see Daddy," she instructed, then bellowed over at her house. "Lou! Watch Desmond!" Lou waved in obeisance and called to his son, then led him to my back deck, where the party sounded as if it was in full swing.

Kim looked at me and folded her arms. "So," she said.

"I know."

"Dennis called me this afternoon," she went on. "Told me the plan, and I want you to know, I did tell him I thought you'd probably prefer a quiet night, oh yeah. Said I wasn't sure you were the public-place-proposal type. Then I called you, like, sixteen times, but you never picked up."

I rubbed my forehead. "My battery died, and I lost the charger somewhere on the prairie. Damn it!"

"So you said yes?" Kim asked. "Harper…"

"I know, I know. But everyone was there…I just couldn't tell him no in front of his whole family and half the fire department!"

"He moved in here, did you know that?"

I grimaced. "Number Four on my list."

"You gave him a list?"

"Don't bother. I've got self-flagellation penciled in for later."

Kim looked out toward the sea. "So what's the status on Nick?" she asked.

"I…oh, crap. This is a gumdaddy of a mess, Kim."

"And speaking of weird Southern expressions, where is BeverLee?"

I closed my eyes. "I don't know. She and Dad are getting a divorce."

"No! You're kidding me!"

"I'm not." I heaved a sigh.

At that moment, a black-clad figure walked up my driveway, the crushed shells crunching under his feet. "Hello, Kim, and hello, Harper!" he said warmly. "*Mazel tov!* I have to admit, I never thought this day would come."

"Hi, Father Bruce," I said. "Um…hi."

He frowned. "Everything okay here? You look awful."

"Yes."

"But…isn't this what you wanted?"

Kim and I exchanged a look. "Well," I began. "It's…I… um…"

"Oh, no," he said. "Did you sleep with your ex-husband?"

"Father Bruce, I am not prepared to discuss that—"

He threw up his hands. "She did. Oh, Kim, I don't believe it."

"Harp!" Dennis's head popped around the corner of the house. "Come on, dude! This party's for us, after all. The happy couple."

WHEN ALL THE GUESTS had finally drifted off around 1 a.m., I was left with Dennis, who, yes, had moved in. Boxes of DVDs, CDs and video game equipment, as well as a few garbage bags of clothes, littered my usually perfectly ordered house.

"This is gonna be so great," Dennis said, slurring a little from where he was sprawled on the couch. I hadn't exactly kept track, but he'd had more than a few beers. His eyes were already closed, his long black lashes giving him a childlike look.

"Honey," I began as gently as I could.

"I'm sorry it took so long for me to get my ass in gear," he murmured.

"Oh, no…it's okay. But Den…" I took his hand, hoping to broach our breakup gracefully. Dennis deserved some gentleness from me, and it was high time I recognized that. "Listen, I thought we were pretty clear about why we broke up."

"I know," he said. "But I missed you. And you were right. I'm kind of a jerk—"

I closed my eyes and squeezed his hand. "No, you're not, Dennis, you're a great guy."

"—and I needed a kick in the head, and you gave it to me." He smiled, his eyes still closed. "And I love you."

Damn it. This was, by far, the biggest shit snarl I'd gotten myself into in some time. "The thing is, Dennis," I whispered. "I just…I don't know if we should get married. You're so sweet, but, um…I think I bullied you into this. There was a reason you said no, don't you think? I mean, when someone loves you, they shouldn't hand you a list of demands like someone holding a bunch of hostages, right? And Dennis, you deserve someone who isn't so… Den?"

He was asleep.

I looked at him a minute longer, his romantic-hero good looks, the ruddy cheeks, curling, glossy hair. "Come on, sweetie," I said. "Let's get you to bed." With some difficulty, I roused him enough to tuck him into my room.

As I pulled up the sheet to cover him, Dennis caught

my hand. "I'm really happy you said yes," he muttered sleepily.

Oh, Den. "We'll talk in the morning," I whispered.

Then, my heart leaden, I went to tidy up the house, sorting bottles for recycling, wrapping up the leftovers, scraping plates, sweeping the floor. At long last, I went out to my deck and looked out over the water. Water slapped at the hulls of the boats, and far off, an owl called, the sound lonely and lovely.

But the peace I'd longed for was elusive, of course. Obviously, I'd be breaking up with Dennis in the morning. His parents had scheduled us an entire weekend of fun—they were like that, family outings and picnics and nights of board-game marathons. It was tempting to give Dennis this whole weekend, to pretend we were engaged till his family left on Sunday, then let him down easy. Maybe I could even make him think our breakup was his idea. But I couldn't last the whole weekend. It wasn't fair. The sooner he knew the truth, the better. Maybe. Or not? I didn't know. To the best of my knowledge, no one had ever praised me for my emotional IQ.

Oddly enough, I wished I could talk to BeverLee, though it was too late to call. Her absence had been horribly noticeable tonight. And I had to check on Willa. God, I hoped she knew about Christopher's problems. It was weird…though we didn't check in daily, I found her silence ominous. Hopefully, she'd be within cell phone range by tomorrow.

I also had to call Nick. That…that was going to be tough. Three days together, and already we were at odds. And already I missed him. Crikey, I *yearned* for him in such a fierce, sudden rush that my chest actually hurt. The look on his face as I got into the cab…it was acid on my heart, that resigned, sad look. The same look he used to get around his father. But before I could figure out what the future might look like with Nick, I had to become unengaged from Dennis.

Crotch.

Coco nosed my hand, reminding me that it was late, and she didn't like sleeping without me. She was right. There was nothing to be done tonight. With a sigh, I washed up, then went into the guest bedroom, earning a confused look from my dog as to why we weren't sleeping with young Dennis.

For a long time, I stared at the ceiling, wondering what to do and how to do it. Finally, with a sigh, I rolled onto my stomach and pulled the pillow over my head. Time to sleep. Surely, morning would be better.

CHAPTER TWENTY-FOUR

Morning was not better.

I rolled out of bed early, sunlight streaming through the windows, let Coco out and started some coffee. Dennis was still sleeping and would be for some time, judging from the number of beers he'd had last night. I cringed at the thought of our upcoming talk, guilt choking me like a forty-foot python. It was 6:45 a.m.; Dennis probably would sleep for another couple of hours. Call me a coward, but I wasn't going to burst in there and wake him with the news that I didn't want to get married after all.

Time to make muffins. Dennis loved muffins, and muffins he would get. If I was going to dump him, at least he could have muffins. I got out a seldom-used cookbook—*The Big Book of Texas Cookin'*, a gift from BeverLee, of course, containing recipes for quantities of food that would feed entire football teams and should thus hold Dennis for at least round one of breakfast—and got to work. I never baked. My mom and I used to bake a lot—cookies, mostly, which we'd eat watching some age-inappropriate movie. Bev liked cooking better—the best present I ever got her was a Fry Daddy, last Christmas. She'd been so happy, you'd have thought it was a month's vacation in the Greek isles. Then again, Bev had always been easy to please.

When the muffins were baking, I checked my newly charged phone. Yep, nine messages from Kim, trying to warn me about the surprise at the airport. One from

Willa, saying only that she'd hoped to catch me. None from BeverLee, though I'd left a message for her while waiting at Logan yesterday. And none from Nick.

I'd have given an awful lot to have heard his voice right about now, and the realization caused an odd stabbing in my chest. Maybe all the heart-strangling food I'd eaten in the past week was catching up with me and my arteries were choked with Swiss cheese. Or maybe I was afraid Nick had already given up on me. That seemed more likely (and also more horrible) than the heart attack theory.

Maybe, though, Nick had sent me an email. I had, after all, left all my contact info, email, work, etc., on his counter in New York, as a sign that I did indeed want us to have further communication. I jumped over to my laptop and waited, my fingers drumming, for it to start.

Nope. As the emails appeared on the list, I saw there was nothing from Nick. The disappointment was a little shocking. As I turned away from the screen, though, something caught my eye.

Huh. It was a message from my credit card company about a recent purchase. United Airlines, $529. Yesterday.

That…that didn't seem to bode very well.

Before the thought was fully formulated, a car pulled into the driveway. I looked out the window with dread… yep. There was Willa, getting out of a cab, eyes swollen and red, blond hair matted and dull.

No sign of Chris.

"Willa!" I exclaimed, lurching into action and running out the door. My sister flung herself into my arms.

"Harper, I'm such an ass," she wept. "You were right! I never should've gotten married in the first place!"

Forty-five minutes later, my sister was showered,

dressed in a pair of my shorts and a Sharky's T-shirt, an untouched cup of coffee at her elbow.

"You want something to eat?" I offered. "Muffin? Toast? Eggs? Ben & Jerry's?"

"No. I couldn't eat." Her face was wan.

"So what happened, honey?" I asked, gnawing on my beleaguered cuticle before putting my hand in my lap.

"Well," she said, forcing a smile, "I should've listened to you. I'm going to tattoo that on my forehead. 'Listen to Harper, because you're an idiot.' Maybe then, I'll learn."

"You're not an idiot," I said. "But obviously something happened." I paused. "Did he…fall off the wagon?"

She gave me a glance. "You found out about that, huh?"

I winced, then nodded.

"No. He's still sober. At least, he was when I left." She welled up again, picked up her cup, then set it down without drinking.

"So what was it, then, Wills?" I asked.

She looked at me, mouth wobbling. "Harper…he wants us to live in Montana, and he thinks I should find a job so I can support him while he, in his words, 'focuses' on his inventions and gets the Thumbie going."

I bit my lip. Honestly, the Thumbie was perhaps the dumbest name for a product I'd ever heard in my life.

"I mean, seriously," Willa continued, wiping her eyes with a napkin. "What am I supposed to do out there? Wait tables? Become a cowboy? So he can stay home and play with his parts? I want to have a baby, not go back to work."

"Um…You've only been married a week, Willa," I pointed out.

"I *know*, Harper," she said tightly. "Look, please don't

lecture me right now. You were right. Christopher isn't good enough for me—"

"I'm quite sure those words never actually came out of my mouth."

"Whatever. You told me not to marry him, and I didn't listen."

I chewed on my lip. "So where's Chris right now?"

"Montana, I guess. That's where I left him." Tears spilled out of her pretty blue eyes. "Harper, I don't know what went wrong. Everything was so great before...then it just went to hell in a handbasket! I mean, our honeymoon sucked, can I just say that? Mosquitoes like something out of *Jurassic Park* during the day, freezing cold at night. And Chris can't cook to save his life—"

"Well, you're a pretty good cook, Willa," I said.

"Not over a fire! I'm not a cavewoman, okay?" She sighed, wiped her eyes and gave me an apologetic look. "I'm sorry, Harper. You're the only one who understands. I leaped without looking, as I always do. I'm an idiot, and I know it."

"You're not an idiot," I repeated, patting her hand.

"Can we not talk about this right now? I'm sorry. I just...I'm exhausted. Can I crash here for a little while? I can't face Mama and Daddy right now. Mama's gonna be heartbroken."

I wondered if Willa knew about the current situation with Dad and BeverLee. It didn't seem that way. "Sure," I said. "Um, listen, Dennis is here, and we're going to need a little, um, privacy later on." Great. That sounded as if Den and I had a booty call planned. "We have to... talk."

Wills gave a weary nod. "Do you mind if I take a nap, Harper? I'm so tired."

"Sure, sure! Come on, I'll tuck you in."

Willa rose from the table. "Thanks for your credit card, by the way. That was a lifesaver."

Five minutes later, my sister was in bed in the guest room, Coco and her bunny snuggled against Willa's back. "Call if you need anything," I said, pulling the shades.

"Will do," she replied, her eyes already closed.

I went back in the kitchen and sat down again. Picked up a muffin and began dissecting it with the butter knife. A new thought was forming in my brain, slowly but with great conviction. Willa was…crap. She was spoiled. She was sweet, optimistic, energetic, friendly…and spoiled.

And I was the one who spoiled her. She'd rushed into three marriages; I'd gotten her out of two (and counting). I'd loaned her thousands of dollars, none of which had been repaid, none of which I'd asked or expected her to repay. I'd ponied up for school…that had lasted three weeks. The paralegal course had endured a bit longer—four. When she convinced me that a stonemasonry apprenticeship was her lifelong dream, I'd paid for that, too, and for her living expenses while she spent two weeks figuring out that it wasn't what she really wanted after all.

In the past, I'd always jumped at the chance to look out for Willa, to guide and offer and protect. But maybe… maybe what she needed now was to sink or swim on her own. How could I have not realized that before now? Bailing her out all the time might have made me feel protective and noble, but maybe…ouch…maybe it was also a little selfish of me. After all, I couldn't be the big sister anymore if Willa actually had to grow up.

Another car pulled into my driveway, a rental. Oh, God! It was Dennis's parents, both dressed in white shorts and pink polo shirts, like senior citizen twins. What were they doing here? It was barely nine o'clock, their son wasn't even awake yet…and I hadn't even had a chance to talk to him yet, as I'd been procrastinating and all. Stifling the urge to hide under the table, I got up and opened the door.

"Hi!" I said. "How are you? Did we have, um… plans?"

"Oh, are those muffins?" Jack asked, kissing my cheek and squeezing past me into the kitchen. "Blueberry, I hope?"

"Yes, they are. Listen, Den's not even up yet."

"Good morning, Harper, honey!" Sarah sang, following her husband into the house. "We wanted to help clean up after the party, but look at this place, it's immaculate! Oh, you'll be so good for Dennis, God knows the boy's a slob. But if he didn't change his ways even with all my nagging, I hope he will with yours!" She chortled merrily and gave me a big hug. "And looky what I have here!" She held up her large straw purse and withdrew several tomes. "Wedding magazines!"

Oh, God, kill me now. "You know, this might not be the best time…um, see, Dennis had a few too many beers last night, and he's still sleeping. And, and my sister just got in, and she's sleeping, too."

"Sure, we'll be quiet," Sarah said at a slightly reduced volume. She plunked herself down next to Jack, who had already finished one muffin and was busy slathering another with butter. "I guess the first thing we need to decide is when," Sarah continued. "I'm thinking June, of course, but you know how I love a spring wedding! Black-tie, too. Can't you just see Dennis in a tux, Harper? Not to toot our horn here, but Jack and I made some beautiful children! Harper, honey, don't bite your nails. Where's your ring, sweetheart?"

I dropped my hand. "Oh…uh…right there. On the windowsill. I was washing dishes…"

"Put it on, put it on," Jack urged brightly. "It's gorgeous!"

I obeyed, wondering if they knew I'd bought it for myself. If they knew I'd said the words "Shit or get off the pot" as I asked their son to spend the rest of his life with me.

"So I thought we'd all have lunch at the hotel later on," Sarah said. "Bonnie, Kevin, the kids, then maybe a family hike, how's that sound?"

"Um…you know what?" I said. "I'm so sorry…I…I'm just gonna dash into the shower, if that's okay. My sister just got back, and I didn't have time—"

"I can't wait to hear about *that* wedding!" Sarah said. "Jack, wouldn't a destination wedding be so much fun? Well, you go shower, honey. Take your time! Hopefully that lazybones son of ours will wake up and we can get down to business."

I fled the kitchen, practically staggering under the weight of all that enthusiasm…and the dread of how they'd feel later today. *I'm so sorry,* I thought. *I'm really, really sorry.*

My head felt like a fighter jet in a tail spin toward destruction. In one room, I had a sleeping nonfiancé. In another, an exhausted and weepy sister. In the third, the two most cheerful people alive. The warm water of the shower calmed me down—a little, anyway. Was I hiding? Absolutely. But just for the moment. It was going to be a busy morning, and I just needed to get my head on straight. First things first: get rid of the Costellos. Next, get rid of Willa, just for a while, anyway. And finally, talk to Dennis ASAP.

I slapped on a little makeup and left my hair down, since I couldn't seem to find an elastic; Coco tended to eat them. Tiptoed into my room and put on a summery yellow

dress, taking care not to wake Dennis. He appeared to be
dead to the world, so at least there was that.

My future not-to-be in-laws were sitting on the deck
when I came out. "Come and join us, sweetheart!" called
Jack.

"Okay!" I answered, taking a deep breath. I smoothed
my hands over my stomach, adjusted the engagement ring.
All I had to do was go out there and tell them this wasn't
a good time, Den would call them later. Then I'd rouse
Willa, send her to Kim's, maybe, and finally wake up
Dennis and—

There was a knock on the kitchen door.

I looked up.

Nick was standing on my porch.

CHAPTER TWENTY-FIVE

"OH, CROTCH," I BREATHED.

"Hey," Nick said. He was smiling. Here. He was here. On the porch. Why were all these men surprising me these days?

He raised a hand to shield his eyes and looked in through the screen door, and oh, that smile! Those beautiful gypsy eyes...And he was here. Crap! But no, it was good, right? So, *so* good...and also very terrible! Horrible, because really could the timing be any worse in any way?"

"I missed you, woman," he said, and damn it, he had flowers. Irises. My favorite. Who the *hell* could find irises in September before 10 a.m. on an *island?* Huh? Who?

I floated over to the door, unable to feel my legs. I did *not* open the door, uh-uh. "Um," I breathed. "Hi."

"I was in the neighborhood," he said. His eyes were happy. Damn it, he looked the way he did the first time he laid eyes on me—knowing and mischievous and naughty and edible.

"What are you doing here, Nick?" I whispered.

"What do you think?"

"Um...peddling the Book of Mormon?" Weak, but apparently, I was brain-dead.

"Wow. It's like you're psychic." He took a step forward, and I jerked back. "Listen, Harper. When you left yesterday, I felt like I was dying. Dying, Harper." He raised an eyebrow, and that little smile, it just killed me.

Crotchety crotch crotch! Of course, under other circumstances, I'd be on him like a tick on a tourist, but... crotch! "Nick, I...um..." Glancing behind me, I could see Jack and Sarah through the sliding glass doors as they sat out on the deck. Sarah was pointing to something in one of the bridal mags. I shifted to hide Nick's view.

"You were right," he said. God! The sexiest three words in the English language, *you were right.* What woman doesn't love to hear that? "I know we have things to work out, and I'm completely willing to—" He paused. "Think you can let me in? I hadn't really pictured kissing you through the screen."

My knees threatened to give out. "Nick, this is...you know...but I have...uh, company? Unexpected company? Can I see you later, maybe?"

"No." His smile faded. "Harper, I love you, and I'm not letting you run away this time. Open the goddamn door so I can grovel and kiss you and maybe cop a feel. And then we can figure things out, okay?"

"Hey!" Kim came torpedoing down the path from her house. Thank the Lord, the Marines had landed. "Hi! Harper! Good morning! And who do we have here! Hi, I'm Kim. Neighbor and friend."

"Kim!" I blurted. "Great to see you. Uh...this is... um...Nick. Nick Lowery. Nick, my neighbor, Kim, mother of four wonderful boys and um...uh...yes. Okay. Maybe you can go to her house?"

Nick squinted at me—who wouldn't? I sounded insane. Nevertheless, he turned to shake Kim's hand. "Hi. Nice to meet you."

"Oh," Kim panted. "Wow. Okay. Yep, I see it now, Harper. Right. Got it. Flowers, that's nice. So you're Nick? Wow." She gave me a wild-eyed glance.

"Kim, I was telling Nick about my *company.* You know. The unexpected recent company?"

"Oh, shitake, yes. Right. Nick, want to come to my house for a little bit? I have children. They're very entertaining. And so well behaved. They hardly break anything."

Nick's gaze swiveled between the two of us women, babbling idiots both, and he narrowed his eyes. "What's going on, Harper?" he asked.

I swallowed. "Well, Nick, I'm so, so happy to see you... but...well, this company? Um..."

"Harper dear?" Sarah called.

"Who's that?" Nick asked.

I was hyperventilating a little. "Actually, see, this is kind of funny—"

"Nick! What are you doing here? Did Chris send you?"

Oh, hell and damnation. Willa had arisen from her nap and came now into the kitchen behind me.

"Willa," he said, though he was staring at me. The warm, hot fudge look in his eyes dried to a hardened lump of tar. "What a surprise."

"Chris didn't send you?"

"And why would he do that?" Nick asked, his voice deceptively mild.

"Because I left him," Willa said, her eyes filling. "Harper was right. He wasn't good enough for me! It was a disaster waiting to happen."

"Those weren't my exact words," I said, cringing.

Nick took matters into his own hands and tried to open the door. I tried to close it.

"Harper, what the hell?" he muttered, pushing it open all the way. Not fair. He was heavier. He stood in the kitchen between Willa and me, looking at both of us in turn before settling his gaze on Willa. "One week? That's all, Willa? You gave him a week?"

"I should never have married him in the first place,"

she said, starting to do that little hitching breath thing again. Kim, bless her, came in as well and took Willa's arm, steering her over to the table. I glanced out to the deck, where Jack and Sarah had turned to look at our little soap opera.

"Nick, listen," I said. "You have to go just for a little while, okay? This is not a good time."

"No, I can see that," Nick said tightly. And he didn't know the half of it. "I thought you said you wouldn't interfere."

"Look, I actually didn't—"

"How did you get home, Willa?" he asked tightly.

"Harper gave me her credit card number, in case things went south," my sister answered, blowing her nose loudly.

Nick's jaw tightened. "Nice, Harper."

"It wasn't exactly like—Oh, crap."

Jack and Sarah had decided to join us. "Hello there," said Sarah, blinking as she came in from the bright sunlight. "We're Jack and Sarah Costello. And you are…?"

"Nick's my brother-in-law," Willa said wetly. "Hi, Mrs. Costello, Mr. Costello, nice to see you again."

"Costello?" Nick said. His voice was very soft.

"What's wrong, dear?" Jack asked Willa.

"Oh, nothing," Willa said, her face crumpling.

I just stood there, unable to figure a way out of this mess, choked to silence by the guilt python.

Then I heard my bedroom door open, and Dennis came in, as well. Wearing boxers and nothing else, his brawny build on full display. "Hey, I didn't know we had a crowd. Hi, Ma, Dad. Hi, Willa, what's up?" He rubbed his eyes, then focused on Nick. "Nick! How's it hanging? You here to offer congratulations or something?"

With terrible slowness, Nick's gaze slid to me. "Congratulations on what?" he asked. I closed my eyes.

Dennis put his arm around me. "Dude. We're getting married."

"And, not to be too presumptuous," Sarah said, leaning forward with one of the bridal magazines, "I think I found you a dress. See? So elegant!"

Nick just stared at me for a minute, and the world seemed to stop as I felt the full weight of his disappointment…no. His disgust.

"Well," he said calmly. "I hope you'll be very happy together." He glanced at his watch. "Sorry to say, I have to run."

And then he was out the door, into the sunshine.

"I would've thought he'd have a little more to say than that," Willa muttered.

"He's not here for—you know what? Be right back," I said, my paralysis shattering. I bolted outside, my sandals crunching on the driveway, little fragments of crushed shells stabbing into my feet. "Nick!" I called. "Wait! Hold on a sec."

He didn't. He was actually on his phone, calling a cab, probably. Or a hit man. "Nick! Hang on! Please!"

I caught up to him at the bottom of my hill, right in front of the dock, where already, tourists were boarding their charter boats for a day of fishing.

"Nick, this is not what it seems." I put my hand on his arm, but he shook it off. "Nick! I'm not engaged to Dennis," I said. The wind blew the hair into my eyes, and I shoved it back.

"I don't believe this," he said. "I mean, I figured you'd have an escape plan, but engaged? Wow, Harper. That was fast. Or maybe not. Maybe you never broke up with Dennis in the first place. I mean, look at you. Your hair's down, you're wearing a pretty dress, a ring that would choke a pony, breaking up my brother's marriage and all set to have a lovely day with your *fiancé* and his family!"

"Nick, come on! I'm not marrying him."

He shook his head, looking at the sky. "Does he have any idea that you've been with me, Harper?"

"By 'been with,' do you mean 'slept with'?" I asked, biting a cuticle.

"Yes, Harper! Does Dennis know you slept with me?"

"Um…well, not really. No."

Nick glared at me. "This is what you do, isn't it? You erase me. You leave me. Our whole time together, back then and right now, one foot out the door. Just in case."

"Nick, he met me at the airport with his whole family—"

"And you just couldn't figure out a way to say no."

I paused. Maybe he did understand. "Exactly. I just needed a few days—"

"You couldn't figure out a way to say no to me, either. That's why you married me. You told me that just this week."

I started to answer, then stopped. "I…it wasn't—"

"So will you marry Dennis because you can't see a way out of it, Harper?" His eyes were molten with anger.

I took a breath. "No. Really, Nick. I'm not even re-motely considering marrying Dennis."

He shoved his hands in his pockets. The wind rumpled his hair, and he stared at me with his gypsy eyes. "Well, let me ask you this, Harper. Are you considering marry-ing me?"

The question hung in the air between us. I hesitated. "Well, I think before we talk about that, Nick, we have to figure out—"

He held up his hand. "Stop," he said. "Just…stop."

I obeyed, forcing myself not to chew on my cuticles.

Nick looked out over the water, past the boats, past the Coast Guard station, out toward the open water. He couldn't seem to look at me.

Then a car pulled up, the same taxi service that had dropped off Willa. "Someone call a cab?" the driver said amiably.

"Yeah," Nick said.

My mouth went dry, my heart clattered. "Nick, don't leave. Don't go," I said unevenly. "Look, it's not that I'm not, you know…it's just that this is all really new and sudden, and it's hard—"

"It's not hard for me!" he barked, causing both the cabbie and me to jump. "Harper, I've loved you all my adult life, but you just can't believe that, and nothing I do will change your mind. You want a guarantee, you want a fucking crystal ball to see the future, and I can't give you one. The only thing I can say is that I love you, I always have, I always will, but somehow that's not good enough for you. And I just can't do this any more." He opened the door, took a breath, then forced himself to look at me. "Take care of yourself."

Then he got in the cab, slammed the door and that was that.

The car pulled away, the seagulls wheeled and cried. A crow called from a telephone wire, and a lobster boat's engine coughed, then turned over.

From my overactive, ever-analyzing brain, there was nothing, and where my heart had been, there now seemed to be an abandoned mineshaft, empty, dark and hollow.

EVERYONE WAS STILL IN my kitchen when I got back. Nick's irises lay on the table next to Willa, who was idly stroking a petal. Kim leaned against the counter, talking to the Costellos, and they all looked up when I walked in.

"Where have you been, honey?" Sarah asked. "Are you all right? You'll get a burn if you don't wear a hat. Do you have sunscreen on?"

"Where's Dennis?" I asked.

"He's getting dressed," she answered. "Why, dear?"

I dragged my eyes up to hers. "I...I need to talk to him." I said. My expression must've been telling, because her mouth made an O of surprise, and a flash of wariness crossed her face.

"Maybe we should catch up with you two later on," Jack said.

"Yes!" Sarah agreed. "Right. Okay, dear. Um...good-bye." I watched them leave, then closed my eyes briefly.

"Willa, why don't we go to my house for a little bit?" Kim suggested.

"You okay?" Willa asked me.

"Um...not really," I said. "I need to talk to Den for a little bit."

"Oh," she said. "Oh, shit. Sorry."

"I'll be home," Kim murmured, giving me a quick pat as she herded Willa out the door.

The quiet of the house was almost palpable. I took a breath, then another, but my heart kept thudding painfully away. Dennis hadn't come out of the bedroom, and after another minute or two, I went in to see what was keeping him.

He was sitting on the edge of my bed, petting Coco, staring at the floor.

"Hey," I whispered.

"Wait," he said. "Hang on a sec." He looked up at the

ceiling and when he looked at me again, his lovely blue eyes were wet. "I did everything on the list."

I pressed my fingers against my lips. Nodded. This was *awful*. I swallowed hard. "I know."

"But you don't want to marry me anyway."

"Den, I'm so sorry," I whispered, sitting next to him.

"So. Nick, huh?"

I nodded, too miserable to speak.

Dennis shook his head. "I shoulda known. The way you two fought in Montana…the way you looked at him." Dennis scrubbed his face. "You never looked at me that way."

A thousand points for Dennis. He might've been a big lug, but he was no dope. I wiped my eyes. Guess the dam had been broken on crying.

We sat there another minute, then Dennis sighed. "Well. I guess I never looked at you that way, either." He glanced at me. "So why'd you say you'd marry me, Harper?"

I twisted my bracelet till it pinched the skin on my wrist, then cleared my throat. "I didn't want to turn you down in front of everyone."

He considered that. "Thanks, I guess."

"I'm sorry," I whispered again.

"I can't believe I cut off my rattail."

I gave a surprised laugh, and Dennis grinned reluctantly. Then he took a deep breath, exhaled slowly and looked at me a long, assessing minute. "I guess we're done, then."

"I'm really sorry, Den."

"Right. Whatever." Neither of us said anything for a long time. Then Dennis spoke again. "I do love you, Harp. You know. In a lotta ways, I do."

It was hard to hear, all that kindness, that generosity. God knows I didn't deserve it. "Same here, Den." Then I took off my engagement ring and offered it to him. Dennis eyed it suspiciously.

"Dude," he said, "you paid for it."

"You've earned it. For putting up with me."

He gave me a sudden smile. "Please. I'm not that pathetic." He stood up. "Well, I guess I'll get my shit outta here."

"I'm so sorry," I said yet again.

"Ah, don't worry. But hey, dude. You mind if I tell everyone it was because you're a heartless bitch and stuff, and not that you fell for your ex?" He must've realized that *heartless bitch* was less than flattering, because he pulled a face. "Sorry. Never mind."

"Den, you can tell people whatever you want," I said, swallowing the lump in my throat.

"Serious?"

"Yeah."

"Great. Thanks, dude. And hey. You can keep the rattail."

"Oh. Uh, thanks, Den." I smiled, then stood up and gave him a gentle hug.

An hour later, Dennis had loaded up his new truck with the still-unpacked garbage bags of clothes.

"I do have to thank you on this," he stated, patting the truck's door. "I'm wicked psyched about this truck. Got a totally sweet deal on it."

"That's good, then," I said.

He got behind the wheel. "All right. Guess that's it. I'll miss you."

"I'll miss you, too," I whispered, and it was true. Sweet, good-hearted Dennis had been easy and fun and pleasant. We would've had a nice life together, had gorgeous kids, probably wouldn't have fought much.

Or maybe we'd have sat there at night, watching the

Sox and stealing looks at each other and thinking, *Is this it?* Either way, I'd never find out.

Besides, Dennis deserved someone who loved him with her whole heart. And that, it seemed, was beyond my reach. I wasn't cut out for couplehood, or marriage, or even children. I didn't have what it takes.

CHAPTER TWENTY-SIX

I WAS NOT THE WALLOWING type. No, I was much more the *work till three in the morning* type, and so, for the rest of the weekend, I sentenced myself to hard physical labor. I cleaned. Furiously. Bleach and ammonia cleaning (not combined...I wasn't suicidal). When my house was free from every grain of sand, every speck of dust and every spore of mold, I decided (at 9:30 p.m.) that the deck could use sanding and got to work on that, too.

Coco watched, her eyes bright, head cocked. "Just doing a little repair work," I called from the roof on Sunday afternoon. "All good."

Kim came over to grill me about Nick, but I told her I was fine. "You know what?" I said from my perch on the ladder as I polished the ceiling fan. "Sometimes I think people want more than other people are capable of giving. And you know, Nick...he's...I..." My breath started to hitch. "Just because you have feelings for someone doesn't mean you get to live happily ever after." That made sense. That was true, wasn't it? Not the stuff of romantic movies, but valid.

"I don't know. I think if you love each other..."

"We tend to go down in flames, Nick and I," I blurted. "I don't like burning. Burning hurts. Burning is painful. I'd rather...just...I'd rather just stay here and clean. Crotch! These lightbulbs are a crime against humanity. Have you ever seen such filthy lightbulbs?"

"You want dirty, I can bring the boys over. Then you will know dirt, and you and dirt will be one."

Relieved that she was letting me off the hook, I continued on my Windex tour, and when I ran out of house to clean, I went over to Kim's and tackled her kitchen as thanks.

The image of Nick getting into the cab kept flashing across my brain like a razor cut, fast and sharp and painless, at least for a second, right before all the blood tried to gush out. Then a rogue wave of…something… would threaten to knock me down and my heart rattled and clattered, my hands shook, and I backed away from that thought as fast as I could. Found something else to clean or wax or iron or nail. Turned on the TV. The radio, too.

But memories kept head-butting the door of my resolve. Nick with his head in my lap after we'd found his father…his smile as we lay in bed talking…the way his face lit up when I walked out of the Bismarck airport and over to his car…and the wave of despair and love threatened to knock me down and keep me underwater. So when those memories knocked and clattered, I shoved them away. I had to. And I was practiced at that sort of locking away. I'd been doing that most of my life, and at least this way, I was safe. Besides, I wasn't capable of giving real, lasting, wholehearted love. I'd proven that, hadn't I? I was my mother's girl, after all. Stunted.

On Monday, I kissed Coco, made sure she had her bunny and enough chew toys to occupy her and drove to work. No bike today. Though I'd missed the Vineyard during time away, I barely saw the bayberry bushes and rock walls as I drove toward Edgartown. The sun beat down, the breeze was gentle, the smell of coffee wafted down the street from the bustling little café. It was a beautiful day, I noted automatically. Just wasted on me.

"Well, well, well, look who's back!" Theo thundered as I walked into the old captain's house that housed Bainbrook, Bainbrook & Howe. "Wonderful to see you. Did you really have that much vacation time coming? Don't ever leave us again. Did you know I had to talk to a *client* last week? I haven't done that for years!" He gripped me by the shoulders and gazed happily into my face. "Well. Nice chat. Back to work!" He did a little soft-shoe back into his office and his beloved indoor putting green.

"You good?" Carol asked, handing me a sheaf of messages.

"So good," I lied. "You?"

"Never better."

"Great." So much for all the gushing and catching up. "Carol, see if you can get Judge McMurtry's new clerk on the phone, okay? I'll also need the Denver file. "

"Yes, master," Carol replied. "Anything else I can do? Wipe your ass? Chew your food and regurgitate it so you don't have to work so hard?"

"That'd be super," I said. "But first the call and the file, Carol." I went into my office, and the fake good cheer I'd summoned slipped away.

My office was very pleasant. Diplomas on the wall. Flowers delivered each Monday. A landscape by a local artist in soothing colors, meant to ease the battered hearts whose owners sat here, weeping or furious or numb…the walking wounded who chose poorly, or couldn't figure out how to compromise, or how to commit to a relationship, or how to accept love…or give it.

Well. Back to work, helping once-happy couples split up. Speaking of, I needed to check in with Willa and see if she wanted to file for divorce. Crap. Maybe I should let her tough this one out on her own.

I also had to see BeverLee. I'd called her twice over the weekend, but my father had been present both times—I could tell because Bev was overly chipper, booming her colloquialisms into the phone. Willa was staying there for the time being, and Bev had her hands full comforting her daughter. So Bev and I hadn't really talked, and we needed to. But the same swell of panic that thoughts of Nick inspired…it happened when I thought of BeverLee leaving the island, too.

It took me a couple of days to really get back in the swing of things. I had lunch with Father Bruce one rainy afternoon, back at Offshore Ale, since the good father liked to have a beer with his burger. He mercifully stayed silent when I told him Dennis and I had parted ways; just nodded, patted my hand, then went on to tell me about the seven couples he had in the pre-Cana class.

"Maybe I could swing by," I found myself offering.

"Like the angel of death?" the priest suggested, taking a sip of his pale ale.

"Voice of wisdom, I was thinking." I paused, toying with my straw. "You know. Give them a little insight into why so many couples…don't make it."

"And why do you think that is?" he asked gently.

To my surprise, there were tears in my eyes. "I have no idea," I whispered.

"Really?"

"Well, I thought it sounded better than 'People are fucked up,' you being a priest and all."

He smiled. "Everyone's messed up," he said. "Note my editing, as I am a man of the cloth and only swear on special occasions. Speaking of that, I have to run. Giving a talk on the priesthood as a vocation."

"And best of luck with that," I said. "I'll get the check, since you're facing Mission Impossible and despite the fact that the Catholic church is the wealthiest—"

"Oh, stop. I've heard it all before," he said, patting my

shoulder as he slid out of the booth. "Thanks for lunch, Harper. Let's talk soon."

When I got back to work, where I'd been logging some serious hours since my return (much to Theo's unadulterated delight), Tommy was standing in front of my desk like a kid about to be caned by the headmaster.

"Hey," I said, hanging up my trench coat. "How's it going?"

Tommy didn't look at me. "I'd like you to handle my divorce," he said.

I froze. "But—"

"She's still sleeping with that guy. The night I came to your party, she hooked up with him. I'm an idiot, and I'm tired of it. So handle my divorce, okay, Harper? Because I just can't take this anymore."

And even though I knew this had been coming, even though I never had any faith in Meggie, even though I knew Tommy would learn from this and grow and hopefully find someone who deserved him…even so, my heart broke.

"I'm so sorry," I said. I hesitated for just a second, then went over to him and hugged him. "I'm so sorry, Tom."

For a long time, I patted his back as he cried, as if he were a little baby, even if he was six-foot-four and I was anything but maternal. All my lines—the heart needing time, the head knowing, the euthanization of a dying relationship—they just weren't enough. Tommy had loved his wife, and she didn't love him back the same way, and all the logic in the world didn't make that feel better.

Later that day, I went into Theo's office and closed the door behind me. "I need a word, Boss," I said.

"Of course, my dear," he said, glancing at his watch. "You have four minutes." He was dressed in a lime-green polo shirt and eye-numbing plaid shorts.

"Hitting the links, are we?"

357

Theo smiled smugly. "Yes. Senator Lewis is in town, dodging the press."

"What did he do this time?"

"Apparently he found his soul mate."

"Oh, dear," I said.

"Mmm-hmm. And she posted their special moments on the Internet. Over three million hits in two hours alone. A proud day."

"Young love," I said, though Senator Lewis was well into his seventies. Made one wonder just who those three million were and why they wanted to burn their souls by watching the withered shanks of a fat white dude getting it on with his former cleaning lady.

"So what is it, dear? Three minutes, twenty seconds."

"Right. Theo, I'd like to branch out."

"From what, Harper?" Theo took a club out of his golf bag and mimicked a putt.

"From divorce law."

He looked up, horrified. "What? Why? No!"

"I'm a little burned out, Theo. I'd still do some, but… it's taking a toll."

"Not you! I thought you were different! You really get it! Sometimes our hearts just need time to accept what our heads already know. "

I inhaled slowly. "Right. But sometimes our heads are just full of crap, Theo."

He looked at me, puzzled. "Well, of course, Harper. What's your point?"

"I need to branch out. Or quit."

He recoiled, dropping his putter or driver or whatever it was. "Don't even speak the words! Oh, you evil black-mailer! Fine. Whatever you want."

"Partner," I said.

"Excuse me?"

"I want to be partner, too."

Theo sank into his chair. "Well, well. Would a raise suffice?"

I smiled, the first genuine smile in ages. "No."

JUST BEFORE CAROL LEFT for the day, she popped into my office. "This came for you. Sorry. It was in with some other papers." She handed me an envelope.

"Thanks," I said, taking it absentmindedly while I clicked through my computer. "Have a good evening, Carol."

"Don't tell me what to do." She closed the door behind her.

I finished with my email, then took a look at what Carol had given me. Hand-addressed, care of the law firm. No return address.

The postmark was from South Dakota.

All the air suddenly seemed sucked from the room.

Slowly, slowly, my hands shaking impressively, I slid the letter opener under the envelope flap and cut it open. Unfolded the letter very carefully, smoothing it out. A one hundred dollar bill fell onto my lap. I took a deep breath, held it, then let it out and looked at the letter. The handwriting was round and loopy, and despite not having seen it for so long, I recognized it immediately.

Dear Harper,
Well, I'm not sure what to say. You really surprised me the other day. I did recognize you, since of course you always did look just like me. I wish you'd given me a little warning—I wasn't ready for a big scene, know what I mean? It was a shock to see you—how can I be old enough to have a grown daughter? Anyway, I looked up your name on Google and found you out there, still on that

godforsaken island. At any rate, looks like you turned out great! A lawyer. You were always smart, I guess.

I suppose you want to know why I left. First, let me say that I'm great! Life has been one wild ride for me, and I wouldn't have it any other way. I never wanted to be tied down and really wasn't cut out for motherhood or island life and all that. I toughed it out as long as I could, but in the end, I had to do what was right for me. I had a lot of plans back before you came along, and it didn't seem fair that I had to stay stuck for the rest of my life. Sorry you got caught in the middle, but we had some good times, didn't we?

Anyway, if you're ever back this way, drop in and say hi. Just call first. By the way, I just didn't feel right taking the money…I'm not the type who likes to be beholden, if you know what I mean. Buy yourself something nice and think of me when you wear it, okay? Take care.

Linda

I read the letter seven times. Each time, it became more repugnant.

Had to do what was right for me. Toughed it out. Wasn't cut out for motherhood.

Holy testicle Tuesday.

Buy myself something nice and think of her? The woman who abandoned me, the woman who pretended not to recognize me after twenty-one *years* of being apart?

Looks like you turned out great.

"Actually, I'm quite a pathetic mess, Mom," I said. My voice seemed overly loud in the quiet.

For a long time, I sat there in the lengthening shadows,

the rain pattering against the windows like a thought wanting to be let in. And then something did creep into my consciousness, carefully, as if testing the waters to see if it was safe. Slowly, very slowly, a new possibility came into my mind.

I'd had enough.

My mother's actions—her one action, really…leaving me—had been a choke chain on my heart…on my whole life…since I was thirteen years old.

Enough.

Looks like you turned out great.

"You know what? Strike the previous comment, Ma," I said. "You're right. I *am* great, no thanks to you."

Before I was even aware of moving, my raincoat was in my hand and I was running down the stairs, out into the small lot behind our building, into my little yellow car. I pulled out so fast the wheels flung gravel, but I didn't care. Breaking every speed limit from Edgartown to Tisbury, I think I touched the brakes only when I veered into my father's driveway. There it was—the house where I'd grown up, the place I'd avoided as much as possible my entire adult life since the second I left for college. I dashed out of the car and inside.

She was here. Looking older and worn out, no makeup today, which made her look oddly blank. She held a ciggie in one hand, and her hair was a couple of inches lower than her usual "closer to God" bouffant. When she saw me, she gave a tired smile.

"Here's a sight for sore eyes," she said. "How's by you, Harper darlin'?"

"Hey, BeverLee," I panted. The radio played some country-and-western ballad; static crackled the reception, but Bev didn't seem to mind. She stubbed out her cigarette, knowing I hated her smoking.

"Have a seat, take a load off. Want something to eat?" She made a move to stand.

"No, no, don't get up. I'm good," I said, pulling out a chair. "Is Willa here?"

"Well now, she was, but she and your daddy are out in the woodshop, I think."

Now that I was here, I wasn't exactly sure what to say. I bit a cuticle, then put my hands in my lap.

"So how you been after seein' Nick and all?"

I looked up sharply, getting a small smile in response. No one else had asked that question. "Um…I'm doing okay, Bev," I said. "But I don't…well, I'm not…How are you, Bev? How are you doing?"

"Well, now, I guess I'm doing all right." She straightened the napkins in the holder, a hideous plastic molded thing depicting a royal flush, then looked back at me. "I heard you and Dennis split up, and I have to say, I was sorry to hear it. But I guess if y'all weren't married after all this time, that said something. Your daddy and me, we only knew each other a week—Well. Maybe not the best example, since we're partin' ways and all." She gave me a halfhearted smile and shrugged.

"Bev, about that. I have to tell you something," I said. "I…" Well, crap. I had no idea what to say. I swallowed; Bev waited; the static crackled and rain hissed against the windows. Some familiar chords were discernible from the radio. "Sweet Home Alabama," the famous Southern rock anthem.

"Oh, I just love this song," Bev said, her eyes taking on a far-off look. "I got this cassette stuck in the tape player in my car, remember? This here was the only song that played all the way through."

A memory drifted to the surface…me watching as Bev pulled into or out of the driveway, Lynyrd Skynyrd's song like a soundtrack for her comings and goings.

"You never wanted to come with me if you could avoid it," Bev said with a faint smile. "But there you'd be, standin' at the window, makin' damn sure I came back. Then you'd run off and hide in your room and stick your nose in a book and pretend you didn't know I was home. Poor little mite. Always so afraid of someone leavin' that you never let anyone get close."

There it was, my emotional failings in a nutshell.

Enough. "Bev," I said again. I reached out and gripped her hands in mine. "BeverLee, listen. I…" The lump in my throat choked off the words.

"What is it, sugarplum?" She tilted her head and frowned. "Oh, my Lord, are you crying?"

I just clutched her hand more tightly. BeverLee had loved me from the first day she saw me, a wretched, sullen teenager who viewed her as a joke. She thought I was brilliant, beautiful…she thought I was lovable. She thought I was the *best*, despite the fact that I'd done everything I could to keep her at arm's length.

But twelve years ago, when I was a huddled mess on a kitchen floor in New York City, she was the one I called. And I'd known without a whisper of doubt that BeverLee Roberta Dupres McKnight Lupinski James would come through for me. And she had. Without hesitation, she'd driven five hours straight, through Massachusetts, Connecticut and New York, found her way to my apartment, taken me in her arms without one single question or recrimination and brought me home.

"BeverLee," I whispered, because my throat was locked. "Bev…you've been more of a mother to me than my own mother ever was." Her eyes widened. "You didn't have to love me, and God knows I didn't give you much to love, but you did. You've always been there for me, always taken care of me, and I'm sorry it's taken me so long to see it. And I want you to know that even if you and Dad get a divorce…" I broke off and squeezed her hand harder. "I will always be your daughter."

Because *this* woman was my real mother. For twenty years now, she'd loved me despite myself, and that was what real mothers did. That was what unconditional love meant.

Bev's mouth opened in shock. "Oh, baby," she whispered. "Oh, my baby, I love you, too."

Then we were hugging, Bev's massive chest oddly comforting, the smell of Jhirmack Extra Hold and Virginia Slims the smell of home. She wept and stroked my hair, and I let her, and discovered that it felt pretty damn wonderful.

AN HOUR LATER, AFTER a cup of tea and a quart of tears, I hugged BeverLee once more. It was a little awkward, all this physical affection…but it was worth it. I could get used to it. I wanted to get used to it.

With a promise to call tomorrow, I went out the back to my father's workshop, a place that smelled of wood and oiled power tools. He was talking to Willa in a low voice, arms folded, face serious. I felt a little pang of envy—Dad had always gotten on better with Willa. She was, of course, much more likable than yours truly, but still.

At the sight of his biological child, Dad broke off, and both of them looked at me.

"Can I have a word?" I asked.

"With me?" Dad asked.

"Um…actually, with both of you," I said, taking a breath. "Okay. Um, Willa. Listen." I bit my lip. "I'm not going to handle your divorce this time. In fact, uh, I don't mean to sound too harsh here, but I can't really bail you out on anything anymore. You're twenty-seven, not seventeen. No more loans, no more credit cards. And I'll just…shut up on the advice front, how's that? You never take it anyway."

"Well, I—" Willa began.

"Actually, one more bit of advice," I interrupted. "Commit to *something*. Whether it's Christopher or a job or a place or school…stick to it, Wills. You don't want to end up just drifting around like milkweed seed, with a bunch of stupid relationships behind you and a whole lot of nothing in front of you. That's what my mother did, and now she's a waitress in South Dakota, with nothing and no one. You don't want that, Willa. Trust me."

There was a heavy silence. My father had frozen at the mention of my mother. Willa just looked at me for a long second. Then she smiled.

"Funny you should say that," she said. "Chris and I are back together. He's gonna work for Dad. So…we're moving here."

My mouth opened. "Really? What about the… Thumbie?"

She shrugged. "I called him that day…the day Nick showed up. He's not going to give up on his inventing, but he sees the upside of regular work, too."

"Oh. Well, that's…great. Good for you, Willa."

She raised a silky eyebrow. "Maybe I don't need your advice quite as much as you think."

I took a breath, then nodded. "Maybe not. Which is a really good thing, Willa. Sorry if I sounded like a pompous ass."

"Why would today be any different?" she asked, mugging to our dad.

"Very funny. Cut me some slack," I muttered. "I've had a rough week."

With that, Willa bounded over and wrapped her arms around me. "So I hear. If you want to talk, I'm around." She smooched my cheek. "Thanks for all the loans and advice and free divorces. I hope I'll never need any again."

"Ditto," I said.

"Gotta run! Thanks, Dad!" Willa blew him a kiss, which he dutifully pretended to catch, and bounded out the door, leaving my father and me alone, twenty feet of wood and machinery between us, the smell of sawdust thick in the air. Rain pattered on the tin roof and the wind gusted outside.

"Crazy weather, huh?" I said, though it was nothing more than a typical rainstorm.

"Yeah."

The silence stretched between us. *Now or never, Harper.* "I saw Linda last week," I said.

"So you said. How was that?"

"It wasn't good, Dad. Not good." I took a deep breath. "She pretended not to recognize me, and I let her."

Dad looked at the floor and said nothing.

"Dad," I said slowly, "listen. I—I always blamed you for not keeping Mom happy enough to stay, or not fighting to get her back when she left. And I hated that you married BeverLee and just stuck her in my life."

Dad nodded in acknowledgment, his eyes still on the sawdust-covered floor.

"I want to thank you for that now."

He looked up.

"My mother is obviously a self-centered, shallow, heartless person. And BeverLee is not."

"No," he said. The wind gusted, rattling a shop window.

"I've never asked you for much, have I, Dad?" I asked gently. "Never asked for money, went through college and law school on scholarships and student loans. Never lived with you after college, never asked for advice."

"No," he agreed. "You've never asked for a thing." A flash of regret crossed his perpetually neutral face.

"I'm asking for something now, Daddy. Don't leave BeverLee. Get some counseling and figure things out. You've got twenty years invested here, and Dad...She loves you. And she...believes in you. I don't think it gets better than that."

He didn't move or say anything for a long moment. "You know BeverLee's fifteen years younger than I am, of course," he said slowly.

I nodded.

He paused, weighing his next words. "Harper, I had a heart attack in July."

My knees gave a dangerous buckle. "What?" I squeaked.

He shrugged. "Doctor said it was minor. But it got me thinking about...the future. I don't want Bev to have to take care of me."

"She doesn't know, Dad?"

He shook his head. "I told her I was fishing with Phil Santos."

"Dad..." My voice cracked. If my father died...

"I don't want her saddled with a sickly old man."

"She loves you, Dad! If she got sick, would you feel saddled with her?"

"Of course not. But...well. I see your point." He didn't say any more. "Still. She deserves someone who can keep up with her. Not a sick old man."

"Are you doing okay now?" I asked.

"Oh, I guess. I take a pill every day. My cholesterol's way down. It's just...you look at your life and wonder what you can do for your family. Seemed like cutting Bev loose was the right thing. If I'm gonna die in the next year or so..."

"God, you men. You're all so melodramatic," I said,

though my legs were still shaking at the thought of my dad being sick. "If you take care of yourself, you'll outlive us all. But Dad, cutting Bev loose is not the right thing to do! Nor is keeping your children out of the loop!"

He gave a half shrug. "Well. You're probably right."

"So will you talk to Bev?" I asked. "Because I'm not keeping this a secret from her, Dad."

He nodded once. "Yeah. I'll talk to her. Been dragging my feet on moving out. Guess that says something."

"It says you love her and don't want a divorce."

He looked at me and raised an eyebrow. "Your day to fix lives?" he asked, a hint of humor in his voice.

"Everyone's except mine, I guess," I said. We looked at each other a long minute.

"Harper, I...You know...well, here it is. I know I haven't been the best father." He sighed. "With Willa, it's easy... she...She's always making mistakes or needs something I can help her with...money, a place to live, whatever. But you...you never needed anything." He paused. "Except a mother. A real mother, that is. The truth was, I was glad when Linda left. I was afraid she'd ruin you."

"Is that why you married BeverLee? To give me a mother?"

"That was part of it. A big part."

God. The past was never what it seemed to be. "Dad," I said after another few beats, "can I ask you something?"

"Is there any stopping you?"

I grinned a little at that. Dad, making a joke. To me. "Well...no. But I always wondered about something. Did Mom name me after Harper Lee?"

"Who's that?"

"She wrote *To Kill A Mockingbird*."

Dad frowned. "Far as I know, you were named after some fashion magazine."

Oh, crikey. *Harper's Bazaar.* Well, hell. I guess that made more sense. And for some reason, it was oddly comforting—my mother had never had hidden depths.

"Can I ask you something else, Dad?" I asked.

"Go ahead."

"Well…" This one was harder. "Dad, if I'd asked for advice all those years ago, what would you have said about me marrying Nick?"

He didn't say anything for a minute, just looked at me as if judging whether or not I wanted the truth. "I guess I would've said I thought that boy was the best thing that ever happened to you."

My heart clenched. "Really?" I whispered.

"Yes."

"You never said anything. I wasn't even sure you approved."

Dad gave a half shrug and looked at the floor once more. "Actions were supposed to speak louder than words," he replied gruffly. "I let him marry you, didn't I? Wasn't about to give my daughter to just anyone."

Then my father looked up, held out his arms, hesitantly, self-consciously. "Come on," he said. "Give your old man a hug."

CHAPTER TWENTY-SEVEN

ON FRIDAY EVENING, I left the office around four and went home to pack.

That took all of fifteen minutes. To stall a little longer, I went to my computer and checked my list.

1. Make plane reservation. (I'd done that already, as well as confirmed it. Twice.)
2. Make hotel reservation. (Also confirmed twice.)
3. Pack. (Just finished.)
4. Write speech. (Done, if highly unsatisfactory and far too long.)
5. Deliver speech. (Not done.)
6. Get Nick back. (Not done.)

"Crotch," I whispered, suppressing a dry heave of terror. Because here was the thing. I may have resolved that I didn't have to be stunted any longer…I may have opened my heart to BeverLee…may have had a little better understanding of my father…but I had no idea if Nick would give me another chance. *I can't do this anymore,* he said just before he got into the cab.

Ah, hindsight. All those times back then, when I'd pushed him away just enough to try to save that most essential part of myself, to wall him out of my heart in case he left me, to preserve myself from damage…I'd hurt myself, and I'd hurt Nick, too. BeverLee was right. I was so terrified of people leaving me that I never let them in.

Add to this fact, I didn't even know if Nick was on

American soil…I seemed to remember a trip to Dubai (or London, or Seattle) on his calendar. I was too cowardly to call his office and ask for his schedule (not that anyone would give it to me, of course), and far, far too nervous to call him. No. Better if I appeared on his doorstep. If he closed the door, I could always yell up at the windows until the police came.

Theo had clutched a fist to his heart when I'd asked for the time, but when he heard my mission, a rather appealing light came into his eyes. "Take all the time you need," he said, twinkling. "I'm a sucker for true love. I've been married four times, after all."

My plan…well, it sucked. But at least it was something. If I had to drop by his apartment every four hours until I found him, so be it.

It was, of course, the final step in the "Harper is a Human" campaign. In this past week, I'd babysat for Kim (I now sported two bruises on my shin and a bite mark on my wrist, but had also learned what Pikachu was). I took Tommy out to dinner and picked up the tab, bought Carol a Dustin Pedroia poster. I even cooked dinner and had Bev, Willa and Kim over for a girls night.

And I wrote a letter of apology to Jack and Sarah Costello, telling them how much I had always loved being included in their family gatherings, and how much I regretted causing Dennis any pain. And yes, I'd checked in with Dennis. He was doing A-okay, it seemed. Good old Dennis. He'd been sweetly surprised that I wasn't back with Nick.

Not yet, I wasn't. But I was going to try. And if Nick wouldn't forgive me, or didn't want me back…the thought caused another dry heave.

"So you're going?" came a voice. Kim, little Desmond on her hip, smelling of sunscreen and salt water.

"Yeah." I pulled a face and zipped my suitcase closed.

"It's good, Harper. It's really romantic, actually."

"Right. Even if it does have that restraining-order feel about it. But I guess it's worth a try."

"'Do or do not. There is no try,'" she intoned.

"Who said that? Winston Churchill?"

"Yoda. Please. I have four sons. *Star Wars* is my life."

"So now the Muppets are giving me advice?"

"Count your blessings. It could be TeleTubbies." She leaned down and gave me an unexpected kiss on the cheek. Desmond kicked me in the ribs, then smiled angelically. "See you when you get back," my friend said.

"Thanks, Kim," I replied. I looked at her and forced a smile, which became genuine after a second. "Thanks."

"Go get him, sister!" she called as she left the room. "Nothing ventured, nothing gained. Worst-case scenario, you'll be right back where you are now."

That was another thing. Here…here was no longer what it had once been. The contentment (the smugness, let's be honest) I used to feel with my life had evaporated like the morning mist, and I was just like the rest of humanity—all of us poor, pathetic dopes battered by the storms of love. Utterly clueless.

I glanced at my watch, tried not to puke, succeeded and got up to find Coco's crate. At the sight of her carrier, she immediately put on her Chihuahua-orphan look. Took a step forward, then held up her front paw as if wounded.

"Your paw is fine," I told her. "What's the problem? Don't you want to see Nick? You love Nick, remember? Is this a sign? Are you trying to tell me not to do it? Speak, Coco. You're much smarter than I am, God knows."

She hunkered down and gave her tail a little wag—

See? I'm so cute, remember? Don't make me go into the evil crate! I'm not a city girl!

Who could blame her? Air travel was punishing enough without being caged. And she'd been so stressed in New York…all those horns and sirens, that eternal roar. With a sigh, I sat down next to her.

"Okay. You can stay. But I have to go, baby. You understand, right? Want to go to Kim's?" Then, thinking of Kim's litter of male children, I winced. "How about Willa's?"

My plane left in an hour and a half. Plenty of time to swing by Willa's—she and Chris had rented a place in Oak Bluffs. I'd seen them a couple of days ago; they still had to get their furniture and stuff from New York, but it was a cute house. Chris seemed good; mentioned AA and the balm of steady work. Willa, for her part, had enrolled in an online class…anatomy. She wanted to be a nurse. It seemed like a good fit for her sunny personality.

I called my sister's cell. "Hey, you," I said. "I need a favor."

"Sure!" she said.

"Can you babysit Coco for a few days? Actually, it might be longer." My legs gave a watery wobble. "Maybe a week, even."

"You bet. Where are you going?"

"New York," I said, swallowing sickly.

"Say again?"

"New York City." I took a breath. "I'm…I'm…I'm going to see Nick."

"Um…Harper? Nick's here."

"What?" I squeaked. "Here? What do you mean, here? Where's here? At your house?"

"Calm down, calm down," she said. "He's on the island."

"What's he doing here?" My heart clattered.

"Chris rented a U-Haul yesterday, drove down to the city and packed up our stuff. Nick drove back with him to help unload. So he's here. But Harper, he just left, like, ten minutes ago. He wanted to catch the seven o'clock ferry out of Oak Bluffs. Then, shit, he's getting a car service to Logan and going to Seattle or something."

I looked at my watch. It was 6:22. "I'm on my way," I blurted.

"Should I call him? Tell him to wait?"

"No! No. Um…he might not want to see me."

I flew out of the house, leaving my dog yapping a reproach for not taking her. In a spray of crushed shells, I peeled out of my driveway, cutting off an earth-raping Hummer with Virginia plates and earning a few enraged shouts. I ignored them, my little yellow car eating up the road. The route from Menemsha to Oak Bluffs usually took about half an hour, more with tourist traffic. Which we had in droves, it being Columbus Day weekend. I'd never make it if I went through Vineyard Haven proper, so I went down past Fiddlehead Farm, through Tisbury, my hands clenched on the wheel. Past the airport. Onto Barnes Road, where I got stuck behind a minivan from New Jersey.

"Come on, come on, come on, don't you have your own shore?" I muttered, chewing my cuticle. When the coast was clear, I passed them, flooring it. Hey. I was from Massachusetts, thank you very much. Speed limits were for other states.

But I hadn't counted on traffic being so damn thick as I came into Oak Bluffs. Short of driving on the lawns (a definite option) and vehicular manslaughter (not so much), I wasn't going to make it. Tourists decked out in Black Dog hats and T-shirts milled around, and the road was packed with cars.

I glanced at the clock. 6:56.

I wasn't going to make it. Not on my own, anyway.

I snatched up my phone and pressed the number of someone known and liked by virtually everyone on this island, someone with friends in high places. "Pick up. Please, please, please," I chanted. My prayer was answered.

"Dude, how's it hanging?"

"Oh, Dennis, thank God. Listen, I have kind of an emergency. I need to stop the ferry."

"Why?"

I hesitated. "To stop Nick. To try to get back with him."

"Awesome," Dennis said sincerely, and I felt such a rush of affection for him with that word, because Dennis's heart didn't have room for resentment.

"But I'm stuck in traffic, and I'm not gonna make the ferry. I thought about calling in a bomb scare—"

"Uncool."

"—I know, and I don't want to get arrested. So. Can you help me? I just need a few minutes."

"Let's see." There was a thoughtful pause. "I think Gerry might be working tonight. I'll make a call, sure."

"Really?" Hope, that thing with feathers, gave a healthy flap.

"I'll give it a shot."

"Oh, thank you. Thank you so much."

"You bet, dude."

"Dennis, you're the best."

"Yeah, whatever. Hey, Harp, listen. You should prob-ably know...I'm back with Jodi."

"Jodi-with-an-I?" I said automatically, veering around a Mercedes whose driver clearly didn't know ass from elbow and was trying to turn onto a one-way street.

"Yeah. We hung out the other night, and it was like old times."

I laughed. "Invite me to the wedding, okay, Den?"

"Dude. Totally." There was a pause. "Good luck, Harper."

My throat tightened abruptly. "Thanks, Dennis."

After what seemed like an eternity, I finally drew within view of the ferry landing. Unfortunately, there was a concert at the gazebo in Ocean Park, and we were inching along. But the ferry was in, even though it was 7:09. Maybe I'd make it after all, and God bless Dennis Patrick Costello. I'd pay for his honeymoon with Jodi, I vowed I would.

Then the air tore with the sound of the ferry's horn. "No!" I groaned. "Oh, damn it." I was still two blocks away, there was nowhere to park, dang it all, and my teeth ground in frustration. But then again, if I didn't catch Nick today, and it was looking as if that was a very real possibility, I could always try some other time.

Except that some other time didn't have the same appeal as right now. Now. It had to be now.

I pulled over, double-parking next to a red Porsche, and hurtled out of the car.

"You can't park there!" called a cop.

"Emergency!" I said, bolting across the street. The ramp to the ferry was a long post-and-beam structure, and tonight, it was full of people taking in the sights or seeing off their friends. "Excuse me, excuse me!" I called, pushing through the crowd. "Stop the ferry! Hold the ferry, please!" My feet thudded along the wooden slats as I ran, then jumped over a coil of rope. A radio was playing somewhere, and my busy brain registered the lyrics. "Sweet Home Alabama." It had to be a sign from God, or Bev, or the universe.

The horn sounded again.

"Stop the ferry!" I shouted. "Please!"

"Too late, lady," said one of the ferry workers as he

tossed a rope to one of the men on board. "No one past this point."

Then I saw Nick. He stood on the lower deck of the boat, staring out at Martha's Vineyard as the ferry inched away, the ever-present wind ruffling his hair, his gypsy eyes distant and...sad.

Well. He wasn't going to be sad anymore, damn it.

"Nick!" I bellowed. "Nick!"

He didn't see me.

"Nick!" I turned to one of the ferry workers. *Leonard* was embroidered over his pocket. "Leonard!" I barked. "Stop this ferry."

"Unless this is a medical emergency lady," he said in a thick New Bedford accent, "or you're packed with explosives, no can do. Sorry."

"Stop it or I'm jumping in!"

"Don't even joke about it, okay?" he said, doing something to the control panel on the boat slip. "You can get arrested for that. And if you get close enough to the propeller, you'll get sucked right under."

The propeller was in the back of the boat. I'd aim for the side.

Do or do not. There is no try.

Egged on by Yoda and the surefire knowledge that I loved Nick Lowery more than anything, I ran as fast as I could for the end of the dock, and when the end came, I kept running, and for one incredible second, I was air-borne and weightless, flying through the air.

Then the outside world went silent as I went under, bubbles roaring past my ears, and, oh, *crotch,* the water was frigid! I kicked to the surface and emerged, sputtering, salt water stinging my eyes, my skin crawling in a wave of goose bumps. I coughed and looked up at the boat. I couldn't see Nick, just the massive hull of the boat about twenty feet away. People on the dock yelled and pointed. Treading water, I pushed the sodden hair out of my eyes.

"Gawddammit!" bawled Leonard the dockworker. I glanced back at him as he pulled out his radio and barked into it. "Hughie, we got a fuckin' nut in the water! Kill the engines!" He looked at me. "Idiot!"

Then there was a splash as a life ring was thrown down from the ferry. I looked up at the boat again. A crowd had gathered, dozens of faces looking down at me. "Nick?" I called. The roar of the engines cut out abruptly, and it suddenly seemed very quiet. "Nick Lowery?" I called again.

There he was, gripping the railing with both hands. "Jesus, Harper, are you all right?" he called.

"Um…sure," I said, though my teeth were starting to chatter.

"Take the life ring, idiot!" Leonard the dockworker ordered. I ignored him.

"Harpy, what are you doing?" Nick asked. "Are you insane?"

"Um…a little?" I kept treading water, though I was now shuddering with cold. "Nick…I had to see you."

"Yeah, I got that," he said.

"Ma'am? Please get out of the water." Great. There was the cop who told me not to double-park.

"Nick…see, the thing is," I began swimming a little closer. Then I stopped. I never did get to memorize that horrible speech I'd been working on.

He waited. The people around him waited. "Mommy, can I have a snack?" asked a kid.

"Shh!" the mom hissed.

"Ma'am, if I have to jump in there to save you, I will not be happy," the cop said.

I looked at Nick, his rumpled hair, his lovely face,

those gypsy eyes that had always done such things to my heart.

"Marry me," I said.

I guess he didn't expect me to say that, because he just stood there, looking at me, mouth slightly open, as if my words didn't quite make sense.

"Marry me, Nick," I said, my voice roughening with tears. "Marry me again. I don't care how it looks or what the plan is or where we are, as long as we're together. I love you, Nick. I always did, I always have, I always will."

He still didn't say anything. The crowd watched. "Sir?" said the cop. "Can you please answer the crazy woman so we can all go home?"

The crowd glanced between Nick and me, and for one long, heart-wrenching moment, it seemed as if Nick was just going to turn away and leave me here in the drink.

Except he didn't. In a quick, neat move, he jumped over the railing, The crowd gasped, the dockworker swore, and with a splash, Nick landed in the water not five feet from me.

"You sure are memorable," he said, and then he grabbed hold of the life ring with one arm, me with the other, and kissed me, a hot, hard kiss, and I wrapped my arms around his neck and kissed him back for all I was worth.

"Idiots," someone called.

I didn't really notice. I had Nick again, the first man I'd ever loved, the only man I'd ever loved. My teeth were chattering too hard to really kiss that effectively, so I pulled back and looked into Nick's eyes and smiled. "I'll take that as a yes."

EPILOGUE

OUR WEDDING DAY—WELL, our second wedding day—
was cold and rainy, the wind slapping against the wood-
shingled Unitarian church, the stained-glass windows
rattling. As my father and BeverLee walked me down
the aisle, the wind howled in full voice.

"Sounds like a warning to me," Nick said, grinning.

"Sorry, pal. Too late to back out now," I answered,
shoving my bouquet at Willa and grabbing both of Nick's
hands.

"Scared?" he asked in a lower voice.

I looked into his eyes. "No. Not a bit. Are you?"

He smiled, and my heart swelled. "What do you
think?"

"I think you look pretty cute in a tux," I said.

"I think if the two of you could manage to quiet down,
maybe we could get started," Father Bruce said.

Because the Catholic church wouldn't touch Nick and
me with a ten-foot pole, Father B. had managed to get
himself appointed a justice of the peace. His bishop wasn't
happy, but the good father said it was worth it to be able to
perform our wedding ceremony. Awfully nice of him.

Chris was best man—hey, guess what? The Thumbie
had been picked up by one of those companies that han-
dles those weird products you see advertised late at night.
So far he'd earned about fourteen dollars, but you never
knew. He gave me a wink, handsome devil that he was,
and I smiled back.

"Dearly beloved," Father Bruce began, "we are gathered here to witness the union of Nick and Harper as they pledge their love and devotion to each other for what we hope is the last time, because I don't know about you people, but I don't think any of us should have to go through this again."

"Everyone's a comedian," I said. Nick grinned.

I glanced out at our guests—Dad's arm was around BeverLee, and she was crying blue tears and smiling hugely at the same time. Theo was there with his latest ex-wife, and Carol, Tommy and the other lawyers from my firm, as well as a few clients (no place like a wedding to meet a potential mate, right?). Dennis and Jodi and her little son sat in the back next to Kim and Lou and the four boys, who were shoving each other. Jason Cruise was there…Nick had insisted, and I was being tolerant. Peter Camden had come too, as well as the other people from the firm; Pete didn't look happy, but I didn't really care.

There'd been quite the little furor over my, er, unusual proposal. Of course, virtually everyone there that day had a camera or a cell phone, so the Martha's Vineyard newspaper had run a montage of the two of us kissing in the water and the adorable headline: "Divorce Attorney Risks Hell and High Water to Win Her Man." Nick had the front page framed and occasionally pointed to it when we started to bicker.

But our bickering was amiable and over things like how much time we'd spend in Boston and how much on the Vineyard. See, Nick had had a long talk with Peter, cut back on his traveling and opened up a Boston office. The joy of owning your own business, he'd said, was supposed to be flexibility. And so, after a life spent in the Big Apple, Nick moved to Beantown, where he amiably mocked the tangled streets, made enemies by wearing his Yankees cap whenever possible and admitted that the seafood was unparalled on the face of the earth. Each month, we'd be spending a few days in what he called "the real city"—but he was adapting. Even broke the speed limit on the Mass Pike one proud day.

For my part, I'd be working for Bainbrook, Bainbrook & Howe's Boston office Monday through Thursday, home on the island the rest of the week. We got a cute little apartment in the Back Bay, and would keep the house in Menemsha (of course!). When we had kids, which we hoped wouldn't be too far in the future, we'd adjust. Nothing was carved in stone, but I had faith.

We said our vows, and this time...this time I knew we'd make it.

"Nick? Do you have the ring?" Father Bruce asked.

"Yeah, Nick. Do you?" I asked. Nick hadn't let me see the ring he'd chosen, which I thought was quite unfair. "You'd think I could've seen it first, since I'm the one who has to wear it for the rest of my life."

"God, does she ever stop talking?" Nick asked. "Yes, I have the ring." He raised an eyebrow. Christopher handed the ring to his brother, and Nick smiled, took my hand and slid it onto my finger.

It was my wedding ring. The first one.

"Oh, Nick," I whispered, my eyes filling.

"I want you to know, I went back for that ring the day after you left me," Nick said. "Had to pry up a manhole cover, go down into the sewer, crawl down a pipe into the storm drain. Couldn't just let it stay there." He paused. "I guess I kept it for a reason."

"I guess you did," I whispered, and then I kissed him, and kissed him, and kissed him some more.

"Well, since no one's waiting for instructions," Father Bruce said, sighing dramatically. "I now pronounce you man and wife. Nick, you may continue to kiss your bride."

BeverLee sobbed, my father chuckled, Willa laughed out loud, everyone clapped and whooped and hollered.

As for me, I was finally back where I belonged, and as I looked into my husband's smiling eyes, I finally understood what happily ever after could really mean.

* * * * *

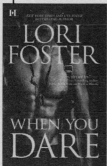
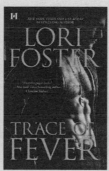

KRISTAN HIGGINS